Neil McCormick is the *Daily Telegraph*'s chief pop and rock music critic. He is an author, radio pundit and television presenter. His memoir, *Killing Bono* (originally published as *I Was Bono's Doppelganger*) has been turned into a feature film and adapted as a stage play (*Chasing Bono*). He lives in London.

BY THE SAME AUTHOR

U2 by U2

Killing Bono (aka *I Was Bono's Doppelganger*)

#ZERO

Neil McCormick

unbound

First published in 2019

Unbound
6th Floor Mutual House, 70 Conduit Street, London W1S 2GF
www.unbound.com

Text Design by Ellipsis, Glasgow

Printed and bound in Great Britain by Clays Ltd, Elcograf S.p.A.

A CIP record for this book is available from the British Library

ISBN 978-1-78352-662-8 (trade pbk)
ISBN 978-1-78352-664-2 (ebook)
ISBN 978-1-78352-663-5 (limited edition)

'My name is Nobody.
Mother, Father, friends
Everybody calls me Nobody'
                    Homer – *The Odyssey*

For my mother, who set me on this wayward path,
with love as my guide.
For Gloria, who lit the way home.
And for Finn, who made the journey complete.

With special thanks to
David Joseph
Marlene McCormick
John McGlue

1

Here goes nothing.

Sing, O Muse, of the fall of Zero, of the hollow king who outran his shadow in the last days of the crumbling empire of poop. Spare no details. We've heard the story before and know how it usually ends.

The Shitty Committee were up before I was, as per fucking usual, rapping a gavel on the inside of my skull. Rat-a-tat-tat, retard. No order in the house. All speaking out of turn, a cacophony of the usual complaints. You're nothing special. You can't fool us. We want our money back. And a few fresh voices to twist the knife, make it really personal. See that porter you tipped a hundred dollars? He called you a cheap prick behind your back. The chef spat in your food. The waiter pissed in your drink. The coat-check girl with the big bazookas you zapped in the cupboard? She faked her orgasm and now she's telling all her Spacebook fiends you were a lousy lay. It's all over Blogoslavakia. Top ten on U-Bend.

Trending on Splatter. Beaming down the wire to a billion mobiles. Tomorrow it'll be front page on the *Daily Rage*. Can't sing. Can't dance. Can't even get it up. Take your punishment. You fake. You loser. You mother—

'Rise and shine, superstar,' sang a voice, not from my dreams, obviously. It was far too nice.

'Fucker,' I groaned.

'Well, that's nice,' tutted the interloper. It was Kailash, known to one and all as Kilo (only not when passing through customs): management lapdog, brown-nosing lickspittle, personal assistant to the talent (that's me), Mephistopheles's little helper, can-do candy man. I wasn't sure where I was or what time it was but I couldn't help noticing that Kilo had already arranged a neat line of pure white powder on a polished bedside table, mere millimetres from my slowly stirring nostrils, Satan bless his evil soul.

I hate drugs. OK, so I'm not exactly a poster boy for Just Say No. But when I was sweet sixteen (or was it sour seventeen? I don't know. Might have been twelve) I made a promise to myself that if I was going to amount to more than a hill of Heinz baked beans I had to stay away from bad shit. Mind you, that was probably while the universe was collapsing after a snakebite and hash binge. Or was it the time I gobbled my guitarist's pills before a Zero Sums gig only to lose all control of my limbs, with the sneaky fucker giggling about K-holes? Which is another very good reason why I fucking hate drugs. Really. It's just that sometimes, well, nothing else will do. Like first thing in the morning after a bad dream in a strange bed when your mouth is dry and your head is soggy and nausea is creeping up your gullet and it's not being helped by your so-called assistant prattling away like it's the first day of spring and all the chicks are hatching.

So I did what had to be done, lifting my head just high enough to snort through a tightly rolled hundred-dollar bill. No one can accuse me of being a cheap junky. I sat bolt upright with a vertigo-inducing lurch, poison kick-starting my heart.

'Fuck,' I said. 'I think I'm going to be sick.'

That's how the day began. Pretty much like any other. Before I was ready for it. The last day of my so-called life.

When I say I didn't know where I was, I'm not joking. I didn't know what city. I didn't even know what country. Somewhere on planet Hotel, for sure. You fall asleep in Berlin and wake up in Beijing and the only thing that changes are the sheets, freshly laundered, air artificially cool and distilled, walls a sea of soothing beige. I've lived in and around hotels all my life. As a kid, I padded along behind the old man, buttoned up in his porter blues, hauling someone else's crap for a shitty tip, and that's if you're lucky. I've done my time with the cockroaches and bed bugs. These days I always get the best suite on the top floor of the finest establishments but chocolates on my pillow don't move me. A hotel is a hotel is a hotel.

'Where are we?' I asked Kilo.

'New York, New York, so good they named it twice: once for the night before and once for the morning after!' he replied in a sing-song that made everything sound as if it's supposed to be a joke.

'What time is it?' These are questions I increasingly found myself starting my day with.

'Six o'clock, so grab your cock!' he said, making a song-and-dance routine of drawing back the curtains. 'You've got a couple of quick phoners with Dublin and London then we'll get you fresh and funky for *Breakfast in America* over at FNY and back to MTV for the launch of Weekend Zero,' he trilled, as if this dreary round of publicity appearances should have me bouncing out of bed with a song in my heart and my dick in my hand.

Six o'fucking-clock. You're probably as sick as I am of celebrities moaning about their hard fucking lives but it really is a long day with no breaks. It was barely light outside. Surely the whole point of fame and fucking fortune was being able to sleep late? My old man used to have to practically drag me out of bed to get ready for school. We both understood it to be the natural order of things, the eternal struggle between parent and child, heaven and earth, moon and sun, old and new, played out daily in a rank teenage bedroom. The dust settled on that battleground when I left home, breaking out on my own for what exactly? So that an over-animated drama queen could waltz into my room without so much as a how-do-you-do and prance around my bed trilling wakey-wakey? I was actually beginning to get upset. Kilo had the curtains open now, infusing the air with fuzzy shafts and shadows of sunrise. 'Ta ra!' he flounced, waving his arms like a magician's assistant proclaiming her master's latest wonder.

And there I was, outside the window, a hundred metres high, staring back at myself with deep, penetrating eyes. I was sort of impressed, despite myself. I stumbled out of bed and stood naked in the middle of the room, basking in the glory of my own personal Times Square electronic billboard. Look on my works, ye mighty, and despair.

My giant reflection was naked too, shot from torso up, lean and mean, a brown-skinned, red-headed, blue-eyed idol. The eyes followed wherever you moved with a laser-targeted gaze. YEAR ZERO said the legend, shimmering above my scrawny chest.

Cornelius, my photographer, had worked wonders as usual but I've never got it myself, not really, if I am going to be honest, and I want to be honest otherwise what is the point? I can fill myself up, puff my chest out, square my shoulders and walk the walk but when I look in the mirror I don't see The Most Beautiful Boy in the World (*American Vague*), Top of the Hotties (*Teanmeat*), Pop's Sexiest Idol (*Virus*) or even the Irish Elvis (*Rolling Stoned*). I see the same skinny, fish-lip, ginger half-breed who's been staring me down in mirrors since self-consciousness erupted in my teenage brain like volcanic acne. I see a walking freakshow, a bully magnet, the playground weirdo still longing for eyes to look on me with something other than curiosity or revulsion. Any eyes. Even my own.

Oh, what I would have given for girls to look at me the way they look at me now, when it doesn't mean anything, when all they see is an idea of me, a shining reflection of their own desire. I was so fucking angry back then, most girls I knew were probably afraid of me. All except for Eileen, of course, lovely Eileen. I tried not to think about her any more, cause just a glimpse of an out-of-focus photograph of us together in some tatty fan book made me want to sink to my knees and prostrate myself in shame. The only girl who ever loved me for myself and I dropped her like a stone, walked away without looking back, mesmerised by a future of silicone groupies with collagen chops. Gave her up for a thousand cheap lays and a shot at Penelope Nazareth.

And, with that, the wave of nausea broke inside me, and I just about made it into the pristine bathroom suite to chuck my guts up.

'You overcooked it last night,' said Kilo, not sounding remotely worried that his wake-up line may have tipped the scales. We had gone through variations of this scene too many times before. Kilo was an expert in the art of chemical balance, a man who had a compound for every occasion.

'I'm feeling better already,' I groaned.

Two little black rabbit pellets rolled onto the gleaming surface next to me. 'These'll clear your head,' said Kilo, 'but wait till you've finished heaving.'

Sound advice. I retched again. 'Did I do anything I'm going to regret?' I asked.

'You were magnificent,' said Kilo, almost as if he meant it.

'Was there something with a coat-check girl?' Maybe it was just another bad dream. I would hate anything like that getting back to Penelope, my so-called soulmate, dearly beloved bride-to-be, who I hadn't seen for over two months and she couldn't even take the weekend off to come to my launch. So she was shooting some fucking Inca epic halfway up the Amazon in a location so remote they couldn't even get a satellite signal, but what kind of excuse was that?

'Beasley took care of it,' said Kilo. 'All she wanted were tickets to the show.'

And the moral of that story is: if you are going to fuck around, you're much better off with a civilian than a stripper, model or groupie. Strippers always go to the press.

I hauled myself to my feet, well, almost all the way to my feet, popped the pills and gratefully accepted the miniature bottle of hotel-branded mineral water that Kilo was holding out. It was coming back to me now. We rode in on a gunship, some fuck-off military helicopter with my tag on the side, 'Ride of the Valkyries' booming out of front-mounted speakers as we buzzed the Manhattan skyline, trailing plumes of coloured smoke, descending like the wrath of God on the roof of the Illium Tower at twilight in a stroboscopic blaze of paparazzi flash. That was Beasley's idea, an apocalyptic vibe to tie in with the whole Year Zero branding: doomed youth, the beginning of the end of the world as we know it, everybody sing along now: *We were never young / We were born into a world you had already destroyed.* Don't try and act like you don't know it, biggest fucking hit of the 21st Century, number one in thirty-four territories, most streamed track of all time.

'Life has just begun / It's the beginning of the end for all the girls and boys.'

My idea, which was a much better idea, was to buy a battleship (I found one for sale on eBay), get the hottest graffiti artists to tag it top to bottom then sail it up the mouth of the Hudson, come in under the Statue of Liberty, dock it at Ground Zero and throw the launch party on the boat. What a fucking photo op that would have been. But, you know, budget, blah blah, permission to dock, blah blah, and this was the clincher: what are we going to do with the boat when the campaign is over, turn it into a floating museum of pop memorabilia? So the chopper was a compromise and not some stroke of genius from my so-called manager, if you really want the truth. But I guess it meant I didn't have to set sail a week before from Southampton which, anyway, would have spoiled the surprise.

Plus, I get seasick.

2

By the time my skinny body had been thoroughly pummelled by the high-pressure shower, I was starting to feel almost human. Either that or Kilo's drugs were kicking in. But my chemically assisted mood kept being hampered by flashbacks from the party, lo-rez mental body shots that made my sphincter clench. Like a bulb popping in my skull, I saw myself posing for a cheesy snap with the wicked witch from *The Scum*, the self-styled 'celebrity's friend' shoving fake tits in my face like we were literally bosom buddies. And after what she said about my movie debut and I quote: 'The CGI effects may be amazing but there's no supercomputer in the world smart enough to animate Zero's face.' I never forget an insult. I should have head butted the two-faced bitch but I went into performing monkey mode as per fucking usual, flirting with the girls, throwing shapes for the boys, singing for my supper.

When The Zero Sums first set sail it was take no prisoners, kiss no ass. But that was before I met Beasley and started to listen to his hypnotic spiel about world domination, that husky whisper echoing like a voice in my own head, saying the things I could never admit to any other living soul. Like how much I really wanted it. And how I would have it, whatever the price. Dance, monkey, dance.

Kilo handed me a phone as I came out of the bathroom in a blast of escaping steam, towel wrapped around my waist, which was just as well because my bedroom was filling up. Hair and Wardrobe. 'Make yourselves at home, girls,' I said, grinning to cover another stab of irritation. Six fucking fifteen and there's already four people in my space, if you count the flunky delivering breakfast as an actual person, which I always do. Linzi had clothes laid out on the bed, Kelly got her fingers straight into my hair while I took the first of the phoners, sipping a double espresso and munching a croissant.

It was an easy one for starters, a mid-morning pop show in Dublin. The DJ, Barry Barrie (just Barry to his friends), tried to come over like a close personal amigo and why not? I used to listen to his show when I was a kid. It was meaningless banter and I'm good at that, the more shallow and vacuous the better.

'How's New York?' he asked, of course he did, of course.

'So good they named it twice . . . once for the night before, and once for the morning after,' I shot back, ignoring Kilo's raised eyebrow, like I should be paying royalties for stealing his crap jokes. It's all about timing and mine is better than his.

It didn't take long to get on a roll. I was talking louder than strictly necessary, firing stealth bombs that surprised myself. It was like the unholy spirit had descended. It doesn't matter if it's Madison Square Gardens or a wake-up call with an ingratiating Dublin DJ, it is showtime and the monkey's got his groove on. But then the insensitive fucker had to go and bring up the subject of Penelope. 'So where's the gorgeous Ms Nazareth while you're taking Manhattan by storm?' was all he said but it was enough to give me a lurch, a pocket of unexpected turbulence. Maybe it was the realisation that every single person I spoke to today was going to ask the same fucking question. And last time I looked we had about a zillion interviews scheduled. I spun a line about how Penelope wasn't invited because 'I don't like being upstaged at my own parties' and we had a good fake chuckle together, my showbiz buddy Barry Barrie and me. Then he hit me blindside. 'So you're still very much an item, despite what some of the more, shall we say, scurrilous scandal sites have been saying about Penelope and Troy Anthony?'

I felt dead airtime opening in front of me. I had to say something before my host was compelled to fill it for me. 'Troy is co-star in her new movie,' was the best I could come up with. 'I'm co-star for life.' It was so cheesy it might have made me puke if I hadn't already emptied the contents of my stomach.

'That go OK?' said Kilo, already consulting his call sheet and lining up the next interview. Linzi was teasing gel through my hair, Kelly was comparing T-shirts, everyone carrying on like it's business as per fucking usual.

I decided to play it cool, which lasted all of, oh, maybe one fifteenth of a microsecond. 'What the fuck are they saying about Penelope and Troy Anthony?'

'You know I never pay attention to that shit,' said Kilo, with the same blank face he pulls walking through customs, although I knew nothing of the sort. Kelly held up an ensemble of artfully torn designer leather jacket and jeans, the anti-bling look they call it, Black Irish (registered trademark), and shot me a reassuring smile. Now she definitely read that shit.

'I think we should go with the branded *Year Zero* T-shirt for *Breakfast* and then change into something more retro for MTV,' she announced, as if anyone was fucking interested. Something was not right but Kilo was telling my next caller he had Zero on the line.

'What time is it in Brazil?' I hissed. 'See if you can get hold of Penelope.' And then I was on air, bright and breezy with some smart-arse motormouth in London, one of those self-amused pranksters who wants everyone to know how fucking clever he is and spends the whole interview trying to make you walk into his punchline. I picture them nodding and winking in the privacy of their own sound booths as they dream up stupid questions. 'So, Zero, if you were never young, how old are you now?'

I mean, what the fuck are you supposed to say to something like that? 'Age is just a number, and as long as I'm number one, who's counting?' I wanted to kick everyone out of my room, pull the covers over my head and sleep for a thousand years. Instead I was bouncing around, jumping on the furniture, trying to do verbal battle with a disembodied voice from the other side of the Atlantic.

'Your new album, out Friday, is called *Year Zero*,' announced my persecutor. 'Love the subtle pun on your name there. Did it take you long to think that up?'

'I have teams of people working round the clock,' I said. Actually, that's true.

'I'll bet you do. Your first solo album was *Zero Hour*, that was another good one. And I hear your old band The Sums are recording an album without you. It's going to be called *Minus Zero*.'

'The Sums did release a record without me,' I said, struggling on. 'You probably didn't notice because it sold zero copies.'

'Ouch,' he said. As well he might. But it got worse. He started telling me about his fixation with Penelope. 'I used to have a pin-up of your fiancée on my wall when I was, well, just a bit younger than you are now, I guess. You know the poster, I'm sure, *Suicide Blonde*, very sexy pose, it was in every red-blooded boy's bedroom back in the day. Did you ever look up at that poster and think "That's the woman I am going to marry"? I know I did.'

I got that all the time, the implication being that I was acting out some adolescent infatuation, and our great romance could be reduced to an act of celebrity stalking. People had a sense of ownership over Penelope. She had been a sex goddess since biblical times, or at least pre-Google, then some Irish runt who was filling nappies when she had her first hit comes along and snatches her away. Well, fuck 'em all.

True love never was predictable, otherwise what would we write songs about?

'Some of us get the women of our dreams and some just go on dreaming,' I said. 'Have you still got that poster, or did your mother make you take it down?'

It was just banter, five minutes of trivia to promote my new album, but daggers had been drawn. I wanted to reach down that phone line and stab him in the throat. But he was too quick for me.

'No, I've got a poster of Penelope and Troy Anthony now,' he said.

I managed to squeeze out a hollow laugh but it was too early in the day for this. I didn't have my force field up yet. Fucking interviewers. They worm their way inside your head, burrow under your skin, probing away for sensitive tissue, armed with erroneous facts and figures, clippings full of every stupid remark you ever made, ready to throw it back in your face. Never trust a journalist. Beasley told me that. 'They'll sing your praises, laugh at your jokes, hang on every word like you are the most fascinating being to walk the earth since Jesus pissed off to heaven, but all they are interested in is a headline.'

This was a whole rap he laid on me when we started out together. 'The media is a whore,' was another one of his maxims. 'You can fuck them any which way you want but they will always make you pay.'

He was full of this shit; his Bad Wisdom he called it when he was feeling particularly pleased with himself, which was most of the time. I don't know why I ever listened to him.

Because he was usually right, I suppose. Or maybe because he was telling me what I wanted to hear. About how we were on a quest, a mission to the stars, strapped to a guided missile blazing its way to the centre of the entertainment universe. And when it detonated, stand back, cause this was gonna be the supermassive supernova of superstardom, not just a global brand but a celestial event, Elvis, Madonna, Mickey Fucking Mouse and Jesus H Himself, all collapsed into one, The ONE, preceded by a dollar sign and followed by an endless procession of Zeros, me to the power of infinity. But, as he never ceased to remind me, you can't get something from nothing. Beasley did what no teacher in school ever managed to: tap my inner workaholic. Life with Beasley was fucking relentless.

Speaking of the devil, the smell of cordite came wafting to my nostrils, the stench of one of his godawful cigars. Beelzebub was in the house. The bedroom door swung open, briefly revealing a clatter and hum of activity (what were all those people doing in my suite?) as my manager made his usual impressive entrance, a big, bald, sweaty human cannonball in slo-mo flight, artfully tailored, stressed cotton suit billowing around him. By any objective criteria, Beasley was a very fat man, but he never struck me as soft. He was tightly compressed, as if he started out larger than life and got packed down, squashed into a body not quite big enough to contain him. The beads of sweat pricking his forehead looked like an early warning system indicating he might spontaneously combust at any moment. Clutching newspapers in both puffed-up fists, jaw clenched tight around his cigar, he glanced imperiously around the room before settling his gaze on me to triumphantly announce: 'We are UBIQUITOUS!'

He tossed the newspapers on the bed. Kilo and the girls dutifully applauded in acknowledgement that my arrival was front page on every first edition. Even the *New York Times* had me stepping out of the helicopter, this descent into blatant populism excused by an ironic headline: 'MAKE MONEY, NOT WAR: Brand Zero Appropriates Military Might for Marketing Assault on America's Youth'.

'Oooh, look, you've pushed the orphans off the front page,' noted Kilo, perfectly aware this was exactly what Beasley wanted to hear. The plight of the so-called Orphans of Medellín, street children devastated by a combination of economic breakdown, political impotence and natural disaster, had become the hobby horse of the hour, with heart-rending pictures of photogenic victims going viral, and had dominated the news for several days running. But not any more.

'They don't buy music anyway,' smiled Beasley, who delighted in affronting delicate sensibilities. Blowing smoke rings, he made a speedy inspection of my appearance. 'Ready to face your public?'

I was ready to get back into bed but Beasley always made me feel I had to rise to a challenge, and that it would be craven to admit weakness or doubt. And to be fair to Beasley (though fuck knows why, I have no reason to be fair to him, of all people) it is hard to complain of overwork to a boss who works harder than you (was he my boss? Wasn't he supposed to be in my employ?). He was usually the last man standing at night and up at the crack of dawn. Fuck knows why, since he had so many minions to do his bidding, many of whom had stealthily assembled in my suite while I was being made human.

Reflecting my status as the biggest swinging dick in town, the luxuriously appointed living area of the penthouse suite stretched the length of one side of the hotel. Which was just as well, since Beasley's battalion of road managers, tour managers, product managers, assistant managers, assistants to assistant managers, assistants of every hue and gender, agents, publicity reps, record company reps and all the other small-credit people deemed necessary to bring my message to the world were colonising every polished surface with their smartphones, tablets, laptops and printers, comparing presentations across leather-topped tables, sticking Post-it notes to a cylindrical glass tank housing a family of exotic jellyfish and making Facetime calls from opposite ends of elongated sofas. My entrance created the usual micro-vacuum as every conversation paused, every eye turned, just for an instant. Then they all started chattering again, slightly louder than before.

I didn't need two guesses whose bright idea it was to turn my suite into the war room. 'If the mountain won't come to Muhammad . . .' Beasley growled, giving me a warning nod as I turned to acknowledge the digicam that had me trained in its sights, webcasting my every move to my most adoring, obsessive, or just plain bored-out-of-their-skulls-with-nothing-better-to-do fans on zero24seven.com.

'Good morning, Vietnam!' I bellowed, pulling a funny face.

It was pathetic, really. I couldn't fucking help myself. My inanity was greeted with gratuitous applause from the busy bees, who have perfected the kind of in-built laugh track that would make them an asset to any sitcom.

I've got to be honest, zero24seven was my bright idea, not Beasley's, and one I had come to regret. Like every other homestar with a cheap mic and an IP address, back in prehistory my bedroom was my stage and the net my only spotlight. At first I wasn't sure if the dark theatre of web dreams was empty or teeming with other lost souls until my hit counter started going haywire. I only formed The Zero Sums so I could fuck some of the honeyz in my inbox, if I'm completely honest, which, of course, I am. Maybe I should have just stayed in my room and ordered pizza, a legend in my own upload time. It was never as pure in the real world, never as easy to control, people kept straying from the script, it got complicated and messy and it all ended in tears. Not mine, obviously. So when Beasley came calling, I told him about my fantasy of webcasting twenty-four hours a day in real time, so that I could find that synthesis between my first and second life, real and virtual, invite people into my space without having to go out into theirs. At least that was the idea. Clearly, I hadn't thought it through.

Everyone's at it now, so it's easy to forget that it was briefly hailed as a zeitgeist-riding nu-media sensation. I was top of the pods before I even released a single. But the 24–7 concept quickly became a royal pain. When I was younger the idea that God was watching my every move filled me with dread.

Would I go to hell if I dropped dead in the middle of a five-knuckle shuffle? But when God Almighty was replaced with an all-seeing digicam and you can't rip a fart for fear of complete strangers wrinkling their noses, or worse still your dad (although in my case that didn't really apply cause my old man was so technophobic he needed the assistance of a child to plug in his electric blanket) then self-consciousness takes on a whole new dimension. The only way I could avoid behaving like a bad actor in the tragicomedy of my own life was to secretly get ripped off my tits behind the scenes (i.e. in any bathroom where I was not contractually bound to let Beasley install a camera). Thank fuck the impossible logistics of getting everyone we encountered to sign release forms put an end to the ideal of the over-examined life. We should be prosecuted under the Trade Descriptions Act because these days zero24seven was full of videos and repeats. I had live content down to a bare minimum, no more than a few hours max of the most public footage, though much of my courtship with Penelope was carried out online because she was never happier than when she was on camera. At least before the blowjob at the BRITs incident, which put her off a bit. Obviously, I hadn't answered my own emails in years. I didn't even write my own tweets.

That was Spooks McGrath's job, among others, a bespectacled, frazzle-haired techie hovering at Digicam Dude's elbow, ready to catch my every wink and stutter and feed it into the voracious maw of the beast. To his credit, in my view at least, he was the only one here who looked as bad as I felt. He had probably been up all night, editing footage and talking to the Chinese branch of the Zeromaniacs fan club while most of Beasley's clean-cut college grads were getting a good night's sleep under chamomile eyeshades.

'Looking forward to the big day?' said Spooks, which was just some inanity designed to get me going, I know, but you expect a better chat-up line from a webmaster and ghostblogger with an alleged IQ the size of a supercomputer.

'Every day is a big day,' I sighed through a fake grin, and looked into the unblinking lens, trying to imagine invisible hordes on the other side. I had to give them something better. 'Here we are in New York, New York, so good they named it twice: once for the night before, and once for the morning after!' That joke wasn't improving with age. 'First we take Manhattan, tomorrow . . . ze world!'

I screamed the last bit, obviously, jumping onto one of the leather coffee tables like a demented dictator and spilling someone's latte. The minions applauded reliably, except for the latte drinker, who was trying to stop a pool of coffee swamping her spreadsheets while smiling apologetically, like it was her fault. Which it was. Now I was standing there like a virgin at an orgy, every face in the room turned towards me and a webcam broadcasting my antics to over 45 million subscribers. How do these things happen? 'My people, my people,' I brayed, waving victory fingers and wagging devil horns. Sometimes, my mouth and body function without engaging my brain at all. 'We will fight them on the beaches, we will fight with their bitches on Coney Island beaches.' All those eyes on me, puzzled but expectant. That's when you either impale yourself or fall into the moment. When the room grows so still you can focus on particles of dust floating in the air. *'Hi-fi, wi-fi, fee-fi-fo-fum, I smell the blood of everybody in the room,'* I spat, falling into a rap I had been working up for the live version of 'Never Young', which made no sense at all in this context but these words, this rhythm was all I had to hold onto, a lifeline tossed out from my subconscious.

Everything accelerating, everybody tired of waiting
For the end of the beginning's the beginning of the end
Approaching singularity, mathematical clarity
Can't see what's up ahead, can't see what's round the bend
Radiation sickness, call Jehovah's witness
Hope they spell my name right in the Big Black Book
Pick a number, any number, odds or evens, dumb or
  dumber
Wake me from my slumber, cut me from the hook
Rich man, poor man, load up your camel
You bring the silver spoon, I'll bring the needle
But you'll never get to heaven in a fuel-injection car
You've got to come . . . to where you are!

Beasley came to my rescue, raising one arm as if to wind up applause while moving deftly in front of the table so I could put my hand on his shoulder and stand there grinning like this was perfectly normal behaviour for a rock-and-roll superstar, which, after all, it was.

'Listen up, people,' said Beasley. 'Zero's right . . .' (I am?) '. . . this weekend in New York is crucial . . .' (It is?) '. . . it is what we have been working towards all year . . .' (Did I say that?) '. . . tour kicks off Monday, album drops in all formats Friday and with our partners at Mount Olympus we've got what is shaping up to be the blockbuster movie of the summer. The single is number one, for which you should all give yourself a round of applause . . .' (They do, of course.) '. . .This year, together, we have the chance to make Zero not just the biggest artist in the world right now but one of the biggest stars in entertainment history . . .' (More applause, they are really getting into it now.) '. . . and we're counting on each and every one of you . . .' (This is just such crap. Where were these kiss-asses when I was holed up in my bedroom studio, carving out the hits?) '. . . to put all your resources behind the final push. . .' (I'd been working on this my whole life, we'd been on the *Year Zero* campaign trail for weeks already and we all knew there was no such thing as a final push, just another push, and then another, and then another.) '. . . there is still everything to play for, the world's media is here, they're watching, so let's do our jobs and make this a weekend New York will never forget.'

The applause was ridiculous, which was par for the course. They were an easy crowd. Probably thinking about their bonuses. But I accepted it on Beasley's behalf, seizing the opportunity to step down from the table. Beasley and Kilo formed a phalanx around me, with Tiny Tony Mahoney, my diminutive head of security (small but lethal, apparently) leading the way towards the door, one of his oversized grunts taking up the rear, while various apparatchiks fell in behind, and the webcrew revolved around, shooting it all. The same thing happened every time I moved from one spot to another: instant entourage. If I got taken short in a public place, there would be a line of my own employees forming behind me at the urinal before I could get my dick out.

Nodding and smiling, kissing a cheek here, patting an elbow there, I worked the room, even though these were my people, for fuck's sake, I didn't have to impress them, they were here for me, me, me, me. Everything is fucking me. We picked up more security at the door, into the lift (ejecting a hapless hotel guest, whose indignation was bought off with a quick autograph for his daughter), through the lobby (security fending off a sudden rush of lurking Zeromaniacs), slipping on some evil logo shades courtesy of Linzi before stepping onto the street where a swarm of stalkerazzi called my name, flashbulbs popping, camera motors whirring, click click clickety click. How many fucking photographs do they actually need? What do they do with all these identical frames of me stunting on sidewalks? How can they even tell one shot from another? Then a voice sliced through my dreaminess: 'Hey, Zero, what do you think of the pics of Penelope and Troy?' Flash. I knew in my sinking heart that was the one they'd use, the rabbit in the headlights shot, as the limo door swung open and I escaped into the soft leather and walnut cocoon, flopping out on the couch, invisible behind the presidential tints.

3

Beasley and Kilo slid in before I pulled the door shut, cutting off the webcrew. Security would ride up front, the rest of my entourage could take the minivan convoy, I needed a moment.

'What fucking pictures of Penelope and that squarejaw cunt are they talking about?' I snapped.

Kilo glanced nervously at Beasley. 'Just the usual gutter provocation,' Beasley shrugged. 'You should know better.'

'Well, I don't know anything, that's the whole fucking problem,' I snapped back, hating the sound of my whining brat voice while Beasley played Big Daddy. I turned my attention to Kilo instead. At least him I could bully. 'Did you get hold of Penelope?'

He started making excuses about time zones, jungle locations, the unreliability of satphones, blah de fucking blah, but I wasn't buying any of it. If illegal loggers and coke barons could run profitable businesses in the rainforest, nobody was going to convince me a Hollywood studio couldn't get a line out for one of their most prized assets. I've seen National

Geographic. Mobile phones come just after ploughs and chickens on the must-have accessory list of the modern peasant farmer. Even the Discovery channel has given up pixilating iPhones out of shots of the Bushmen of the Kalahari. I bet there's an Internet cafe in every shanty town in the third world. Meanwhile, it had been a week since I had heard from Penelope, a fucking cinematic icon, and even that was a broken-up, digitally stuttering, incomprehensible cackle, the underlying theme of which had been the nobility of suffering for your art. She claimed to be living on location in a tent but Penelope's idea of camping bore little relation to the waterproof sheets we used to crawl inside for respite from pissing rain on so-called seaside holidays in the west of Ireland. Our tents didn't have built-in toilet facilities with hot running water. If you wanted a piss you braved the elements or went in your sleeping bag for extra warmth. I got Kilo to look up Penelope's location one night on Earthmap. It was a fucking Bedouin city. Her so-called tent was built like a wedding marquee. She had a fucking walk-in wardrobe, for fuck's sake.

And less of the fucking language, as my old man would say. I always did have a bit of a Parental Advisory sticker mouth. My English teacher, Ms Pruitt, wrote in my report that I had a flair for language but all of it was bad. When my old man read that he went thermonuclear and he had a flair for language that would have made Ms Pruitt's ears melt. But I mean, sometimes nothing hits the spot like a true blue fuck fuck fuckity fuck.

Beasley broke into Kilo's excuses, holding his right index finger aloft, six inches from the end of my nose. 'Is this going to be an issue? You've got to focus.' He took some training from a hypnotist once and always used the same tricks to assert authority.

'I'm focused, I'm focused, fuck's sake, I'm fucking focused,' I whined. 'Why the fuck aren't we moving?'

My unflappable PR, Flavia Sharpe, had broken through the scrum and was rapping a bony knuckle on our tinted windows.

'The world is watching,' Beasley reminded me as he opened the door and flashes popped.

And then the limo earned its stretch, filling up with people, my people, so many of my fucking people that I relented and waved Spooks McGrath and his crew in. The world was always fucking watching. That was the whole point. One of these days it was going to watch me taking a dump, get an anal probe and shove it up my sphincter, check out if there was any truth in the rumour that I had Penelope's name tattooed on my liver.

'Welcome to my humble abode,' I declared, magnanimously. 'There's champagne on ice if anyone's got the stomach – at this time of the morning. H_2O for the wetwipes among us – I'll have one of those, thank you. . .' (At this point I had to fend off offers of mineral water, selecting a bottle proffered by a smiling woman I didn't recognise, looking impishly dishevelled in a two-sizes-too-small dress topped off by a shock of unkempt hair dyed a near reflective blond) '. . .And in case you've missed breakfast, I think you will find I have been supplied with an excellent bunch of bananas, though I've no idea why.'

'It's on your rider,' said Kilo, a touch sulkily, I thought, maybe because I didn't take his water bottle.

'I don't even like bananas,' I snorted.

And everyone laughed. Like I said, your own employees are an easy crowd. Someone was quietly snapping pictures, and not my usual photographer, Cornelius, who had done the limo ride too many times to care, and was watching streets glide by with an air of ambient awareness, as if, should some particular juxtaposition of light, form and content manifest, he would suddenly spring into action, which, in fact, I had seen him do many times before. I liked having Cornelius around, cause he took pictures that made me look like the person I imagined myself to be, rather than the person I saw in the mirror. Not every photographer can do that, which is why this interloper, a small, leathery-skinned Latino with a stupid soul patch goatee and a fish eye lens was making me agitated. I hadn't even seen his portfolio, for fuck's sake.

Sensing my displeasure (which was, after all, part of her job), Flavia affected introductions. A team from *The Times* was travelling with us to make sure our US invasion got covered back in the UK. The blonde was feature writer Kitty Queenan, who smiled demurely and said, 'You won't even notice we're here.' I doubted that, somehow. Her eyes were lasers. Her byline seemed familiar, which must have meant she once wrote something nasty about me.

'Wouldn't it have been cheaper for your parents just to buy a cat?' I said, by way of making conversation.

'Kitty is a common form of Katherine,' said Flavia, instinctively smoothing away my habitual rudeness.

Kitty herself was unperturbed, looking at me with sporting amusement, like a gladiator sizing up a lippy Christian, if you can imagine an overweight gladiator in an ill-fitting lacy dress. 'It's a pen name,' she said. 'My friends call me Pussy.'

I knew who the enemy was now. Queen Bitch was her column; she specialised in hyperbolic put-downs and never let facts get in the way of a good pun. What the fuck was Flavia doing letting this monster loose behind the lines? She was scribbling in her notebook, which made me wonder what I had done that she found worthy of recording. I'd have to deal with her later. The photographer was Bruno Gil, a New Yorker stringer. As soon as Flavia mentioned the magic words 'We have picture approval', I lost interest. Snap away, buddy. If I didn't like what I saw, I wouldn't approve a single frame and *The Times* could make do with one of Cornelius's iconic shots just like everyone else.

Flavia was running through my itinerary. It wasn't good, my day parcelled into fifteen-minute blocks covering six A4 pages, each and every block filling me with silent dread. Flavia was a stick insect styled like Dracula's lawyer (sleek, tailored black with non-specific religious trimmings) but she exuded imperturbability, which is what Beasley liked in the people he hired, the sense that no matter how wild the hurricane was blowing, with enough hairspray everything would stay in place. She was usually surrounded by a coven of midget witches, all, in fact, frighteningly competent PR girls for Sharpe Practice, adept in the dark arts of media manipulation. I wanted to ask Flavia what the gossip sites were saying about Penelope and Troy in the jungle. She would give it to me straight, or at least make it sound palatable in her silken English tones. But I couldn't raise the topic in front of the vulture from *The Times*, still scratching away at her notebook, as if a ten-minute limo ride was the stuff of *War and Peace*. So I listened to Flavia's midget assistants recite their litany of evil, complete with radio station call signs, genre specifications and time allotments: 'WRDW in Philly, top forty station, ten minutes with Joe and Steph, we've spoken to them before, they're easy'; 'WFLC in Miami, adult hot, five minutes with the T2 girls, Julie and Tamara, flirty and fun'; 'WNYU, New York college radio, up to fifteen minutes with Tyrone Adamski, he's going to want to talk about music. . .'

'Not music, God forbid!' I snorted.

They smiled indulgently and continued churning out press-conference arrangements, one-on-one interviews, TV slots. I stared out the window, craning my neck to quietly marvel at this towering metropolis glittering in the morning sun, a dizzying spectacle that always set my country heart aflutter. New York's skyline spun me all the way back to the cliffs of Moher, day trips by the Irish seaside. I was momentarily overloaded by the vertical rush and horizontal buzz, a stream of bodies rising from subways, dodging traffic, snatching cigarettes, yelling into phones, grabbing coffee and pastries and newspapers with stories about me and Penelope and fucking Troy fucking Anthony. I tried to let it all wash over me.

'Donut asked if we can absolutely ring-fence rehearsal time,' interjected Eugenie Arrowsmith, Beasley's personal assistant. Duncan 'Donut' McCann, my perpetually stressed tour manager, was given to complaining I spent more time talking about music than making it, which, of course, was true. With days to go before showtime, we still hadn't managed a full dress rehearsal of the whole set. Actually, that's not fair, I am sure the band and crew had been through it dozens of times without me.

'I thought we could bring some international press over for that, give them a bit of colour,' suggested Flavia.

'Donut really wants Zero's undivided attention,' said Eugenie.

'Everybody wants Zero's undivided attention,' retorted Flavia.

That's right, talk about me as if I'm not here.

We had only got as far as page two of my schedule when the limo pulled up at FNY studios, where the sidewalk was cordoned off for photographers and Zeromaniacs. They had probably hot-footed it over the few blocks from the hotel, New York being quicker by foot than limo. Not that I was ever allowed to walk the streets for fear of spontaneous outbreaks of civil insurrection or something that wasn't covered by insurance.

An FNY news crew was on hand to shoot my arrival, so we gave it the full service, stony-faced security clearing a path as I ran the gauntlet, touched some hands, scribbled on scraps of paper and allowed myself to be whisked through revolving doors into a vast atrium of air-conditioned sanctuary. I paused in the filtered light to look back at the hysteria unfolding soundlessly on the other side of reinforced glass. For one brief moment, it felt like they were the monkeys in a cage, not me. Then a door exploded open as one tearful Zeromaniac broke the cordon, eluded a uniformed doorman and came screaming across the polished floor. One of my security grunts, moving quicker than I would have credited, took her down. It was not a fair contest. She was a girl not much younger than me, suddenly embarrassed and scared to find herself pinned beneath a creature the size of a sumo wrestler. She stretched out a hand to try and catch her spectacles as they skittered across the tiles.

Tiny Tony began to move me away from the action but I was transfixed. What forces were at work that could detach a girl from her ordinary inhibitions, her sense of herself in the world, and turn her into a quivering hysteric? Was I responsible for this illusion or just part of it, equally in thrall to the music and marketing, the lights and smoke and mirrors, the power of suggestion, the demands of role play? Don't you people know by now that the famous are just like you, they shit like you, spit like you, piss like you, and lie in bed at night wishing they were someone else, like you?

She was a pretty girl, someone I might have been too shy to ask for a dance just a few years ago but maybe, if we had got to talking, she would have let me walk her to the bus stop, and we would have discovered what books we both read and what music we loved and where we dreamed life might take us, and who knows, who knows? She reminded me of Eileen, just a little. But there she was, spreadeagled, making whimpering noises and blushing furiously. I was the one who should have been embarrassed. I broke free to pick up her glasses, then waving away the grunt, bent down and helped her to her feet, walking her back to the entrance while she wept uncontrollably.

The FNY TV crew caught the whole thing, and it was swiftly edited together to provide a dramatic clip to introduce me on air. 'I bet that kind of thing happens to you all the time?' winked our host, Gordy, the perma-tanned, blow-dried, silver-haired anchorman of the top-rated East Coast breakfast show.

'Only when I come here,' I twinkled back. 'She was looking for you. She wanted me to ask for your autograph.'

He laughed but I could see the idea appealed. He was seated on an excessively bright orange couch, next to his new sidekick Mindy (Gordy got through co-anchors quicker than I got through personal assistants, and probably for the same reason: an inability to keep his dick in his pants).

With big hair, dimples and lively smile, Mindy was a weather girl riding the updraft, an impression compounded by newly installed breast enhancements. Mindy played not-quite-as-dumb-as-I-look blonde to Gordy's statesman-about-the-house, tossing jokey remarks and laughing in all the right places, but there was a raptness beneath the make-up. She was making me nervous as we faced each other across a small potted plant and MacBook perched on a modernist glass table, items intended to symbolise the show's unreliable mix of hard news and cosy chit-chat. Only a glass wall separated the studio from the busy news floor. By some trick of lighting it glowed white and opaque until a story broke, when it would gradually become transparent, revealing a vast room full of journalists frowning into computers and gesturing at rolling footage on flatscreens.

Gordy famously made his name in the thick of the action, donning flak jacket and helmet to file reports from war zones. But in his new domestic niche, he was savvy enough to understand that it was early, guests were doing him a favour turning up at this hour and viewers were only half awake. He asked the kind of questions you could answer with a bashful grin and well-honed anecdote. Softball, they call it. Mindy was a loose cannon, though. I could tell she was dying to ask about Penelope and it wasn't long before she lobbed one in. 'With girls throwing themselves at you wherever you go, that must put pressure on maintaining a relationship.'

'I have my security guards to keep them at bay,' I smiled back.

'As we've just seen,' grinned Gordy, who felt it necessary to underline gags in case they went over the sleepy heads and low IQs of his target audience.

'And what about Penelope, does she need security?' smiled Mindy.

'Penelope can look after herself,' I smiled back.

'So I've heard,' said Mindy, raising one eyebrow knowingly, a look she must have practised for fucking hours in the mirror. Fuck them, fuck them all, grinning at you while they toss grenades. I noticed Gordy didn't bother underlining that one. I wanted to kick over the fucking table and dump the ridiculous potted plant on Mindy's head. I wanted to let out a banshee howl that would shatter the glass wall and carry on the wind all the way from New York to the Amazon jungle, where Penelope and Troy fucking Anthony would look up to see the burning eyes of monkeys gathering in the trees and know, with a chill in their filthy hearts, that I was on to them. But instead I winked at Mindy and said, 'Do you think you could make it past my security? You look like you've got a few moves.'

'Oh, I used to be a cheerleader, I've definitely got moves,' she flirted, moving Gordy to interject with a jocular, 'Come on, you kids, this is a family show.'

'"Come On, You Kids",' I said. 'That's genius. That's gonna be the title of my next song.' And I started to sing, 'Come on, you kids, let's rock and roll, but keep it clean, it's a family show,' while Gordy and Mindy laughed indulgently and we were best of friends again, filling airtime until, at a prearranged signal, Gordy invited me to perform my latest single.

'I actually didn't know Zero played piano,' wittered Mindy, just to say something while I crossed the studio floor, as if she had only just noticed the fucking great instrument set up by my advance crew. Oh this fatuous fucking showbiz universe, this brain-numbing entertainment game.

'I'm not just a pretty face,' I said, sitting down and laying my fingers on the keys, making the studio resonate with a deep, satisfying C chord. Nine million units of my debut solo album shifted worldwide, I played every fucking instrument on there, and still I got this crap. Didn't these people ever read the credits?

'He's a very talented young man,' said Gordy, as if he actually had the faintest idea what he was talking about. Gordy, who looked like he still listened to Andy Williams, maybe a little Neil Diamond if he was in the mood to get racy. Gordy, born middle-aged and proud of it.

'This one's for you, Gordy,' I said, and ripped into 'Never Young', attacking it like the piano was a weapon of mass destruction, like the song could annihilate the world and rebuild it in its own image, right every wrong, end every war, cure cancer. Sometimes it happens. You lose yourself. And you know that is as good as it gets, you might never sing that song so well again. But as I hurled myself into the second chorus, I looked up to see Gordy staring into the middle distance, finger to his earpiece, mouthing something to his invisible controllers. Then the white glass wall slowly became translucent, revealing industrious figures in the newsroom. The floor manager was waving for me to wind up. I just kept playing, they could turn me down in the mix, the fuckers.

'I'm afraid we're going to have to interrupt Zero for news from Colombia,' announced Gordy, putting on his gravest face as he stared into his autocue. 'Reports are coming in of a second earthquake in the region, dealing a severe blow to aid efforts for the orphans whose plight has touched the world.'

Next to him, Mindy had taken on the demeanour of a saint in torment. 'Those poor children,' she said.

'Let's go to our man at the Medellín orphan camp . . .'

Those poor fucking children. I executed a dramatic descent back to the C and closed the lid of the piano. I hate leaving a piece of music unresolved.

4

'That went well, I think,' said Flavia. 'It hit all the spots. Great opening footage. You were charming, sexy – did you catch Mindy blushing, poor dear – it was a little bit edgy and you wrapped it up with a splendid performance of your song—'

'Half a fucking song,' I snapped.

'Half a song is more than enough at this time of morning,' said Flavia, who had Beasley's attention. 'It is not a music show, it's short-attention-span chat, and the biggest sin is to give viewers an excuse to go and make a cup of tea. The Medellín thing was great, really. Newsy and dramatic, people will remember it. A number of stations have been cutting "Never Young" with disaster footage and something like this will drive that connection home, give the whole thing the zeitgeist factor.'

Beasley, who had just got through threatening a hapless TV producer with a lawsuit, looked thoughtful. 'You could be onto something,' he murmured, whereupon the minions all started falling over themselves to second that motion.

It wasn't the fucking orphans that bothered me, though. I waved Kilo towards the toilets, stationing a meathead outside with strict instructions not to let anyone else in. Even superstars are entitled to privacy when they take a piss.

'Rack up a line,' I instructed Kilo. 'Make it a high-speed railway line. Make it the fucking Tokyo bullet train.'

I was never sure how much Beasley knew about the full extent of services Kilo provided, but not much got past His Satanic Majesty, so it was perfectly possible narcotic provision was part of the job description. I asked Beasley once why we had hired a Hindu homo from Hoxton and he said it was because I kept screwing all my female assistants and then requiring Beasley to replace them. Which was fair enough.

I took the rolled-up note from Kilo's hand and snorted greedily. 'That's what I'm talking about,' I groaned, leaning against a sink while spots danced before my eyes. 'Do you really think that went all right?'

'It was wonderful,' Kilo gaily reassured me, rolled-up note applied to one nostril. 'Live TV's always more exciting when things don't go to plan. You were in your element.'

'What about the Penelope thing?'

'What Penelope thing?'

'That bitch Mindy was going on about Penelope.'

'She asked, like, one question.'

'You didn't see the thing with the raised eyebrow?'

'You're reading way too much into it.'

That's not how it felt when I was out there alone, in the cameras, under the lights, with only my wits for weapons. It felt like they were probing for weakness, forked tongues and talons scratching about in the soft underbelly of my secret life, closing in on an exposed nerve, jabbing it, waiting for a reaction, licking their lips.

'Penelope's a goddess,' Kilo was saying in that happy-crappy sing-song, where every sentence ends on an uplift, perpetually suspended between sarcasm and delight. 'You're engaged, you've made a film together . . . it's bound to come up.'

'You really think I'm being oversensitive?'

'Just a touch.'

'So get Penelope on the phone.'

'I'll keep trying.'

Oh, he almost had me there. Almost. 'You can't get her on the phone?'

'I'm on the case, trust me.'

'What the fuck is going on? Get Flavia in here.'

'It's the men's toilets.'

'Yeah? Well what the fuck are you doing in here, then? Get Flavia.'

Look, I'm not proud of it, but there you go. These people were supposed to work for me.

My publicity rep looked a little nonplussed to be summoned for an audience among urinals. 'I wonder what our friend from *The Times* is going to make of you turning a gentlemen's facility into your office?'

'It's the only place I can fucking talk without her scribbling everything down in that fucking notebook,' I snapped. 'Whose bright idea was it to invite Queen Bitch along for the ride?

Didn't she write that "Nothing From Nothing Leaves Zero" piece?'

I told you, I never forget a bad review.

'Which is precisely why she is perfect for this,' insisted Flavia. 'Katherine's opinion swings from one extreme to the other, that is her entire rationale: there is nothing she likes better than contradicting herself. We're giving her the opportunity to perform another of her infamous reversals. She's around for one day, she's susceptible to flattery and, apparently like every other woman in the Western world, she thinks you are the hottest thing on two legs. So be nice. You'll charm her, she'll write something extremely clever and funny, it'll get a big splash in the paper with a handsome colour photo, and you will never need to think about her again.' We stood in silence for a moment, Flavia wrinkling her nose at the odour of disinfectant. 'Can we go now? I believe they're waiting for us at MTV.'

But I hadn't dragged her into the toilets to discuss some hack from a British rag. 'What is going on with Penelope and Troy Anthony?' I asked, nervously.

Flavia contemplated me with a steady, even gaze, as if weighing up what it was safe to tell me. In which case I must have looked truly pathetic, because something approaching sympathy actually crossed her poker face. 'There are pictures circulating of Penelope and Troy embracing. I believe they are stills from the film they are shooting, which our friends, the gossipmongers, are deliberately misrepresenting. It goes with the territory, as you should know by now. It would be a mistake to make too much of it. Just keep batting it back. You're handling it fine.'

My heart was pounding so hard I thought I could hear it echo off the tiles. Maybe it was just the coke.

'Wipe your nose,' Flavia instructed. I did as I was told, removing powdery leftovers. 'Shall we go?' she asked.

'Ladies first,' I replied.

The phalanx formed and we rolled on out, but not before Mindy caught up with me in the corridor during a commercial break. The way she said she hoped to see me later at the *Generator* awards, suddenly she didn't seem so scary. And she did have great tits, even if they were fake. I didn't really care. Reality had no place in the world we inhabited.

I did a quick phoner in the car but the deflector shield was fully operational now.

'Penelope's a goddess, I've been watching her make out with movie stars since I learned to operate a remote control.'

'So you're not even a little bit jealous?' asked the disembodied radio host on the other end of the line.

'You should ask Troy's boyfriend how *he* feels.'

Kitty Queenan snorted quietly, scribbling in her notebook. She was going to be bored of hearing that line by the end of the day.

The thing about Penelope was, I didn't even know why I was so upset. It was Hollywood rules. It didn't really matter if we stayed together or split, expressed eternal fidelity or fucked around, either way we got headlines. The more trouble, the more publicity, I understood that. Why else get engaged except to make mischief? It's so fucking old-fashioned, from an era of lace curtains and roses, when courting couples were still necking in the back seat of somebody else's car, back in the mists of time, when my own folks were wide-eyed and innocent, if they ever were, which doesn't bear thinking about. Penelope was practically primeval. I was half her age and had a whole life of sex and drugs and rock and roll in front of me.

We met on the film set, a classic location romance. My trailer or yours? You know the plot, *#1 With A Bullet*, basically a reverse-gender sci-fi *Star is Born* with kung fu and explosions. It wasn't even my idea to cast her. I thought Madonna would be perfect for the part of the fading pop queen who sacrifices herself for a young gun but she refused to play a woman her own age. Penelope stepped into the thigh-high black leather boots and my fate was sealed.

I can't explain the effect she had on me. It wasn't just fantasy fulfilment, a desire to notch one up on the bedpost. In the flesh, she was sexy and wise, her womanliness enveloping me in a way that was so emotionally overwhelming I couldn't get through rehearsing a scene without a hard-on. Which, as it turned out, never proved much of a problem. But I wanted to talk to her even while I was inside her, I wanted to thrust right into the heart of everything she knew, because it was like she knew everything about me, as if she could see all the secrets pulsating beneath my skin, all the things I kept hidden, even from myself. And for reasons I never understood, she found that exciting. She wasn't turned off by my youth and naivety, any more than she was turned on by my celebrity. Fame was meaningless to someone as famous as Penelope Nazareth. She called me '*l'enfant sauvage*', her very own wild child, and we did get wild, we got carried off in a torrent. And so we announced our engagement to the press in a storm of emotions, pledging our troth on a gambling trip to Las Vegas after consuming a dozen Es. Since which time I had hardly seen her. In six months, our schedules had coincided for a few weeks at most, days snatched here and there, transatlantic flights for a night of passion interspersed with lots of phone sex, dirty texts and soul-to-soul conversation. But you can't touch someone on Facetime. I longed to talk to her. I wanted to see her. I needed to feel her. And the thought that someone else might be doing all of that was making me sick to my stomach.

We ran the gauntlet at MTV, where New York City's finest had erected barriers to stop the crowd from shutting down traffic on Times Square. We were filming news clips, guest spots and sound bites for an online special, since even MTV wasn't commercially suicidal enough to actually put music on TV these days. But they still liked to pretend they cared, so it was all wisecracks and japes with reality nonentities, frippery and tomfoolery, quips and chit-chat, stuff and nonsense (well, I was Stuff and they were Nonsense), a scene so shallow I almost started enjoying myself. I gamely introduced some of my videos (which I could never actually bring myself to watch), led competition winners in a singalong of 'Never Young' (music is a universal gift, I truly believe that, but God save us all from overconfident screechers who wouldn't know what a key was if you used it to lock them up for life) and subjected myself to an interrogation about as probing as a skin polish with a feather duster. 'Where do you get all your brilliant ideas for songs?' Oh ask me another one, ask me another one, ask me another one, do. Some interviews are like being strapped to a chair in Guantanamo Bay and having your teeth pulled out through your sphincter by a sadistic marine armed only with pliers and a jar of K-Y. But mostly it's just toothless sycophants trying to gum you to death. Sure, Penelope's name came up but it was friendly fire and I was on my game now, fuck 'em all. Whenever things were getting dull, I could stroll over to the panoramic windows and stir some hysteria on the sidewalk. I couldn't actually hear the screaming through the reinforced glass, just see open mouths and tears. The background static in my brain was fading, perhaps aided by the sheet of codeine pills Kilo slipped me to take the edge off the coke. He said take two, but what good has moderation ever done anyone?

When we weren't on air, I was fielding phone calls, disembodied voices asking questions so old and overdone I only needed to tune into one or two key words to dial up the appropriate answer:

Press one if you want to hear amusing tales about Zero's tough childhood without a mother's love in the barren hills of Ireland.

Press two for how Zero came by his unusual name.

Press three for the latest on the hot romance between Zero and movie legend Penelope Nazareth.

Press four for the young philosopher king's inanities on the power of music to heal the world.

Press five for the hidden pain behind worldwide hits 'In The Stars', 'Make It On My Own', 'Amnesty' and 'Never Young'.

Press six to hear those anecdotes again.

Ad fucking infinitum. You should never believe what you hear about me anyway, cause it's all lies, and I should know, I tell them.

There's a Zeropedia which is supposed to collect every known piece of information about me from my first breath (one dirty morning on a table in the kitchen of Castlerea Hotel, or so I'm told) to my last known sighting (in the bathroom mirror, while taking a piss, half an hour ago, though I don't think you'll find that on the net, at least I hope not). I have been known to check the Zeropedia sometimes to find out what I am supposed to have done on such and such a date, and it usually leaves me feeling there must be another me out there living my so-called life in a parallel pop universe where Elvis is on the throne and all is well in his kingdom. And that is why you should never read your own press: the essential facts may be the same, significant dates coincide, but nothing rhymes. No bells start ringing. Events have been twisted back to front and had bits grafted on and you're left with this kind of Frankenstein fiction lumbering around, made up of bits of you and bits of other people's fantasies and bits of God knows what, space junk and landfill. Next thing you're talking about yourself in third person. 'That's not the kind of thing Zero would say,' I might say, and then immediately think, shit, who said that? Was it Zero, or was it me? What kind of name is Zero anyway? It says Pedro Ulysses Noone on my passport, which is also a fucking ridiculous name, but no one calls me Pedro any more, except close family and officers of the law.

And while we are on the subject, we might as well get this name business over and done with cause I've heard a lot of stories about how I came to be Zero and told a few myself. The favourite fansite theory is based on my surname: Noone becomes No One, i.e. nothing, nada, zilch, zero. Like kids are that smart, well, maybe they are, but not where I grew up. I've been Zero since I was seven years old. It was just a basic racist insult, because I was the only brown-skinned boy anyone in Loserville, Roscommon had ever laid eyes on. Even my brother got my old man's Irish pale face. I just got his ginger hair. All my life I had to answer to stupid Spanish nicknames. I've been Carlos, Cheech, Chong, Wah-Wah (as in Chihauha) and Torro (at first I thought that wasn't so bad. But whenever I said anything, my tormentors would shout out 'Bull-sheet!' in a stupid accent). So when *The Mask of Zorro* popped up on Saturday morning kids' TV, every pint-sized bigot in the play-ground started calling me Zero. It was only later, when I really started listening to hip-hop, I learned you can neutralise an insult by treating it as praise. Which is how come nigga became a term of endearment but only from one person of colour to another. I don't recommend any honky hipsters using it out of context cause it's still a millimetre away from starting a race riot. Anyway, as an authentic brown skin Paddy, Kilrock's first and only nigga, I wore the name Zero as a badge of pride. But try explaining that in a five-minute phone call between traffic bulletins on a breakfast show. I usually stick with the lies.

I was spinning more nonsense over the phone when Honey Pie came gambolling down the corridor, a burlesque teen beauty queen hemmed in by suits, minders and hangers-on. 'Hey, Zero!' she called out, with a camp, delighted chuckle, and blew me a theatrical kiss. She was too much of a pro to interrupt an interview but she made the universal 'call me' sign before moving on about her business. Which was nice. I had never met Honey before in my life, but we pop stars stick together. 'Honey Pie just went by,' I told my caller, inciting fake orgasmic excitement in the grey hinterland of Midwestern radioworld as the DJ stoked listener fantasies of celebrity nirvana, just out there, beyond the veil, over the rainbow, down the yellow brick road. 'Breeze Black just arrived,' I added, catching sight of a dark fury in a rainbow shock afro wig striding out of a lift with her own entourage. My announcement caused more squeals of incredulity down the line. Could life really be this glamorous? Then the pale, slender figure of movie star Gena Claudette emerged from a studio, looking dreamily distracted amid another welter of people although it was hard to tell whether they were her people or her rock-star husband Adam Monk's people, or maybe they shared people in a happy marriage of entourages: Do you take these people to be your lawfully wedded people?

We do. I couldn't help but notice, with a twinge of irritation, that my people (who had professionally ignored Honey's people and Breeze's people) were starting to twitch about Gena's people, exchanging discreet nods and smiles, probably wondering how cool it would be to work for a movie star. That's the problem with people. No fucking loyalty.

It may have been Weekend Zero but clearly I didn't have the music station all to myself. The stars were in town for the *Generator* magazine tenth anniversary awards (only in America could entering double digits be viewed as a milestone achievement), which (in one big daisy chain of mutual media masturbation) all major networks would be covering, MTV would broadcast live online, and at which I would be performing, as well as picking up several richly deserved gongs for my outstanding contributions to music and culture and civilisation as we know it, to add to all my other gratefully and humbly accepted statuettes, which presumably my manager kept, though fuck knows where. At this stage he'd have to have a warehouse. I must have had at least one gong from every TV station, pop radio station, celebrity website and music magazine in the known universe, or at least in every territory where Beasley considered a prime-time appearance to be worth its weight in additional sales and endorsements. I could spend the year just travelling from one award show to another, and last year it felt as if I did just that, perfecting the act of surprise for whatever honour was being bestowed when I knew perfectly well I had won because otherwise why would I even turn up? Critics may have fulminated, panels debated, viewers, listeners and readers voted, but Beasley negotiated.

'Hi,' said Gena, who had been discreetly lingering till I finished my call. So I said hi right back, and we did some cheek-pecking, and I tried not to think about the see-through underwear she wore in the cyberpunk remake of *Pride & Prejudice* when she strips for Mr Darcy, which is the only bit of the film worth watching. YouTube it. 'How's Penelope?' she asked and I reeled slightly until I remembered they did a movie together and were bonded for life in the sisterhood of the set.

'She's fine,' I replied. Not how the fuck should I know, the bitch never calls. 'She's shooting with Troy in Brazil.'

'That's what I heard,' sighed Gena. I was watching closely for telltale signs, in case she *had* actually heard anything. But if she had, she wasn't giving it away. Fucking actresses.

Then her husband appeared, bouncing around, all high-wire energy, eyes popping, clapping me on the shoulders. 'Just the man I wanted to see. Hey, how are you, we need to talk, can we talk?'

Much as I dug his band, Softzone, I had my suspicions about Adam Monk. He exuded the happy-clappy energy of a Born Again using the Holy Spirit to override shyness. I kept expecting him to break out in prayer or try to interest me in a copy of *The Watchtower*. Now he was propelling me away from the safe haven of my people, wheeling me down a corridor, babbling enthusiastically. 'I love "Never Young". It feels like a song the world needs right now.' He broke into a snatch of chorus, as if I needed reminding: '*We were never young, we were born into a world, you had already destroyed . . . Genius.'* Glancing back to see two sets of entourages trailing, with MTV's cameras and my own zero24seven crew capturing this collision of heavenly objects for live transmission, he tried an adjacent door then, finding it locked, ushered me around a corner. What the fuck was this about? 'You know what the world really needs? You know what we have to do?' he continued, breathlessly.

If he was a fan, my security would have had him pinioned to the floor with a truncheon rammed up his back passage, but because he was a fucking celebrity they didn't seem in the least concerned. I wished I felt as confident. Where was Tiny Tony Mahoney's taser when you needed it most? Adam opened another door onto a room occupied by MTV desk jockeys, all looking up from monitors to be confronted by superstars on walkabout. 'Sorry!' he sputtered, backing us out. The staffers broke into spontaneous applause. 'Over here!' Adam declared, pulling me through a door marked with the universal logo for men only. Another fucking washroom confab for Kitty Queenan to scribble about in her notepad. Before closing the door behind us, Adam showed the palm of his hand to the pursuing pack, which brought them to a shuffling halt. As ranking superstar, he was firmly in control.

So there we were, alone at last, a couple of pop stars in a toilet and not a gram of coke between us. I half expected him to whip out a crucifix and start demanding repentance. Instead he burst into another snatch of song, singing directly into my face. *'You make me feel like a motherless child.'* I had not the first fucking idea what he was on about, but smiled and nodded, as you do when confronted by potentially dangerous lunatics. 'A song for the orphans!' he said, as if it was the most obvious thing in the world. 'Everybody's in town, this is the moment, we've got to do it, we've got to do *something*, show those children that we care. I've been working something up, a new version of "Motherless Child". You know "Motherless Child"? Of course you do, everybody knows it: "*Sometimes I fee-ee-eeel like a—*"'

'I know it,' I assured him just to stop him breathing into my face.

'We've got some new verses. I've already roped the sainted Bono in, I am sure we can get the Boss, Madge, Sir Elton, all the old guard. I just caught up with Honey and Breeze in the lobby and they're up for it. If you get on board we'll have critical mass. We'll get everyone who's in for the *Generator* show – Dean from The Smoking Babies, I'm sure we can count on him, the guys from Safety Boots, Ed Spectrum, Ca$$andra, Premier Cru can do a rap and if he does it Cristal will do it . . . Can you imagine Cristal singing that chorus? It's going to be amazing, we've booked a studio, Softzone will lay down a track this afternoon, Atomic Dog are going to come and do their thing, then after the show just get everyone to put down a vocal, set up a feed at the ceremony, we can have this thing on iTunes by Monday. It'll be Live Aid all over again, 'feed the world', this'll be the biggest song on the planet and all proceeds go straight to the kids in Medellín. What do you say?'

What do I say? What the fuck was I supposed to say? Those fucking orphans. Hadn't they heard it was Weekend Zero?

I fucking hate charity records. You want to give to the poor, give to the fucking poor, don't make a song and dance about it. Songs are intimate, songs are personal, songs are the sound of a human voice expressing their innermost secrets, not a fucking celebrity rabble swapping lines for effect. And don't talk to me about saving starving Africans. I watched Live8 on TV and even at eleven years old I wanted to puke at the sight of all those preening peacocks puffing up their social consciences then stuffing their gullets on a backstage buffet. And you know what? The Africans are still fucking starving. Yea, the meek shall inherit the earth but not until the rest of us have fucked it for all it's worth. Live Earth was even worse: fly a bunch of pop stars around the planet to tell us to stop flying around the planet cause we're doomed, we're doomed, we're all fucking doomed, like we didn't know already, we grew up doomed, cause you had it all, you fucking users, you had it, you ate it, you snorted it, you burned it, you spent it, and now you want us to pick up the tab. Well you can fuck right off, cause like the song says, we grew up in a world you had already destroyed. You want to sing along? I've got a good one for you. *I feel no pain.* All the children sing with me now. *I feel no pain.* Let me hear you, Adam, let me hear Bono, let me hear you, Brucey baby. *I feel no pain like my pain, feel my pain, feel my pain, feel my pain* . . .

That's not what I said to Adam Monk, though. I told him I would do whatever I could to help, and he gave me a hug, and we left the washroom to the embrace of our entourages. We were whisked away for an on-camera love-in, in which we declared how much we admired each other's work, joked about the domestic hell of being married to movie stars ('Even on our honeymoon, Gena insisted on a body double' was such a good line, I filed it away to use myself) and dropped heavy hints that we planned to record together, all to be revealed in due course. Then Adam went into a huddle with MTV execs and I corralled Beasley and Flavia and their favourite minions in an empty boardroom. I filled them in on the proposed charity record while throwing down mouthfuls of pasta covered in some kind of basil emulsion as Kelly fussed over my hair. There was general inane enthusiasm about Adam Monk's idea from the minions, although Beasley's face was unreadable. He would be fiercely calculating whether this would put a positive spin on our campaign or steal our thunder. 'Well, I don't want to do it,' I said, just so they knew how I felt, as if they even cared.

'Given that you practically just announced it live on MTV, it may be a little late to start expressing reservations,' noted Flavia.

'Download the lyrics of "Motherless Child",' Beasley instructed his assistant, Eugenie. 'If we're going to do this, I want to make sure Zero gets the money shot. Let's identify the key line and make sure our boy is singing it. And get Adam Monk's manager on the line. My artist doesn't get railroaded by anybody, I don't care how big they think they are.'

'It's for the orphans,' said Kelly, timidly.

'The orphans are not our concern,' snapped Beasley. Oh, he was a man after my own black heart.

5

We staged a mass exodus to the Pilgrim Hotel for award rehearsals, an MTV crew expanding my entourage. Any normal person of sound mind and limb would walk the fifty metres across Times Square but we went twice round the block so that I could be transferred from limo to blacked-out people carrier and sneaked in through the rear goods entrance. The Zeromaniacs, of course, were way ahead of us, screaming and banging on the side of the van as it drove past production trucks into underground parking. I was hustled like a presidential candidate on assassination watch into a staff elevator, almost colliding with Sting as the holistic superstar made an exit after his own rehearsal. 'Have you been roped in by the do-gooders to save the orphans?' he enquired, while my people faced off his people, mobiles at the ready.

'I hate charity records,' I muttered.

'We all hate charity records,' the greying Adonis laughed. 'It's the things that test us that make us stronger.'

Then we were on the move again, emerging amid a cackle of walkie-talkies into an enormous ballroom, the ceiling a sea of chandelier glass blazing in the glare of TV lighting. One wall bore a blow-up of the latest *Generator* cover, featuring yours truly, naked from the waist up, with a Superman logo painted on my chest beneath the headline 'From Zero To Hero'. I was introduced to camera crews, stage managers and TV directors, tragically hip men the age of my father squeezed into clothes two generations too young. One was even wearing my own brand tailored trackies, which of course I complimented him on, even though they made him look like a lardass loser. Not the feel my designers were going for, I suspect.

A tall, nervous, middle-aged effete in mod suit and ponytail turned out to be *Generator*'s editor. 'Hope you enjoyed the cover feature,' he murmured. 'Brian Spitzer is America's finest contemporary music writer and I really think he's done you proud.'

'I never read my own press,' I said.

It's not true, of course, but why give them the satisfaction? But I had to wink and show him I was just joking. I am so weak.

Our host for the evening's event was lured out of his dressing room to pay his respects. I could see him switch into on-mode, casual stroll turning into shoulder-rolling, street-hustling slouch. Willard Meeks was a black American online comic with a hyperactive persona and a rep for tweeting the untweetable. I had caught his act on U-Bend and he was pretty funny but I was already cringing in anticipation of assault.

'Yo, Zero, wassup, bro?' he started in, like we were old friends. 'You left my girl Penelope in the jungle with Troy

Anthony? What's wrong with you, man? You think she won't go for a man her own age? Ain't you watched any of his movies? Goddamn, his ass oughta have its own agent. He must be, like, contractually obligated to drop his pants every movie or the ass goes on strike. You got to respect an ass with the clout to swing a shower scene in a biopic of George Washington. Only man in the world I'd recognise by his buttocks. If he came into the room now, buck naked, backwards, I be like, "Hey, Troy, thanks for coming on the show." You better pray those Amazonian mosquitoes are sucking the blood out of his white ass, cause I don't like to think what else is getting chewed up, you know what I'm saying?' Then he let out a big yuck of trademark laughter to remind me we were all show buddies here, just trading banter.

I have never understood people who think it's a testament of character to be able to laugh at themselves. Why would I want to laugh at myself? It's hard enough getting out of bed in the morning without starting with the premise that life's a big fucking joke and I'm the punchline. I had enough of it in school, I had it all my fucking life, and I didn't claw my way to the top of the fucking hit parade just to take more fucking abuse from fucking self-styled verbal vigilantes. But it's no use trading one-liners with a comedian. It was either smile or punch him in the throat. I'd have a word with Beasley. No jokes about Penelope tonight or we'd pull the show.

My band was already onstage, with Donut McCann fretting about the suitability of the hired backline, our own equipment being in a studio in Queens, where, he reminded me at least ten times, I was scheduled to do a full dress rehearsal at four. 'What do you need me for, Donut?' I chided him. 'I know all the songs, I wrote them.'

'Then don't come crying to me on Monday night if you stand over the wrong trapdoor and get a firework up your arse in front of a full house at the Garden,' snarled Donut.

He had a point, I suppose.

We ran through 'Never Young' a couple of times for camera blocking. The bright sparks at *Generator* had proposed bringing in a choir of infants dressed like war refugees to join in the chorus, which Beasley opposed out of concern that it might be perceived to be crass in light of the Medellín orphan situation, and Donut opposed on the more practical basis that you should never work with children, especially on a tight schedule. So we came up with a choir of septuagenarians, the oldest gospel singers we could find that could stand without a Zimmer frame and hold a note. Dressed in white robes, they looked like a choir of ghosts. The backdrop was supposed to be black-and-white footage of children in peril, in wars, famines and refugee camps throughout the last century, finally freeze-framing on a particularly appealing Medellín orphan, but when they sat down to watch the edit, no one could get through without bawling their eyes out. Well, no one except Beasley, obviously, but he pulled it on the grounds it would create negative associations. So instead, someone hastily assembled global-warming disaster footage, floods, fires, stranded polar bears and pictures of the Earth from outer space, ending with a newborn baby being held up to his mother for the first time. Her expression as she pulled this tiny creature to her breast still got me, to be honest, but I didn't have to look at it, I was on the mic, back turned to the big screen. I wasn't playing an instrument for this, just standing very still and singing my heart out, dropping to my knees for the finale. At the end, the studio techs broke into applause, which is usually a good sign.

The old folks didn't have the faintest idea who I was, which was nice. They just smiled at me benignly like I was a clever child who could sing. When I went over to say hello, only one man asked for my autograph, for his granddaughter, and then glowered intently when I scribbled in his book, before asking, 'What's that say?'

'Zero,' I said.

'Your name, son, write your name,' he insisted, rather fiercely, and had to be helped back onto the choir stand by Donut and my musical director, Carlton Wick.

For a moment I stood and stared at this motley assembly of worn-out skin and bone, liver spots, rheumy eyes, wrinkles so deep they were like scars on the surface of the earth, and had to pull my gaze away with a shiver, a cold tremble running up my gullet. Was that where we were all going? I've never really known anybody old, not really old. My Irish grandparents were gone before I was born, or before I remember anyway. And my mother's parents were an abstraction, I had never really given them any thought. I don't know if she even had parents, maybe she was an orphan, or there was some big disruption with her family back in the mists of time, I don't remember her ever talking about them, I don't remember her ever talking, I don't really remember her at all. She never got old. Live fast, die young, leave a beautiful corpse. That's rock and roll, isn't it? My mother must have been rock and roll. Did she leave a beautiful corpse? I stared up into the choir, all these craggy faces, beauty long since having taken a leave of absence, all that was left was life, a fierce will to survive. Why couldn't I remember my mother's face? How could I forget something like that? She looked like me, that's what my old man said, that's why he found it hard to look at me sometimes.

I sat down at Carlton's piano. 'I need some water,' I announced, to no one in particular, and then chose from an array of bottles pressed upon me. I felt the cool, clean liquid glide down my throat. Sometimes there is nothing like water. And sometimes you need a little twist of something extra. It had been a long day and we weren't even halfway through yet. 'Are we done? What the fuck are we waiting for?' I snapped at Carlton.

'Just waiting to hear if they have got everything they need, then we'll wrap it up,' replied my long-suffering musical director. Carlton was a former one-hit wonder from the Eighties. You must remember 'Komsi Komsa' by Zen Twister? Carlton was that very same trustafarian with tatty dreadlocks who fashioned a jingle out of misspelled French and cod philosophy and has survived on the royalty cheques ever since. He was brought in on my first solo album to add a bit of polish to my home production and stayed on to enjoy finally being acclaimed a genius, when all he really did was transcribe my parts and use communication skills honed at Eton (and wasted for decades trying to follow up his only hit) to organise a team of top session musicians, who could have probably organised themselves just as well for a twelve-pack of beer and a couple of grams of coke.

Since we had a few minutes on our hands, I asked Carlton if he knew 'Motherless Child'. 'Of course,' he replied, as if I was impugning his professional integrity. 'Everyone knows "Motherless Child".'

'Well, I don't fucking know it, Carlton,' I sighed, although there was some vague melody lurking in the back of my mind. 'Would you mind playing it for me?'

I pushed over on the piano stool to make room, and Eugenie came dashing forward with the lyrics on her tablet. There were just three verses, doubling as choruses, and they only had a couple of lines in each, with lots of repetition. I wondered how Adam Monk thought he was going to get his A-list chorus to share this around? Carlton was laying down some simple, soulful gospel chords with an underlying minor melancholia, and as the notes rang through me I realised I did know this song, fuck knows from where or when or how, perhaps it was imprinted in my neural circuits like an ancestral memory. I started to sing, softly, tentatively, to myself, feeling my way through the lines.

> *Sometimes I feel like a motherless child*
> *Sometimes I feel like a motherless child*
> *Sometimes I feel like a motherless child*
> *A long way from home . . .*

Something strange was happening, something moving across the stage like a breeze, the way that music can, the way that music does bring everything together. The old folks stirred. They were swaying gently with the chordal movement. And they started to sing along, at first a soft hum, rising with confidence to a mournful sigh.

> *Sometimes I feel like I'm almost gone*
> *Sometimes I feel like I'm almost gone*
> *Sometimes I feel like I'm almost gone*
> *Way up in the heavenly land*
> *True believer*
> *Way up in the heavenly land . . .*

Those old folks could sing. Their voices had the cracks and patina of age, they had the stretched thinness that years wreak on vocal chords, the dry timbre of kindling that might catch fire at any moment and disappear in a crackle and puff, but blended together in harmony the effect was awe-inspiring, a cathedral of sound, climbing up to the chandeliers and beyond. Everyone in the room stopped what they were doing to watch and listen. Even me.

> *Sometimes I feel like freedom is near*
> *Sometimes I feel like freedom is here*
> *Sometimes I feel like freedom is near*
> *But we a long way from home . . .*

'Are you all right?' said Carlton, his face suddenly looming before mine, snapping me out of my reverie.

'I'm fine,' I said, then realised I wasn't. My eyes were swimming. There were tears pouring down my cheeks. My whole face was wet. Carlton had stopped playing and the choir resumed chatting among themselves, as if nothing had happened. But I couldn't stop crying. I didn't even know where the tears were coming from. Kilo was at my side now, Kelly was dabbing my face with a tissue, my people were closing around me, cutting me off from prying eyes. 'I'm fine,' I protested. 'It's just . . . the lights . . .'

In the privacy of a washroom, Kilo warily chopped out another line. I felt the nostril burn, the neural explosion, the adrenalin shot to the heart, then I rubbed my tongue across the delicious numbness of my gums and clapped my hands together, filling the washroom with an explosion of sound. This was more like it. 'What next?' I grinned.

Did I really need to ask? We had half an hour before an international press conference scheduled at the neighbouring Enlightenment Hotel, where an advance party were already setting things in motion. In the meantime, there were more radio calls and Bruno Gil, *The Times* photographer, was pestering Flavia for ten minutes to shoot a classic New York skyline photo on the hotel roof. She had turned him down flat but I was feeling munificent now, cocaine crashing through my blood, and what the fuck, I could talk on the phone, ride an elevator to the roof and pose for photographs at the same time. Hell, I could even chew gum.

So that's what we did, although the elevator only took us as far as the Pilgrim's forty-fourth floor, then we had to walk up several steep flights. I took the stairs two at a time, laughing to see my so-called bodyguards hauling their sumo blubber after me. Bursting onto the roof terrace, the view was spectacular, a 360-degree looping vista of craggy towers poking into the blue. I ran whooping to the edge, while Flavia sternly admonished me to slow down and the sumos puffed to keep up, then I leaned over the balcony and spat my chewing gum out into the wind, imagining it flying through the air to attach itself to the head of one of the unwitting ants hustling across the streets below.

Bruno Gil started shooting as soon as he got close. I threw my arms out against the balcony and leaned back like a Hollywood starlet, laughing with childish glee at this absurd moment of near freedom. 'Top of the world, Ma!' I shouted. 'Top of the world!'

'That's nice, that's nice,' the photographer murmured, issuing a steady stream of come-ons, like he was seducing a model. My bodyguards stationed themselves far enough away not to intrude but close enough to intervene if Bruno should go psycho and try and tip me over the edge. Kelly and Linzi hovered discreetly, occasionally intervening to adjust a hair or tuck in a stray bit of clothing. Flavia and her midgets occupied Queen Bitch. Kilo was talking to a hotel manager. Spooks McGrath and his digiman recorded zero24seven footage while a late-arriving MTV crew set up to shoot the photo shoot. You are never alone with an entourage.

'Where you from, man?' asked Bruno. He was just keeping up the patter, I know, holding my attention, but it was a stupid question, everybody knows where I'm from, don't they?

'Ireland,' I said.

'You don't look Irish.'

Like I didn't know that. I look like a fucking alien. 'My mother was Colombian,' I said.

He seemed pretty excited by this. 'Yeah? Mine too! What I mean is I'm Colombian – mother, father, the whole works, *es un mundo pequeño*, eh?'

'I don't speak the language,' I admitted.

'Really, why not?'

'We spoke English at home.'

'They speak English in Ireland?'

'They speak English everywhere, don't they?' I snorted. 'They probably speak English in fucking Colombia. You speak English pretty good.'

'What part of Colombia she from?' he persisted.

'I don't know.' I was starting to regret granting him ten minutes.

'You don't know where your mama's from?'

'She's dead.' That was always a surefire conversation stopper. But not this time.

'I'm sorry, man, I'm so sorry. My mama too, God rest her soul, before I came here. Life's hard down there, *siempre duro . . .*'

'La Esperanza,' I said suddenly, surprising myself.

'What's that, man?'

'That's where she was from. La Esperanza.'

'I don't know it.'

'I don't even know how I know that.'

'It's in your blood, man. You got relatives?'

'In Ireland.'

'Colombia, man, your mama's family?'

'No. I don't know. I don't think so.'

'You don't know?'

'I don't know.'

'You don't know much, man.'

Who the fuck was this guy? I tried to catch Flavia's eye. It was time to wrap it up.

'My family's from Medellín,' he continued. 'It's not good what's happening down there, with the orphans.'

'Yeah, I guess.' I started clicking my fingers, trying to signal to someone to pull me out. Fucking people watch you like a hawk all day, then the moment you need them they are all cooing over the view.

'People don't protect their own kids, you know their soul is in trouble,' said Bruno, snapping away. 'The kids got nothing, they homeless, fucking death squads running around treating them like vermin. That country's gone to shit, man. I never go back there, never. It's good what you're doing with the record, man, giving something back, I admire that . . .'

How the fuck did he know about the charity record? Could nobody keep a secret round here?

Kilo had finally woken up, and stepped in with a phone, saying I had to take a call, we had to keep moving. Bruno accepted his fate graciously. 'Thanks, man, *el Dios esté con usted*,' he said, putting the camera down.

'Yeah, God be with you too,' I said.

'I thought you didn't speak the language, man?' Bruno grinned.

'I don't speak the language,' I said.

6

We rode the people carrier all of a hundred metres to the back of the Enlightenment, pulling into the rear, where I was escorted through kitchens and corridors, all the time talking to some DJ on a West Coast radio show. 'What's the weather like in New York?' he wanted to know. They always ask about the fucking weather, like it makes any fucking difference to me as I am transported by luxury vehicles from one air-conditioned room to another, from Timbuktu to Reykjavik.

'It's hot,' I said, gazing at people in shorts and shirtsleeves. 'It's hot everywhere. That's why they call it global warming. Here is the weather forecast for the next hundred years: hot and getting hotter.'

'It's snowing in LA,' he said, cheerfully.

'I bet it's hot snow,' I said.

I liked that image, I could use it for something. I thought I ought to write it down but the phone was plucked from my hand and I was led into another overlit ballroom to applause from massed ranks of journalists, seated on row after row of fold-up chairs, leaning forward, notebooks in hand, ready, willing and eager to record my every inanity. And there was going to be some inanity spouted this afternoon. I sat behind a raised table bristling with microphones, smiled graciously and prepared to answer the most stupid questions I would hear all day.

International press conferences really are the bottom of the barrel of global communications, a room packed with stringers from every second-rate media outlet in every corner of the globe, intent on reducing the burning issues of the hour to its parochial essence so they can go back to their editors with at least one line of provincially relevant copy. And so it began.

'Hi, I am Sumiko from *Asahi Shimbun*. You have many fans in Japan who share your concern for the future of young people on the planet Earth. What is special relevance in your song "Never Young" for people of Japan?'

Yeah, how about stop dressing your hookers up as schoolgirls, that would be a start. There is no pornography in the world more disturbing than Japanese porn, and I should know, I've whacked off to enough of it. And while we're at it, how about you leave the whales alone? What have whales ever done to you? In fact, we've got to talk about this whole sushi business. Haven't you heard the seas are going to be fished out by the middle of the century? What are you going to eat then? Cucumber rolls?

I didn't say that, of course. I said, 'I love Japan, Sumiko. Tokyo is one of my favourite cities in the world. It feels like the future is already here, and when I'm gazing up at that awesome skyline I think maybe, just maybe, there is hope for us all.'

'Hello, Zero. Jouko from *Helsingin Sanomat*. Is there a special reason why you chose Finland to launch the European leg of your tour?'

Yeah, because it's the middle of fucking nowhere, the weather is shit, the transport links are terrible, the media won't be busting a gut to get there and it's nice to get a show under the belt before we hit a major capital. That's the truth. But what I said was: 'Hi, Jouko. Finland is a very special place. I once played a midsummer festival there with The Zero Sums, which was weird, all these kids trashed out of their minds on that local moonshine, stumbling about under the midnight sun, it was like a post-apocalypse teenage zombie party, which seemed absolutely right for this record. And I always find Finnish audiences to be very appreciative. They really give you a great reception.' I didn't add the obvious point that they should fucking appreciate it because no other major star ever goes and plays there, it's such a fucking dump. Next question.

'*Bonjour*, Zero, Thierry Grizard, Agence France-Presse. You play the Stade De France, two dates, your biggest shows in mainland Europe – do you have a special relationship with the French people?'

I don't know, Thierry, I've fucked a couple of French hotties in my time but the waiters are kind of rude, *non*? Wrong answer. 'Paris is one of the great cities, it's one of the only places I ever visited outside Ireland before . . . well, before all this, did you know that? I went on a school trip, spent a day on a coach and a ferry, to see some exhibition about the

European Union, which was kind of boring to be honest, but we took in all the sites: Eiffel Tower, Notre Dame, Sacré-Coeur, the hookers on Montmartre.' This got a laugh, which is a dangerous thing, because it only encourages me. 'A couple of us bunked off and spent an afternoon trying to find the grave of Jim Morrison but we just got lost and had to be brought back to the hotel by the gendarmes. My teachers were not amused, I can tell you. I took a beating for France, that day.'

That was Eileen and me, what a day that was – we made love in a park under the shadow of a national monument, ate crêpes and drank café au lait down by the river, then ran off without paying, laughing like lunatics, which is how come the gendarmes got involved. I hadn't thought about that in a very long time, and the way it opened up before me now I felt like I could just fall into the past, go tumbling back to a bridge across the Seine, where I couldn't quite believe I was standing in the sunshine with the prettiest girl from Kilrock, and I loved her and she loved me, and I was happy, I was happy, I was really fucking happy. I blinked hard, snapping back to the present and all those expectant faces. 'Vive la France!' I shouted, stupidly.

'Hi, Zero, Kay Darling from the Sun . . .' announced a startling figure beneath an enormous mane of black hair. She was dressed like she was auditioning for the role of high priestess at a black mass, with the kind of plunging décolletage you could hurl yourself into from an Olympic high diving board and survive the fall.

'Hello, *Darling*, what's your question?' I knew Kay well, Darling by name but not by nature, poison princess of British gossip, the so-called 'celebrities' friend', she would dazzle you with cleavage while stabbing her six-inch stiletto heels through your heart.

'Given that your fiancée has opted to Carry On Up the Amazon with Troy Anthony rather than joining you in New York for Weekend Zero, I was wondering what advice you would give to any of my readers who may have already gone to the expense of purchasing wedding gifts? Should they hold on to their receipts?'

You had to watch out for the Brits at these things, they prided themselves on the art of provocation. 'You can tell your readers Penelope has all the cutlery she needs, thank you, Kay. So why not claim a refund and send the money to the Medellín orphan's appeal?'

'So are we to take it wedding plans are on hold?' she persisted.

'One question each, Kay, you know the rules', interrupted Flavia. 'There are a lot of territories to get through.'

'We haven't set a date but when we do, you'll be the last to know,' I snapped. 'Why does anyone still think this is an interesting story? Famous actress on location with famous actor. Love scenes thought to be involved.' There was a smattering of laughter and applause. Oh, don't encourage me. 'I knew what I was getting in for when I got together with Penelope. I've got the director's cut of *Suicide Blonde*.' More laughter. 'You should see the pre-nup her lawyers handed me. She reserves the right to send a body double on honeymoon.' I was lapping it up now. 'If we ever split, she gets to keep the five houses, I get the tent up the Amazon with Troy.'

I should have known better than to goad a hack.

'So I take it you haven't seen the evening edition of the *New York Post*?' smirked Kay Darling. 'I believe they're running a series of shots of Penelope and Troy in what used to be known as compromising positions.'

Fuck that bitch. I wasn't going to give her the pleasure of seeing me flinch. 'Compromising Positions? Isn't that the name of Troy's new movie? You should see if they've got a part for you. I think it ends with a ritual sacrifice of the truth. You'd be perfect for it.'

Someone else had the microphone now. 'Hi, it's Sven from Sweden. Last year you had the biggest selling album in Sweden, your Stockholm show has sold out in under ten minutes – what do you think is the source of your special connection with the Swedish people?'

Thank fuck for Sven from Sweden. 'I love Sweden,' I said with feeling. 'Abba, The Cardigans, I grew up on Swedish pop music . . .' Blah de fucking blah. I just wanted to get out of there, but I had another thirty territories of foreign cock to suck.

Afterwards, I posed and grinned like a model on MDMA for a photocall in front of logos of our tour sponsors, then I was led out front, pressing flesh with a screaming crowd before hurling myself into the back of the limo, where I slumped across a leather couch to be transported to rehearsals in Queens, mirror shades pulled down over tired eyes. I gave Kilo the cutthroat signal. Minions and media could ride coach, I needed a moment alone. Well, when I say alone, there was Kilo, Beasley, Flavia, Eugenie and Cornelius, which is about as alone as I ever got. Oh and Tiny Tony and the driver up front.

Beasley and Flavia dived straight into forensic analysis of the press conference, but I wasn't listening. Too many stray thoughts and images were chasing each other around my head, knotting together in ever more complex permutations, circles and loops of memory and projection, Eileen fucking Troy fucking Penelope stabbing Kay Darling with cheap cutlery while fucking orphans cried for their mothers, Jesus fucking Christ, I was tired, I was tired, I was so fucking tired, I needed drugs, I needed sleep, New York framed in the limo window, endless faces, cars, buildings, everything passing by in an unfocused blur, deli, record shop, news vendor . . . 'Stop the car!' I yelped. 'Stop the fucking car! Just stop. Stop right fucking now!'

The driver did as he was told, traffic behind beeping, everybody in the limo staring at me like I might be having a heart attack, Beasley demanding, 'What's the matter?' as I threw open the door and made a beeline for a news stand.

'The *Post*, gimme a *Post*,' I demanded. A sad-eyed vendor handed over a newspaper then started yelling for his dollar fifty as I turned away, leafing through the pages. The orphans had bumped me off the front page again, a post-earthquake shot of carnage and desolation, but that's not what I was looking for.

There it was. Page five. A strip of grainy photos of my bride-to-be, naked from the waist up, kneeling in front of what looked a hell of a lot like Troy Anthony's world-famous ass, and even with the wonders of pixilation there was no question where she was putting her beautiful mouth, dear God. Alongside it was a photo of Yours Truly stepping out of a helicopter giving a victory salute to the New York skyline. The headline was 'LOVE MINUS ZERO As Popstar Boyfriend Takes Manhattan; Penelope Seeks Comfort With Troy'.

'You're him. You're him, aintcha? You're him.' Some gangly, corn row black youth overwhelmed by outsize sports clothes was pointing at me. 'Shit, dude, I know you're him.' Tiny Tony hit the sidewalk running and tried to get between us while the guy snarled, 'Don't put your hands on me, motherfucker, I know my rights.' Smartphones were clicking, drivers were cheering. 'Way to go, Zero!' shouted a red-faced bruiser leaning out the passenger window of a battered delivery van. 'You give Penny a shot for me!' My own people poured onto the street. A scraggy homeless loon, all bug eyes and beard paced around, shouting, 'Can I get some attention here? Can I get some attention?' A birdlike oriental woman in a canary-yellow tracksuit demanded an autograph. 'For my daughter,' she kept saying, 'For my daughter,' and when I didn't respond she started yelling, 'What's wrong with my daughter, you son of a bitch?' Tiny Tony wrestled her away. In the people carrier access-all-fucking-areas Queen Bitch was licking her lipstick like the cat who got the cream. The news vendor was still yelling for his dough until Kilo slapped a ten-dollar bill in his hand. It felt like something was spitting in my face. Hot snow, maybe. I looked up but the sky was blue and clear, the blinding white orb of the sun peeking between skyscrapers, light bouncing off windows, my face was wet again, I was crying for the second time today. What the fuck was wrong with me? Tiny Tony led me back to the limo, the door shut behind us, and we started moving.

Nobody said anything for a while. The newspaper lay on the floor, with my beloved in her adulterous nakedness for all to see. People would be poring over those very pictures right now, all over New York and the rest of the world too, downloading them, uploading them, turning them into funny little animated gifs to share with their friends on Spamchat and Snarkr. By Monday, they'd be selling them on T-shirts outside my gig. 'Open the bottle of vodka,' I instructed Kilo.

'Is that wise?' said Beasley, gravely.

'No, it's not fucking wise,' I snapped back. 'We're way beyond wisdom here. I need a drink.' Kilo was hesitating. 'I would like a drink of vodka from my drinks cabinet, please,' I announced, firmly. Beasley gave a subtle nod and Kilo unscrewed the lid of a bottle of Absolut Citron, took a glass from the cabinet and poured me a shot.

I knocked it back swiftly, tasting the bitterness in my mouth, feeling the hot burn in my chest. 'You can chop me a line of coke, now,' I said. There were sharp intakes of breath. 'Oh for fuck's sake,' I groaned. 'It's rock and roll, not the fucking priesthood.'

When Beasley gave another nod, Kilo took out his stash and started chopping white powder on the polished walnut of the limo sideboard. I accepted a rolled-up bill, bent down and inhaled deeply. Then I slumped back, heart crashing against my ribcage. 'Go on,' I waved expansively. 'Help yourselves.'

For a moment nobody moved, then Cornelius shuffled up, bent over and snorted a line. Kilo looked at Beasley warily, then followed suit. Eugenie too was watching her boss. He rolled his eyes and she got down on her knees and snorted. Then Beasley, with a shrug of his shoulders, heaved his fat behind off his seat and, with surprising grace, leaned over the table and hoovered. Flavia's lips were pursed, her expression inscrutable. For all her gothic styling, there was a taut rigidity to Flavia, something vicarious about the way she operated in the entertainment industry. She was like designated driver at a rave, determined to keep her wits while all about her were losing theirs. But she shook her head, muttered, 'Oh, fuck it!' in that prim English voice, and dived in.

Then somehow we were all laughing, hooting at our ridiculousness, Beasley's body vibrating with compressed mirth, Eugenie giggling girlishly, Cornelius sniggering merrily, Kilo softly yukking, Flavia uttering involuntary high squeals that embarrassed her so much it made everyone laugh even more. I slid to the floor, close to hysteria. I knew I had to clamp it down as I sucked in deep breaths, slowly regaining control. Calm, calm, calm. I let out a long, steady sigh, and picked up the *Post*. There were tears in my eyes but I couldn't tell if they were from crying or laughing, I didn't know if I was happy or sad, and anyway I had my shades on, so it didn't matter, no one could see me, not really, not the real me, if there even was such a thing, if I hadn't stopped being myself years ago, and slowly metamorphosed into this other Zero, this creature of awards shows and gossip rags, absolute Zero, Nothing to the nth degree.

'Are you all right?' asked Flavia.

'There might be some film stills of Penelope and Troy *embracing*, you said. Embracing is what you do when you meet your auntie, you don't grab Auntie's tits and take her up the arse. Shit. She looks like she's embracing his cock.'

'I didn't think anyone would publish them,' Flavia replied. 'And if you value my opinion, Zero, I stick by what I said, I think they are fake, inasmuch as I suspect they are scenes from the film surreptitiously shot by one of the crew. It is pure mischief and the *Post* should know better.'

Cornelius had picked up the paper and was examining the evidence. 'I don't know. They look like they've been shot with a long lens in low light, which wouldn't suggest a film set.' Beasley glowered at him. 'Just trying to help,' drawled Cornelius, scooping up some stray coke to rub on his lips before retreating to the front of the limo.

'Get Irwin Locke on the line,' Beasley commanded and Eugenie was immediately speed-dialling the Hollywood studio boss. 'Who is Penelope's agent? Marisa Powers. Let's patch her in. And get hold of Norris Sheehan, I want to examine legal options.' Within minutes he was locked into a conference call with producers, agents and lawyers, stroking egos, concocting strategies and issuing understated threats, oblivious to everyone around him. There was nothing like a crisis to get him going. Then again, this was nothing like a crisis for Beasley. He was already calculating column inches. He had never liked the idea of his golden boy being led down the aisle. For all the charm he could muster, he treated Penelope more like a rival than a new member of the entourage. Now my affair of the heart was crashing and burning in spectacular fashion, a whole new blaze to keep the publicity inferno roaring, and he would have me all to himself again. Fuck. When he reached over and patted my knee, murmuring, 'It's going to be fine, you'll see,' I realised he always thought it would end like this. For all I know, he fucking planted the pictures. He'd done worse before.

We crossed Queensboro Bridge and pulled into the parking lot of Mightybeat warehouse rehearsal studio complex. 'I'm not getting out,' I announced, to general apoplexy.

Inside one of these vast hangars, a revolving circular stage was set up like a giant target zero, with full lighting rig, an enormous LED screen curtain that raised and fell throughout the production displaying a dazzling array of 3-D digital imagery, various off-lying platforms where dancers would strut their stuff, and in the centre of it all a Perspex bubble, inside which I would descend from the ceiling at the speed of a bungee jump for the intro, and in which, at the climax of the show, I would float into the air and apparently disappear in a black hole supernova of lasers, dry ice and assorted pyrotechnics. It was, as Beasley frequently reminded me, one of the most expensive musical productions ever to be staged, only made possible by our friendly sponsors at Budweiser, Apple, Mastercard and, incongruously, Max-Mart, a budget store chain trying to raise their global profile (Can't pay the groceries this week? Make up the money you blew on a big night out with savings on generic household products). The production had been installed in Queens for a month, we were about to launch this spectacular in two days, and I still hadn't managed to get through a full dress rehearsal. Carlton became so frustrated with my absences he hired a stand-in to work with the band, an *American Idol* reject from Seattle called Jan Duran who had achieved fifteen minutes of fame doing an impersonation of me on prime-time TV almost perfect down to every detail, apart from the minor problem that she was an overweight lesbian African American.

'Jan can do the rehearsal,' I whined, as Beasley subjected me to his most lethal glower.

'And should she do the show at Madison Square Gardens on Monday as well, or do you think people might notice?' my manager replied in his quietest, most commanding voice. He was doing the hypnotic thing with the finger again but I wasn't falling for his tricks. I complained that I was tired, overemotional, my voice was sore from talking all day and I needed a short break to gather my strength for this evening's awards show, all of which was true, and none of which was really the issue.

I had developed a growing dread of rehearsal. I had a recurring dream that I was onstage and couldn't remember the lyrics of any of my songs (which had never happened, and anyway, Carlton had installed hidden autocues to scroll through lyrics for my understudy). And another dream where I was halfway through my big opening number when I realised I was naked from the waist down (which my audience would probably enjoy). I affected nonchalance but I was secretly as perplexed as everyone in my team. I had never experienced stage fright in my life. I took to performance like I was born under the glare of the spotlight. Singing onstage I could sail free, liberated from the incessant barrage of my own thoughts, released into the beat until I was part of the music, a human conductor for soundwaves, not really there at all. Nothing came close, not even drugs, not even sex, not even a double-header orgy on crack cocaine and ecstasy with Penelope and a thousand-dollar-an-hour Vegas hooker, which had happened, and if the tabloids ever got hold of that we could kiss the sponsors goodbye.

The thing is, I had never really toured live without The Zero Sums. My solo career had all been TV and Internet slots, awards shows and one-off promo specials, where everything was focused on the event. This arena tour of the States was like starting all over, and it didn't really matter how many stage crew it took, how many virtuoso musicians we employed, how many special effects we dreamed up, I felt like I was going out there naked, with nowhere to hide if anything went wrong. I mean, I had a great band, but they were hired hands, they weren't really a band at all, no one cared about them and they didn't care about each other, it was all me, me, me. The way I had wanted it all along. But the closer it came, the more terrifying it seemed.

Carlton was trotted out to plead that the band needed me. I argued that I knew the songs inside out (true); that I had gone through the whole set on many occasions (sort of true, just not in one go, in the right order); that I was at my best when improvising (debatable, but winging it certainly added an edge); and that anyway, we still had another couple of days' rehearsal, which I solemnly promised to attend. Donut turned up, declined to get into the air-conditioned limo, just stood in the hot car park and shook his head in disgust, muttering that I shouldn't expect him to bring me grapes in hospital when they were surgically removing firecrackers from my arsehole.

Flavia confessed that she had arranged for select members of the press to walk through during rehearsal, at which Beasley rolled his eyes and said, 'Screw the press, they're not exactly doing us any favours. They can see it on Monday night like everybody else.'

So that was settled. The convoy turned around and headed back to the hotel.

7

Up in my suite, I picked at a buffet without an appetite. A whole hour of unscheduled time to myself was almost unheard of – I should have been leaping for joy or, better still, catching up on sleep, but instead I was pacing the floor, listening to alternative club mixes of my next single, 'Life On Earth', at head-throbbing volume and flicking through channels on the wall-mounted flatscreen.

'You should try and relax,' Kilo shouted above the din.

'Yeah, you got anything to help me?' I fired back eagerly.

'I think you've done enough,' shouted Kilo.

But his job was not to question but to serve. 'Enough is never enough!' I yelled, as he tossed me a plastic pack of pills. 'What are these?'

'They'll bring you down a bit,' shouted Kilo. 'Take two.'

I took four washed down with a tumbler of vodka. I felt the beat of the remix pound through me and waited for the wobble, the blurring of edges, anything to tune down the static fizzing through my mind. I watched the Starship *Enterprise* boldly go where no man had gone before, then pressed the remote and my own picture came up, news footage of my hyperactive exit from the press conference, some clips of Penelope and me from the trailer of *#1 With A Bullet* and a shot of Penelope and Troy at the Oscars where they seemed to be holding hands. How the fuck had I never noticed that before? Then there was some phone footage of me standing in the middle of traffic, reading the *New York Post*. Shit. Everyone was paparazzi these days. It cut to the photospread with all the offending bits digitally obscured. I snapped out of my trance and changed channel, only to wind up smack in the middle of a rerun of *Darker With The Day*, right on the scene where Penelope emerges from a swimming pool in slo-mo wearing that one-piece black swimsuit, water dripping down her skin, shakes her wet hair and looks right at the camera, that scene where everyone fell in love with her. She must have been younger than I am now and she already looked like she knew everything worth knowing, that she *was* everything worth knowing. I felt the first ripples of deep space open up in my chest and then it cut to Michael Douglas in mirrored aviator shades leering lasciviously, so I changed the channel and watched a crocodile with its mouth open while little birds fluttered in and out, picking at parasites between its teeth. The music was still pounding out. *'And I wonder if you know just where you are? / In the palaces of Mars or a dirty astrobar?'*

There had been some strategising on the ride back about how to handle the Penelope crisis, and another failed attempt to reach her on satellite phone. Irwin Locke stuck to the line that the film crew were doing deep jungle location work and were temporarily uncontactable. Well, I knew exactly what kind of deep jungle work that faithless bitch was interested in. He said there were plans to send a chopper in. Oh, I'd send a chopper all right, I'd send a chopper to chop off her head. My voice sang out in stereo, swimming around my brain, *'It's a blessing, it's a curse / So beautiful it hurts / Do you believe . . . in life on earth?'*

I lurched into the bedroom, lay down and tried to get the images out of my mind but it wasn't working. All I could see were endless permutations of Penelope and Troy and Eileen fucking like monkeys on heat, and what the fuck was Eileen doing in there anyway? She was way out of her league getting it on with a couple of Hollywood superstars.

Last time I saw Eileen, she was standing in my old man's living room in Kilrock, crying her eyes out under the painting of the sacred heart of Jesus. She had just given me a blow job in my bedroom, and then I told her I wouldn't be coming back any more, and that I cared for her and would always care for her but that it was over, over, over, Kilrock was too small for me, I had places to go, things to do, and I was leaving the past behind for good. It was after that last shitty visit to London when she turned up with a big red suitcase and caught me with a couple of groupies in my hotel room, after the abortion, after that terrible, terrible day lurking outside that fucking awful clinic, not knowing if I was worried for my babe or sick for my unborn baby, or just feeling utterly nauseated at having come that close to being sucked into a life of domestic drudgery just as I was reaching escape velocity. I had hooked up with Beasley by then and made up my mind to split the band. The Zero Sums had returned from a European tour in disarray, nobody was talking to me anyway. I went back to Kilrock to get my things and break some hearts. I didn't care if I never set foot there again. I didn't have the courage or the meanness to tell Eileen before. Or maybe I was just greedy and wanted to feel her going down on me one last time.

Actually, that wasn't strictly the last time I saw her. Cause my brother Paddy came in and looked at me like I was dirt, and said he'd take Eileen home. I watched from the window as they got into Paddy's car, a beat-up piece of rusting shit that he treated like it was a fucking latest model BMW. And she looked back up at the tenement at that very moment, and saw me, and blew a kiss, and shook her head, like I was making the biggest mistake I would ever make in my life, and then I ducked behind the curtain. And that really was the last time I saw her.

I've never been back to Kilrock, not even to visit the old man in his new house on the hill, bought on the advance for my first solo album, or Paddy in his little boutique hotel, paid for by my first American number one. I heard Eileen left soon after. Went to live in Dublin, or maybe it was London. Cut herself off from everybody, her own family, her old friends, and I can't blame her. There was really nothing for people like us in that fucking town.

It was actually a relief when Kilo came in with a call from Flavia, anything to stop the memory-jacking. He handed me a bottle of water with the phone, then practically tipped my head back and poured it down my throat. Flavia proposed a damage-limitation exercise on Kitty Queenan, a half-hour exclusive interview, during which I would let it be known the pictures were just movie out-takes and melt her heart with tales of how hard it was being subjected to pernicious media assaults. 'Give her the full charm offensive,' instructed Flavia.

'I'll charm her fucking pants off,' I said, although I was worried my head was starting to float away from my neck.

'Are you fit to do this?' Flavia wanted to know. 'Put Kailash on.'

Kilo spoke briefly into the phone, assured her I was fine, then chopped out a couple of lines. I greedily snorted them both. 'One of them was for me,' sighed Kilo. But I was feeling better already, if you discounted the slight twitch in my left eye. I put my mirror shades back on.

Kitty wanted to interview me in my suite for the full at-home-with-a-superstar experience, hotels being as close to home as most superstars ever get. Kilo let her in, made sure we were plentifully supplied with hot coffee and iced water, then made himself scarce. My interrogator appraised the room with a sweeping gaze that seemed to suck in every detail before coming back to rest on me. For someone who should have been physically unimposing, a short, middle-aged woman swathed in a jumble of lace, patterns and costume jewellery, I was struck again by her aura of mischievous sharpness, as if the frumpy glamour of loud make-up and

clashing layers was a disguise, something to blur her dangerous edges. When she was done admiring the hotel artwork
and contents of the jellyfish tank, we settled on either side of
one of the elongated sofas, digital recorder perched between
us, notebook in her lap.

'Would you mind taking your sunglasses off?' she enquired.

'I don't think so,' I said, while she warped in front of my
stoned vision, a wolf in hippie clothing. There was something
intimidatingly sensuous about such ripe confidence. Her eyes
were predator sharp, and when she spoke, I got the uncomfortable feeling I might be the main course.

'This business with Penelope and Troy is obviously bother-
ing you, yet it goes with the territory of celebrity unions,
so . . . what is it about this particular story that has upset
you so much?'

'I wouldn't say I'm upset,' I lied. 'Take the celebrity out of it,
I'm just a guy in love with a girl, hearing horrible things said
about her . . .'

'Can we really take the celebrity out of it? I am not sure you
are just a guy, and she's certainly not just a girl, she's one of the
most famous women in the world, and there is a twenty-year
age gap. She is old enough to be your mother. . .'

'You're old enough to be my mother,' I pointed out.

'Not quite,' she retorted, a little wounded.

'Half the women I meet are old enough to be my mother,' I
said, to smooth things over. 'Usually the most interesting half.
I'm drawn to character, I'm drawn to experience – girls my
own age have nothing to teach me.'

'Your own mother died when you were young, didn't she? I notice that you never talk about her.'

'I don't actually remember her,' I said. 'I was very young.'

'Nine is not that young.'

Fuck, she was tough. 'I think I was eight,' I said. 'My father was the dominant character in my life, anyway. He raised me really.'

'So would you say he was both mother and father to you?'

I laughed out loud. 'No, I wouldn't say he was a mother at all. Not much of a father either, sometimes. He was just my old man. He was what I was running away from when I ran into music. I wanted to find something I could make my own, a place where I was safe, and music was that place.'

'A kind of womb,' she suggested.

I didn't like where this was going at all. 'A womb with a view,' I joked, trying to divert her. 'And the view was the whole world. Music wasn't just about cuddling up somewhere nice and warm, it was about getting out in the world, getting away from Ireland, seeing new things, having new experiences, meeting new people, like you. Smart people, educated people, people I could relate to. That's a nice dress.' I reached forward and touched the fabric of her billowy frock. There was a trace of a blush in her cheeks but she wasn't deflected for a second.

'Thank you,' she said, smiling indulgently. 'So do you think the fact that you never really mourned for your mother has shaped your attitude to women?'

Fuck sake, she was like a dog with a bone. 'I am sure I mourned my mother,' I said. 'Everybody has to bury their parents eventually. Death's part of life, that's what my old man used to say.'

Was it? Did he really say that? I don't know where that came from. I don't remember him ever talking about death at all, certainly not my mother's.

'Look at the orphans in Medellín, they've got nobody, but they survive, living on the streets, fending for themselves, it's what you do, that's what being "never young" means. You're forced to grow up fast.'

'When you were having your photo taken this afternoon, my photographer, Bruno, asked about your mother's family . . .'

She didn't miss a trick. 'My mother didn't have any family. We were her family. I am her family.' I could feel panic rising – it was time for desperate measures. I reached out and touched her arm. 'Why are you so interested in my mother?' I said.

'Maybe because you don't seem to be.'

'I don't think about her very often,' I said, and reached forward and turned off her recording device. 'Can we go off the record for a minute, is that OK? If I wanted to go to analysis, Manhattan's full of shrinks. And they've got diplomas from medical school, not journalism courses. I just don't believe in navel-gazing. Music is therapy and I've got music coming out of every orifice. I can fart and it sounds like a symphony. Please don't quote me on that.'

'Are you trying to be obnoxious or does it just come naturally?' said Kitty, with a sly, mocking smile.

'I'm just kidding with you, you make me nervous,' I said, gently stroking the back of her hand and holding the tips of her fingers. I picked that move up a long time ago. If she pulled away, I could pretend it was just a friendly gesture. But if she lingered, we both knew it was on. The truth is, they never pulled away. Not any more. So I was a bit flummoxed when she reached forward and turned the recording device back on.

'Why would you be afraid of a few questions, you've been batting them back like a pro all day?' she said. 'I've been watching you. You don't let anyone under your shield.'

'It gets exhausting talking about yourself all the time,' I pouted, caressing her fingers again. 'Why don't you tell me what you think about me instead?'

'Oh, I think I better save that for my readers,' she smiled. 'When was the last time someone said no to you?'

'I've got a feeling someone just did,' I said, letting go her hand. The woman confused me. I was usually good at this. But I couldn't tell where her questions where leading, or how to bamboozle her with my bullshit.

'Are you happy, Zero?' she asked, with a quiet intensity that left me reeling behind my shades. I felt her warp in my vision again. This time she didn't look like a wolf in sheep's clothing, she looked like the holiest little sheep you ever saw, as meek and mild as the lamb of God itself, soft bright eyes dewy with concern for my well-being. Maybe I had taken too many drugs.

'What kind of question is that?' I retorted, my mouth dry.

'One that people ask themselves all the time,' she said.

'I've got everything I ever dreamed of,' I said, getting up to refill my vodka glass. 'I'm only twenty-four, for fuck's sake.'

'Twenty-five,' she corrected me. Jesus fucking Christ, where does the time go? I was getting old. Pop stars are like dogs. Every year counts for seven.

'I'm ludicrously rich,' I continued, making a joke of the whole thing. 'I'm ridiculously famous, engaged to the most beautiful woman on the planet. And you're asking me where it all went wrong?'

'That's not what I asked,' she smiled. 'But let me put it another way. When was the last time you clearly remember being happy?'

I stood gawping like a beached fish, my mouth dry despite the swill of vodka. I could see stretched reflections on the surface of the jellyfish tank, where luminous, transparent blobs drifted blindly in their liquid element. Outside, through slanted blinds, my billboard loomed in the sunlight, giant eyes following my every move. All the while, Kitty sat calmly absorbing my discomfort, quietly scribbling in her damned notebook. I was supposed to be charming her, seducing her, recruiting her to the cause, but I couldn't even talk to her. I knew I needed to give her something. So I just told her the first story that came to mind.

'When my brother and I were small, I don't know what age, we mitched off school,' I said. 'It was a beautiful day, just like this one, the sun was out, and we just couldn't stand the idea of being cooped up indoors.' Where was this story coming from, suddenly so vivid in my mind? 'I don't know whose idea it was – probably Paddy's, he was older – or what we were doing, really, roaming about the hills, we were going to get into so much trouble. But then the strangest thing happened. I don't think I've ever told this story to anyone. You'll have an exclusive. There was this truck, rattling along in the middle of nowhere, on the road down below us, we weren't paying it much attention, but suddenly it jack-knifed. I don't know what happened, maybe the driver fell asleep, maybe its wheels went into the ditch along the side, maybe it hit something, but it just tipped right over, crash, came skidding to a halt below us.'

Kitty looked up at me curiously. But I didn't feel like I was talking to her any more. I was just remembering, with a sense of wonder. 'It was a pretty remote place, Kilrock. There was nobody around, just us and some sheep and this fucking truck lying on its side. I didn't know what to do. I was only little. But Paddy ran down, he didn't hesitate, he clambered right up on the side of the thing, and he got the door open, and he was calling me to help him, but I don't know what help I would have been, I was just a lad. Paddy wasn't much bigger himself. Next thing, he's pulling this guy out. He's all bloody and dazed, the driver, but Paddy gets him out. He gets him down. I just stood there watching. I was terrified. The truck is on fire now. Paddy's dragging the guy as far from the truck as he can, like it's going to blow up, like in the movies. It didn't blow up but that cab was burning, the flames were licking everything, he'd have been gone for sure if we hadn't been there, mitching off school. So he has a phone, and we call the police, and soon the place is crawling, there's an ambulance and fire truck, everybody's there, even the headmaster, and we're like these great heroes. You saved his life, boys! You saved his life. We got a medal, I think. Or anyway, there was some kind of presentation in the school hall later, like a while later, a couple of weeks, with the mayor and all. And that's what I really remember. Cause it was the first time I'd ever been on stage. That's the truth. The first time I'd ever been up there with people applauding and flash lights going off from photos being taken. It was in the papers. The guy's whole family had come. Jeez, even my dad was happy, and he should have been tanning our backsides for skipping school. And I was happy on that stage, really happy, I remember that. I felt like I belonged up there. It was electrifying, standing above the audience, looking down at them, while they're clapping and cheering. Electrifying. Still is. But you know what else I was thinking, the whole time?'

I waited. I had her now. And if she asked, I'd tell her the truth. 'What were you thinking?' she finally said, breaking my stage-managed silence.

'I don't deserve this,' I said.

She smiled sympathetically. That's when I knew I had her. Still, she had to push it. That was her nature. 'Was your mother there?' she asked.

'I don't remember,' I insisted. But she must have been, mustn't she? You'd expect your mother to be there, on the greatest day of your life. But maybe she had vanished already by then, faded out of my life, as if she'd never been there at all. Just a black hole, where love should have been.

8

'How did that go with Katherine?' enquired Flavia.

'I think it went well,' I said.

'She seemed happy,' said Flavia.

Oh, I hope she was happy. I hope, at least, someone was happy.

I was starting to come down from whatever plateau the drugs had put me on, but I wasn't ready to crash, I preferred it up here, gliding high above my emotions. So I summoned Kilo into my bathroom and we did a couple more lines, then Linzi and Kelly got me suited and booted: dark Black Irish jeans, classic Converse, impossibly thin fake calfskin leather YSL three-quarters hooded frock coat and a retro *Suicide Blonde* T-shirt to send out the message that Penelope was still mine, the latter being Flavia's idea. We headed for the limo to drive a hundred yards to the hotel next door and make a red-carpet entrance for the *Generator* awards, working the crowd in the early evening sunlight. Flavia guided me by the elbow, pausing to offer sound bites to big-toothed boys and girls carrying oversized broadcast mics: 'Penelope's fine, thank you for asking, I'm more worried about Troy, he seems to have nothing below the waist but pixels.' Blah de fucking blah.

I exchanged a knuckle-banging salute with gold-plated trap sensation EgoPuss, while he flashed a mouthful of jewel-encrusted teeth and croaked, 'S'all good, know what I'm sayin', s'all good.' I had no idea what was supposed to be so fucking good about it but I smiled right back. A lean, tattooed, spiky-haired quartet of lookalikes gave me the two-finger devil-horn salute from the top of the stairs. I hadn't the faintest idea who they were supposed to be but I flashed those devil horns right back at 'em. My path intersected with Elton John at the doors, the legendary songwriter done up like an overstuffed peacock in a crushed velvet coat, and we briefly admired our own reflections in each other's sunglasses. Elton grabbed my shoulders, whispering, 'Dear boy, dear boy,' with a warm, gap-toothed smile, 'Don't let the bastards grind you down.'

Then it was into the lobby and somehow I had a glass of champagne in my hand, and on into a vast antechamber where long-limbed models in low-cut gowns and plastic porn babes in lacy mini-frocks and dirty record-biz girls in butt-hugging skirts all swished about. There were hot girls everywhere, eye candy for the candy factory, hovering at the edge of my entourage, laughing too loudly at the attention of men in black designer suits (the stars came in character, everyone else was dressed for a ball), catching my eye with blatant come-hither stares, a circus parade of gorgeous women breathing electric perfume in the air. But Beasley wanted me working the room and only bigwigs and famous names made it through my tight ring of people.

The pecking order was subtly graded: stars surrounded by celebutantes, scenesters, liggers, posers, has-beens, wannabes and fifteen-minute wonders from the bottom of the alphabet trying to get flashed with the A-B-Cs. You could always tell which way the big dicks were swinging. Swirls and eddies formed around us as we moved like centres of gravity through the swell, occasionally merging in a star-crossed melee of air-kissing, back-slapping, shoulder-hugging and small talk. Most of which was about whether we were taking part in Softzone's charity project, like anyone was going to say no to the orphans.

Saint Bono, Irish superstar, statesman and God's celebrity representative on Earth, was holding court in a rock-and-roll epicentre, an uberfame vortex into which all other celebrity eddies would eventually and inevitably be consumed. I had met my countryman a few times, bathed in the mega-wattage glare of his touchy-feely compassionate charisma, been given the famous Bono talk about how to steer a true artistic and moral course through the dark terrain of fame, and felt irradiated by the holy spirit of his undivided attention, but I was rather dreading it now. I steered a course towards the safer shores of Amber Smack, the lairy Scottish soul diva, with whom I once got absolutely hammered and sang a karaoke duet of Frank Sinatra's 'That's Life' backstage at an LA radio festival. 'Fuck sake, Zero,' Amber brayed, air-kissing. 'Don't wanna get lipstick on your cheek, know what I mean? Oh my

God, are you going to sing on this charity thing? I've gotta give out a gong and get the fuck out before they catch me.'

'We can blow the joint together,' I grinned. 'I've got champagne on ice and a karaoke machine in my suite.'

'I'm a married woman,' she sniffed, indignantly. 'But thanks for asking. I hear Baby BooBoo's gonna give it a go, did you hear that?' And she sang a sexy, sinuous blast of 'You make me feel like a motherless child'. 'It is a chewn, oh God, that is a chewn.'

'So you going to do it then?' I asked.

'Shit, it's for the orphans,' she sighed.

Oh, Amber, I thought, not you too. And then we were moving again through rounds of introductions and interruptions till I didn't know who I was talking to and what I was talking about, while beautiful hostesses refilled my champagne glass and I felt myself being sucked into the maw of the beast, until he was there, before me, in blue wraparound shades, giving me a bear hug and rubbing stubble against my cheek. 'Are you all right?' the sainted Bono whispered in my ear. 'You know I am always here for you.' And I felt a little lurch, like I was in danger of bursting into tears right there, throwing myself bawling at his feet and begging for forgiveness. Maybe because he reminded me of the parish priest who had once led the flock in Kilrock, Father Martin his name was, he had the same gift of empathy, a way of making you feel you were the most important person in a room, the only face he saw in a crowd. And he had come and put his hand on my shoulder once, in the harsh fluorescent light of a hospital room, smoke was hanging in the air, there were tubes and coloured liquids and blinking lights, and he said those exact same words, 'I am always here for you.'

Fuck. Where did that come from? It was as if a crack had opened up in the middle of the room that no one else could see, a fissure in my personal space–time continuum, and I was clinging to the present by manicured fingernails, feet kicking above the abyss, trying not to spill my complimentary champagne. Bono's lips were moving but I couldn't hear a word he was saying. I was transfixed by the silver crucifix dangling around his neck, just like another crucifix, swinging at the end of black rosary beads in Father Martin's hand, the smell of antiseptic in the corridor, my father howling like a wounded dog, Paddy weeping, everybody weeping. 'I am always here for you.' But he hadn't always been there for me, had he, the fucking liar? He was drummed out for making one of his congregation pregnant, a girl in sixth form at Kilrock Comp. And we got fire and brimstone Father McGinty instead, who assured me one day I was going to go to hell for all my acts of vandalism on church grounds, sticking a cigarette in the mouth of the Virgin Mary, chopping down his Christmas tree and dressing the statue of Christ on the cross in a T-shirt bearing the legend THE POPE SMOKES DOPE. 'You go to hell yourself, Father,' I told him, 'and say hello to Mother Teresa when you get there.' I wasn't worried about God. I had long since given up on Him. But not before He gave up on me. I was more concerned about how my old man would react but he was so fucking unpredictable, he listened to McGinty's complaints and just said, 'Ah, the boy's a bit high-spirited, Father,' and sent him on his way. I heard him in the kitchen later, muttering, 'The pope smokes dope,' and laughing out loud. Mind you, even he had stopped going to church by then.

Adam Monk had joined us now, and was enthusiastically explaining that a makeshift recording studio had been set up backstage. Stars would be walked through one at a time as we came offstage and legendary producer Ezra Wise would be on hand to guide us through a vocal take. 'The track is a monster,' enthused Bono. 'You'll do it proud.' Then Madonna arrived and the centre of gravity in the crowd shifted again, and I was able to back away, accepting another glass of champagne, feeling the bubbles fizz on my tongue, ignoring the acid burn in my gut. The waitress's smile was dazzling, she had the most perfectly even white teeth, and gorgeous dimples, and her pneumatic breasts were straining at the leash of a sleek, low-cut silk and chiffon dress that rose and fell in all the right places. They must pay waitresses in New York a lot if they can afford enhancements like that, I thought.

'I hoped I would see you here,' my waitress was saying, clinking her glass against mine, and I realised it was Mindy, lovely Mindy, FNY TV's jumped-up weather girl.

'Mindy!' I shouted with delight. 'It's been so long!'

'About twelve hours,' laughed Mindy. What lovely laughter, it rose up and floated in bubbles all around me.

'A lot can happen in twelve hours, Mindy,' I said. The background music was blending with the chatter, light was refracting, Mindy was talking but it was hard to concentrate.

Someone was hovering, waiting for an opportunity to interrupt, but I shut them out, focusing hard on Mindy's mouth, champagne foam fizzing on her voluptuous lips as she took another sip.

'I'm sorry,' said Kilo, breaking in. 'Excuse me, Lamont Walker wants to say hello.'

I turned to see a huge, white-haired man in baggy Armani, my American label boss, one of the most powerful men in the music business, but no way as pretty as Mindy. I grabbed her elbow to keep her by my side while paying my respects to the man Beasley referred to as The Money. Or maybe he was paying his respects to me, The Cash Flow, it was hard to tell. I couldn't understand a single word Lamont was saying, all I could see were numbers and dollar signs spilling out of his mouth. I was struck by the certain revelation that this was how The Money heard music: not as a flowing series of notes, melody and harmony and rhythm coming together in a confluence of sonic beauty, but as pure mathematics, the cosmic order of the cash register. I watched with amazement as the numbers danced in the air and flowed mellifluously into the ear of Beasley, who smiled as if he understood, then opened his own mouth and distinctly said KER-CHING!

'How did you do that?' I said.

'What?'

'Ker-ching!' I said. Beasley and Lamont looked puzzled, as if they had missed a punchline.

A disembodied voice boomed, 'Ladies and gentlemen,

please take your seats in the main ballroom, the show will commence in five minutes.'

'I want to go look at the backstage studio,' I announced, then casually, to Mindy, 'Want to come backstage?'

'We should take our seats,' suggested Kilo.

'We've got time,' I said. 'When did these things ever go to schedule?' The entourage started to move with me. 'Everybody doesn't need to fucking come,' I snapped, then glanced guiltily over to make sure my display of temper hadn't shocked Mindy. But I could have pistol-whipped a paraplegic fan and she would have stood there, smiling. Kilo flashed his Access-All-Areas pass at security, I flashed my famous face, and Mindy held on to my arm as we waltzed beyond the cordon. Behind us the ballroom lights were dimming.

Technicians milled around backstage, clutching clipboards and walkie-talkies. Willard Meeks was shadow-boxing in a corner, talking to himself out loud, building up for his performance, while a girl in a black baseball cap struggled to adjust his radio mic, pleading, 'Mr Meeks, Mr Meeks, can you just stay still?'

'I'll stop when I'm dead, bitch,' said Meeks, then yukked loudly. 'I'm sorry, sweetheart, I didn't mean that. I thought I was talking to my mama. I'll stop when I'm dead, Ms. Is that better? Ms Be-yatch!' Yuk, yuk, yuk.

We were directed down a hotel corridor, where another team of people hovered at a door, indicating that we should be quiet, yet excited enough by my arrival to softly open up and usher us inside. I nodded for Kilo to wait behind.

In an ordinary hotel room, where you might expect to find a bed, blonde bombshell Cadence Butterscotch stood in front of an elegant Brauner VM1 microphone, surrounded by portable bafflers, eyes shut, ears encased in giant headphones, belting out a chorus of 'Motherless Child'. A bearded, balding producer smiled beneficently while his young, hollow-cheeked assistant watched a digital display on a Powerbook. That's modern recording for you. It lacks a certain romance. An MTV crew had set up in one corner to capture performances for posterity, while behind them a couple of what were presumably Cadence's people studied their iPhones. Cadence opened her eyes, taking a moment to come back from whatever musical zone she had lost herself in, then registered another famous face and waved. 'Hi, Zero, wow, are you up next? Awesome. Wait'll you hear what Softzone have done. Totally, like, inspirational.'

'I just wanted to take a look,' I said, shaking hands with the production team. 'I'll come back later. What's through here?' I indicated an open door. They shrugged. I led Mindy into an adjoining room, a mirror image of the other, except it contained a bed. I shut the door behind us and gently turned the lock. She giggled. Nothing needed to be said. We kissed hungrily, my hands ran up her thighs, underneath her dress, sliding beneath the silky fabric of her underwear. She groaned. We sank onto the bed, and I buried my face in her state-of-the-art breasts, while she struggled to get the strap of her dress down, and I wrestled to release one breast from its constraint, finally being rewarded with the emergence of a nipple, which I licked and nuzzled and . . .

. . . do I need to go on? Reader, I fucked her. I even used a condom, at her insistence, which was helpfully supplied as part of the hotel's standard guest amenities range in a basket above the minibar. And then we opened the bottle of minibar champagne, and drank that, and I sank into her, and I lost myself, I lost myself, which is all I ever wanted, and stars streamed across my vision, and bells rang in my ears, and I expelled myself from myself, until I was empty, and panting, collapsed in an entanglement of sticky flesh, but the bells were still ringing, and she was saying, 'Someone's at the door,' and grabbing her clothes, half on, half off, and stumbling towards the bathroom, where she locked herself inside. I pulled up my pants and peeked through the spyhole, to be greeted by the vision of Kilo waving my mobile, which he always carried with him.

I opened the door. 'This better be—'

'It's Penelope,' he said. And handed me the phone.

I lurched several paces back to sit down on the rumpled bed. 'Hi, babe,' I said, weakly. I could hear my own voice echo back, hollow and deceitful.

'Sweetheart,' said Penelope, or at least an electronic approximation of her voice. 'Poor baby, what must you have been going through today?'

'It's been hard,' I said. And my voice came back to me. It's. Been. Hard.

'I heard about the story. We are going to sue them, we are

going to take those jerks to the cleaners. Troy's people are on it and they're the best.'

'How is Troy?' How. Is. Troy?

'You know I would never do something like that to you, don't you? Troy is a dear friend and a trusted colleague. You love me, don't you? You trust me, like I—' The line fizzed and crackled. Her voice took on a robotic timbre. Trust you, I suppose she said. Like I trust you. Mindy's silk underpants lay on the floor. I picked them up and tossed them to Kilo.

'I read the script, babe, remember? There's no sex scenes.' It was hard to talk through the echo, my words bouncing back like accusations. Kilo rapped softly on the bathroom door. When Mindy opened it, he handed her the underwear. 'Thank you,' she said, disappearing back inside.

'We've been adding and improvising, there's rewrites every day, it is the most intense and revelatory experience . . .' Crackle, fizz. '. . . you know what Marcus is like, God, the man is a genius, I swear, he's bringing things out of me I didn't even know were there . . .' Crackle, fizz.

'You never call me.' You. Never. Call. Me. Even I thought I sounded pathetic.

Crackle. Fizz. '. . . up the Amazon on a boat, can you imagine that, a whole film crew going places Western civilisation has rarely ventured, the people here, they are so innocent yet so wise . . .' Crackle, fizz. '. . . life-altering experience . . .' Crackle, fizz.

'Why don't you come back, babe? Just come up to New York for the opening night. It would mean a lot.'

Mindy slipped out of the bathroom, looking radiant, looking untouched by human hands. She smiled at Kilo without a trace of embarrassment, blew me a kiss and let herself out the room. Kilo's face was a mask.

'I can't do that. Please don't ask me to. I'm an actress and this is my life, this is my work . . .' Crackle. Fizz. '. . . crucial stage. It is changing me, it is changing me in ways I would never have imagined possible.'

'I don't want you to change,' I said. And my voice said it back to me, but it didn't sound like I meant it.

'Zero, sweetheart, we have to talk when this is over, when I am finished shooting and you've got your tour out of the way. Maybe this break has been a good thing . . .' Crackle. Fizz.

'What do you mean by that?' I knew what she meant by that. Everybody knows what it means when your lover suggests a break might be a good thing.

'You're so young, you've got so much to learn. You've got your whole life ahead of you. I'm old enough to be your mother . . .'

'You're not my mother.' You. Are. Not. My. Mother.

'Troy says . . .' Crackle. Fizz.

'Let's leave Troy out of this,' I snapped. But there was no echo this time. The line was dead. I would never find out what Troy said.

9

'Fuck,' I said, handing the phone back to Kilo. 'See if you can get her back.'

'She called us,' he said. 'It's a satellite thing. There was a twenty-minute window, apparently.' He looked away, not wishing to confront me directly. 'I was looking for you for ten minutes.'

'Just fucking try,' I ordered, shocked by the harshness of my own voice. 'I'm sorry. Please try.' And I realised I was crying again, tears rolling down my cheeks, for the third time today, or was it the fourth? I was losing count.

Kilo looked uncomfortable. 'You are due to pick up your first award any minute. Come on, guy. You have to get it together.'

'Have you got that coke?'

'You're first up, we are not even going to hear them call your name back here,' said Kilo.

'Just give me the coke,' I insisted.

He started to fumble with the plastic bag that contained his stash. His walkie-talkie crackled. 'I've got him, we're on our way,' he announced. I grabbed the bag out of his hand, poured some powder on the bedside table and started to chop it with my Amex Black, the only item of financial transaction I ever carried. I didn't even have a banknote to snort with. Kilo handed me a rolled-up hundred and I knelt down and worshipped at the shrine of the Great God of Oblivion. I felt like I was sliding downhill backwards, gathering speed as I pitched into the abyss.

Kilo hauled me to my feet and we started walking, picking up the pace as we approached the ballroom entrance. The lights were blinding, my pupils must have been like saucers. 'I've dropped my sunglasses,' I said, panicking.

Kilo fished in his jacket to pull out a pair of Bulgari prototypes. He always kept a spare set for emergencies.

As we entered the ballroom, Bono was onstage, pulling a card out of an envelope and theatrically pausing as he read the contents. 'You know, this is not an award I could ever win, and for that I'm grateful, cause, you see, I've got a band, the greatest rock-and-roll band in the world, and whatever happens, I've got my friends to stand beside me, we share the glory and we take the blows, together, there's strength in numbers. But this guy is out on his own, he sings, he dances, he plays every instrument you could imagine and some you might not imagine. I have it on very good authority he's a dab hand on an accordion, I kid you not, he can play a mean jig and a reel, cause he's a fellow Irishman, and I'm proud of him . . .' There was a cheer as the crowd acknowledged that he was talking about me. 'But when he goes out there with his music, he goes out solo, he doesn't have a band to share the burden, he doesn't have friends to lighten the load, and some of you, particularly some of you in the media, have been giving him a hard time today, of all days, you've been hitting below the belt. There's been some very underhand stories about the love of his life, a lady we all know and admire, Penelope Nazareth . . .' There was a big cheer. 'But he's still standing, he's not letting it get to him, he's here tonight, because he is all about the music, this guy, and what music, these are anthems for our times, he was never young, may he never get old, the winner of Best Male Solo Artist is—'

The anticipatory roar of the crowd drowned out my name. Cameras circled around the table where I was supposed to be sitting, spotlights darted across the room, alighting on my empty chair, then moving off, in a panicky search action. On the big screen, I caught a glimpse of Beasley's face, looking like thunder. Then a camera found me, as I made my entrance from the side of the stage, fist aloft, bounding up the stairs. Bono hugged me, Willard Meeks hugged me, there was always a lot of hugging at these things, like we actually knew each other, like we actually cared. A pretty woman I hadn't even noticed stepped forward and I hugged her, whoever she was, while she pressed a coiled silver object in my hand covered in baffling hieroglyphics. I think it was supposed to represent an electrical generator but it looked more like an old bed spring. I waved it aloft anyway, and stared into the lights, and blinked behind my shades, and felt the whole world grind to a halt. The noise of the room faded into the background, all I could hear was a tidal wave of blood rushing in my ears, the boom-bang-a-bang of my heart pounding fit to burst. After Bono's introduction, I had to say something profound or funny, I had to say something, for fuck's sake, I'd had all week to work it out. I was due to pick up four awards tonight and Flavia's people had drafted a selection of speeches but when I opened my mouth there was nothing there, just my sandpaper tongue and a row of tombstones that might have been my teeth. Somewhere beyond the blinding light spreading across my vision I could sense dark eyes, weighing me up, judging me, and beyond them a black hole of vampiric desire, sucking me in, eager to swallow me whole and lick my bones dry. Then Bono patted me on the back and the bubble burst and the words, 'This one's for Penelope!' exploded out of me like a belch.

I was led backstage for photos with Bono in front of a *Generator* logo. Journalists shouted questions I couldn't understand. Bono filled the empty space with some spiel about 'Motherless Child' and finally I was released into the care of Kilo and Tiny Tony Mahoney, who led me back through the ballroom. Attention had mercifully shifted to the stage and a Willard Meeks routine for the female artist award. 'Do girl groups all get premenstrual at the same time? Don't pretend to be shocked, you *know* you always wanted to ask that.' *Yuk yuk yuk* 'Why you think they always in such a hurry to go solo?'

There were high fives and congratulations as I reached my table but there was no mistaking the cold undercurrent of Beasley's stare. 'There's three more of these things to go. I think I'll save the big speech for the end,' I said, sliding in next to Carlton.

'I thought for a minute I was going to have to go up and accept on your behalf,' grinned my musical director.

'You wish, Carlton,' I snipped, picking up a glass of champagne, cue for everyone at the table to pick up glasses and clink them together. I ignored them and guzzled mine down so quickly that liquid fizzed up my nose and spilled on my chin. Kelly jumped up to dab me. I looked around the table, at all the faces so familiar yet so alien, like bodysnatchers in human guise. Who were these people, my people? What did they do before they met me? Where did they grow up, what were their families like, what did they believe, who did they love, and, let's cut to the chase here, what did they really, really think of me, me, me? I knew nothing about any of them, nothing substantial, nothing personal, certainly nothing nice, nothing you could say at a funeral to make their mother feel better, if they had mothers, or to offer solace to their children, if they had children, except to point out that they were professionals. Oh yes, they were all very professional. They did a good job. They were, dare I say it, the best in their field, though to be perfectly honest I wasn't even sure which field we were wallowing about in. My mind was suddenly filled with the image of the crocodile on TV and I started to laugh, so everybody else started to laugh, and I wondered if somebody had said something amusing. It's called a symbiotic relationship. You see, I did learn some things at school, Ms Pruitt. It takes a whole flock of Egyptian plover birds but just one croc, and it didn't take a film crew from National Geographic to work out who was the big beast here. 'Do I look like a crocodile to you?' I asked Carlton. And he laughed, just in case I was making a joke. Poor Carlton Wick, so eager to take credit for my inspiration because he was bereft of any of his own. But he was, let's be fair, very professional.

A winner must have been announced because everyone was cheering, like they actually cared which underdressed autotuned aerobicised stage-school graduate was this year's designated best female. Jan Duran was slapping her hands together like an overexcited seal. The rest of the band were ensconced somewhere else in the building, probably eating with the TV crew, certainly not invited to join the feast, but Jan had been given a place at the table as reward for all her anonymous work as my understudy. At least she looked like she was enjoying herself, dreaming that someday all of this would be hers. And she was welcome to it. She'd just have to lose a few pounds, get some liposuction and breast implants, wear a wig and pretend she was hetero. The world was her oyster.

Next to her sat Kelly and Linzi, make-up and wardrobe, so interchangeable I suspect even they got each other mixed up. And there was Cornelius – how many pictures had he taken of me? How long had he stared at my face, looking for a way to capture an exposure of my soul, if it existed, if it wasn't already hurled into eternal damnation like Father McGinty promised. And when I looked back at Cornelius what did I see? A lens.

Next to him sat Spooks McGrath, my ghost, whose job it was to translate my thoughts into witty tweets and posts so perfectly nuanced even I couldn't tell which bits were me and which were him. Maybe he couldn't tell either, maybe he had forgotten what his own opinions were, become so absorbed in the minutiae of my life that he had lost the sound of his own authentic voice. He once told me he dreamed of Kilrock, even though he grew up in Belfast.

Flavia was a dry stick, her sole visible emotion a kind of quiet pride. She was all about the client and offered a poker face to the rest of the world. She was working now, as always, absorbed in mutual iPhone tapping with one of her identikit underlings, whose names I could never remember. Next to them sat Kitty Queenan. Who the fuck had invited her to the table? I felt a stab of shame as she looked up and smiled. Was that sympathy? I didn't need anyone's pity. It was a relief when she turned her head to continue talking to Tiny Tony Mahoney, who had obviously drawn the short straw, the small hard man offering nothing but a tight smile as her words wafted over him. He wouldn't touch his food, wouldn't take a drink, he was working too, scanning the crowd for danger, in case Sting or Elton, outraged at being passed over for Best Male Solo Artist, should suddenly launch an attack armed with hotel cutlery.

Kilo drummed his fingers on the table, almost as coked as me and probably as bored, my little shadow. Did Kilo actually have a life? He was there when I woke up in the morning, there when I retired at night – when did he fit in his own life?

What did he do for thrills? What did he do for love? Did he slip away for secret assignations with handsome men he met on his travels, and if so, what would he do if his beeper started flashing because I urgently needed an iced mocha caffè latte with an extra shot? Would he zip up, make his excuses and leave? I would expect nothing less.

The tattoo boys from the red carpet were onstage now, roaring through some cacophony of splintered metal, speed riffs, pummelled drums and werewolf howling, not so much music as a swift boot in the solar plexus. It was the kind of crap my old amigos in The Zero Sums thought was cool before I came along and blew their fucking minds by teaching them to play in tune and in time, by showing them the secret power of sweet harmony. But this was fine, it suited my mood. Apparently they were up for Best Newcomer, some rock delinquents out of Akron, Ohio who called themselves Utopia Avalanche, which sounded like something they had selected from a random-band-name app. Judging by sheer repetition, the song was called 'You Can't Handle The Truth' and the only other words I could make out were 'Apathy will kill us all', which sounded about right. They were signed to the same label as me, which might explain why Lamont Walker, The Money, had numbers drooling out the corner of his mouth. He was sitting with his wife, Mrs Money, who smiled back in diamonds and pearls.

And Beasley, my partner in crime, what did I know about him, except he blew into my life and whispered in my dreams like my own bad angel? He had a wife and child stashed away in London, but even when he paraded them at big events they barely registered. Mrs B was an X-ray, transparent but for designer accessories. The boy was fat and wrapped in an invisible cloak of sadness, never took earbuds out of his ears or eyes off his phone, an eight-year-old with the demeanour of a depressed adolescent. I once asked what he was going to be when he grew up and he said, 'Rich.' And I was letting this parental role model guide my life? Before he managed me, Beasley had been all round the business, specialising in quick turnover boybands who started in stage school and ended in rehab, making money for everyone but themselves. Carlton Wick was his first protégé and look at Carlton, a middle-aged university-educated white man still wearing his receding hair in fake dreadlocks. Next to Beasley, and next to me, sat Eugenie, consulting a folder of A4 sheets and tapping into her phone. She was an adjunct of Beasley, clearly extremely competent, though she lacked his predatory intensity. I sometimes thought he only kept her around so he would have a pretty girl to administer sadistic shocks to as he sounded out his savage humour.

These were my people.

My fucking people.

All eyes were on me, and it dawned on me that I might have said it aloud. 'I just want to thank you all for everything you have done for me,' I improvised, now that I had their attention. 'All the years of human sacrifice, rape, pillage and bloodletting, without which I would not be here today . . . I'd probably be home in bed in Kilrock, getting a good night's sleep, utterly oblivious to the honour of receiving one of these . . .' I held up the silver gong '. . . things, whatever it is.'

My people tittered, and clinked glasses, as you would expect, and I joined them and gulped down more champagne, though it was starting to burn, like drinking acid, and I couldn't help but notice that Beasley wasn't laughing, he wasn't looking amused in the slightest. 'Just practising my speech,' I said.

'Well, I would go easy on the rape and pillage,' Beasley growled.

'What's that?' I said, pulling the A4 folder from Eugenie's hands. 'My schedule?'

I flicked through the pages, sheet after sheet of more of the same shit: a six o'clock start, breakfast television, interviews, lunchtime television, rehearsals (tightly ring-fenced with red marker), a sprint across Manhattan for a photocall at the opening of an exhibition by some wunderkind of the New York art scene who made mock-ups of famous atrocities using old album covers (I was apparently depicted in a triptych of the siege of Leningrad, being sodomised by Nazi stormtroopers led by Marilyn Manson while Madonna cradled me in her arms and wept), an evening chat show, a series of satellite television interviews, it kept going all the way up to midnight, when I would be graciously allowed a few hours half-sleep before the whole thing began again.

'I need a piss,' I announced.

Several members of my entourage immediately stood up. 'Which one of you wants to hold my cock,' I said, and they sat down again.

Beasley gave Tiny Tony the nod and he stuck close as I made my way backstage and into the VIP restrooms, with Tiny stationed at the front door, in case anyone not quite as important as me was caught short and dared to attempt to join me at the urinal. A wizened black man sat in the corner, waiting to spray my hands with unctuous fluids. I fumbled with my fly but I was having trouble with the buttons. My fingers felt thick and useless. I leaned my head against the tiled wall and tried to concentrate. Maybe I should have let one of the serfs come and help me out after all. I wondered how the toilet attendant would feel if I asked for his assistance. I always made it a point to tip hotel staff in honour of my father and his lousy life, so I fished about in my coat pockets and realised I still had Kilo's hundred dollar bill (well, technically it was mine, since I footed all the bills in the end) and his bag of coke (ditto). I dived into a cubicle, shut the door, poured some powder on the seat, chopped it out with my Amex Black, and snorted deeply.

A shudder passed through me like a ghost. I sat on the toilet seat. This wasn't making me feel any better. It occurred to me for the first time that day that it might actually be making me feel worse. I needed to take a dump. Yeah, even superstars need to take a dump sometimes, but I'll spare you the details. It's just that I was sitting there, trousers round my ankles, all this pressure building, and the door in front of me began to vibrate and shimmer and disintegrate into coloured dots, and the dots swirled and coalesced into an image of Penelope, in the swimsuit from *Darker With The*

Day, obviously, and she said, 'I'm not your mother.' Why would she need to say something like that? She looked nothing like my mother, if I could just remember what my mother looked like. But the dots were dissolving and reconfiguring and for a moment there I swear I could almost see her face, my mother's face, coagulating like a blood mask. I reached out to touch her one last time, there was a crucifix swinging, and Father Martin saying, 'Are you all right in there?' Only it wasn't Father Martin, of course, it was Tiny Tony, knocking on the door of the cubicle.

'Give me a minute,' I said. Fuck's sake, a man can't even get some peace to take a shit. They never tell you about that when you're queuing up to audition for *Pop Idol*.

'I am but a bird in a gilded shithole,' I announced to the attendant on my way out.

'Ain't we all, son,' he replied, with weary stoicism, and proceeded to spray my hands with eau de cologne. I gave him my last hundred-dollar bill, which I hope he appreciated.

10

'I need some air,' I told Tiny Tony. He conferred on his two-way, then said we had ten minutes.

As we passed the recording room, Ezra Wise and Adam Monk were conversing with EgoPuss. 'It's a great line, Ego,' said the producer, carefully, 'but I don't think "motherfucking motherless child" is gonna work in this context.'

'Fuck contex', man, keep it real, keep it street, y'all can bleep the motherfucker out later,' snuffled EgoPuss.

'Hey, Zero,' said Adam, looking relieved to see me. 'You want to take a run at this now?'

'Later,' I said. 'Just . . . air, I'm . . .' I couldn't talk to him, I had to keep moving.

We rode the elevator down one level, came out in the underground parking, where four Puerto Ricans in dirty white overalls were leaning against a wall, blowing cigarette smoke into deepening shadows, framed by reflections of the burning twilight sun. A goods van reversed in under the grill to unload, watched by two security men, both over six feet tall, pumped-up bodybuilders in black MTV logo T-shirts with matching shiny bald heads. 'Could you take those guys, Tiny?' I said. 'I bet you could take them.' Tiny just grunted and looked at his watch. 'Do you mind that I call you Tiny?' I wondered.

'Everybody does,' he said.

'It doesn't bother you?'

'Size doesn't matter,' he said.

'I knew it, you think you could take them,' I said.

The security guards were laughing about something unseen and one lightly punched the other on an overblown bicep. Beyond them, at the top of the parking ramp, lay the street, New York City, America, freedom. A steady stream of traffic shunted past, random snatches of music floating in the air. I hung back in the shadows watching stray passers-by, some craning their necks to see past the broadcast trucks into our sanctum of fantasy and privilege. They didn't linger, everyone exuding a sense of being about their own important business. All except for a small olive-skinned boy who couldn't have been more than four or five, dressed like a miniature indie slacker only with those too crisp and over-bright clothes you get in kids' shops: orange bandana, camouflage baggy shorts and a T-shirt with a familiar face on it. The same one I saw in the mirror every morning. The boy peered right into where I was standing and stopped, smiled happily and waved. I waved back. Then a plump white woman in an African print dress and frizzy hair hove into view, grabbing his wrist, laughingly admonishing him, 'Whatchadoin? Y'gonna gimme a break-down. I tol' you – stick close to Mama.' He protested, pointed, said, 'Zero', at which she laughed, picking him up in her big arms, and, not even glancing in my direction, kissed his forehead and swept him out of my sight forever. I wished that had been me, clinging to that bosom, safe in those fleshy arms, being carried away from all this. A slow ache was spreading outwards from my chest, tentacles unfolding through my stomach, reaching down into my groin and up into my brain, as I was gripped by a sense of loss so terrible I thought it might floor me. I rocked on my heels, and briefly considered dashing out after the kid and his mother.

I just wanted to see her face again.

If only I could remember what she looked like.

'We ought to get back,' announced Tiny.

'Do you have kids, Tiny?' I asked.

He grunted, non-committally.

'Fuck, man, you never say much, do you?' I complained. I was stalling for time – I didn't want to go back in there, didn't want to pick up any more awards, didn't want to sing for my supper, didn't want to drink any more champagne, snort any more coke, fuck any more groupies, sleep in any more hotel beds and wake up in a cold sweat to do it all over again.

'I have four boys at home in Dublin with my missus,' said Tiny. 'I don't see them enough. I've spent half their lives on the road. The eldest is just a few years younger than you. Wants to be a pop star. I tell him it's overrated. No offence, but this is no life. We ought to head back in.'

It was the most I had ever heard him say in one go. 'I don't want to go back,' I said, because it was the truth. Tiny returned to grunting, like this wasn't even worthy of a response. 'I only wanted to make a record and fuck the local beauty queen. How the fuck did I get here?'

Tiny laughed, like I was making a joke. 'Let's go back. You can pick up your awards, take a bow and go and get a good night's sleep.'

'I never sleep,' I whined. 'I'm so fucking tired, just give me a minute here.'

A flicker of concern crossed Tiny's features. I knew it wasn't for me, though. It was a work thing, the stirring of a notion that I might be serious, and he was going to have to find a way to deliver me to the podium on time with the minimum drama. 'We've got to go back,' he said, tersely.

'Who do you work for, Tiny?' I asked.

'Beasley pays the wages.' So it was like that.

His two-way crackled. 'No, no problem,' he spoke into it. 'We're on our way.' The exit was right in front of me, five metres away, I could just walk out, join the civilians on the sidewalk, let New York swallow me. 'Shall we?' said Tiny, as if inviting me to dance. But I was sick of dancing.

'Have you got a cigarette?' I asked.

'You don't smoke,' he replied, warily.

'I wanna start,' I said. 'I've tried everything else.' He shook his head and smiled, humouring me. 'I'm serious, can you get me a cigarette? Ask those guys. I'll smoke it on the way back,' I offered.

Tiny hesitated for a moment, then, choosing the path of least resistance, strolled over to where the Puerto Ricans were smoking. They turned to him warily, perhaps worried he was management dragging them back to their shift. But they visibly relaxed as he made his request, welcoming him into the international fraternity of smokers. Tiny glanced back, then turned to his new friends as they fished a cigarette out of a crumpled pack.

And I walked.

I stepped behind the reversing truck, smiled at the astonished security guards, and I was on the sidewalk. I don't think I had ever been in the open air in New York without my entourage and the very idea was making me giddy. My momentary sense of liberation was infringed by the startled yelps of a group of passing teenagers. I dodged between two broadcast trucks and dashed across the road to the screech of brakes and a horn blast, then broke into a trot, not looking at anyone to my left or right, eyes focused dead ahead. I knew Tony was coming now, coming fast, but if I could just make it to the next junction, if I could just round the corner and get into the Broadway crowd, I had the insane belief that I would be free.

Heads were turning, people calling my name but I kept running, trying to stay ahead of a ripple of recognition. The crowd was heavier on the next street but if I thought I was going to blend in I was mistaken, it was getting harder to dodge down the sidewalk and the slower I got the more people reacted, some turning to follow, laughing like it was some kind of game, hands trying to grab hold of me, halt my movement. There was a barrage of cries, hey, hey, hey, voices firing in my face, someone took hold of my shoulder, I spun to see Tiny Tony running into the street, registering the crowd, knowing with the eye of a pro exactly what he would find at the epicentre of this human swarm. I tried to push on, shove through the wall of people, and I could hear outrage escalating, 'What's your problem?', 'Zero', 'Hey!' 'Hey!' 'Hey!' I had a sense things could turn ugly very quickly but I couldn't stop now, I had made it to Times Square. There were lights exploding around my head, neon and LED, traffic accelerating, a cop blowing his whistle as the crowd spilled off the sidewalk. I stumbled forward, looked up to see a mass of oncoming cars and threw myself into their path, arms in front of my face in an absurd, involuntary attempt to cushion the blow. In that moment I really don't think I cared if I lived or died, I didn't care what happened next, I was ready . . .

. . . but the traffic screeched to a halt in front of me and around me. It was as if the whole of Times Square had paused to watch me, while I looked up to see myself, a hundred metres high, an idealised billboard icon towering over the whole ridiculous scene. I started running again, through the traffic, dodging between cars, running even though there was nowhere to run, nowhere I could hide from overwhelming, all-consuming, irresistible fame. I could see a space on the sidewalk, glass doors sliding open, and I hurtled through, into a cinema atrium, colliding with a yelping girl and sending her flying in a shower of popcorn, stumbling on, throwing myself up the escalator two steps at a time, while shouts of outrage turned to exclamations of amusement. An usher blocked my path then stepped back incredulously as I skittered past a life-size cut-out of myself, pistols drawn in a sexed-up combat pose advertising my own forthcoming attraction. There was no escape. 'What are you doing here?' said the bewildered usher.

I glanced back and Tiny Tony was in the foyer heading for the escalator, but he wasn't having the free run I had as ushers attempted to intervene. I took off down a corridor, turned a corner and opened the first door I came to, stepping into darkness, the only light emanating from a big screen. Temporarily blind, I walked towards it, stumbling down the central aisle, lungs burning from the sudden exertion, a pain drilling through my chest, tongue swollen in my mouth. As my eyes adjusted, I turned into a seating row, stood on somebody's toes to sudden curses and flopped down in the first empty seat.

I wondered how long I could hide here in the darkness of the cinema, while on screen trailers played, flashes of racing imagery, dazzling colours, jump cuts, explosions of sound, everything too fast for me to register. What was going on back at the *Generator* awards? Were they calling me to the stage to accept 'Single of the Year'? Spotlights and cameras seeking me out in the crowd? Was Willard Meeks stalling for time, yukking it up, making jokes about pop stars being caught short? Was Beasley smiling his most frozen smile, issuing icy commands to Eugenie while she worked the walkie-talkie, sending a security crew to Tiny's aid? Was Carlton shifting in his seat, wondering how long he should leave it before volunteering to accept on my behalf, secretly dreaming of glory? What the fuck had I done? How was I going to get out of this one?

And then, because it had to happen, because there really was no escape from the world of me, me, me, because, like Beasley had crowed this morning, I had achieved ubiquity, because you can run but you can't hide, because the universe can't resist a cosmic joke at the expense of a fool, because instant karma's going to get you, because ... because ... because, I don't fucking know, maybe just because, my own beats kicked out of the speakers and a deep, ominous voice announced, 'A HIT MAN LOOKING FOR REDEMPTION ...'

And there I was on the big screen, larger than life and twice as ugly, a brown-skinned redhead dressed in black, swinging two ridiculous guns like I actually knew what to do with them. I shrank in my seat.

'... A WASHED-UP SUPERSTAR LOOKING FOR A HIT ...'

My heart gave a little lurch. There she was, my love, Penelope Nazareth, sexy as hell in thigh-high black boots, looking right at me, the way she always did, like she could see deep into my coal-black heart and loved me anyway.

'... IN HIS MOTION PICTURE DEBUT ...'

I was cringing so much I almost convulsed in my chair.

'... ZERO!'

My onscreen doppelganger came crashing and karate-kicking in gravity-defying CGI-animated flight through a crowd of disposable extras, winding up in a close-up clinch with Penelope, gun pressed under her chin.

'AND SCREEN LEGEND PENELOPE NAZARETH . . .'

'Are you gonna kill me or kiss me?' she drawled.

'I haven't decided yet,' I said.

It was so fucking corny, I could feel my cheeks burning in the darkness. My screen self spun around, pistols blazing, and a CGI bullet rippled through the air towards me. Shot by my own gun. I wished it would put me out of my misery.

'*NUMBER ONE WITH A BULLET*,' announced the man with the gravel voice.

I could sense eyes boring into me and sneaked a look sideways to find a round, bearded boy my own age staring, an enormous grin on his face. 'You're him,' he said.

'Shhh,' I whispered. 'I'm trying to go incognito.'

'No problem, man, no problem,' he reassured me, shaking his head in amusement. 'Shit, man, you really are him.' He started to nudge his girlfriend.

On screen, Mickey Rourke was facing me in a gleaming hi-tech office, walls conspicuously bedecked with framed discs and posters of Penelope in her prime. 'There's only one thing you need to know about this business, son,' smirked Rourke. 'The artist is the enemy.' He reminded me of Beasley. Cut to Penelope, drop-dead gorgeous, throwing a drink in Rourke's face in a nightclub, drawling, 'You don't own me. Nobody owns me.' Cut to Rourke, screaming down a phone in a helicopter, specks of spit flying from his lips. 'She's over, she's finished, bring me the bitch's head on a silver disc.' Cut to me, kneeling in a confessional: 'This is the last one, Father. After this, it's over.' Cut to Samuel L. Jackson as the priest, pulling a knife from beneath his cassock. 'It's never over, son.' There was an inferno of explosions on the screen as my stunt double wreaked carnage through the city of LA, and then I was at a piano on a blacked-out stage in a single spotlight, singing my big ballad hit 'Make It On My Own'. Cut to Penelope. 'You really can sing, you know. Maybe there is a way out of this.'

It sounded like a promise.

'This is my girlfriend, Nicola,' said my neighbour.

A fleshy girl leaned over to grab my arm, saying, 'I got all your tracks, all of them, we love you.'

'She's telling the truth,' insisted her boyfriend. 'Every one.'

'I appreciate it,' I whispered. 'Just . . . we don't want everyone to know I'm here.'

'Not a whisper,' she said.

Somewhere behind us, the cinema doors opened, admitting a beam of light against which an usher was briefly silhouetted, and beside him, the unmistakeable form of Tiny Tony. Onscreen, Penelope was sliding out of her dress to reveal a shadowy hint of those voluptuous and entirely natural breasts, and I was grabbing her, throwing her back onto the bonnet of a sports car.

'So what's up with Penelope and Troy Anthony?' my new friend wanted to know. The usher's torch probed the darkness.

The interminable trailer continued with me performing the title song in a heaving nightclub. Mickey Rourke snarled, 'You got talent, kid, but a man's only as good as the clauses in his contract. Do the deed. Then we'll talk.' Cut to me, gun in hand, racked with badly acted anguish, woodenly proclaiming, 'The only thing standing between me and everything I ever wanted is the woman I love.'

'Jesus Christ, I can't believe they left that shot in,' I muttered.

'You look good,' said the girlfriend. 'Very handsome.'

'I'd go and see it,' agreed the boyfriend.

People were shifting in their seats, necks craning, a ripple of Chinese whispers spreading through the theatre. Sam Jackson stood before a statue of the Virgin Mary, swigging from a bottle of communion wine, pistol held to his own head. 'If you won't do it for me, do it for your mother,' he wailed. Cut to me, gun cocked, approaching Penelope on an empty stage. Cut to Mickey Rourke in a limo screaming, 'Retire the bitch!'

'Keep it down back there,' said someone in the row in front of us.

'It's him. It's Zero,' explained the girlfriend, helpfully.

Onscreen, Penelope was a vision of wounded sexiness, eyes only for me, a look of lovelorn betrayal burning through the celluloid. 'I knew you'd let me down, you sonofabitch,' she spat.

The usher's torch lit up my face.

I stood and vaulted the seat in front but, without the aid of a Hollywood special effects department, I caught my foot on the back of the chair and crashed to the floor. Someone let out a yelp. People were standing up to see what was going on. I crawled under a seat, squeezing through into the next row, where I had a clear run to the end of the aisle. I bolted. Tiny Tony called my name.

'Shuddup!' bawled an irate patron.

'Siddown!' yelled another.

'Zero!' screamed a third.

'*NUMBER ONE WITH A BULLET*,' said the voice-over artist.

I made it to the glowing exit sign and pushed the doors open. I could hear Penelope saying, 'If you want me, you're gonna have to come and get me.' I didn't hear my riposte, but I knew what it was.

'I'll track you down in hell, babe.'

I threw myself down the stairwell three steps at a time, banged through a fire exit and out onto the street. An elderly black man stepped back, startled, but his stare was blank, without recognition. An old people's home, I thought, that's where I would be free. An old people's home for the blind, deaf and dumb, just to be on the safe side. I put my hands over my face, covering my features the only way I could, and hurled myself into the lengthening shadows, running like a madman, ducking down the first adjacent alley, diving into the next street, mingling into the pedestrian traffic, trying to see through the spaces between my fingers. I bounced off someone. 'Lookwhereyagoin, yafugginmoron,' he snapped. 'Whassamatterwidu?' I pushed on, walking blind, the silliest disguise, but it was working, I was getting away with it, I was getting away. But then I glanced back to see a trail of curious faces following me, the murmur going up, 'Is it him?' 'It's him,

I think it's him.' I picked up my pace, and they picked up too. I turned another corner, dropping my hands and running, but I was on Broadway again, right in front of the Pilgrim Hotel. How the fuck did that happen? Was there no way out of this nightmare? There were spotlights beaming into the early evening sky, and a crowd of fans pressing against crash barriers. I was running as fast as I could, about to be sandwiched between a pursuing horde behind and Zeromaniacs in front. The thought flashed through my mind that I could just run straight up the red carpet, race through the ballroom and, who knows, maybe I could still get onstage in time to pick up my award. Make a joke of the whole thing. 'I went to take a leak, turned left when I should've turned right, and I've just been twice around Times Square pursued by screaming fans.' Maybe they would buy it. Maybe it would be a headline grabber, which would keep Beasley happy.

And then, like a vision before me, I spotted my white stretch limo, parked on a double yellow, the driver leaning against the bonnet, idly smoking. What was his fucking name? Why didn't I ever get to know the staff? 'Driver!' I shouted inanely, making a beeline for him.

He casually glanced up, then jolted to attention.

The Zeromaniacs had spotted me. The New York mob were hot on my tail.

'Gimme the keys!' I screamed as I reached the limo.

'I can't just—' he stuttered.

'Gimme the fucking keys or you're fired,' I snarled.

He handed me the keys and I threw myself behind the

wheel. I heard a plaintive plea of, 'Are you insured?' as I started up. Hands were banging on the windows, faces pressing against the glass, but I was driving, I was moving, I was gliding into the traffic, I was on the road, I was leaving it all behind, I was accelerating, I was gone, I was real gone, I was real, real gone.

I was free.

11

It was a long, long time since I had driven myself anywhere and I can't say my handling was particularly smooth, what with the last blast of the setting sun bleeding into my eyes and light flashing and bouncing off every surface, other drivers honking, silhouetted pedestrians yelling abuse as I cut through red. Or maybe that's what driving in New York is always like. It probably didn't help that I was shit-faced on booze and worse but I grew up in Ireland, for fuck sake. I learned to drive while drunk. How else were we supposed to get home from the pub? But I had no idea where I was going, just away from THEM, just towards HER, and the car phone kept ringing while I was trying to get to grips with the automatic pedal action on a vehicle at least three times the length of my brother's jalopy, which was the only thing I had ever driven before. Did I mention that I don't have a licence? Anyway, there was no way I was going to pick that phone up, I knew exactly who it would be, but the fucking thing wouldn't stop, it just kept ringing, ringing, ringing, so I tore it out of its mounting and (after pressing every visible button just to wind down the window) fucked it out onto the street. Goodbye, Beasley.

Somehow I found myself in a long, wide tunnel, hemmed in by slow-moving traffic, fumbling with buttons and levers, turning on windscreen wipers and indicators in an effort to switch on the lights. I looked up just in time to slam the brakes without rear-ending the car in front as traffic ground to a halt. I wouldn't have relished getting out to swap insurance details. An elderly woman sitting stationary behind the wheel in the next lane turned towards me and bared her teeth alarmingly. I had a moment's panic but she was just admiring her reflection. Thank Christ for tinted windows. Then I was out into the dusk, the darkening sky streaked with pink and purple, everything picking up speed, road signs flashing past before I could get a fix on them, shiny articulated giants with tyres twice the height of my crawling limo overtaking with stern blasts of their pipes, like I should get a move on and stop hogging their highway. A vast, flat industrialised wasteland spread out to my right, a cityscape of distant towers off to my left, and it dawned on me that I had left Manhattan behind. A giant spotlit billboard on stilts directed me to an Adult Super-store next exit, where every temptation of the flesh was on offer, while directly opposite, an equally big black-and-white billboard informed me HELL IS REAL. As if I didn't already know that.

I had to get off this road, which was dividing and multiply-ing, adding lanes as if there was no limit to the amount of cars it could handle, traffic merging from every direction, a river of white lights coming towards me, a river of red tail-lights swimming ahead, but I was at a loss as to how I was ever going to stop this thing now. And then the traffic bunched and slowed and I realised I was heading into a trap, a long line of gated toll booths blocking my escape. I thought this is it, my flight is over before it has even begun. I never carried money. That was Kilo's job. I hated anything to spoil the line of my trousers. But I reached into my pocket, more in hope than expectation, and pulled out my credit card and coke. My heart gave a little leap, although I doubted either would be acceptable currency to a toll-booth operator. But as I pulled up, ready to promise autographs and tickets and dia-mond-studded watches for a free exit, the gate raised and I kept moving. The limo must have been equipped with some kind of auto-pass. I laughed aloud. I was settling into my rhythm behind the wheel, comfortably looping around to merge with another traffic stream. Could I drive all the way to Brazil, Highway 666, straight to hell, boys, Amazon here we come, drive all night into the cheating arms of the woman I love? I had no fucking idea. All I knew was that if I stayed between the white lines I'd be OK.

Talking of white lines, I opened up the packet. It was a little difficult to manoeuvre so I just stuck my snout in and inhaled. I was surging now, inside and out, foot down on the accelera-tor, burning through the disappearing world. Out of the dark-ness, brightly lit signs indicated I was on the New Jersey Turnpike, heading towards Philadelphia. That sounded all right to me. That sounded like a song. I reached over to turn on the radio, flinching slightly in case the first thing that greeted me was one of my own hits. But it was the Boss, telling me that tramps like us, baby we were born to run.

And even though my hands were shaking and my teeth were grinding from the cocaine and fuck knows what other chemicals were coursing through my system, I started to feel OK, I mean really fine, for the first time that day, fuck it, for the first time in as long as I could remember. The sheer focus of driving was engaging all functional parts of my brain and the radio was colonising the rest and there was no room left for anything else. Just song after song, the lights of the road, the looming darkness of the continent beyond. I didn't even have to think about what I had done because The Who were doing my thinking for me, telling me I was the seeker on a wave of power chords, searching low and high. The Eagles were there to remind me that life in the fast lane would surely make me lose my mind. Tom Petty chimed in to sympathise that love was a long hard road and the Rolling Stones let me know that though you can't always get what you want, if you put in a bit of effort you might get what you need. There's a philosophy to live by. I would have been happy to drive all night with classic rock for company but brash salesmen kept breaking in to bombard me with offers of new-model mobile phones, low-emission high-performance vehicles on easy payment schemes and better health insurance, terms and conditions may apply, so I flicked channels, quickly passing over pop and news and settling on everything country, a warm cushion of plush harmonies, silvery guitars and homespun wisdom. I felt safe there for many, many miles until some old fool started singing about the last time he saw his mama and I felt a catch in my chest and then she let go of his hand and my eyes suddenly filled up so I could barely see where I was going. 'Mama are you there?' he wailed. I hit search and found some grinding metal and that was better, I could go numb in the noise.

I don't know why music has this effect on me, but I suppose if it didn't I'd still be back in Ireland working the family trade as a cap-doffing, back-scratching, shit-eating bag-carrier. Sorry, hotel service worker. And maybe I would be a whole lot happier. It is as if things don't even come into focus unless there is a soundtrack attached. Parts of my life are a fog, a vague mist I can sort of detect shadowy shapes moving about in, and that's OK with me. I think of that as pre-music, like prehistory, like when they used to teach us about the world Before Christ, and all the dates counted backwards, which must have been fucking confusing for the denizens. But play me certain tunes and everything sharpens up, I am overwhelmed by sensation; I can smell, taste, touch and see things long since left behind, each memory triggering another memory in a chain reaction. Like, I can't even remember my own mother's face but I could tell you the first CD I ever bought. It was *Resurrection* by Tupac, the ghost rapper. I haven't heard it in an eon but it is still bouncing around the inside of my skull, with its tight beat and mournful rap predicting Tupac's own death that squeezed my little heart so tight I thought I was going to burst. I can even describe the inside of the shop in Galway where I bought it, an Aladdin's cave of pop junk, every inch of its walls thick with posters, layered up over one another, like nothing was ever taken down, just a new poster slapped on top. In some places the paper would be torn or peeling to reveal a mysterious glimpse of an image underneath, a portal to unfashionable fads and last year's models. It smelled of paper too, musty and damp like a cat's dirty litterbox. There was this one poster of a creature with a white face, black eyes and blood-streaked tears like the devil incarnate but it was torn right down the middle and you could just make out this raven-haired, blue-eyed icon in a gold suit shining like an angel trying to break through the darkness. I stared at that poster for ages, transfixed. I didn't know who either of these deities were but I was pretty sure it had something to do with biblical battles between the forces of Good and Evil that Father fucking McGinty was always hammering on about in church on Sunday. And I remember a man with the sideburns cut at an angle and one silver tooth, who came out from behind the counter and explained that the devil was Marilyn Manson and the angel was Elvis Presley. That was actually the way he put it. He said that heavy metal music was the path to corruption but Elvis would always be there to light the way back home. Then he laughed and the light glinted off his silver tooth. He had a black T-shirt that said GREAT BALLS OF FIRE and a pair of tight denim drainpipes with a chain hanging from his belt. He pulled a face when I said Marilyn looked like he had just eaten Elvis for breakfast and I could tell he really wasn't at all impressed when I asked him for the Tupac CD but he sold it to me anyway and winked and said, 'Rock and roll will never die,' as he handed over my change. I remember all of that but I don't know what I was doing there, or who took me, or where I got the money to spend on rap records and what my old man thought about it all. That's just the way it is.

I was lost in my reverie, I must have been driving in a daze for hours, but traffic was building up, tail-lights trailing on every side, and I could see a black on black geometric silhouette in the distance, tiny coloured lights winking in the night, the city of brotherly love. I had been to Philadelphia before, of course. I had been to every urban population centre in the United States at least half a dozen times, criss-crossing the country in the back of aeroplanes, riding coach, every day a different state, every state three different cities, every city God knows how many radio shows, TV shows, record store signings, club appearances, local press, fan club meet 'n' greets. We did four US stints, eight months in America working that first solo album and I swear it felt like I shook a hand for every unit sold. And in all that time I had never gone anywhere on my own. Never driven up, stopped the car and stood on the sidewalk without an itinerary. Without someone to carry my bags, mop my brow and wipe my backside, should it be required. What was I going to do? Where was I going to go? What would people say when they saw me, lost and helpless, with no idea how a human being was supposed to behave?

I veered between lanes, horns shrieking in dismay. And then I was following an exit and somehow the streaming intensity of the interstate was just gone, like it had evaporated, and I was rolling through a wide, empty grid of suburban dreamland, past perfectly square lawns and blank-faced wooden houses lit like a movie set waiting for someone to say action. I switched off the radio. Crawling past row after row after row of identical plastic postboxes, I turned down one street, then another, and it was all the same, as empty as a model village. If there was any life here it was going on behind those dumb walls, in cosy family units where something as alien as a drug-crazed pop star on the verge of a nervous breakdown would never ever set foot, where Mom was doing the dishes and Dad was treating himself to a hard-earned beer and kids were hunched over laptops, phones and TV sets, flicking channels and fighting over the remote, perhaps idly pausing on reports of an award show where the headline act had mysteriously vanished. Occasionally I glimpsed someone watering plants or taking out garbage, but even they looked like they had been posed by a town planner trying to make his model more authentic. A group of pale teens from central casting gathered beneath a street light. They glanced up to watch me cruise past.

I kept driving, through mile after mile of relentless sameness. There was nothing for me here. Street lights grew fewer and further between, the houses and yards pressed closer together. Black boys shot hoops, spotlit behind wire mesh, grunting and shouting into the night. Some houses were boarded up, others sported broken windows like black eyes. There was rubbish piled in yards, discarded refrigerators and burned-out ghost cars. The more beaten up and abandoned the place looked, the more people could be seen, sitting on stoops or gathering in streets talking and laughing, or drinking from brown paper bags outside a store bristling with barred windows and branded neon. A red sports car with the muffler removed from its exhaust roared past and screeched as it whipped around a corner. Multi-storey tenements loomed ahead, forecourts lit like prison yards, walls tagged with elaborate graffiti. I felt conspicuous in my white stretch limo but as I turned down one street and then another I just seemed to be getting deeper and deeper into the urban jungle. The fuel gauge was blinking on my dashboard. When I paused at an intersection there was a sharp rap at my window. A black face loomed at the glass, lazy eyes, a livid scar across a dented nose. I pressed a button and the window rolled smoothly down. 'You lost, dawg?' enquired my visitor.

'I am lost,' I nervously admitted. He wasn't any older than me, tall and gangly but muscular, standing proudly in the middle of the wide road dressed in a baggy vest that bore the slogan HEADZ YOU LOSE. He wore a black stocking cap over his skull. A thick faux-gold chain hung round his neck as far as the hem of his boxers, poking out over low-slung baggy jeans. Behind him, on the sidewalk, a gang were gathering, oversized boys in supersize clothes and skinny girls in next to nothing, thongs pulled high, jeans dropped low, lots of cheap bling, bandanas tied round heads and hats worn backwards, sideways and inside out. Maybe accelerating out of there would be the smart move. But a bone-rattling roar alerted me to the return of the red sports car, a heavy-set Mitsubishi pimped up with rims, spoiler and underside neon, which came down the cross street and screeched to a halt in front, blocking my exit. 'Who you carryin' back there?' asked Scarface.

'Nobody,' I said. He did a double take and his poker face was replaced by an incredulous grin. 'What the fuck, man! You on MTV, I know you. What the fuck?' Behind him, one of the girls started to squeal and jump up and down.

'Zero, omigod, it's Zero!' And that was a cue for everybody to move forward till the car was completely surrounded, and there was nothing for it but to open the door and get out.

I'd been in the thick of crowds before but usually I had bodyguards to keep them at bay. Hands were feeling the cloth of my coat, patting me on the back, banging my knuckles and engaging me in elaborate hip-hop shakes. Questions and exclamations popped in my ears. Girls pushed forward to get pictures taken by friends wielding mobiles, one small curvaceous babe shoving her rocket breasts at me. 'Touch them if you want, they're real,' she assured me. A man mountain of lardy flesh pushed her unceremoniously aside to demand I listen to him rap. 'You gonna want me on your nex' beat,' he insisted in a squeaky voice. 'I'm undiscovered, brother, hear me spit you won't recover! Never ever love another, hit the pitch, bitch, don't even bother . . .' The tall scarface who stopped the car made an attempt to assert proprietorship by throwing a long arm around my shoulder and declaring, 'Give a dawg some space.' The doors of the red sports car were open and a big, burly man with long, swinging dreadlocks approached, surrounded by swaggering homies. The small crowd parted. He had a few years on everybody else, deep-set panda eyes, neat little goatee beard, smoothly decked out in black baseball jacket and clean white T. 'What we got here, boy?' he said in a deep, ominous growl but the threat quickly subsided as he too broke into a grin, prominent gold flashing in his mouth. 'Zero! Come here, cuz!' he declared, wrapping me in a bear hug like we were old amigos. 'Welcome to the hood, cuz. Welcome, welcome, welcome.'

Right on cue, with a boom-shaka-boom, beats started dropping, like some unseen choreographer was staging an urban musical: hey, kids, let's put the show on here. A humungous ghetto blaster with bass bins emitting subsonic frequencies that could loosen your bowels was hoisted onto the roof of the limo, and Fat Boy started urgently rapping at me in a high, quickfire voice while girls danced lasciviously around, eyes swivelling to make sure I was checking out the cargo. A party was breaking out in the warm night air. The crowd around the car was swelling by the minute, someone opened the passenger doors and people swarmed through, fighting their way in, grabbing bottles of champagne and vodka. Even the bananas were doing the rounds. I was squeezed between dreadlocks (who the others respectfully referred to as Sinner-Man) and Scarface (who introduced himself as Hard Head), who formed a spontaneous security detail, backed up by SinnerMan's posse, Evildoer, Assassin and Karnivor. The fat rapper was Master Beatz. The girl with the bazookas was

Bountiful. 'Of course,' I said, laughing. That's why I fell in love with hip-hop: the self-invention. Everybody can be their own superhero no matter how shitty their circumstances. I should know.

Lights were going on in surrounding buildings, more and more people pouring into the street. The liquor store was soon doing a roaring trade. There were children running about while girls who didn't look old enough to be mothers half-heartedly tried to corral them. Everybody was talking to me at once. I pressed flesh, signed autographs, posed for pictures. I might as well have been back at the *Generator* awards, only with more elaborate handshakes, all double-clutching and slithering palms. A pretty prepubescent in a pink tracksuit hopped giddily around, brimming with childish glee as she sang 'Never Young' at the top of her voice. Somebody held up a baby for me to kiss. I laid one on his little bald head. 'A'ight, Zero, one for good luck,' gushed his young mother. 'I'm never gonna wash his head again. My little superstar gonna be as rich and famous as you one day.' Be careful what you wish for, I thought. But I let the feeling subside, it was too much fun watching Master Beatz sweating and gasping in verbal battle with a muscle-toned rival who announced himself as Roc Bottom, while a skinny girl with multicoloured pseudo-dreads jumped onto the hood of the limo and started spinning in wild circles. Growing up I had no one to do hip-hop battle with but my reflection. No bitches, no hoes, no guns, no gangstas, just me and my mirror, spitting vengeance at playground bullies.

'Is it always like this around here?' I asked my self-appointed protector. Apart from some washed-out and wasted oldies, most of the real adults were women. Although he probably hadn't hit thirty yet, SinnerMan was a man among boys.

'MTV don't live on these streets,' he replied, passing me a bottle of my own champagne. '*American Idol*, shit, they don't run auditions in the projects. For mos' these kids, you stepped right out of television, cuz, you know what I'm sayin'?'

I took a swig from the neck, bubbles fizzing up my nose.

'Hey, Zero, you gonna show us what you got?' shrieked a big-ass girl, shaking her booty in ripples of flesh. I could feel the monkey rising. He was never far away. What the fuck. All the world's a stage, after all. I swung up onto the bonnet next to the Asian dancer and the crowd started clapping along and whooping. *Zero! Zero! Zero!* The local rappers were doing a good job but I was way beyond local. I was global. I started laying it down. I had so many rhymes, so many lines learned in my bedroom flying solo, so many couplets cooked up in the classroom when I was supposed to be studying mathematics or geographics or anything that would have kept me in an honest trade and out of trouble back in Kilrock, where I was the only nigga on the block. I could freestyle like a downhill racer in an avalanche.

My people, my people
Let's all count to Zero . . .
You get NOTHING for the money

NADA for the show
And MINUS ZERO to go man go
Let's roll, let's blow, let's rock the joint
Drop the taunts, what's the point?
It's a new way of talking – s'alphabetti spaghetti
Droppin' rhymes like confetti, emergency spit
I can keep up this shit, baby, all night long
You can say it don't make sense but you can't tell me that
   I'm wrong
Let me tell you my story, the pain and the glory
There was nothing before me, and nothing came after
But tears and no laughter, the things that you haveta
Do to strike lucky, lie down and let ya fuck me
Like a paparazzi Nazi stickin' cameras up my ass-y
Play me like a patsy, suck on the lens, boo
'Was it good for you, too?' Smile and swallow
There's more to follow, so where do I sign?
Show me the dotted line, sell your soul to Satan
For silk and satin, can you see a pattern?
Moët on ice, that's nice, limos on call
We havin' a ball, we havin' it all, blowin' bubbles
With this year's model, it's a doddle, the latest thing
Ten sex symbols on the head of a pin
Sub-atomic fashion under your skin
Who says there's no such thing as an original spin?
What goes around runs aground
You got your mind made up but your knickers down

Cause I been looking for a reason, I been trying to come
    clean
I've been looking for salvation in a dirty magazine
Help me, Father, I'm fallin', can't you hear your child calling?
No excuses, no stallin', no more bangin' and ballin'
Cause Nothing from Nothing leaves Nothing
Even a Zero need a little something
So here's the prize, guys, look in my eyes
What you see inside will not be denied
You can run . . . BUT YOU CAN'T HIDE!

I could spin it out all night if I wanted. So what if it doesn't always make sense, it's the flow, it's the show, it's the braggadocio. The Philly kids understood that, at least. Master Beatz took up the battle and I jumped down from the limo, SinnerMan's posse manoeuvring me to the sidewalk, where we set up a command post in a tenement stairwell. He kept the shimmying girls at bay by showing the palm of his hand while his homies glowered threateningly. 'No cameras,' snarled Evildoer whenever someone whipped out a smartphone. I wish my usual security had been half as effective at deterring selfie-seekers.

An enormous spliff appeared and was ceremonially handed to SinnerMan, who sparked a light, sucked in, held it tight, then seemed to vanish for a moment in a blue cloud of exhaled smoke. 'So what's a five-star motherfucker like you doing on my turf?'

It was a reasonable question but how could I explain that I

was running away from everything these people were running towards, especially when I didn't understand it myself? I shrugged helplessly.

'You drive your own ride these days?' he pressed, handing the spliff to me.

'My old lady says you run out on a TV show,' sniffed Hard Head. 'She seen it on the news.'

'Your mama too busy suckin' on a crack pipe to follow *Scooby Doo*, never mind CNN,' sniggered Assassin, whose short stature and fluffy moustache belied his name. All the other homies laughed, including, curiously enough, Hard Head.

'Woman's fucked up,' he agreed. 'Wha'm I gonna do? She my mama.'

'I fuckin' heard that, you little cocksucker,' shouted a rake-thin, drawn-faced, half-dressed woman at the bottom of the stairs, before hurling a beer bottle that smashed somewhere behind us. 'When yo' daddy get out, don't think you so big he can't paddle ya backside.'

'He doin' life no parole, Mama,' Hard Head pointed out. 'We all be dead before he get home.'

Everybody laughed some more, though it may have been the saddest wisecrack I ever heard. I pulled on the joint and felt the whole world lurch.

'What's in that thing?' I coughed, heart pounding and the stairwell turning 360 degrees.

'Little skunk, little rock, little smack, you know,' sniggered Assassin. 'It's a SinnerMan special.'

Shivery pulses ran through my body. Fuck, that was nice. If only the world would stop helicoptering. 'I'm driving to Brazil to find my woman and tell her I love her,' I groaned.

'I'd say you a little fuckin' lost, a'ight, dawg,' said Hard Head, to more laughter.

'You in trouble, cuz?' enquired SinnerMan.

I felt like I was melting through the floor but otherwise I couldn't think of any immediate danger. 'I just had to get out of New York,' I said. 'It's complicated.'

'What you gonna do 'bout Gorgeous Troy when you get there?' said another of the homies, I think it was Evildoer, to more sniggering. Oh but news travels fast in every direction these days, doesn't it?

'I'm gonna fuck him up,' I announced, lifting my head with great effort. 'The only movies he's gonna be making from now on are horror movies.'

'You bad, dawg,' grinned Hard Head, high-fiving me.

'Whole world's fucked up,' announced the previously silent Karnivor. 'Every day it just gets fucked-upper, fucked-upper and fucked-upper until one day it's gonna get so fucked up we gonna go, oh shit, it's on. Armageddon time. Pestilence. Leprosy. Plagues. Zombies. We're gonna have all type of shit. Earthquakes in South America, shit, right on our own border, orphan kids running round get whacked by they own peeps? S'already happening, man. It's coming. We treat the world like shit, one day it's gonna come and smack us right in the grill.'

'That shit's raw,' concurred Assassin.

'Karnivor's a philosopher,' explained Hard Head.

I looked back to see Karnivor glowering in the shadows of the stairwell, a slack-jawed, oval-eyed, scowling Bad Buddha. His eyes burned into mine. 'You think you got troubles, superstar? You got the cheese, the ride, the bling-a-ding-ding, you gots everything all these peeps pray to Jesus Christ and Allah for every night. You may have had a hard day, but we talkin' about hard lives. Years of hardness, that's the American nigga experience. Does that sound like some sort of philosophy to you? No, it's the truth.'

'You gotta stop smokin' all that weed, bro,' rumbled Sinner-Man. 'It's making you depressing.'

'You make your records, talk all that shit you don't even give a fuck about and make all that dough but the kids hear it and they believe it. Because TV tell lies,' Karnivor continued, spitting poison darts in my direction. He had a slight lisp, which added peculiar weight to every word. I could feel his animosity pierce my skin, pumping paranoia round my system. 'See those kids dancing at your feet, they believe your shit cause they got six hours a day watching that glass tube, you know what I'm saying? TV's the biggest drug of all. Kids sittin' there watching that shit all day, television programmes – who's being programmed, the TV or the person watching the TV? Real life ain't never allowed on TV. This is real life, right here, us talkin' here. You can't even get this much time for talkin' on TV, you get maybe one minute of real life surrounded by a bunch of illusions. These kids is watching the videos, it's programming they minds, man, they watching

MTV, it ain't never like that, never like TV.'

'Leave the nigga be, he just working his side of the street, like all of us,' growled SinnerMan.

'He ain't no nigga, they ain't got niggas in Irishland,' whinged Karnivor. 'Brown-skin Latino motherfuckin' fake-ass superstar.'

He had me till he started in on the skin. I'd been listening to that kind of crap all my childhood days. 'Brown is beautiful, haven't you heard? Or you too busy getting your cape ready for Klan meetings?' I shot back. 'You think I grew up in a TV set? Maybe in a crib in a Beverly Hills sitcom with a comedy butler? I grew up in a place just like this, bro. Home sweet fucking home.' It was true. It might have been on a smaller scale and a whiter shade of pale, but a tenement in Kilrock is as salubrious and inviting as a tenement in Philadelphia. Rusty swings and broken glass in a children's playground. That's always a sure sign no one cares any more. Not even the people who live there.

SinnerMan yukked with laughter. 'You see that. You see what I'm saying? He's a nigga all right.'

'I gotta take a piss,' said Karnivor, who turned his back and started urinating in the stairwell. The yellow liquid ran round his sneakers and formed a puddle, dripping down the concrete stairs.

'Dirty motherfucker,' yelped Assassin, jumping out of the way. Everybody got to their feet.

A police cruiser rolled cautiously past, two pinched white faces staring out at the street party. There must have been fifty or more people down there now, dancing round ghetto blasters, facing off in rap battles, passing around bottles, kids clambering in and out of the limo. The cruiser stopped opposite the throng at the bottom of the stairwell but when a group of sullen young men faced it off, the squad car crept on.

'They callin' it in,' said Evildoer.

'We gots to go,' nodded Assassin.

SinnerMan turned to me. 'Listen up, cuz, I gotta make a delivery. My uncle waiting on me. How about we ride together? Take the limo, travel in style, you know what I'm saying? It'll take a while but you will see things that will blow your nigga mind. You think this is a party? They got a party going on down there like no Irish motherfucker ever witnessed. There's a cat so old, he can remember the blues from when they was still green.'

'That's what I'm sayin',' agreed Assassin.

'He one scary old motherfucker,' concurred Evildoer.

'This cat came over on the boats with our grandcestors. You can see the scars where motherfucker broke his slave chains. You want some philosophy? You want some history? Come meet my man, he'll show you where the hip-hop was born, make you feel like you still a jellybaby in Mama's belly. Play you blues so old and cold it'll make your blood freeze.'

'Where is this place?' I asked.

'South,' said SinnerMan.

'South's good,' I agreed.

12

We loaded up on supplies at a petrol station, restocking a booze cabinet cleaned out by party jackers and laying in an impressive stash of emergency snacks and junk food, while Hard Head, who nominated himself chauffeur, gassed the limo. I paid for it all with my Amex Black, the inevitable staff hysteria and selfie requests dampened by SinnerMan glowering with lethal intent. 'We go dark,' he warned his posse. 'No text, no tweet, no selfie, no damn Fakebook Live with the talent here or we gonna have the whole damn country up in our business and not just the po-po. You feeling me, Hard Head?'

Hard Head looked up sheepishly from where he was tapping into his phone. 'Aww, I wuz just updating my Insta profile, Sinner,' he grumbled. 'You know how many followers our boy got on there?'

'You want to be followed, dope, give your name to the feds,' growled SinnerMan.

'I tol' you before, motherfucker, I see any pictures of me in there, I'm a delete your account. Permanently,' snarled Karnivor.

'I ain't take pictures of you, cause I don't want to crack my lens,' scowled Hard Head, reluctantly tucking his phone away.

By ten o'clock we were on the road to God Knows Where, the back of the limo degenerating into a rolling den of iniquity, sound system pounding out R'n'B and hip-hop, in-car flatscreen displaying some generic action blockbuster with the sound turned down, SinnerMan blowing clouds of reefer smoke so blue and smoggy you could get high on secondary inhalation while Assassin passed round a crack pipe fashioned from a glass tube and Brillo pad. Karnivor shaped what was left of my coke into a large spiral, chopping and scraping with compulsive intensity and unable to disguise his irritation whenever anyone snorted a section of his elaborate design. Evildoer, despite his protests, was assigned the task of following in the Mitsubishi. I was so wasted, all I could do was lay back and look at the girls, hand selected by SinnerMan from a dozen volunteers. Bountiful and her equally stacked homie Azure were pressed up against each other, asses shuffling on the leather seats, grooving mock-lasciviously to the beats like a low-rent lesbian floorshow at a mobile lap-dancing club. Their scrawny, doe-eyed friend Ella-X curled up against me, false white nails idly scratching my thigh while she asked endless questions, apparently not even expecting answers, just excited to be touching the hem of someone who had breathed the same air as her celebrity sheet pin-ups: 'So what's Cristal like? Have you really met Premier Cru? How about D'Bonair? He's so hot . . .' Names of stars tripped off her tongue and I grunted whenever I recognised one, which was enough to keep her happy.

SinnerMan leaned in and handed the spliff to me. My senses were so scrambled I kept alighting on one thing after another, sucked into a bass beat and blown out the other side by a snatch of conversation, honing in on Bountiful's bouncing breasts then free-falling into the TV screen where the action mixed with the music and guns fired slo-mo bullets rippling across the limo and into my skull, till I snatched myself back with a shudder, took the spliff and inhaled deeply, because I didn't want to appear weak in front of the gangstas, the kind of street hoodlums I dreamed of hanging with as a kid. I sucked my craving for approval deep into my lungs and let it course through my bloodstream, breaking out of my skin in a prickly sweat.

'Everybody just tryin' to be on top of that pedestal, that's all it is,' SinnerMan was saying as I tuned into his low, rumbling monologue. 'But there ain't no top. Cause once you get there somebody's comin' up behind you. Just get your money and keep movin', that's my truth. It don't mean nothin', cuz, don't mean nothin''.

He had taken off his jacket and shirt, and was sitting in a vest that revealed a thick, muscular body going to fat, covered in black etched tattoos of winding snakes, snarling tigers and roaring lions. 'One plus one is two in any language,' he continued. 'That's what truth is. It's the same wherever you go. The truth is indisputable. The truth is universal. And the truest truth is unspoken, it's just lived out, you know what I'm sayin'?' The animals moved with the ripples of his biceps, and as I stared the voice seemed to be coming from the mouth of the lion. 'A superior being is known as something that's survived, and it's smart, inventive and attuned to the planet,' quoth the beast. 'Cause if you losing touch with the planet you thinking you better than the planet itself, which is impossible, you was brought from this planet right here and you can't defeat the laws of nature.'

'Have you met Chastity Lock?' wondered Ella-X.

'I kissed Chastity,' I grunted.

'No way! That's all-the-way hot,' gasped Ella-X, whose false nails were raking across my crotch.

'Man kissed Chastity Lock,' yelped Assassin, who was attempting to pour champagne down the front of Bountiful's shirt.

'Fuck you, nigga,' screeched Bountiful.

'Lick it up, bitch,' sniggered Assassin, nudging at Azure, who pressed her face in Bountiful's cleavage till the car took a bounce and they slipped off the seat and collapsed giggling on the floor.

'The black man is the original people of this planet,' continued SinnerMan, rolling on his own sweet way as if assured everyone was paying attention. 'If you don't believe it, you go through your history. Lock yourself in a library and you will find out the hard way.' Smoke billowed from his nostrils and mouth as he spoke, making fantastic twisted shapes. 'I ain't saying we superior, I'm not prejudiced. You can take superiority through force, or you can take superiority through nature.

Everybody's dominated in certain ways. But we are the original people. Before us there was nothin' but—'

'Zero!' roared the black ink lion.

'What?' I snapped, jerking awake. Where had I been? I could feel a pulsing in my loins and looked down to see Ella-X's head buried in my crotch, soft lips and tongue working hard. She looked up with big eager-to-please eyes to see if she was doing the right thing. What age was she, I wondered? I hoped she was legal. I wanted to tell her to stop, I wasn't worth her adoration, but I felt as powerless as a sleepwalker, unable to scratch the surface of conscious volition. Further up the limo, about a million miles away, her friends were squatting around the crack pipe, greedily sucking their own poison. Bountiful had divested herself of her wet shirt and Assassin pawed her breasts.

'The Chinese the only people who kep' they culture,' Karnivor was saying. SinnerMan nodded, eyes closed, in a cloud of dreams. But Karnivor wasn't talking to him. His eyes were locked on mine. 'They dint get Americanised, they dint get Irishinised, they dint get Britishised, they stuck with they culture. They dint get stripped of nothing, they jus' kept it. Mos' peoples has been manipulated outta they culture. Look at you, fake-ass Irish nigga, where's you culture? I don't see no whiskey and potato, all I see is US penny candy, you nothin' but glucose, fructose and corn syrup. You artificial colouring, faggot. Glazed shit. Agent orange. Sugar and poison, makin' all the kids hyper and stupid.'

I was flat on my back, under attack. It had been a while since I had been exposed to such naked hostility. These days, I assumed people mostly bitched behind my back. What was making it particularly confusing was the warm sensation surging through my loins. I felt like I was about to explode and disintegrate. 'Fucking culture bullshit fuck,' I croaked, struggling to string a response together. 'The whole fucking planet is carpet-bombed with American shit, fucking cowboys in Iraq and Mickey Mouse in your precious China. Fuck. I grew up eating Big Macs with Bart Simpson, are you saying I can't take a piece of that great big fat apple pie and eat it? Oh Jesus.' I had reached escape velocity. 'We're all fucking Americans now.' And I came in Ella-X's mouth, brain fizzing and shattering.

'That's the truth, right there, cuz,' growled SinnerMan. 'My culture was stripped. My grandcestors was brought to America hundreds of years ago, we was slaves, we was stripped of language, we was stripped of everything. Now we just trying to get what's coming, grasp the things that we is owed.'

Ella-X looked up and wiped her lips.

'Shit, you swallow that, bitch?' sniggered Assassin. 'Why dint you tell me you a meat-eater?' This cracked him up.

'I eat nothin' that is dead,' intoned SinnerMan, eyes shut, head rocking back and forth. 'No dead birds, no dead cows, no dead flesh.'

'You eat dead vegetables,' Bountiful piped up.

'Vegetables don't die, woman,' growled SinnerMan.

'You eat eggs,' said Azure, who was wrapping her fingers through SinnerMan's dreadlocks.

'I don't eat fertilised eggs. I told you I don't eat dead flesh. What you tryin' to test me for?'

'This is not a test,' I mumbled to myself. Lying back, looking up through a passenger window, I could see an ocean of stars in a black sky. I was slipping into another world. Where did I come from, I wondered? I was staring down the wrong end of a telescope, everything was tiny and faraway. The past just wasn't talked about in my house. There were no photos. No stories. No gay remembrances of happy families. It was strange now that I thought about it. I was self-invented, an orphan adopted by Elvis and Marilyn. Before that, there's nothing. And after that, nothing but trouble. That's when things came into focus, just when you might wish they would blur. The ripe beery smell of my old man's breath when he'd been drinking, rambling on talking to himself, conversation zig-zagging from one point to another until no one can follow him but he doesn't care, he just keeps right on jabbering away. Not that he was drunk very often but when he was, watch out. Cathal Kelly, that fucking schoolyard bully, I can still see his leering swagger in every threatening stranger, feel his rough knuckles rubbing on my scalp, hear his sing-song taunts, 'You gonna run home crying to Mammy now? Oh, I forgot, you don't have one, smelly brown shit.' Smelly! Oh, the fucking shame. That pungent pile of clothes I used to pluck my school uniform out of, searching for a pair of socks and pants I hadn't worn too many times before cause somehow the laundry never got done in our house, the dishes didn't get washed, the sheets didn't get changed, everything reeked of disinterest and neglect, of boys' sweat and my old man's fags. That endless chain of roll-your-owns that he would sit and patiently assemble, spitting on his fingers and licking at the papers, picking at the strands of tobacco, too fucking trashed after a day scraping and bowing to do anything but slump vacantly in front of the TV and chain-smoke. 'You boys go out and have some fun, Daddy's tired.' Daddy was always tired.

Like I could go out anyway without getting more aggro, fucking gangs of little racists chasing me down tenement alleys and across fields, tossing dried dog shit and puerile invective, the same fuckers who turned up at The Zero Sums homecoming gig, wanting me to sign their girlfriends' posters. 'Ah, those were the days, Zero, when we all used to play round the back of the estate, eh?' Those were the fucking days. I wanted to bite off their noses, piss in their eyes and fuck their girlfriends in front of them, but, of course, I signed the memorabilia and thanked them for coming.

I got Cathal Kelly, though, in geography class, in front of everybody. I'd had my eye on the paperweight globe for a while. I liked the heft of it, I sensed it could do some damage. There was a map of South America tacked on the board and stiff old Mr Burns was looking right at me as he talked about the geological history of the region, as if I might have some special inside knowledge of plate movements in the Andes. I was waiting for Cathal to open his smart mouth and when he did, I grabbed that thing and swung it, cracked his fucking skull with a noise you could have sampled for a snare drum. I can still see the mottled skin of Mr Burns, that sanctimonious old prick, ashen-faced as I ran riot in his classroom, kicking over tables and chairs, screaming who cares, who cares where anyone comes from, we're all stuck in this shithole together. And the hushed voices in the head's office as they looked over at me then turned to gather in a huddle, like I didn't know what they were saying: the poor boy hasn't got over his loss. What fucking loss? How can you lose something you never even knew you had?

Paddy was called in to take me home that day. My big brother, Patrick Jesus Noone. Neither of us had much luck when it came to names. He was three years older than me . . . and still is. He might be a hotel proprietor now while I am a world fucking superstar who made joint number one with Cristal in Spacebook's poll of the Sexiest People on the Planet but, when it is just us together, he is Big Brother and I know my place. I remember asking Paddy about our mother and he would look at me and say, 'Daddy doesn't want to talk about her.'

'I'm not asking Daddy, I'm asking you,' I whined.

Oh, I got into a whole dumptruck of trouble as per usual. But one punishment blurs into another after a while, so I couldn't tell you for sure if that was the time I got spanked, whacked, screamed and sworn at, stretched on a rack and hung, drawn and quartered or if it was just my old man sighing and giving me a look of complete and utter disappointment. That same old weary-eyed gaze that said, you've fucking let me down again just like I knew you would, you little shit, my cross, my burden, bane of my fucking life.

As for Cathal Kelly, he was sent to hospital for an X-ray and returned with a bandaged head and black eyes. They said nothing was broken but he and I knew different.

That's right, Cathal, open your fucking wet mouth and say it again—

'Jakes, fuck! Lose the stash.'

I don't know how long the home movies had been playing on the inside of my eyelids. I pulled groggily around. White light was flooding the car, which was cruising slowly to a halt. Ella-X had moved off, I noticed, somehow replaced in the crook of my arm by Bountiful.

'How'm'I lose it? Ain't nowhere to flush,' Assassin was yelling. 'Yo, yo, Zero, where's the shitter in this fuckin' zine?' There was an air of wild panic. Assassin was pulling his trousers up while simultaneously trying to gather his crack pipe and bag of rocks. Ella-X was raising her head next to him, wiping her lips.

'Out the window, nigga,' growled SinnerMan, waving his arms in the blue clouds of smoke. 'And kill the fuckin' music.'

'They ain't blind, fuck, we busted, we busted,' wailed Assassin.

The limo stopped on the side of a dark road, black hills rising beyond us. Something was casting a pool of light all around the car. 'Turn off the ignition and step out of the vehicle,' crackled an electronic voice. Hard Head had the chauffeur screen pulled back. 'Wha'm'I do?'

'I ain't goin' back in da house,' said Karnivor. He had something blunt and metallic in his hand. With a lurch of horror, I realised it was a gun.

'What the fuck, guys?' I yelped.

'Shut the fuck up,' commanded SinnerMan, peering out the rear window of the limousine. 'It's police. This tinted, right, they can't see in?' He too had a gun in one hand.

'Yeah, right,' I said. Bountiful was scrabbling round on her hands and knees now, looking for her shirt.

'It's a state trooper. He's on his own,' noted SinnerMan.

'We gonna cap him?' asked Assassin. He had a gun out too. 'Shoot a cop, that's federal, that's the chair, right there, no plea.' He looked rigid with fear. The girls all gathered at the front of the limo, huddling silently together.

'Fuck right, I'ma cap him,' snapped Karnivor. 'No way I'ma goin' down on this joyride.'

'Driver, step out of the car, please,' the state trooper ordered through his loud hailer.

'Wha'm'I do?' Hard Head bleated.

'Get out the car and show him your paper. Don't do nothin' stupid,' ordered SinnerMan.

'I ain't got no licence,' whimpered Hard Head.

'Put the guns away,' I said. My heart was racing and my mouth was dry. I was supposed to be in my hotel bed right now, clutching a pile of gongs and dreaming of tomorrow's schedule, not getting dragged into a gunfight with a posse of gangstas. What was I thinking of? But I had seen Beasley, Tiny Tony and Donut handle police checks before. The trick was to play it like any other meet 'n' greet. 'I can take care of this,' I insisted, straightening my clothes.

SinnerMan glanced around at his posse, then nodded.

'Fuck us over and I'ma shoot yo fake ass first,' snarled Karnivor.

'Put it away,' said SinnerMan, slipping his own gun in his trousers.

'You're my manager,' I said to SinnerMan. 'What's your name?'

'You know my name, cuz,' growled SinnerMan.

'Your name, man, tell me your real name,' I insisted.

'Brian,' said SinnerMan, with obvious reluctance. 'Brian Sweeney.'

'Fuck, man, you're more Irish than me,' I said, opening the limo door and stepping into the police lights.

'Do NOT move, sir,' insisted the trooper. 'Raise your hands, please. Only the driver—' There was a pause. I blinked into the white light. I could make out the police car, and an indistinct figure standing next to it. 'Sir, could you step towards me, please?' asked the trooper, his tone notably altered. 'Heck . . .' He started to laugh, a weird electronic sound amplified by the loudhailer.

'What's the problem, officer?' I shouted over to him.

The trooper put down his hailer and came towards me. 'What the heck are you doin' out this way?' he said, vigorously shaking my hand. 'My girlfriend, Jenny, she is not gonna believe this. She's got us tickets for your show in Washington DC. How about that? I'm more of a country man, myself, but

Jenny is such a fan.' He was only a few years older than me, all starched and proper in his uniform, but smiling ear to ear, pumping my hand as he shook it. Still, the holstered gun and utility belt bristling with batons and handcuffs was making me nervous. I could feel Karnivor's deathray stare lasering into us.

'Well, maybe we could invite you and Jenny to come and say hello backstage,' I suggested.

'I hope you are not trying to unduly influence an officer of the law,' said the trooper, and for a moment I thought I might have blown it. But his eagerness to impress his girlfriend overcame any scruples. 'But that would be very nice. Jenny would be so pleased. She's such a sweet girl. Real pretty too. You'll like her.'

'I'm sure I will,' I agreed. I called my manager Brian out, and though I could tell the trooper was surprised to be greeted by a six-foot-two dreadlocked black man with gold teeth, he took it in his stride. SinnerMan suited this role, pumped up but polite, power personified, clapping me on the shoulder, shaking the trooper's hand, asking what he could do to help, officer. Azure was summoned to take the trooper's details.

'My personal assistant,' nodded SinnerMan, smugly. In the absence of a pen, she gamely tapped into her mobile, asking him how to spell his fiancée's name. I saw the trooper cast a curious eye over the denizens of the limo.

'Bodyguards,' I explained.

'I imagine you need them,' nodded the trooper.

SinnerMan explained that we were on our way to shoot a video in Charleston, and the trooper helpfully informed us we had taken a wrong turn and would have to back up many miles and get on I-79. 'I thought it was funny seeing a limo up here in these mountain roads,' he laughed. 'We don't get too many big stars in West Virginia.' There was a brief, sticky moment when he explained that we had been travelling nearly twenty miles over the speed limit and he was going to have to cite us.

'I'm sorry,' I said. 'We don't have a speed limit in Ireland.'

'I heard that,' nodded the trooper, thoughtfully. 'I myself am one sixteenth Irish.'

'Is that so?' I have never been sure how Americans work these fractions out. All I knew was that I was some kind of fucked-up mongrel hound dog genetic mutation that was surely never meant to occur in nature, a carrot-topped Irishman cross-fertilised with some mysterious race of brown-skinned natives from another continent. How did that happen? 'I could tell you were Irish,' I lied. 'You've got the gift of the gab.'

'Gee, I don't know about that,' said the trooper. 'But we are trained to talk to the public.'

We were nearly home and dry. But then he had to walk up to the passenger door, look inside and sniff the smoky air thoughtfully. I could pick up the aroma of crack and weed from where I was standing. He turned to look at me. Behind him, Karnivor reached stealthily into his waistband. God no, please, not that, I shuddered. We were all going to wind up bleeding to death on a roadside in the middle of nowhere.

'Rock 'n' roll?' said the trooper, knowingly raising an eyebrow. I could have kissed him. Instead we posed for a selfie on the trooper's mobile. 'Jenny is just not gonna believe this,' he grinned.

A roar came echoing down the road. Two beams of light were fast approaching through the blackness. We all stood and watched as the noise grew louder, bouncing around the hills. Then the red Mitsubishi tore past, Evildoer at the wheel, ripping it up like Formula One.

'You see that?' boomed SinnerMan, in tones of mortal outrage. 'He musta been doin' a hundred and twenty.'

'I gotta go,' snapped the trooper. 'Duty calls.' And he ran towards his car. 'See you in DC,' he shouted, jumping in. His siren wailed as he screeched off into the night.

The posse whooped it up as we continued our journey, Assassin retelling the incident in ever more dramatic detail, as if we hadn't all been witness to it, claiming credit for calling in Evildoer on his mobile, SinnerMan chuckling and congratulating me on being a stand-up soldier, Karnivor suggesting it would have been easier to just pop the cracker cop and roll him off a mountain. I sat subdued and shell-shocked, waves of sharp white fear coursing from my burning brain to the tips of my frazzled toes, making my skin feel electrified with sensitivity. To top off the celebrations, the stash was intact and Assassin struck up another crack pipe, while SinnerMan hauled out a sports holdall I hadn't even noticed and from it pulled a large plastic zip bag stuffed with weed, and another fat with powder. 'You smoke some'a' this, you be chill, cuz,' he assured me. The holdall was bulging with plastic bags. Now I understood what kind of delivery we were making. It wasn't pizza. I kept seeing the trooper's face, with the smile wiped off and blood pooling around him. How would his Jenny have felt identifying the body? And would I have been left beside him, full of holes, or hauled up in court as an accomplice? I wondered if I could get hold of one of their mobiles, call Beasley to come and get me. They could send out a chopper. I could still make rehearsals.

'What's a matter, *thug*, never been in a bust before?' sneered Karnivor, twisting the thug, spitting it like an insult. 'Shit, this is real reality right here, no pussy-ass mediaised MTV version. So what you got, gangsta? You gonna show me some showbusiness?'

But I had seen the panic in Karnivor's face, and fear in Assassin's eyes. I recognised it for what it was, because if there was one thing you learned in showbusiness it was how to put on a mask.

'Why'n't you leave Zero alone,' piped up Ella-X. 'He saved yo' nigga ass.'

'Shut the fuck up, ho, you wanna suck my dick too?' Karnivor snapped back.

'Cops don't carry guns in Ireland, ain't that so, Zero?' Ella-X bravely continued. 'I seen it on TV. It was beautiful, all green and shit. Everybody friendly. I want to live in Ireland one day.'

I smiled at her, wishing I could step right into her pipe dream.

'You believe everything you see on TV, bitch?' sneered Karnivor.

'It was on National Geographic,' insisted Ella-X, defiantly.

'They got animals in Irishland?' pondered SinnerMan, striking up a spliff.

'Some,' I said. 'Like what?'

'Tigers and lions?' speculated SinnerMan. 'I always wanted to live somewhere they got lions.'

We cruised on through the looking-glass night in our mobile wonderland, so many lost children, armed to the teeth and stoned to the eyeballs. The limo crept like a white ghost through a sprawling town, wide roads empty and silent, down streets of shuttered stores, boarded fronts and vacant windows. And we rolled out the other side, easing through silent suburbs of clapboard houses. And on till the street lights tailed off and habitations became fewer, further apart and ever more isolated, winding our way into the black mountains, bumping down twisting lanes, past ill-lit shotgun shacks. Then at last we turned into the yard of a sprawling, ramshackle flat-top bungalow, pulling up alongside Evildoer's Mitsubishi. Lights of red and blue and yellow flickered and flared inside. Bodies milled about on the porch, chattering merrily, swigging and smoking. From the house came a deep vibration, a boom-boom-boom that made the windows rattle. The car clock blinked 04:09.

A shadow peeled away from the rickety porch. The passenger door opened. A wiry old black man stood there in a crumpled suit and stained wifebeater vest, face like a burned peach, white hair shaved tight to his scalp, cigarette dangling between his lips. When he opened his mouth, a single precious stone glinted in his teeth.

'Unka Jimmy,' beamed SinnerMan.

'Get your blues on, boys,' Uncle Jimmy announced in a sandpaper croak. 'Party's started without you.'

13

The building might have been standing for a century, slowly spreading out in a forest clearing, acquiring extensions with passing decades, each more loosely assembled than the last. Some kind of fake brick veneer peeled from the walls, mossy grass grew on the roof and ivy twisted and dangled in spidery limbs that lent it the look of a shaggy dog. A rough, hand-painted sign hanging over the porch read C U BURNSIDE, decorated with childlike images of a guitar and bottles.

Uncle Jimmy led us past drink-sodden outdoor revellers into a tatty parlour dominated by an industrial refrigerator, chain and padlock securing its door. From a big, battered vat on a table covered in a vinyl sheet, he poured misty liquid into disposable plastic cups. 'It's on the house. I have ridden high, now I'm goin' down slow!' Uncle Jimmy declared, tossing his drink back.

'What's in this?' I asked, sniffing suspiciously. I looked over at SinnerMan for guidance. His cup was already empty. I took a breath and drained mine in one.

It seized the back of my throat like an acid snake and

burned its evil way down my gullet. I knew the sensation. My old man used to keep a bottle of poteen hidden at the back of his wardrobe. I had made myself sick as a mangy dog on that Irish moonshine many times, topping the bottle up with water to disguise my incursions. Which worked fine till he took a tipple himself. I don't know what was worse, the toxic hangovers or the beating that followed.

'Skull cracker, stumphole, cat daddy, ruckus juice, it go by many name but the outcome is the same,' chortled Uncle Jimmy.

'Tell me you didn't drink that, cuz?' SinnerMan whispered. 'I tossed mine. That stuff'll kill you slower than a bullet to the head but just as dead.'

I was experiencing aftershocks, shuddering lurches into new levels of insobriety. Even at that time of the morning, the room was hot and chokingly close, a single slow-moving fan stirring clouds of cigarette smoke. Extension cords stretched across the ceiling in every direction. Blinking Christmas lights were strung around cracked signs for Budweiser, Jack Daniels and Coca-Cola. Walls were covered with newspapers, varnished to a hard sheen. I looked at the spread closest to me. 'MINERS TRAPPED; CHANCES SLIM.' It was dated October 24 1958.

Our entrance had created barely a stir among the few chattering denizens, who were either too old to recognise a superstar in their midst, or too drunk to care. I wondered how Beasley would feel to learn there were still outposts of rural America resisting ubiquity. One loose-limbed younger man in dungarees and bandana unpeeled himself from the makeshift bar and fist-bumped SinnerMan, calling him cousin (Sinner-Man called everyone cuz but I gathered this one might actually be related) before staring into my face. 'Do I know you?' he slurred but I was already moving away, irresistibly drawn towards the music.

It was coming from an adjoining room, a booming blues thump that made the whole place vibrate. I followed a slip-sliding middle-aged woman in a canary-yellow dress as she negotiated the crowded doorway. It was a big, dark space, stifling and fetid, jammed with bodies, elbows sticking out, feet shuffling, everyone in the grip of a communal sway. The raw beat seemed to be sweating from the walls. I forced my way further in, Bountiful and her girls sticking close by my side. At the far end, through the throng, I could make out a band on the floor, comprising a tall man hunchbacked over an upright piano and a toady guitarist wrapped around a battered semi-acoustic plugged into a tiny amp. The sound was so distorted it was as if the strings were rusty and the speaker cones bashed in. The guitarist was seated on a square bass box, pounding out the beat with the heel of his right shoe. There was a fiddler too, ancient and white-bearded, whose frenzied playing was abetted by a tiny young girl in a flowery print dress, standing on a chair behind him and whacking the strings with a pair of knitting needles.

The music sparked lightning in my amplified senses, as free and fine and wild and weird as anything I had ever heard. A sinewy arm reached out and grabbed hold of Bountiful as an old man in vest and trilby hove into view. 'Damn, you a fine-looking woman,' he cheerfully leered. 'Come and make Daddy happy.' And he pulled her into the groove, to which she uncertainly surrendered. Other men snatched at Ella-X and Azure, and soon they too were dancing.

I was jostled from behind and turned to find Karnivor sneering. 'You think that shit's tight, gangsta? Slave music, that's all. These country fools never gonna lose they chains. Rotgut and rhythm, that's all they got to be free.'

I shrugged him off. I had thought blues was dead man's music, just scales to be practised by rote. I couldn't wait to get past them when I was learning to play, eager for melodic adventures. Shows you how much I knew. I was free-falling into another dimension, where decades of crusty reverence fell away and the music burst into life, broken, bleeding and true. Ebony faces and limbs swam around me, it was the blackest throng of human beings I had ever been in. I felt pale and alien, just an Irish boy with a tan, but I kept moving towards the players, focusing on the irresistible lure of a row of harmonicas on top of the piano.

As one blues ended another kicked off, gutbucket low and nasty. The guitarist pulled a stand towards him. The microphone lead was plugged into the same small, distorting amp as his guitar. He started to moan and groan, his voice crackling and fuzzed up. '*Got up this mornin', got up this mornin', blues standin' in my door, dog-gone-you,*' the toad wailed, flaps of his neck shaking, voice surprisingly high and sweet. '*Woke up this mornin', blues standin in my door.*' The groove uncoiled like a slithery viper. '*Says, "I've come here to stay with you, ain't gonna leave no more."*' The rhythm of the room shifted into a slow, sexy groove.

'*I said, "Blues!" I said, "Blues why don't you let me 'lone,"* oh, Mama,

I said, "Blues why don't you let me alone,
You been follerin' me ever since the day I were born!"'

The crooked pianist smiled quizzically as I stepped up, grabbed a G harp and started to blow. Oh, man. The harmonica was the very first instrument on which I learned how to chase the notes in my head and I wailed on that thing like a lost banshee crossing the wild blue yonder. The band picked up the pace. Bountiful, Azure and Ella X pushed up front, popping and gliding, dropping and spinning like a trio of hip-hop cheerleaders. Onlookers whooped and hollered. As the band settled into a railroad funk, I blew quivering, gasping, floating, shuddering, shrieking, moaning refrains till I was breathless and dizzy. At the song's clattering conclusion, I slid to the floor. The guitarist gave an almost imperceptible nod. I beamed with helpless joy. And there was applause. Oh, how the monkey loves applause. It just wants to roll over on its back and let admirers tickle its stomach. Until I realised the applause wasn't for me.

An elderly woman was helped onto centre stage. Her skin was mottled like a two-tone palomino, she had a black do-rag wrapped tight to her head, thick spectacles, rheumy eyes, her sagging body encased in a shapeless, shiny brown dress buttoned to the neck. She seemed to have some difficulty walking and was breathless and still as the fiddler adjusted the microphone stand. A sense of anticipation swelled in the room.

'You got it, Alberta?' the guitarist gently enquired, picking out a low, stately blues.

'Oh yeah!' someone called out.

The pianist joined in, playing resonant, harmonising chords. The fiddler stroked a long, tremulous, plaintive note then sat down on a fold-up chair. Rocking unsteadily on her heels, eyes closed, Alberta began to groan and whimper, a strange, unearthly sound rising from between her thin old lips. She was feeling the rhythm, waiting for the spirit to descend. I understood. Then she opened her eyes. Magnified by her glasses, they looked eerily large as she turned, stared right at me and began to sing.

You broke your mother's heart, Lord when you runned away,
You broke your mother's heart, Lord when you runned away,
She said, 'He's a hard-headed child, I know you is gone astray.'

A cold wind blew through me. 'Sing it, Alberta,' a voice yelled.

Mama said, 'Son, oh son, way you carryin' on is a low down dirty sin,'
Mama said, 'Son, way you carryin' on is a low down sin,

*You done run away and left me, but you comin' back
home again.'*

Her voice was crushed velvet and whiskey, bittersweet and
lived-in. Anybody can move notes around but some people
open their mouths and you can hear every sin, every act of
mercy, every victory, every regret, all the love and all the
shame. That's what it sounded like to me, anyway, winding
through the alcoholic fog. How did she know my secret heart?
Was she some kind of witch?

*I'm coming home Mother, please don't cry when you see
me,
I'm coming home Mother, when you see me don't you cry,
I was a hard-headed boy, now your son's coming home
to die.*

I blew into the harp, soft and low and hurting. A mournful
wheeze. A lonely sob of self-pity.

*Ooh Mother, oh Mother, remember I'm your child,
Cryin' Mother, oh Mother, remember that I'm your son,
Mama, please forgive me, all the things that I have done.*

When Alberta made her exit, I couldn't move, I was too
drained, squeezed like a bitter lemon. The band picked up the
beat but when I looked closer I realised this was a whole different set of players. People seemed to have stepped off the

floor and taken over the instruments. The pianist was hollering out a call, and the crowd yelled the response. *'My gal is red hot!'* *'Your gal is doodly squat!'* *'I said, my gal is RED HOT!'* *'Your gal is doodly squat!'* I didn't know much about the blues but I was pretty sure they didn't belong in the Appalachian mountains. I needed to find Alberta. I wanted to ask what was going on. And I really wanted to find out where she learned to sing like that and if she could teach me.

From a door at the back of the stage, I found myself in a narrow corridor, lit by a single red bulb. The first door I tried opened onto a small room where six men were seated round a table, in the centre of which lay a pile of stray bills and small change. Smoke hung in the air, the pungent whiff of marijuana. Everyone was holding cards and the chatter was loud and raucous.

'So what you been doin' hanging round Mrs Colbie's place, Henry? cause you sure ain't been teachin' her how to play poker.'

'I've been pokin' somethin', sure 'nuff, ain't quite figured out what, that's all. I just keep pokin', hopin' for the best.'

'You've got a dirty mouth, Henry. Mrs Colbie's a good church-going widow.'

'Well, it ain't the Lord been puttin' a smile on her face. I'll tell you what, these niggers around Scarsdale, they been lyin' to me all these years when they say white women can't fuck.'

When the laughter petered out, one of the men noted my presence. 'You got bidness?' he asked.

'I'm with SinnerMan,' I said.

He sniffed, apparently satisfied. 'Out back,' he said, tipping his head towards another door, next to which Hard Head was stretched on a couch, fast asleep. I walked carefully past him, measuring my steps so I didn't stumble.

Everything froze as I entered. SinnerMan and Uncle Jimmy were standing over the hold-all, counting out bags of coke and weed. Evildoer and Assassin were slumped on a sofa, mouths agape, looking at me like I had materialised in a puff of smoke. The bricks of money on the table put the poker game next door to shame. Behind them all stood another man, smartly turned out in a dark suit. His face was so wide, hard and stony, he looked like he might have been the original model for the Easter Island statues. 'I'm sorry,' I said, knowing I probably wasn't supposed to be seeing this.

'Who's this motherfucker?' asked Stoneface.

'He's cool,' SinnerMan reassured him, shooting a dirty look at Assassin and Evildoer, who were half-heartedly attempting to escape the sofa's gravitational pull.

'I'm cool,' I vouched for myself.

Stoneface didn't seem convinced. 'Miles Davis is cool, motherfucker. Who the fuck are you?'

'Why'nt'cha all relax, now, my very, very good friends,' said Uncle Jimmy. 'This here's my nephew's ride, ain't that right?'

'I *know* you,' said Stoneface.

'I get that a lot,' I said.

'You're that fuckin' pop star. Zippo. My daughter plays your records. What the fuck you doin' here?'

'It's a long story,' I shrugged, uneasily.

'You really a pop star?' said Uncle Jimmy. 'That's nice.'

'Is this s'posed to be some kinda fuckin' joke?' snarled Stoneface. 'Candid fuckin' camera?'

'You famous?' asked Uncle Jimmy. 'I don't really keep up with the records these days.'

'What kind of fool brings a fuckin' pop star to a meet. You got a yearning to be on TV?' said Stoneface. 'Maybe *America's Most Stupid*?'

'Don't be callin' me no fool, nigga,' snarled SinnerMan, looking a little sheepish.

'Take care of your friend,' said Stoneface. 'We got business.'

'I'm'a take care of this one,' said a voice, soft and close to my ear. I twisted to see Karnivor, who had come in silently behind me.

'Where the fuck you been, bro? You supposed to be on the door. Shit!' said SinnerMan.

'Hadda take a piss,' said Karnivor.

'Why'n't you just piss on the door, like you do at home,' sniggered Assassin.

'Shut your mouth, halfpint, or I'm'a piss all over you,' sneered Karnivor.

'Jesus Christ, I'm not interested in whatever shit is going down here,' I interjected, maybe too forcefully. Even in my pathetic state, I was acutely aware of how finely balanced the tension in the room was. 'I'm sorry to intrude. I'm just going to leave you to it, OK?'

'You can't be leavin' already,' complained Uncle Jimmy. 'You gotta say hello to old Honeyboy. He be very pleased to meet a fellow musicianeer.'

'Honeyboy?' Who the fuck was Honeyboy?

'Clarence Urreal Burnside,' announced Uncle Jimmy proudly. 'Greatest bluesman you never heard with your very own ears. He been playing this juke since before I was born, and that was a long time ago, let me tell you. Peoples call him Honeyboy but I can't rightly say why. He ain't sweet iffen he ever was and he sure as hell ain't a boy no more. Names stick, I guess.'

'Are we fuckin' done with the history lesson?' growled Stoneface.

'You sit tight, cuz,' SinnerMan instructed me. 'Drink some more of Uncle Jimmy's juice. I'm'a take care of business here, then we pay our respects to the man. Evil, take our boy outside, buy him a drink.'

'I don't want another drink,' I said. Ever, I might have added. 'But I could use some of that.' I pointed to the bags of powder on the table.

'That's how it's goin' down, is it?' said Stoneface.

SinnerMan looked at me like I was a stone idiot. I felt craven and ashamed but I desperately needed something to straighten my head. Or at least that's what I was telling myself. He pulled a little baggie from inside his jacket and poured the contents on the table. 'What you waitin' for?'

'Uhm . . . you got a dollar bill?'

'Shit, you s'posed to be a rich motherfucker,' muttered Karnivor. 'Now we payin' this bitch to bump our coke?'

SinnerMan peeled a fifty off one of the stacks. I didn't look anybody in the eye as I rolled it up and did what I had to. Not that it made much difference. I was still ripped to my tits, I just didn't feel the desperate need to crawl away somewhere and sleep any more. I let Evildoer escort me out.

'Hey, Zippo!' called Stoneface. I turned back. 'Don't be runnin' off nowhere.'

'Well, I, for one, am glad my nephew is consorting with a better class of people,' smiled Uncle Jimmy.

I needed air, so Evildoer led me down the corridor and out back, all the while asking questions about how much you get paid for making a track, who collects your royalties and whether it was worthwhile having management. 'My rap is fresh,' he assured me. 'I'm ready to blow up. You wanna hear?'

'Not right now,' I politely requested. But he went right ahead anyway, peppering the warm night air with sloppy verses about capping niggas and banging hos, hands chopping like he was engaged in a karate fight with an invisible assailant. I looked up at the almost full moon, wrapped in a radiant halo, glowing like a promise above dark, ancient trees. The aroma of the forest filled my nostrils, damp and mossy and green, the smell of my own faraway homeland.

'Something's wrong with you, baby, you got an evil stranger in your midst,' said a voice out of the darkness. Evildoer nearly jumped out of his baggy pants. Gun in hand, he whipped around in alarm.

Alberta was sitting on a fold-up chair, pale and still in the moonlight. She had removed her scarf and an electroshock of grey hair sprang wild and wiry from her head. Her magnified eyes seemed independent of her, moving about in the spectacles like bloodshot globes. When she smiled at me, her teeth, what were left of them, were crooked and furred. I could tell by the way Evildoer was recoiling that he was intimidated by the old crone. But whatever was inside her, straining against the shell of age and infirmity, had cast a spell over me. I moved forward to sit at her feet.

'Where did you learn to sing like that, Alberta?' I asked.

'Life is all the teacher you need,' she said. 'Never had no education. I was born a triplet, seven brothers and sisters before me. When Daddy seen what Mama brought into the world, he was not a happy man, cause he had too many mouths and too little food to put in 'em. You had to live very scarcely back then, you know, just bread and meat. They was hard times. So he said to my mother, "Come and pick the one you want, cause I'm gonna drown the other two." Course, Mama, she couldn't choose between her three little babies, so Daddy says, "Whichever one of these fellers bawls the loudest, that's the one we gonna keep." And I been bawlin' ever since.'

I saw Evildoer cross himself as he backed into the house. I don't think I had ever heard a story so terrible, yet the old woman told it like she was passing the time of day. 'I been near to death all my life and it ain't got hold of me yet,' Alberta continued. 'Mama passed when I was six years old. That's just about the earliest thing I can remember. Daddy put her in her grave. Said she'd been messing round with Holt Watson, fella on the sharecrop next but one. I don't know nothing about that. All my brothers and sisters were running around, crying and begging. I remember that. "Please, Daddy, don't kill Mama, Daddy please." He never was one for listening to us children. Killed old Holt Watson too, they say. Burned the house right down, them inside it. That's when I caught the blues. It's a feeling deep inside, so deep you can't possibly get to the bottom of it. *You* know.'

Oh, I knew. I sat hugging my knees, listening as Alberta talked about her life, so much trouble and pain, 'hard lived and easy told', she said. Her daddy had been on the chain gangs, but he turned up every few years to bring fresh misery into her existence. The community dated back to the civil war. 'Coloured time, the slavery,' as she called it. Virginia sided with the Confederacy, West Virginia stuck with the Union, and escaped slaves settled in the foothills of the Appalachian mountains. 'Grandma was born the second year of surrender.' Life was hard up here for the white folks, even harder for the blacks, but at least there were no lynchings, mostly people were too tired working to bother with hating. Alberta worked in the fields and she worked in the railroad, she worked as a cook on the coal mines and a dishwasher in the sawmills. 'I have done just about everything a person could name to make that money for living.' Then her daddy got out of jail the last time and took her to sing with him in juke joints. 'He could raise a big mess but the people did love to hear him holler.' She fell pregnant, even though she said she 'never knew no man but Daddy'. Alberta gave birth to twins but her father sold them to a childless couple in Chicago, at least that's what he told her. Some nights she dreamed of her babies fighting their way out of a sack in the river and woke up so wet with tears she thought she was drowning herself. 'I prayed they growed up big and strong and never had to sing the blues. You know.'

And even though the world she described was a million miles from my own, that part I did understand. 'No man nor woman in good spirit and pure heart can sing the blues,' said Alberta. Her disembodied eyes shone with tears. 'Never has been, never will be.' And she started to sing, softly.

You can fill your eyes with silver, fill your belly full of gold
You can buy an ocean liner, sail it all around the world
You can climb a ivory tower, you can fall down on yo'
  knees
But when Mama Death come calling, you come crawling
  back to me

Soft hand claps sounded as SinnerMan and Uncle Jimmy emerged from the shadows. 'You putting the fear of God in the boy with your stories, Alberta?' called Uncle Jimmy, grabbing me around the shoulders. 'Alberta and the truth are very distant relations.'

'What would you know about that, Jimmy?' sniffed Alberta. 'I'm proud of my life, cause I come through with my skin on. And if I had to live over, I'd live it all over again.'

'We're gonna borrow your young man, sister, I hope you don't mind,' smiled Jimmy. 'He's gonna pay his respects to

Honeyboy. This fella here is a noted musicianeer hisself, ain't that right, Zip?'

'You take care now, child,' said Alberta. 'There's two sides to the road, no needs to walk on the wrong one.'

'You know Honeyboy, Alberta?' I asked. She looked up at the moon but didn't answer.

'Everybody knows Honeyboy,' insisted Uncle Jimmy, evasively.

'He's my daddy,' said Alberta.

Clarence Urreal 'Honeyboy' Blindside was laid out like a corpse in a room at the furthest extension of the building's random sprawl. He was tricked up in a sharp black country-and-western suit with elaborate silver woven patterns, white shirt buttoned to the neck and a bootlace tie with native American clasp, lying dead still on a double bed with a black mahogany headboard carved in the form of an eagle. Sharp screws protruded hazardously from the bedposts. Roaches skittered up the panelling on the wall behind. He was a big man, wide and thick-set, though the skin of his broad face had loosened with age and hung in saggy folds. His eyes were closed. Two women sat either side, like mourners keeping watch. They glanced up anxiously as we entered, as if our presence might disturb the spirits.

Uncle Jim coughed hesitantly. 'Uh-hum . . . is he awake?'

'I am the Black Ace, I am the boss card in your hand,' the corpse announced in a bullfrog croak. The women stared at us balefully.

'Brought someone to meet you, Honeyboy. He is a noted musicianeer and popular star.'

'That so?' croaked the corpse. And he opened his eyes. One was watery grey and bloodshot, swimming in yellow and flecked with black spots, which was nonetheless an improvement on the other, bleached white and blind. He lay there examining me intently with his functioning eye for a while. Then he sniffed, loudly and dismissively. 'I got but one eye and part of my lung is gone, but my fingers is still live. I been shot, I been cut, but nobody can take me down. Some niggers say I can't fight as good as I used to but if Honeyboy gets his hands on him, he belongs to me. I'm the wolf, baby, take my time prowlin', wipe my tracks with my tail.'

Uncle Jimmy smiled benignly, as if all this made sense.

'Help me up now, dear ladies, I got to keep moving, got to keep moving, blues fallin' down like hail,' Honeyboy commanded.

It was quite some operation for the women just to get him into a sitting position, feet on the floor, through which he grunted and cursed under his breath. As he moved, his trouser legs shifted, revealing white scar tissue around his ankles. The women said nothing, as silent as the devil's hand maidens. They had the look of sisters, middle-aged with a sad-eyed beauty. He patted one on the ass, letting his hand linger. 'Whoa, it smoke like lightnin', yeah, but shine like gold,' he croaked. 'Don't you hear me talking, pretty baby?' The ancient figure seemed to be propelled by a kind of malevolent vitality. 'Who sent you down here, boy, what did you break in this jail for?' he enquired. I wasn't sure if he was addressing me or just reciting half-remembered lyrics. Beckoning me closer, he gripped my arms tightly with big, bony hands. 'You look like a man who would kill your mother. Oh boy, what did you kill that old woman for?' Then he laughed, a sound like torn sandpaper.

'Where did you get those scars?' I asked. Just for something to say. The women gasped as if I had blasphemed in front of the pope but Honeyboy seemed unperturbed.

'Well, I can't rightly remember if that was the state farm in Mississippi or the chain gang in Wisconsin, what would you say, Jimmy? Black nigger baby gonna take care of myself, always carry a great big razor and a pistol in my vest. Turn that nigger round and knock him on the head, cause white folks say, "We're gonna kill that nigger dead." Uh huh. Take a drink with me, boy.'

Jimmy fished a couple of tin cups through a pot of liquid. A visible shudder passed through Honeyboy's body as he sank his but it was hard to tell if it was pleasure or pain. I held the cup in my hand uncertainly but when he turned that one gruesome eye on me I poured the burning fuel down my throat. Honeyboy's rank breath hit me like a heatwave. The musical vibration of the house thudded in my ears. I stared into the tiny black iris of his one good eye and saw it bloom like an ink blot, sucking me in with the gravitational pull of a black hole. 'I'm a crawlin' king snake and I rule my den,' Honeyboy croaked, his laughter echoing around my skull. 'Oh, I'm blue, black and evil and I did not make myself!'

'Play Honeyboy one of your popular songs,' Uncle Jimmy urged, handing me a hollow-body Gibson semi-acoustic guitar, scratched and worn but with beautiful pearl inlays and elegant f-holes. I tried to make excuses. The guitar is not really my chosen instrument. I can make my way around it if I have to but it helps if I am sober.

'You ain't one of them crack-smokin' jive-talking rappers, is you, little boy?' Honeyboy growled suspiciously, as I fumbled with some chords. 'In this latter day here, with all this education, in this here space age, when everybody's lookin' up, the whole world turning back to front, you got the white children trying to be negroes, and the negroes trying to be white, and everybody wants blood but nobody wants to spill it. Keep it real, Urreal, young niggers tell me, but blues is reality and I am the blues, that's right. They ain't seen the things I seen, trouble, trouble, trouble all over the world.' Spittle was dribbling from his mouth, he seemed to be chewing himself into a state of vitriol. 'If you was white, should be all right, if you was brown, stick around, but as you is black, git back, git back, git back. What is so damn wonderful about reality?'

I started to sing 'Make It On My Own' in a shaky voice. It's got a lot of chords and I was showing off, though they weren't falling under my fingers right and the Gibson was thin and dull without amplification. The chorus soars through the octaves, technically it's quite hard to sing and probably not the wisest selection on a tin cup of 100-per-cent-proof bootleg whiskey but I stood up and belted it out.

Baby there is something you should know
I want you to stay, I don't want you to go
But if you should leave me,
You better believe me, baby
I can make it on my own.

SinnerMan applauded loudly when I finished. 'That's my nigga,' he announced. No one else responded. The women were waiting for Honeyboy's lead while Uncle Jimmy seemed discomforted, as if I might have been trying to show Honeyboy up. The man himself just snorted indifferently.

'How you gonna leave me, baby, with my pistol in your mouth?' he croaked. He seemed so pleased with that, he repeated it a couple of times, chuckling, then stuck out one hand and wrapped it around the neck of the guitar. 'One of these days, people, and it won't be long, you gonna look for me baby and your daddy be gone,' he announced. The women helped him to his feet. 'The ice man's calling, baby, I give it to you cold.' One of the women placed a black cowboy hat on his head. 'I can hear my black name ringin', oh hurryin' on down the line. I never been satisfied, and I just can't keep from crying.' He started to move off, embarking on a long, slow walk down the red-lit corridor, supported by the women.

'That's one bad motherfucker,' whispered SinnerMan.

'Watch your mouth,' said Uncle Jimmy.

'My mother died and left me reckless, my daddy died and left me wild,' Honeyboy called out. 'You gotta treat me better, or it be your funeral, and my trial.'

Honeyboy's arrival onstage caused a commotion. Everything was bent out of shape, everyone seemed crazier and drunker, and that included me. Hands grabbed at my coat, spinning me about, voices blurred around me. Hey, Zero. Zero. Zero motherfucker. Seems I'd been rumbled. I found myself in the centre of the room, propped up by complete strangers, directly in front of Honeyboy, who was seated at the microphone, guitar across his lap. The band were poised and ready. A hush descended, electric with anticipation. 'This is for all my children,' croaked Honeyboy, staring right at me. 'Wherever they may be.' Then the ancient bluesman let out a raw-throated, blood-curdling, death-rattling, spirit-summoning hoodoo howl that ripped right through me. The crowd erupted in a body-crashing frenzy as the dirty riff took hold. *'Come here little fella, come sit on Daddy's knee,'* he roared. I was being buffeted about but Honeyboy kept me in the range of his evil eye. *'I tell you the truth, cause truth will set you free.'* I wasn't sure if I wanted to hear Honeyboy's truth but I was powerless to stop him. *'Somebody's gonna get hurt and it won't be me.'* And he howled like a werewolf racked with bloodlust. The room was spinning but everywhere I looked there was Honeyboy's eye. It was staring out of the walls and the ceiling. It was glaring up from the floor. It was scowling at me from the single light bulb.

Took care of your brother Billy, took care of sister Mary too,
Took care of your cheatin' mama, you know I did what I
*   had to do,*
Now somebody's gonna get hurt and it might be you.

I lurched and staggered, barely staying upright. Hands pushed me away. Teeth bared in feral grimaces.

Why d'you come down here, why'n'tcha let me be?
You ought to lock that door, you better throw away the key
Somebody's gonna get hurt and it won't be me.

I tried to make my way to the door but someone held onto me tight. 'I'm'a like that coat, Irish,' Karnivor whispered in my ear, tugging at the arms of my frock coat till it worked off my shoulders. I stumbled to the floor as he slipped the $5000-dollar garment onto himself. 'You won't need this where you're goin', clown.' The music raged like a storm around the dance floor, a gale force blast picking everybody up and tossing them about.

There's a black ghost rising, there's a ship sailing with no captain or crew,
There's just you and me and the devil and the old deep blue,
Well, somebody's gonna get hurt and it might be you.

I lurched across the pitching floor, clawing my way to the exit. Hands grabbed me and spun me around. By the time I got my bearings, my coat was vanishing through the front door. I threw myself after Karnivor, snatching at the hem and tumbling over the porch, till I was kneeling outside in the dirt, looking up into a small circular black hole. I blinked as the barrel of Karnivor's gun came into focus.

'Might be you got SinnerMan fooled but I ain't gonna be your fuckin' bitch,' he screamed. 'You must think we all dumb-ass niggas fucked up on rock so little wigga can play gangsta. Where you be without the streets, MTV? Never Young, mother-fucker? You ain't never gonna get old.'

My mouth was a desert. My heart was a volcano. A tsu-nami of blood crashed through my veins. The world shrank to a single thought: what a stupid way to die. I closed my eyes.

I felt the ground open up beneath me. I was tumbling through the universe, stars beneath my feet, galaxies unfold-ing, supernovas exploding, my whole being separating into cosmic dust and the last thing I saw . . . the very last thing I saw . . . was a distant constellation coalescing into a face, so familiar, so strange, so beautiful . . .

'Mother?' I whimpered.

But the stars faded. I opened my eyes. I was kneeling in front of the house. Karnivor was standing in my coat by the limo, next to SinnerMan. The lights were on and the passen-ger door open.

'Should have stayed where you was safe, MTV,' laughed Karnivor.

I looked helplessly at SinnerMan. He shrugged and climbed into the limo, which was already occupied by his posse. Kar-nivor shut the door behind them and the vehicle gently eased off, Hard Head behind the wheel.

'Hey!' I yelled, jumping to my feet. The fuckers were stealing my car. I started to run after it but I was caught in a blinding flare of bright white light as the Mitsubishi came roaring towards me. Evildoer spun the wheel at the last possible moment, dirt and gravel flying in my face, the wind of the speeding car gusting across me.

And then I was alone beneath the stars.

'Fuck,' I sighed. I stood in my jeans and T-shirt looking at Uncle Jimmy's juke joint, twinkling with fairy lights and vibrating to the blues, wondering what I was supposed to do now. I didn't want to go back into Honeyboy's malignant orbit. But where else was I supposed to go? I looked down the dark road, stretching to an infinity of blackness. I guess I'd have to walk.

As I wearily turned to leave, a voice called out. 'Yo, don't move, motherfucker.'

Stoneface was standing on the porch. 'We got unfinished business.'

I contemplated a dash for the trees. I might just be able to make the cover of darkness before Stoneface caught me but I was so drunk and tired, I didn't even have the will to save myself. The grim-faced drug dealer came striding towards me, hand reaching into his jacket. Here we go, I thought. People were queuing up to kill me today. That's the price of popularity. My stomach clenched involuntarily, as if all those gym-toned muscles would help me now.

Stoneface pulled out a pen and shoved a beer mat into my hand. 'You weren't gonna split without signing something for my daughter, were you? Her name's Jewel. Make it nice and personal.'

My hand was shaking as I scrawled, 'To Jewel, it's been a pleasure doing business with your daddy. Love, Zippo.'

'All right,' said Stoneface, approvingly. 'Nice doing business with you, too.'

We shook hands awkwardly. He turned back to the house and I started walking down the road.

14

I walked into the town of Siren Creek, Pop. 643, at thirteen minutes past seven by my Patek Philippe Rose Gold Nautilus watch, the luminous dial of which was all I had to light my way for the first pitch-black hour of my hike. The temperature had dropped, the road kept rising, I was cold and tired and frightened and locked into frenzied mental ping-pong, cursing my stupidity and fantasising alternative endings, the same wretched thoughts bouncing back and forth and back and forth until my mind had run me ragged. Shame, shame, shame, sang the evil chorus line. How long have you been shooting blanks, bad boy? All those gangsta dance moves, all that CGI martial artistry, all the fame and all the applause, and just one look down the barrel of a gun and you turn into a little bitty baby boy crying for his mummy. You fake. You loser. You . . . know how it goes.

But somehow, as a fuzz of dancing particles began to fracture the darkness, and the faint outlines of trees and mountains appeared out of the gloom, my spirits lifted incrementally, at least far enough to be thankful I had made it through the night in one piece. Pretty soon pastel hues of pink and cyan brightened the sky and the Blue Ridge Mountains filled out in all their craggy glory. And you know what? They really are blue. A bird chirruped overhead, the smell of pine was sweet and heavy, the road dipped into a river valley, the incline easing my aching limbs, and by the time I reached Siren Creek, with the climbing sun starting to radiate some faint heat, the thing foremost on my mind was where to get something to eat.

It was not promising. From a distance, the town looked pleasant enough, a few streets protruding from a central drag, set in the midst of scrappy plots of farmland and bisected by a small river. But up close it looked like Siren Creek was either shut or abandoned. The road surface was cracked and weeds edged the pavement. I walked past a garage with a single lonely petrol pump, metallic paint flaking. Car wrecks in various states of decay lined the side of the building, many with FOR SALE painted inside their windscreens. There were a couple of stores, window frames warped and cracked, shelves almost entirely empty. A barber shop carried faded photographs of haircuts that had gone out of style before I was born. The post office was boarded up. It was so quiet, I could hear grass rustling and the distant bray of competing cockerels. But it was early, and the Sulphur Spring Tavern at least looked like it might have been freshly painted sometime this century, the lurid shade evidently chosen to match its enticing name. Directly opposite stood Rita May's Stop N Shop, with a stars and stripes in the window and a confusing array of signs:

'TOURISTS WELCOME' and 'PUBLIC RESTROOMS' hanging alongside 'NO LOITERING' and 'SPITTING PROHIBITED'. While I pondered whether waiting for a shop to open could be construed as loitering, a dented Ford the colour of burnt rust trundled up the street and stopped in front of a pink clapboard store. A skinny girl got out, spat on the dusty sidewalk in direct contravention of Rita May's public ordinance, unlocked the front door and disappeared inside. I strolled over. The sign announced SIREN CREEK DINER, or would have if all the letters had been in place. Actually it said SIR REEK DIN R. But it was good enough for me.

A bell announced my entrance. There were six Formica tables in a room cluttered with product signs and tacked posters, the largest featuring American icons Elvis Presley, Marilyn Monroe and Vanilla Ice, the original white rapper out of his league even in a rural diner. 'We ain't open,' a lilting voice called from a kitchen hatch behind the counter. I sat in a corner contemplating a lurid oil painting which appeared to show a colourful feathered creature of indeterminate species sitting in a tree strumming a guitar, although the brushwork was so poor it could have been almost anything. If I squinted, it turned into a mermaid on a rock playing a lyre, an impression reinforced by the addition, in black magic marker, of two large breasts with prominent nipples, out of which emerged a speech bubble saying, 'This town ain't big enough for the both of us.' I was so tired, I might have laid my head on the table and slept if my stomach wasn't protesting so loudly. I picked up a red plastic tube and wondered what tomato sauce tasted like on its own.

'I said we ain't open,' repeated the voice. 'I only stopped by to let Jimmy in to fix the oven hood, damn thing keeps blowing when it's supposed to be sucking, iffen you know what I mean. Course he's late. Shit. I s'pose I could fix you a cup of coffee and maybe a sandwich but chef ain't coming in today, not that that's gonna make a whole lot of difference, he don't come in till ten most mornings, iffen then. Says it's so dead out there, no one will notice. Well, *I* notice and I ain't no one.'

I looked up to see the skinny girl, mousey hair tied back in a ponytail, her freckly, high-boned face almost exquisite if it hadn't been for eyes that were small and wary, and tight lips that looked like they never smiled. In a crisp white shirt and tartan skirt, she looked an angel of mercy to me. 'Coffee and a sandwich would be amazing,' I said.

'Omigod!' she gasped. Then louder. 'Oh my God!'

There's not much you can say to that.

'You're him,' she screeched.

'I am,' I admitted.

'Oh. My. God,' she repeated, with dramatic pauses. 'I saw you on TV last night. You was on an awards show but they said you run out. How d'you get here?'

'I ran all the way,' I said.

'Shit. No way. You're pulling my leg. Did my momma put you up to this?' She prodded my hand, as if to make sure I was real. 'Oh my God! Shit.'

She could turn shit into a two-syllable word. There was something familiar about her Appalachian drawl and not just from countless cinema cowboys and country singers. Something about it reminded me of home. I liked her straight away. It took me a while to persuade her there were no secret cameras filming our encounter, but eventually she accepted that pop stars had to eat too, and retired to the kitchen to cobble together whatever she could find, although she couldn't promise it would be up to much. There was a lot of clattering and the occasional 'Omigod!' and one almighty crash, but she returned in due course with some sandwiches of square white bread, butter, processed cheese, tomatoes and salad cream, augmented by a packet of crisps and a bottle of Coke – on account of the fact that she had dropped the coffee pot and smashed it. To me, it was a feast. While I tucked in, she pulled out a chair and sat opposite, furiously chain-smoking cigarettes and telling me random things about her life.

By the time I finished eating, I had learned that her name was Devlin Perry, she was seventeen years old and had lived in Siren Creek all her life and dreamed practically every day of getting away; she wanted to be a singer but didn't know if she was any good; she lived with her mother and aunt Velma, who sort of owned the diner, although it really belonged to her daddy who had run off with a schoolgirl from the neighbouring town of Scarsdale and even though it was only six miles away she almost never saw him again; she much preferred my early singles to my new one but she was gonna buy the album anyway, especially now that she had met me for herself; her granny died last year and left her a trailer up in the woods, where she stayed when she wanted to get away from everyone, which was more often than not; the town was dying on its feet especially since they built Walmart in Scarsdale; there really was a sulphur spring and the mayor (who also owned the tavern) had tried to turn it into a tourist attraction but it bubbled up green and let off an awful stink which had been kind of a hard sell; she wanted to turn the diner into an Internet café but Aunt Velma said all that men around here were interested in was tractors and porno, and she was damned if she was gonna run a farm sex emporium; and she wasn't supposed to smoke at work but since we were the only two people there, what the fuck?

'What the fuck,' I agreed.

'You want one?' she said, proffering the pack. When I politely declined, she said, 'I know you don't smoke.' She read all the celebrity magazines and knew practically everything there was to know about me, apparently. She had cried when I got engaged to Penelope, and wondered what did I see in an old woman like that anyway? The bitch was much better suited to Troy Anthony. Before I could thank her for the vote of confidence, Devlin solemnly informed me that she herself was single and open to offers but there were no boys worth dating in Siren Creek and anyway they all thought she was a lesbian just cause she was saving herself for someone special.

I looked at my empty plate. I had dined in the finest restaurants in the world, but couldn't remember the last time I had eaten so voraciously, and finished every last morsel. Was my break for freedom over now? Should I just find a phone and meekly surrender? I couldn't see what else I was supposed to do, in the middle of nowhere, with no transport, no possessions and no idea what I was really trying to achieve. The glare of the sunlight dazzled my eyes. I was too tired to think. 'How much do I owe you?' I sighed, fishing out my Amex Black.

'Do we look like we take credit cards?' Devlin laughed, mirthlessly.

'I don't have any cash,' I admitted.

'Shit, it's on the house. Shit. I can't believe it's you. Shit. It really is you.'

'It really is,' I agreed.

'Shit.'

'You got a phone I could borrow, Devlin?' I enquired. The question tasted of defeat in my mouth. But I was spared a reply by the bell ringing over the door. Devlin frantically stubbed out her cigarette as a bearded man in a blue work shirt and jeans entered. 'You smoking, girl? Your momma catches you, you'll get what for.'

'I got a customer!' said Devlin, jumping up, frantically indicating that the cigarettes were mine. I grabbed her hand, shifting so that she blocked me from the new arrival. I couldn't face another scene.

'Listen, Devlin,' I whispered, pulling her towards me. 'Please don't tell anybody I'm here. I'm trying to lay low.'

'Well, that's gonna be a hard secret to keep. Shit. I don't believe there's ever been a famous person in Siren Creek, like, ever! They say Clint Eastwood was in Scarsdale once, so they say, he stopped for gas and said hi to everybody and signed autographs, but Momma says it was just a lookilike. You ain't a lookilike are you?'

I assured her I wasn't.

'I know you ain't. I read the magazines. I'd recognise you anywhere.' The bearded man had disappeared into the kitchen. 'You don't need to worry about Jimmy,' she assured me. 'The only magazines he reads are the ones with naked girls on motorbikes. I don't think you're in them magazines.'

'You never know,' I said. I was ubiquitous, after all.

'What the hell you been doin' back here, Devlin?' called Jimmy.

'Making a sandwich.'

'What kinda sandwich would that be, girl? Broken glass and coffee grinds? Remind me never to ask you to cook for me.'

'Listen, Devlin,' I said. 'I really need somewhere quiet to lay down and just get my head together. What about that place of your grandmother's you told me about? Do you think I could rest up there?'

'Shit. You wanna stay with me?'

'Just for a little while.'

'Shit. Well, all right then.'

While she swept up in the kitchen and fed Jimmy some story about going to get a replacement coffee pot, I examined the oil painting a little closer. If it was supposed to be a nude portrait, Picasso himself couldn't have made it more unfathomable, yet there was something violently seductive about it, as if it had been thrown together in a mad frenzy by an eroticised primitive.

'You like that picture?' asked Devlin, sceptically. 'Aunt Velma painted it herself. She took lessons, you know. I reckon she could use a few more but I ain't gonna be the one to tell her.'

'What is it?' I asked.

'Shit, can't you tell? It's me.'

Life was stirring in the little ghost town – kids playing on a garden swing, a dog snuffling around some garbage, a couple arguing as the man tinkered under the hood of his car, a woman hanging washing. We drove into the hills, where the small dwellings became progressively more run-down and spread further apart. We finally pulled into a forest clearing that was a cross between a junk yard and a smallholding, dominated by a dirty white oblong box standing on bricks. 'I don't even know why they call it a mobile home,' said Devlin. 'It ain't never been nowhere but here and I don't suppose it's going nowhere else.'

We picked our way past stray items of furniture, a discarded fridge, a rusted bicycle bent in two, a car with no wheels or windows, a broken toilet with plants growing in it and other bits of random domestic detritus. 'Grandma was kind of a hoarder,' explained Devlin. 'People would come round to see if she had anything they could use and buy it off her. Since she passed, the fuckers just use it as a dump. Shit.'

She opened the trailer door onto a grotto of bric-a-brac. Shelves were overcrowded with figurines, mostly religious, lots of Jesuses, Marys and Josephs, but also animals and birds, especially eagles and owls, and elaborate clocks, all set at different times. Walls were papered in tin foil and pinned with pictures, some domestic snapshots, some religious icons, some black-and-white scenes from bygone eras featuring priests and nuns torn from the pages of magazines, and a few framed portraits of John F. Kennedy, Mother Teresa, the bleeding heart of Jesus and various popes. There was also an enormous range of crucifixes and a slightly smaller display of American flags. It was like stepping into the exobrain of a hallucinatory Catholic.

'Wow,' I said.

'I can't bring myself to take them down,' said Devlin. 'It would be like sacrilegious. Wait till you see the bedroom.'

It was even more intense. Pictures had been stuck on top of other pictures and religious icons on top of them until every inch of space was covered, and family members appeared to poke around Jesus's shoulder and struggle for space with saints and angels. There was a small plastic Christmas tree, fully decorated, and a twelve-inch Mary draped in rosary beads. Pride of place, over the headboard of a small single bed, went to another of Aunt Velma's garish paintings of a psychedelically colourful, anatomically challenged naked woman.

'You?' I enquired.

'Oh no!' Devlin protested. 'How could you think that? That's my momma.'

I sat on the side of the bed. I just wanted to lie down now, shut my eyes and enter oblivion, but my brain was throbbing, the moonshine hangover kicking in before I'd even got to sleep. 'Your granny wouldn't have something here for a headache, I suppose?' I asked.

A sly smile faintly tugged at the edges of Devlin's serious mouth. 'Grandma didn't hold much truck with medication but I might be able to help.' She bent down and reached under the bed, pulling out a locked metal box. 'You won't tell no one about this, right? The doctor gave Grandma a prescription for her cancer but she wouldn't touch it, so I got to picking it up instead.' She opened the box with a small key. There was a veritable medicine cabinet inside, from which she selected a small bottle of pills. 'I can get a thousand dollars a piece for each one of these little bottles, can you imagine that? One day I'm just gonna sell the whole lot and get the hell out of here, maybe go to Hollywood and audition for one of them TV singing shows, cause you never know what can happen if you get on a programme like that. I could be a star, just like you. Maybe we could do a song together. Shit. That would be something.' She popped the lid and handed me two pills. 'Just suck off the outer layer, then chew it up.' She briefly contemplated the contents of the bottle, before tipping out a couple of pills for herself. 'What the fuck,' she said.

'What the fuck,' I agreed. The taste was bitter.

'Just wait there a minute,' she said. She went into the other room while I flopped back on the bed. Devlin returned with a cheap acoustic guitar, dragging a chair. 'I'm gonna sing for you. I never sung for no one but Momma and Velma before. They think I'm the best, but what do they know? All they listen to is country music. You can tell me whether I'm good enough for *American Voice*. I wrote this all by myself. It's called "Not For Sale".'

She strummed the soft nylon strings, a single, ham-fisted downbeat. A warm glow was spreading through my body. My headache faded so quickly it was hard to believe it had ever been there. The guitar was slightly out of tune but it didn't matter. She started to sing.

Conjure me, dream me up
Put your lips on my lips, your hips against my hips,
Drink from my cup, drink it all up
Take my heart, take every other part
Take everything I am, take it while you can
Just take me somewhere nice.

Her voice was thin and high, sharp in some places and flat in others, but that didn't matter either. It was beautiful.

You've seen me walking the street, don't deny it,
You think you know what kind of end she's going to meet,
*   that's right*
With her red shoes and her red lips
And her red eyes and her red slips,
And red running like blood through everything she does
I'm going to run like rain down your window pane

Run like a rat down your drain
But I'm not for sale
Not for sale.

The song was beautiful. She was beautiful. The room was beautiful. The world was beautiful. Jesus, Mary and Joseph were watching over me, and everything was going to be fine.

Stretch out my hands, pale in the light
I feel so frail I might blow away tonight
I'll be carried on the wind, carried on the stars
Don't imagine I'll get very far
Not long on this planet now, never cared for it much
  anyhow
We'll all be gone before we know it
So take my heart, take every other part
Take what you can get while you can find it
I'm free-falling, on hands and knees I'm crawling
But I'm not for sale
Not for sale.

I opened my eyes. I wasn't sure how long I had been drifting. It could have been a microsecond. It could have been all day. Devlin was standing over me, wide-eyed with wonder.

'I can't believe you came,' she said.

I smiled.

'I always dreamed something like this would happen, and now it has,' she said.

I felt so good I wanted to laugh. I thought my heart would burst with pleasure. I wanted to melt into the universe.

Devlin started to take her clothes off.

'What are you doing?' I said. Then laughed at the sound of my voice, floating through the air.

'It's fate,' she said. And climbed into bed with me.

Days passed like that. Devlin would come and go, it didn't really matter to me as long as I had the OxyContin. Kilo never supplied me with anything like this. It left me blank, null and void but dreamily, euphorically so, blurring the past, extinguishing the future and soft-focusing the present, wrapping me up in a big fuzzy blanket of now. It was the perfect antidote to life and the great thing was it was prescribed by physicians, so it didn't really count as taking drugs at all.

During the days I would lie in bed and stare at the walls, or, if I was feeling more energetic, walk around the trailer and stare at the walls. Grandma had done an outstanding job of interior decoration. All those Jesuses, with their glowing halos and sacred hearts and shepherd crooks and flowing robes and gentle, compassionate eyes. The way he shepherded the little china sheep across the shelves made my heart burst with joy. I loved those sheep and spent hours turning them around in my hands. Each one seemed to have his own woolly character. I named them Dozy, Cheeky, Mushy, Cutey and Beasley, the fat one at the end, who looked pompous and pissed off. Even nailed to little crucifixes, our Lord's suffering never hardened into hatred for his persecutors. His eyebrows were knotted nobly together and his blue eyes always raised upwards, as if he could see right through the roof of the mobile home to a better life beyond. If only Father McGinty had passed out OxyContin during communion, maybe I would never have strayed from the righteous path. But better still were the Marys, lovely ladies with alabaster skin, draped in white and blue and gold, with gentle eyes and mysterious mouths, hands outstretched, palms upturned to welcome me, hold me, wrap me in a cocoon of cotton-wool love. My favourite picture was a gold framed 3-D postcard of Mary tenderly holding baby Jesus to her breast and when you tipped it a certain way, Jesus actually seemed to be suckling. I wondered how Mary had dealt with her son's halo during breast-feeding.

If I tired of the religious icons, there were always the insects. The mobile home was crawling with them. Brown moths fluttered about, banging blindly off walls, battering wings against tiny windows. Armies of little black and red creatures crept from behind foil walls and roamed about the ceiling. Cockroaches charged across the floor then dashed under the bed when I stamped my feet. Best of all were the spiders, patiently spinning webs. I watched as they tucked their tiny prey up in silver blankets, as if putting them gently to sleep.

It was hot and airless in the trailer and I sat for hours in the breeze of a portable electric fan. There was no TV or radio. If I wanted music I would pluck at the guitar and listen to bubbles of sound float up and fade away, testing how long I could make a single note linger in the air. Or I would go out for a walk. A few steps beyond the junk pile, the forest was electric with life, laden with heady scents of home but edged with something otherworldly. Wildflowers of scarlet and purple sprang through mulchy floor, luminescent moss bristled like green fur on blue rock, thick ferns weaved through craggy tree trunks, sunlight rippled the canopy of leaves. A spring turned the earth to rich red mud. I listened to water tinkling like bells and tuned into an outdoor choir, bass croak of a bullfrog, French horn in the breast of a blue jay, raucous jazz of crows, contrapuntal melodies of mating birds, clickety percussion of crickets, mournful saxophones of distant cows. I stood for hours, dazed by the symphony of the woods. I remembered this music. I had heard it before, as a child.

After work, Devlin arrived with food from the diner and we would have sex. I liked kissing her, she tasted of cigarettes and I spent a long time exploring her teeth with my tongue, puzzling over her curious flavour of burnt butterscotch and whiskey. Between bouts, she smoked and talked about her future in Hollywood, in a mansion with jewel-encrusted fixtures, a games room with a full-sized pool table for me and a row of one-armed bandits for her, cause she liked to gamble but there was nothing in Siren Creek but an old fruit machine in the Sulphur Tavern which the mayor didn't let her play any more cause she worked out how to beat it by listening to the tones. She had her heart set on a jacuzzi with gold taps and flatscreen TVs built into walls on either side, so we could sit face to face being squirted by warm jets of water and both watch TV at the same time, which was something she had seen on MTV *Cribs*. J-Lo had one, apparently. I didn't say much, I would fuck her and stare at the walls. Jesus kept a close eye on me while I took her from behind. Even Mary failed to avert her gaze as I licked and nibbled between Devlin's legs. She was a noisy, voracious lover, multiple orgasms rippling through her, sometimes seven or eight in succession, her body detonating fireworks, sparks firing behind her eyes. When she popped a strawberry-flavoured condom in her mouth and expertly worked it over my erect cock using only her lips, I began to suspect she wasn't quite the virgin princess patiently awaiting Prince Charming. 'I thought you refused to have anything to do with the boys around here?' I recalled.

'They ain't all boys,' she said. It was the only subject on which she was guarded. She talked a mile to the minute but there remained something hidden behind her unsmiling face, only released during orgasm. 'Velma always says there ain't nothing else to do in Siren Creek but smoke and fuck,' she told me. 'I figure you can do that anywhere in the world. I'm gonna do my smoking and fucking in Hollywood.'

She would sit and play her songs, naked but for the guitar. The songs were peculiar and her singing unlikely to impress the panel on *American Voice* but if she kept her clothes off I thought she might stand a chance. I didn't tell her that. I just smiled and clapped.

On Wednesday her period started. Not that it made any difference to us. We ground the OxyContin into a powder and snorted it, then fucked on the floor under the ever watchful gaze of the holy family. Afterwards, I sat staring in horrified fascination at my blood-covered penis. 'Shit, looks like there's been a murder,' said Devlin. 'What would Grandma think?' She led me to the tiny shower and scrubbed me clean. I could have stayed in there forever, feeling the water prick my skin, watching my pale-skinned Appalachian girl wash my sins away.

The next morning, I woke feeling a little rough. A car was pulling up outside. I wondered what Devlin was doing there so early but when I tried to move, it was as if my bones were rubbing off each other. I felt about for the bottle of pills but it was empty. 'Fuck,' I groaned. I heard the trailer door open. 'Devlin,' I called out. I needed the precious key to the medicine box. The bedroom door opened.

'I knew the little bitch had something going on up here,' said a woman standing in the doorway. Slim and tan, with too much make-up and dark roots showing in auburn hair, she had the warrior sensuality of an ageing waitress who still relies on looks for tips. It was hard to tell if she was amused or upset. 'So you gonna introduce yourself?' she enquired.

I groaned by way of reply.

'Jesus fucking Christ,' she said. 'It's you. Jesus, half the fucking country's looking for you. What the fuck has she got herself into now? You been on the TV every night.'

'I'm ubiquitous,' I croaked.

'I don't know about that but you are just about everywhere right now.'

I threw back the quilt and rolled out of bed naked. 'My Lord,' she said, in shock or appreciation I don't know. I fumbled under the bed, grabbed the medicine box and locked myself in the cramped washroom. I looked for something to force the box. There was nothing. It felt like my flesh was melting. I stumbled to the kitchenette, squeezing past my visitor in the tight doorway. 'Shouldn't you ought to put some clothes on?' she asked. I found a fork and started trying to lever open the lid of the box. The fork bent. I grabbed a knife and poked at the lock. When there was no movement I sat at the small table and stabbed the lid. 'Here,' the woman said, gently touching my shoulder. 'Let me do that.' She took the knife from my hand, carefully worked it under the rim of the lid and prised the box open. I snatched a bottle of pills, popped it and poured some in my mouth.

'What's wrong with you?' she asked, handing me a glass of water.

'I'm ill,' I said. But I was OK now. I relaxed back, waiting. It wasn't long before I felt the first wave wash over me.

'What have you been doing with my daughter?' enquired my visitor.

'So you're Momma,' I smiled. I liked the way that sounded. Momma. 'There's a painting of you in the bedroom.' Another wave lifted me up and carried me away. I was drifting into the middle of an ocean of tranquillity. I don't know how many pills I had taken but it was good, it was better than good. I looked at Momma. I could see the family resemblance now, high cheekbones, tiny love-heart dink in the top lip. Her face was fuller, eyes creased, but she had an ease that Devlin lacked, a sense of being in the world. 'You look better in real life,' I said.

'Well, thank you. I'll take that as a compliment. You don't look so bad in real life yourself.' She lifted an eyebrow at my naked body and we both laughed. She sat quietly, sizing me up. 'People are worried about you,' she said.

'There's nothing to worry about,' I replied. 'I'm fine.'

'So what are you doing hiding out here?'

'I'm running away.'

'From what?'

'Myself,' I said.

She sighed deeply. 'Don't we all wish we could do that sometimes.'

She had a tattoo just about visible above her cotton slip, over her left breast. I couldn't quite make it out. I reached forward and shifted the slip aside. It was a mermaid in green, black and pink, hair piled up like a storm, her elemental tail winding round the curve of the breast and out of sight. 'My husband was a sailor,' she said. 'He got lost at sea.'

'Devlin says he went to live in Scarsdale.'

'Same fucking difference.' She put a hand over mine, perhaps intending to stop me going any further but the effect was only to press me into her breast. A pulse crossed the table between us. I tugged the slip down a touch, uncovering more of the mermaid's tail. The ink work was so delicate and intricate, I had to follow the twists and curls as it wound around her breast, the arc of the tail framing her nipple. She moaned softly. 'Are you sure you want to do this?' she said.

'What?' I asked. I just wanted to follow the mermaid.

Later, as we lay squashed and sweaty on the small bed, she said, 'I wouldn't like you to get the impression I do this kind of thing all the time.'

'I do,' I admitted.

'I've never even met a famous person before. What's it like being famous?'

'It's like being a little boy in a candy store,' I said.

'I don't know about that. Too much candy'll rot your teeth.'

'And worse.' I ran my fingers across the stretch marks on her stomach. 'Is this from when you had Devlin?'

'I hate those marks, they're unsightly.'

'I think they're beautiful,' I said, full of genuine awe. 'They show that you made a person in there. Don't you think that's amazing?'

'You can't tell my daughter about this, or she'll never talk to me again,' she said, her face suddenly stricken.

'It will be our secret,' I promised.

'Come to Momma,' she said, pulling me towards her.

When Devlin returned that evening she climbed into bed and nestled into my still naked body. 'What's your mother's name?' I asked.

'Bitch,' she said. So I didn't pursue the matter further.

The next day a pick-up truck pulled into the yard. I had been studying a particularly interesting spider wrapping up a moth on the window sill, its tiny legs still flailing, but I broke off as a blonde in orange paint-spattered overalls climbed out of the truck then struggled to remove a wooden easel from the back. She dragged it over to the trailer, hauled it up the

stairs and clattered into the living room, where I was standing, still naked.

'You must be Velma,' I said.

'How d'you figure that?' she asked, amused.

'Wild guess. Your sister said she wasn't gonna tell anyone.'

'She has no secrets from me,' she said, casting a cool,
appraising eye over my body. 'I'd like to paint your picture.'

She set the easel up in the middle of the floor and laid her
brushes and tubes of paint out on the small table. I watched
with fascination. Every action was methodical – she was sure
of herself in a way neither Devlin nor Momma were. She must
have been the senior member of this family unit. Velma's skin
was pale, a washed-out quality shared by hair dyed the colour
of straw and eyebrows that existed only as faint pencil lines.
The effect served to emphasise the brilliant blue of her irises
and lips painted letterbox red. Despite the work clothes, there
was nothing remotely masculine about Velma.

'How do you want me?' I asked.

'Naked is just fine.'

She set to her task with zeal, mixing up colours that bore
no relation to anything in the room, and applying them with
vigour. 'Can I see what you're doing?' I asked.

'Wait till I'm done,' she said. Such was her seriousness, it
was easy to imagine some masterpiece taking shape, though
my expectations lowered when she said, 'You kind of remind
me of Vanilla Ice.'

'Fuck, no. Don't say that. I'm not white.'

'Well, you ain't exactly black,' she said, mixing red and yellow into a bright orange. 'Anyway, what's wrong with the Iceman? I always kinda dug him.'

I spat lines from her hero's only hit, some nonsense about speakers that boom and poisonous mushrooms. I don't know why all these couplets stick in my head. I could do a master in hip-hop history.

'Yeah well, it was the eighties,' she grinned. 'Things were different in the eighties.'

'How different?'

'Everything hadn't turned to shit yet.'

'Like what?'

'Like everything. There was none of this global warming to worry about. Damn, I mean if this place gets any hotter we might as well move to hell. No Isis terrorism. No war. Ain't that what your song is about? I hear it on the radio and I feel sorry for your generation. At least I was young once and too dumb to know it wasn't gonna last. I went to New York and rode all the way up to the top of the Twin Towers, how about that? I had a cocktail in the Skybar, that's what they called it. Highest bar in the world and man, did I get high in it. The city all spread out, like it was mine for the taking. I'll never forget that.'

'So what happened?'

'To the world?'

'To you.'

'Some asshole. Nothing unusual about my story. There's broken hearts in every street in every town on this damn planet, I expect. There's certainly enough around here.' She lit a cigarette, inhaled deeply, and examined her work so far.

'I don't know if I can hold this position much longer,' I complained.

'That's OK. You can move.'

'Are you finished?'

'It's abstract. It don't matter what exact position you hold. The thing is to capture the essence.'

'How's that going?'

'I'm not sure. Your essence is kinda confused.'

'That sounds right,' I said, stretching. 'When did you take up painting?'

'A person should have an interest,' she said. 'There's nothing else to do in this town.'

'Except smoke and fuck,' I quoted.

'That's what I always say. You want a cigarette?'

'I don't smoke.'

'Bully for you.' She stubbed hers out. 'They say each one of these things takes five minutes off your life. I'm counting on it.'

The session lasted several hours. I lost interest after a while and went back to studying walls. There was always something new to find, a rosary made out of baby teeth or a sequinned crucifix. The snapshots showed only women, who I identified as Devlin, her momma and Aunt Velma in various stages of development, from nappies to nylons, and another who shared their features, often in faded black and white, presumably

Grandma herself. Wherever men might have featured, heads had been carefully cut out.

Finally, Velma announced she was finished. 'What do you think?' she asked.

'Is that my essence?' I felt there was cause for concern. The canvas was frenzied and violent, crawling with ugly shapes and strange hieroglyphics. What might have been a small naked boy with big eyes held a giant, erect penis as if it was his last defence against night terrors. It was hard to distinguish any particular resemblance, since his head was wrapped in a kind of gauze.

'I paint it as I see it,' said Velma.

While it was drying, we went into the bedroom and fucked.

Afterwards, she lay back and smoked a cigarette. 'You ever been to Paris, France?' she asked.

'Many times.'

'They know how to appreciate fine art there.'

'Have you been?'

'Not exactly. But I went to Las Vegas once.'

'How was that?'

'They got a replica of the Eiffel Tower and a whole Parisienne shopping mall.' And she laughed bitterly, and blew smoke rings in the air.

I went for a walk after she left, hiking high up into the woods, and watched the sun set over the mountains, a raging inferno of scarlet and purple, the very colours Velma used to capture my essence. By the time I got back it was dark. Devlin was sitting in the kitchen with the lights off. 'Where you been?' she asked with desperate sullenness.

'Nowhere,' I said, honestly. As far as I could figure, that's where I lived now. Smack in the middle of it.

'Velma's been here, ain't she?'

I didn't say anything.

'I knew it,' she sobbed. 'I seen the painting. It's you.'

'How could you tell?' I asked, genuinely puzzled.

'I know every inch of you. You're mine. When are you gonna take me out of here? I'm sick of this place. I'm sick of that shitty diner. I'm sick of all the men here, looking at me all the time, wondering when I'm gonna give up dreaming of better and settle for what they got. Shit. I wanna go to Hollywood with you, like you promised.' She raged and pleaded, wept and wheedled, cosied up and shoved me away, blew around me like a storm. I sat there uncomprehending. I liked it just fine in the trailer in the woods. It was way better than Hollywood.

'Anyway, I'm pregnant,' she said, after a while.

'You're in the middle of your period,' I pointed out.

'Well, I coulda been pregnant. What would you have done about it then?'

I was still thinking about that when a car pulled into the yard. Devlin opened the door of the trailer and screamed, 'Go away!' at the top of her voice. Then she sat down crying while her mother and Velma came inside.

'It's no use sitting there bawling, girl, we've got to decide what we're gonna do about him,' said Momma.

'You ain't gonna do anything about him,' cried Devlin. 'He's mine.'

Momma glared at me fiercely, while putting protective arms around her daughter's shoulders, as if I was the one responsible for her unhappiness. I suspected Momma had a head start there. I looked to Velma for some support but she averted her eyes. She had changed into a cotton summer dress and looked like a movie star who had wandered onto the set of a terrible TV soap and wasn't sure what her lines were or if she could bring herself to say them. She was carrying a folded newspaper, which she kept shifting about in her hands.

'How long do you think you can keep this little love nest a secret? He's just about the most famous person in the whole damn world,' said Momma.

'We were doing fine till you come along,' whined Devlin.

'Yeah, looks like it.'

'Don't think I don't know you been here. I could smell you on him,' hissed Devlin.

That stopped them in their tracks. Me too, for that matter.

'There's been reporters asking around in Scarsdale,' said Momma, after a while. 'They say your fella was at some negro party, ain't that right, Velma? If we're gonna work this situation, we gotta do something about it now.' She moved, as if to take hold of my wrist, but her daughter threw herself in front of me.

'Leave him alone, he's mine!' screamed Devlin, her face red with fear and rage.

'Yeah, well, Daddy was mine, and that didn't stop you,' her mother spat out. 'Nor Velma's Jackie.'

'That's enough, Marcy,' warned Velma.

'So your name's Marcy,' I blurted out. She glared at me like I was an idiot.

'I didn't have too much say about that, did I,' wept Devlin. 'I was twelve years old.' And she collapsed back on her chair, crying so much her body was shaking.

'I know that, darling. I'm sorry, baby. I didn't mean that,' said her mother, gently.

'Zero and me, we're gonna go to Hollywood and make records,' sobbed Devlin. 'He's gonna get me on *American Voice*.'

'There's a reward,' said Velma, throwing the newspaper on the table. She still wouldn't catch my eye.

Marcy unfolded the paper. 'See, baby. We can collect the reward. One million dollars for information leading to Zero's safe return. See that.'

'A million dollars?' said Devlin. And she actually laughed through her tears, her voice practically tinkling with childlike wonder, as if the entire sum was raining down like fairy jewels before her very eyes.

'That's what it says, right there. One million dollars.'

'Shit,' said Devlin. Now that was more like her.

'All we gotta do is take him down to Sheriff Baxter, hand him over and we're gonna be rich, baby.'

'One million dollars,' repeated Devlin.

'You going to split it three ways?' I said.

Velma flashed her blue eyes at me, defiance a thin screen for guilt. Of all people, she should have known you can't hide your essence.

'Well, I found him first,' said Devlin.

'D'you mind?' I said, picking up the paper and retreating to the washroom. I locked the door and sat on the toilet. My hands were trembling. Did I really think I could just turn my back on all of this? I was all over the newspaper. It was worse than ever. 'STILL MISSING: IS ZERO ALIVE OR DEAD?' Pride of place went to a paparazzi picture outside the Illium Tower in New York, looking haunted and hunted, the rabbit in the headlights shot. 'NEW SIGHTINGS FROM ALASKA TO MEXICO CITY'. There was an artist's impression of what I might look like with a handsome beard. I rubbed my chin. It had been nearly a week already and I barely had any stubble. There was a picture of me posing with the state trooper and another of SinnerMan and Karnivor in handcuffs. 'GANG MEMBERS ARRESTED IN PHILADELPHIA DRIVING ZERO'S STOLEN LIMO'. Served the fuckers right. There was a photo of Beasley, holding up a cheque for a million dollars. 'SIX-ZERO REWARD'. What the fuck was he up to? That was my money. And it turned out pre-orders for the album were breaking the Internet. That should have been enough to keep him happy. I turned the page. There was a picture of Penelope, in widow black with sunglasses, built for mourning. Just behind her, a familiar figure had his big, dirty hand on her shoulder. 'All We Can Do Is Wait And Pray,' Says Penelope. 'ZERO'S FIANCÉE COMFORTED IN BRAZIL BY TROY'.

My hands were shaking so much I could barely hold the paper. I needed my OxyContin. I pulled the pill bottle from my jeans pocket – I never let it stray too far from me now. Outside I could hear the Siren Creek bounty hunters arguing about how to divide the spoils. I looked at my reflection in the mirror, pupils dilated, dark shadows under hollow eyes. I was a pale shadow. How did I get here? As I popped the lid of the OxyContin, I dropped the bottle. Pills spilled all over the floor. The mirror shimmered, my reflection divided. What happened to me, I wondered? I felt like I was waking from a dream.

'Let's just get this over with,' I heard Velma say.

There was a small window in the washroom, which I could reach by standing on the toilet. It was tight but I could just about get my head and shoulders through. I got stuck for a moment, looking out into the darkness. I heard the door handle turn behind me.

'It's locked,' said Devlin.

'You might as well come out, kid, there ain't no other way this is gonna end,' said Marcy.

I gave an almighty shove and wriggled through, falling awkwardly on the hard dirt below. I lay there winded.

'Open this door or I'm gonna kick the fucking thing down!' commanded Marcy.

I picked myself up. Behind me, I heard a thump and a crash. I started to run.

'He's gone, Momma, he's gone,' cried Devlin.

I made it past the junk and into the dark road. I paused for a moment to look back. Devlin was standing at the door of the trailer. 'I love you,' she wailed. 'Don't leave me like this.'

I turned and ran.

'Take me with you,' she cried, voice desolate with abandonment. 'Take me away from here.'

15

Afraid the coven would come roaring after me in Velma's truck, corral me, lasso me, and drag me kicking and screaming back to Beasley, I dived off the road, crashing through dark Virginia woods in a state of night blindness.

Big mistake.

Long, thin arms whipped my face and snatched my hair, roots grabbed my ankles, the darkness grew dense and heavy, its pitch impenetrability panicking me so that I stumbled, crashing through spikes and colliding full force with something solid and unyielding. On balance of probabilities, let's assume it was a tree.

I don't know how long I lay there, struck out on my back, dazed and winded, tasting the metal of blood in my mouth. Slowly, very slowly, as the adrenalin shot faded and my racing heartbeat subsided, something else began to demand my attention, something worse than concussion, something more worrying than the possibility of recapture, something low and grim crawling through the marrow of my bones and fibre of my muscles, inching up my intestines, dragging around my groin. Dread seized me. Why had I tossed those fucking pills? One little dose of hillbilly smack would keep the pain dogs at bay. I lurched to my feet, trying to find my balance in the darkness. Surely Penelope could wait? What was a day or two more between star-crossed lovers? I could go back to the cabin, make up with Devlin (so I fucked her mother and aunt, but look on the bright side, at least her family liked me) and kick my little pill habit tomorrow. But which way was the road? I spun helplessly in a void, stepped forward and crashed into an invisible force field that left me sprawling.

You know that expression you can't see the wood for the trees? What about when you can't even see the trees? People go on about the beauty of fucking nature but it doesn't look like shit in the dark without night-vision goggles. While I lay groaning, trying to catch my breath, the immediacy of fresh pain blotted out the aches of withdrawal, and I began to think I could do this, Keith Richards style: one night, knuckle down, cold turkey, be a man, shake this monkey off my back, stand tall, beat my demons, hit the road and reclaim the woman I love.

That lasted until an icy hand closed spectral fingers around my interior organs and tried to drag them out through my sphincter. Everything I touched was supersized: a leaf brushing my face like the raspy tongue of a hound, tree bark like mountain crags beneath my fingertips. And what the fuck was that rustling behind me? Did they have mountain lions in Virginia? I suddenly saw how this was going to end. The disappearance of Zero would be a mystery forever unsolved. I'd be a twilight zone legend, dinner for wolves and vultures.

But what right did I have to feel pity for myself? The question sounded out loud and clear, ringing in the echo chamber of my skull. Eileen, lovely Eileen, flitted across my vision, a startled deer lit by hunter's headlights, but then she was gone, and other faces peered from the dark undergrowth. I knew who they all were even if I couldn't make them out, the boys in the band I ditched, the girls I fucked and forgot, Paddy, Daddy, everyone who ever loved me, receptacles of all the shit and hurt I spewed in my wake, rampaging through life like some monstrous ego unleashed, like the only three things I ever cared about were me, myself and I . . .

. . . am sorry, I'm sorry, I'm so fucking sorry and I want to go home . . .

It was a night that stretched in every direction, a night that would not end. One moment I was on my knees, dry-retching, prostrating myself for forgiveness from a God I had never forgiven, then I was on my feet hurling abuse at a merciless universe, determined to see this through the hard way and pay for my sins like a man . . . but I wasn't a man, I was an open wound, a throbbing nerve, a bawling baby, lost in the woods. I raged and gurgled and roared and wept and banged my head on the ground, trying to knock myself unconscious, rolling over and over, wrestling myself to exhausted defeat.

I must have passed out somewhere along the line, because the last thing I remember was a vision of an angel of mercy, perhaps even Mother Mary herself, silhouetted in saintly splendour against the glorious moonlight, reaching down to mop my brow. But when I opened my eyes the dark shape towering over me was animal, predatory, hairy, mean of eye, sharp of tooth and claw, a fucking bear, I swear. I tried to scream but no sound came out. It was so close I could make out individual hairs on its pelt, lying along rippling muscle. I smelled rank, meaty breath on my face. Then it was gone, with a snuffle and a shuffle, and I had to wonder if I had dreamed it too.

I lay shaking, aching, staring at a dawn sky, absurdly glad to be alive, cold and battered and exhausted, but still here, feeling damp foliage beneath my body, smelling the rich, wet aroma of the forest, still part of the world.

I headed downhill, just because it was easier, driving ever deeper into a mossy green world, my mood as slippery as the pink and grey sky. I was hopelessly lost but beginning to accept this might be my natural condition. The cramps were more tolerable if I kept moving, and even with an icy headache and dry-bone cough, I had a sense the very worst was over. In the clear water of a burbling stream, I washed my hands and face. Dried blood flaked from beneath a tender nose. I prodded it carefully, wondering if it was broken. I imagined Beasley yelling, 'Not the face! Not the face!' and laughed out loud, a mad dog bark startling a bird out of the trees. I watched as its wings carried it into the blue beyond.

At last, through thinning pine, I made out grey asphalt. And there was something else, a battered chrome-and-white motorhome parked at the border of a grassy clearing. Smoke hung in the air, the crackle of a small fire, the roasted, thick smell of coffee percolating. I lingered at the edge of the treeline. Even from a distance, I could see the man hunched by the fire was big, a hulking, bald, bearded slab. I contemplated whether I should make myself known. He could be a hunter. He might think I was in season.

'You gonna come and get some coffee or stand there admiring my RV all day?' the man called out in a deep, vibrating baritone.

I inched forward, breaking through a mass of serrated leaves at the edge of the clearing. 'How d'you know I was here?' I asked.

'My little brothers and sisters told me you was coming,' he replied, holding out a metal cup from which steam rose enticingly. 'Been waiting this past half hour. You took your time. Coffee's getting cold.'

I looked around but couldn't see anyone else about. I wondered if he was mad. He had grave, sad eyes, which studied me intently from beneath a craggy, furrowed brow. His nose was bent and gnarly. Thick lips were mostly hidden by a neat, greying beard. The man was as ugly as he was big, standing at least six foot six. Tufts of hair sprouted wildly from the neck of his sweatshirt, and when he held out the mug, the back of his enormous hand was thickly matted. Vines of dark hairs curled around his wrist, retreating under his sleeve. I suspected his head was the only hairless part of him.

'Where are your brothers and sisters?' I asked, cautiously accepting the coffee.

'Here's one of them now,' he gestured. I turned to see a squirrel inquisitively edge into the clearing before dashing back to the security of the foliage.

'You talk to squirrels?' I sounded stupid even to myself.

'You been disturbing the wildlife, son,' he explained, smiling. 'I could track your movements just from the birds scattering overhead.'

'Oh,' I said and drank my coffee, feeling warmth spread through my chest. I must have looked quite a sight, scratched and bruised and wasted, dressed in torn T-shirt and dirty jeans, bits of twig and leaf caught in my clothes and hair, but he didn't comment. He obviously didn't recognise me, which was something, but then you probably don't expect to come across a pop star on the side of a West Virginia mountain. 'Are you a hunter?'

'No, no, I wouldn't say that, not a hunter, not exactly,' he replied, then smiled a cryptic smile. 'I suppose you could say I am a fisherman. Or a fisher of men.' He waved towards the recreational vehicle. There was a line of coloured letters painted along the top of the cab: REV TYLER SALT – TRAVELLING REVIVAL – SINNERS WELCOME. 'Are you lost, son?' the Reverend asked.

'Aren't we all?' I replied.

'Amen to that,' said the Rev. Then he added, 'I was lost, but now I am found.' We stood together, silently pondering this nugget. Can found really be a permanent state of being? Do you find yourself, or does someone else find you, and what happens if you move after you've been found? 'Where are you heading?' asked the Reverend.

Every question seemed loaded with existential meaning. 'I don't know,' I admitted. 'You?'

'Anywhere and everywhere,' said the Rev. 'Anywhere they'll have me, and everywhere they need me. The spirit leads, I follow, God and gas prices willing.'

'Which direction is the spirit pointing today?'

'South,' he nodded. The Lord, it seemed, was going to be my shepherd after all.

Reverend Salt was on his way to an annual gathering in Moody, Alabama, known as the Heavenly Picnic, a big date on the calendar of the itinerant preaching community. I could tell he was trying not to be pushy, refraining from asking direct questions about what I was doing wandering about the woods battered and bewildered. He simply noted that I appeared to have no worldly belongings and opened the passenger door for me, inviting me to ride as far as I wanted. A bumper sticker on the windscreen read: IN CASE OF RAPTURE, THIS VEHICLE WILL BE UNMANNED.

Clambering up, I was startled to see a ghostly figure raise itself from an unkempt bed that dominated the dilapidated interior. Grey-skinned, skeletal and sunken-eyed, the creature lifted a hand to point at me. I stared in horror as it croaked two syllables. 'Ze . . . Ro.' The ghost was gasping. Two thin tubes emerged from its nostrils, running to a squat machine humming by the bedside.

'It's all right, Ma,' said the Reverend, pushing past. 'We

picked ourselves up a lost sheep along the way. We're going to give the boy a ride, lend a helping hand, praise the Lord.' He knelt beside her, gently stroking her hand and muttering soothing phrases, while I hung nervously back in the driving cab. There was some fumbling with the breathing apparatus and administration of medication. All the while the old woman's rheumy, unfocused eyes never strayed from my direction. Zero, I felt sure she kept saying between gasps. That's Zero. Eventually, she sagged back, trembling, her gaze becoming unfixed.

'Don't mind her,' said the Reverend, settling into the driver's seat. 'She suffers bad in the mornings but she'll be good after she's slept some more, God willing.'

'What's wrong with your mother?' I asked, cautiously.

'My mother passed over to the other side,' said the Reverend. 'It's OK. She's been dead nearly three years now but we will be reunited in the bosom of the Lord. Could be any time, which is why we must always be ready. We shall be snatched into the clouds into the meeting place of the Lord in the air, it says in the letters of Paul. You heard of the Rapture? It's coming.' And before I could open the door of the RV and throw myself on the mercy of the bears in the forest, he started the engine and shifted into gear.

I glanced fearfully back at the creature behind us as we drove. 'She doesn't look dead,' I said, although, come to think of it, she actually did, lying there slack-jawed with sightless, open eyes, mottled arms crossed on top of the covers like a cadaver awaiting burial.

The Reverend started to laugh, dry, heaving, shuddering booms. I shrunk deeper into my chair with each terrifying guffaw. 'I'm sorry,' he eventually succeeded in saying. 'Marilyn's not my mother. She's my wife.' And he hooted and chortled some more, until tears ran down his cheeks. Recognising that this might not be an ideal state for driving, he made a visible effort to pull himself together. 'Hoo-ha, I haven't laughed like that since . . . oh . . . well . . . it's been a long time.' The fleeting memory of his last laugh seemed to sober him. 'Laughter's good,' he announced. 'It's a gift from God.' He seemed uncertain of this and I got the impression he was searching for an appropriate scripture to justify hilarity. All I could bring to mind was 'Jesus wept.' It was the only phrase from the Gospels I ever remembered accurately and that was because my old man used it all the time, though not in a religious context.

'You called her "Ma",' I pointed out.

'Yes,' said the Reverend. 'That's what we are together, Ma and Pa, the most important thing we share, along with the love of Christ. Even if our beloved offspring don't always see it that way.'

He seemed to have completely lost his good humour but at least his driving improved. The huge vehicle wound down the mountain road at a stately pace. 'Emphysema,' he said, after a while. 'The lungs are gone, really. Only the Lord is keeping her alive now, Christ's love and oxygen tanks, when we can afford them. But it is not for us to question human suffering. The

Lord moves in mysterious ways. "If ye have faith, nothing shall be impossible to you." I sank into my seat, laying my throbbing head against the glass, the movement of the world outside a distending blur. Somewhere in the distance, I could hear the Reverend predicting the coming of the Rapture, when true believers would be beamed up to a heavenly Kingdom while legions of the faithless (fornicators, idolaters, adulterers, sodomites, pretty much anyone who knows how to have a good time) languished in hell on Earth, which sounded like your average global-warming weather forecast: ominous signs in the sun, moon and stars, distress among nations, people fainting from foreboding of what is coming upon the world. Since the Reverend apparently thought newspapers unfit for wiping his nether regions, considered television the entertainment medium of the devil himself and judged the Internet a superhighway straight to hell, I wondered how he could be so sure we hadn't already passed the point of no return? In which case, he and his missus must have been left behind with the rest of us sinners.

I was briefly stirred by the sound of the radio, an explosion of country joy, a fiddling bluegrass band praising the Lord over a clickety-clacking, tambourine-shaking rockabilly beat, with lots of yelled call-and-response vocals.

> *I'm heaven bent (heaven bent)*
> *I've said my prayers, I've paid the rent (paid the rent!)*
> *For a room at the top of the stairs,*
> *I've been dying to meet Saint Peter,*

Why, you must be the grim reaper!
Come on boys, take me to your leader –
I'm heaven bent!

The jolliness faded as a DJ preacher bellowed over the outro: 'The Jesus I love is not a hippy, no! He is not a limp-wristed, smiling do-gooder come to pay the Earth a condolence call. Mine is a Furious Christ, ready to confront the Armies of Darkness . . .'

I drifted in and out, opening my eyes to watch a blurry crucifix swing hypnotically from beneath the rear-view mirror, then shutting them hard again, as Father Martin and the antiseptic white of a hospital room materialised around me, like a bad dream that wouldn't let go. That cowardly priest had a mouth like the grill of an old wireless radio, crackling in a southern drawl, 'And Jesus said, "Do you suppose I came to establish peace on the Earth? No indeed. I have come to bring dissension. From now on, families will be divided, father against son and son against father, mother against daughter and daughter against mother . . ."'

And I was in the room I never wanted to go back to, the room I could never escape, smoke hanging in the air, the howling of my father echoing into the distance, silence rising like a wave that might break over me, silence louder than thunder, and all I could see was that bed, that bed, that long white bed, stretching to the horizon, a smooth ocean of crisp linen, and all I could focus on was a hand, her hand, laying still on the white sheet, brown fingers cold to the touch, and I couldn't breathe, I was drowning, fighting for air, lungs on fire as I struggled to the surface, bursting through the liquid skin of consciousness as the preacher savagely brayed, 'Hide ye in the blood of Jesus. Get washed in the blood of the Lord.'

'Help,' I gasped.

'Satan is real!' crowed the voice.

The RV was stationary, parked at the side of a two-lane highway, neat green fields and rolling hills stretching into the distance, the sun high in a perfectly blue sky. Someone was gasping for breath but it wasn't me. I twisted to see Marilyn wheezing desperately, sunken eyes wild with fear, while the Reverend murmured soothing platitudes, 'got it under control, Ma, just hang in there', placing a thick plastic mask over her face and pressing a vial of blue liquid into the rattling machine. She sucked and sucked, mouth opening and shutting like a fish out of water, body in spasm, hands flaying in panic. Then suddenly she caught the air, pulling it into her lungs, letting it fill her up with the relief of a junkie, every muscle slackening as she sank back into her pillows.

'There, there, Ma, just breathe, keep breathing, praise be the Lord,' whispered the Reverend, his big, hairy hand stroking her white hair. Glancing up, he caught me watching, and smiled. 'Come sit with Ma a moment, son, I need to fix some food. Come on. She's just having a turn, that's all. Ain't nothing to be scared of.'

Oh, but there was everything to be scared of. Everything. Because if this was where life was leading, if this was the final destination, going out the way we came in, kicking and screaming, then what was the fucking point of this perpetual struggle for air? It was all right for the Reverend with his plastic Jesus promising eternal love in the ever after but when I looked into Marilyn's worn-out face, all I saw was dust settling in random patterns then blowing away like so much smoke in a hospital room. The old lady sat forward in the bed, skinny fingers grasping my wrist. 'I know who you are,' she hissed. Then she lay back just as quickly, as if the effort of speaking had worn her out.

'That's nice,' said the Reverend. 'She likes you.'

'I need a cigarette,' Marilyn croaked.

The Reverend turned from his gas stove, which was spitting oil and issuing smoke. 'Now, Ma, you know it's cigarettes has put you here.'

'It's you who put me here, ya sonofabitch,' muttered Marilyn.

'You don't mean that, Ma,' sang the Reverend. 'It's just the pain talking. You know, Jesus Christ our Lord loves you . . .'

'I wanna die, Tyler, why won't the Lord let me die? Everything I took from you, wasn't I punished enough? I should be at home with my children. Where are they now, Tyler, where are they?'

'They'll always be with us, Ma, in our hearts and in our prayers,' intoned the Reverend, shovelling yolky eggs and burnt steak onto a plate. 'Someday they'll come around, I know, the Lord will open their eyes.' He laid a tray across her lap, on which a pill bottle took pride of place. The label shone like the holy grail: OxyContin. 'With the Lord's grace, we will live as a family once again, by His side.'

'I don't wanna live no more, Tyler,' moaned Marilyn, but there was feral eagerness in the way she held out her hand for the pills. She swallowed greedily. Her husband held a glass of water to her trembling lips while he recited grace in a mumbling stream, *Bless-us-O-Lord-for-these-Thy-gifts-which-we-receive-from-Thy-bounty.* I wanted to fall to my knees, yell praise the Lord, stick my tongue out and demand communion. But the Reverend had other ideas. He nodded at me. 'We'll take our food outside.'

We sat in the shade of the RV, eating our greasy meal on a fold-out table. Fields of green stretched away in graceful order. Heat vibrated in the air. Watching a wide-winged bird swoop and dive for the sheer joy of it, I almost laughed aloud to find myself here, on the road with this fucked-up family, experiencing a sort of mad freedom I had forgotten was possible.

'She wasn't always like this,' said the Reverend, chewing noisily. 'She's a good woman, a beautiful woman.'

The eye of the beholder is a wonderful thing and I should know. I find it hard to look in the mirror, yet I'm a certified sex symbol.

'That darn oxygen machine is so expensive, excuse my French,' the Rev continued. 'The meds eat up our savings, everything we ever worked for, every cent we put aside, spent just to keep breathing – well, it ain't right. Health insurance been nothing but trouble. Paid dues all my working life, then they invoke some clause about self-inflicted harm. I do believe they are in league with Satan, them, the tobacco companies, the federal government, all in it together. They're gonna get theirs come the day. Come the day.'

His fists were clenched, knuckles white, his craggy face scrunching up. Wariness stiffened my body. I had seen that kind of transformation in my father. But then the Rev breathed out heavily, crossed himself and his expression softened. 'I got an anger in me, sometimes. I used to lose my temper, Marilyn knows, to my great regret. But that was before I accepted the Lord Jesus Christ into my heart.' He laid a big hand on my shoulder. 'You have that anger in you, son. You can't hide it from one who knows. What you running from?'

'Not the law,' I said.

'Your folks?'

'My mother's dead,' I said, and almost choked. I didn't even know why I would offer that information.

'What about your father? When was the last time you spoke to him?'

I couldn't remember. I must have called him this year, surely? Or did we just communicate by bank order these days, the regular payments Beasley made to his account on my behalf?

'Your father loves you,' said the Reverend.

'How could you know that?' I demanded.

'Because a father always loves his child. We just have a hard time showing it, that's all,' said the Reverend. I guessed he wasn't really talking about me at all.

I rode the next leg in the back. The Reverend said it brought his wife comfort to have company but she didn't even seem to be aware I was there. The radio played gospel, the Rev singing tunelessly along above the bass hum of the engine. We must have gone hundreds of miles before Marilyn slowly stirred from her opiate trance, watery eyes gazing at me. 'You look a lot like that boy,' she said.

'Who?'

'The one's gone missing.' She touched her nose, conspiratorially. 'He don't think I know nothing about what's going on in the world but I have my sources.' She lifted her blanket and there, beneath the covers, was a tiny, handheld square box with a screen of wobbly lines and static. 'Soaps is about all that keeps me going out here, when I can get 'em. Don't get me wrong, I love my Lord Jesus Christ with all my heart, yes I do, but the way I figure it, if the Lord had meant us to be bored, he wouldn't have given us television.'

I laughed, and with it my fear of Marilyn's age and infirmity receded. I glanced up to make sure the Rev was still lost in song. 'What did you mean when you said he put you here?' I asked.

'Oh, I didn't mean nothing by it,' she sighed. 'When the pain gets real bad I say things. It's the devil, I know, puts bad ideas in my mind. Pa understands. He's a good man. Wasn't always that way. But he's a good man.'

She wanted to tell the truth about the Reverend. All she needed was a little prodding. 'So what way was he before?'

'He used to lay his fists on me,' she whispered. 'Broke just about every bone in my body at one time or another. Times was tough then, raising a family. Tyler worked the rigs, real work, you know, dangerous. He used to drink hard. But then he found Jesus and asked for His forgiveness, and for mine, and I had to give it. When I see the way Tyler changed, that's when I truly realised miracles happen. The kids still find it hard to forgive. Our boy Johnny, he's a elected sheriff down in Texas, you know, he's doing all right, gonna run for mayor. Our girl, well, she ain't doing so great. I'd like to help her, but we put everything we got into this rig. Pa says the Lord has a plan for us and I have faith in him. I've got to have faith. I just get so tired of this life. Don't understand why there's got to be so much pain. Pass me them pills, will you?'

I didn't know if I could trust myself to pick up her OxyContin. The bottle felt like it was burning in my trembling hand. 'I am going to leave this broken body behind,' said Marilyn, snatching it from me. 'I am going to sit with the Lord in Paradise one day.' Her fingers fiddled furiously with the lid, then she shoved the bottle irritably back. 'Open that, will you? Damn fingers. Can't do nothing for myself no more.' I popped the lid. The pills glowed like unholy orbs, chattering on a frequency only I could hear, promising not the Earth and all its kingdoms but nothing, sweet nothing, pure oblivion. Marilyn's eyes drilled into me as I shook a couple into her outstretched palm. She recognised the need, the way addicts always recognise one another. 'You want some of these? It'll ease the pain,' she said.

Would every waking moment from now on be like this, I wondered, a battle for my soul? 'I can't,' I grunted, snapping the lid back in place.

'Suit yourself,' she said. 'If you'll excuse me, it's time for *Almost Heaven*, got to find out if the young doctor ran away with the dentist's wife, if I can pick up a damn signal.' She disappeared under the covers to watch her TV. The last words I heard were a muffled, 'Lord, I'd kill for a cigarette.'

I moved up front, next to the Rev. 'Better days are coming soon,' he announced. 'But first there will be a war between the forces of good and evil. You have to decide which side you're on, son.'

'I wish it was as easy as that, Reverend,' I sighed.

I sat, vacantly entranced by the highway. Tree-covered hills hinted at home but on such an epic scale my memories were dwarfed. It was like Ireland reconstructed by a megalomaniac. The sky was vast, the hills endlessly undulating, the fields mathematically multiplying. I was lost in the landscape. I was a bug on the windscreen. When I snapped out of my waking dream, dusk was filtering out the detail, my vision degenerating into static. Still we drove, engine humming with subsonic familiarity beneath me, taking me back to the cocoon of the road, so many journeys in vans and coaches to the promise of a stage, a spotlight, an audience, a moment when I might exist outside of my own imagination, inside someone else's.

'I think we'll pull in for the night,' said the Reverend. Out of the darkness loomed the artificial lights of a sprawling truck stop. A gang of bikers briefly swarmed around us, flags and bandanas trailing, as we crept past shadowy canyons of parked rigs. I covered my face as a beefy motorcyclist glared in the window, made the sign of the cross and peeled away.

The rigs stretched on, forming a craggy skyline, cabs perched atop enormous wheels, a mobile city that had ground to a halt. The avenues of vehicles loomed deserted and dangerous, as if all human life had withdrawn to the neon-lit hub of gas tanks, diners, bars and stores, lit up like a twenty-four-hour retail village in the centre distance. We kept moving, crossing into a compound behind a tall wire fence, where at least fifty motorhomes were parked in neat, orderly rows. The Rev expertly slotted in between a luxurious Sundowner and a gleaming Airstream, his battered RV with hand-painted signs lowering the tone of the neighbourhood. A blind rattled up next door and a red, round face peered out, nodded at the Reverend then retreated. 'There's a motor chapel here, where I can do a little of the Lord's business,' announced the Reverend. 'Replenish the coffers.'

I looked out warily. Where did I go from here? 'Wanna get something to eat?' offered the Rev. My stomach jumped to attention. But the café was bustling with truck drivers and travelling salesmen, and I had a vision of conversations breaking up mid-sentence, even the jukebox grinding to a halt. So I politely declined, while my stomach growled in protest.

'Well, all right, I'll bring you something back. Just keep an eye on Ma for me.' The Reverend looked me up and down carefully, before pocketing the RV keys. 'There's nothing here worth stealing, son,' he said.

'I wouldn't steal from you, Reverend,' I protested.

'I have looked into your heart, and I believe what you're saying is true,' said the Rev.

Almost as soon as the door shut behind him, Marilyn groaned theatrically, leading me to suspect she had only been pretending to sleep. 'Come here, son. Fix me some of my medication.' As I sat down, she snatched my hand. 'Where are we? Oh, it doesn't matter. Another truck stop, I know. They all look the same after a while. You play cards?'

'Not really,' I admitted.

'That's fine. I'll whip your bony ass.' Marilyn smiled, and through the wrinkles and rheumy eyes, something coquettish flashed, a feeble memory of long-faded sex appeal. 'You got any money?'

'I thought the Church frowned on gambling.'

'What he don't see don't hurt him.'

'Doesn't God see everything?'

'I'm talking about the Reverend,' she laughed, then had to lie still for a while to catch her breath, her fingers gripping mine as tightly as she could. After a while, she recovered enough to fish about beneath her blankets, emerging with a pack of cards.

'What else have you got down there?' I asked.

'Wouldn't you like to know?' she snapped back coarsely, then brayed with laughter which quickly turned into a hissing, airless cough. I waited for her to breathe again but her mouth popped like a fish flapping out of water. Every scratchy sound was an exhalation, her eyes wild with panic. I stared helplessly as she jabbed a finger towards the oxygen machine. There were knobs and buttons, but which should I turn, which should I press? She snatched weakly at the plastic oxygen mask and I clumsily fixed it around her face. But there was no oxygen catching. She gestured limply at a liquid tube by the bedside. She was sinking fast. What had I seen the Reverend do? I fumbled with the tube, trying to slot it into the machine with thick fingers, but it wouldn't fit.

'Fuck!' I yelled, the sound of each death rattle booming in my ears. Her eyes made an almost imperceptible blink of confirmation. I snapped the bottle into the slot. Now which button? I banged the reddest, most urgent-looking one, and the machine spluttered into life. Marilyn's body arced as her throat opened and she sucked precious oxygen into her lungs with shuddering relief.

She flopped back, feeble, pathetic, old and broken. I sat, drained and shaking beside her. She nearly died on my watch. I felt like I had been here before, that I was always here, crammed to my gills with guilt and fear. As the oxygen machine heaved and groaned, mist filled my eyes, blurring my vision. Tears again. Who knew I had so many locked inside? Marilyn croaked something in a faint whisper.

'What's that?' I said, leaning closer.

'I need a . . .' But I couldn't catch the last word. I moved my ear to her cracked blue lips. 'I need a cigarette,' she hissed.

I almost shook her off in dismay. She had just put us both through that horrific gasping for air, and now she wanted to fill her tattered lungs with smoke? 'I can't do that,' I insisted. 'The Reverend . . .'

'Fuck the Reverend,' she snarled. She clung to me with a fierceness that belied her wasted appearance. 'I want a cigarette. I want a damn smoke before I die. Get me some cigarettes . . . *please.*'

'No,' I said, trying to wriggle free of her desperate fingers.

'I'll tell Tyler who you are,' she whined. 'I'll tell him, and see what he has to say then. That's right. I know who you are. I know.'

I pulled myself away. 'I'm nobody. I'm just hitching a ride.'

'You're him,' she pressed, angrily. 'The singer. Don't think cause I'm old I don't know nothing. Everyone's looking for you.'

'I never asked them to.'

'I don't care about that. All I want is a cigarette,' she pleaded. 'Just one cigarette. I won't tell Tyler nothing if you get me a cigarette. It'll be our secret. Look, I'll give you the money. I'll trade you my pills if you want.' She reached for a purse, and poured some change out on the blankets.

'All right.' I reluctantly snatched the money. 'It's your funeral.'

'Yes it is,' she sighed. 'I pray for the day.'

I made sure the coast was clear before stepping into the night. I had all of four dollars in change to my name but I didn't think I was going to spend it on cigarettes. I would have liked to say thank you and goodbye to the Rev but it was time to move on. I skulked between motorhomes, seeking out shadows in the spaces between tall orange lamplights. From inside thin walls, I could hear TV sets, radios, muffled conversations. I crossed an overlit ramp towards the dark alleys of parked rigs, but halted as a bearded, shabby road tramp shuffled into the sodium glare. 'Spare some change, friend?' he muttered, swigging from a brown paper bag. There were shapes moving in the spaces between vehicles, hookers and hobos, hustlers of the forecourt. I had to keep moving, but not towards the lights of the gas station, nor the neon cross of a chapel where The Rev was plying his trade. I headed for the wire periphery, with the tramp shouting half-hearted abuse in my wake.

And then I saw Elvis, across the interstate, beckoning me, a saviour in my hour of need. Well, a gaudily painted, twenty-five-foot giant fibreglass Elvis, with a jaw like a lantern and a gaping hole in his side, apparently made by some kind of vehicular collision. He listed badly to the left but was unmistakably the long-lost firstborn of rock and roll, an impression confirmed by a flashing sign: RIDE WITH THE KING. LED letters raced across the flat-top building behind him: KING'S AUTOS: USED & NEW. 24 HOURS. I scuttled across the empty interstate. I still had my Amex Black. I could buy a car and get the fuck out of Dodge. I'd be dust on the highway before anyone realised what was going on.

The sole occupant of the brightly lit lobby was a soft, round, egg-shaped young man, tightly squeezed into a faux gold suit. Perched unconvincingly atop his head was a jet black Presley pompadour that might have been fashioned out of plastic string. He was fiddling at a vending machine as the glass doors slid open. With a candy bar clutched guiltily in one fist, he looked like he didn't know whether to give me a sales pitch or call security. I guess I was quite a sight, a scrawny, bruised, brown-skinned tramp dressed in the same jeans and ragged T-shirt I had been wearing for a week. 'I wanna buy a car,' I yelled, to make it easier for him.

'Uh, uh, welcome, welcome to the Graceland of automobiles,' he announced, remembering his lines. 'We can fix you up with a ride fit for a king, whatever your budget.' He tried to shove his candy bar into a jacket pocket, but it was sewn shut. 'Uh, uh, what kind of vehicle did you have in mind?'

'Something I can drive straight out of here,' I said. There was a sleek, low-slung canary-yellow sports coupé parked in the foyer. I patted the roof. 'This'll do. What is it?'

'Uh, uh, please don't touch that, sir. It's kind of a display thing. This here's a classic Dodge Viper, belongs to my boss. I don't know if it's really for sale . . .' He peered at me a little closer, and blinked slowly. 'You're Zero,' he announced.

'And you must be Elvis,' I said.

'Uh . . . uh . . . uh . . .' he stuttered.

'It's OK,' I said, before he could get his brain in gear. 'Don't believe what you've been reading online. It's all a publicity stunt.' I needed to make this as easy for him as possible. I pulled out my Amex Black. 'You know what that is? I want to buy a car. I'll take the most expensive car you have on the lot. I'll pay top dollar. I'll put a little extra commission on just for you. The only condition is I want to drive it out right now, with a tank full of petrol.'

'Uh, well, uh, I guess, we got a 1996 Cadillac De Ville, uh, really good deal, or I could offer you a great price on a Lincoln Continental, very nice family car. Got one on the lot for under six thousand dollars.'

'You're not paying attention. What's the most expensive car you've got here?'

'Well, that would be the Dodge Viper.'

'I'll take it,' I said.

'Don't you want to know how much it is?'

'How much is it?'

'Eighty-eight thousand dollars. My boss said if anyone asked, eighty-eight thousand is the price he would let it go for.'

'Great,' I said. 'Sounds like a bargain. Let's round it up to ninety grand for your commission, fill it up with gas, shove some of the candy snacks from that vending machine in the boot, and get it on the road.'

I waved the credit card in his face, and he came out of his trance and took hold of it. 'Well, uh, thank you very much,' he said.

'That's more like it, Elvis,' I grinned.

'So this is really a stunt?' he said, hopefully, as he pushed the card into his processing terminal.

'Yeah,' I said. 'It was my manager's idea. Pretty good, huh? You can't buy this kind of publicity.'

'Can I get your autograph? Uh, uh, for my wife?'

'Sure,' I said, grabbing a pen from his desk. 'Would that be Priscilla?'

'No. C'mon. I'm not the real Elvis.' Then he blushed. 'You know that.'

'Just kidding. Have you got something for me to sign? Who should I write it to?'

'Sandy,' he said, shoving a car brochure into my hand. 'Can you make it personal?'

'Whatever you want.'

'How about, "Sandy you're a star."'

I scribbled his request. Out of the corner of my eye, I could see Elvis frowning at the card machine.

'Ninety thousand, right?' he said.

'There's no limit on that card, Elvis. I could buy an aeroplane with that. I could buy your whole lot.'

'I'll try it again.'

'Nice suit,' I said, trying to keep him talking as we waited for the bleeps.

'Uh, it doesn't really fit me too well,' he stammered. 'I'm just the Night Elvis. See, uh, the Day Elvis, uh, he's a bit slimmer.'

'Your boss makes you share the suit?'

'Day Elvis is the boss. My uncle, really. I'm just, uh, helping out during college break.'

'At college and married already? Way to go, Elvis.'

'Truthfully, I'm not married.'

'So who's Sandy?'

'I'm Sandy,' he blushed. 'I'm afraid the card has been declined.' He looked crestfallen.

'There's obviously been a mistake, Sandy.' I knew exactly what had happened. Fucking Beasley had stopped my credit. 'You know who I am. You know I'm good for it. Why don't you just give me the keys to the car and I will have my accountant come around in the morning and sort this out.'

'I can't do that, sir.'

'OK, well, maybe not the Dodge Viper. How about that Continental? Six grand, you said. I spend more than that on lunch. C'mon, I'll mail it to you, Sandy, how about it?' I could see he was wavering. He wanted to help. Everybody wants to help a celebrity. 'I'll throw in some concert tickets. VIP.'

But then the penny dropped. 'There's a million-dollar reward for you,' he said.

'Just give me the card back,' I said.

'I'm sorry, sir. I have to retain it. I've got to call American Express. You just wait here now.'

'Fuck,' I snapped.

'There's no need to be like that, sir. I'm sure we can sort this out.' He started to dial.

I turned tail.

'Stop!' he yelled, in high-pitched panic. 'I've got a gun here.'

I spun around to be confronted by a fat, red-faced Elvis pulling a stubby black shotgun from under his desk. I raised my hands in surrender but kept walking backwards. 'Are you going to shoot me, Elvis?' I said. 'For what? Running away from home?'

'There's a reward,' he said, voice trembling.

'I don't think it's Dead or Alive.' I heard the sliding doors open behind me, stepped back, turned and ran.

I hammered through the lot and across the interstate, startled for an instant by the headlights and horn blast of a passing vehicle. I dashed for cover among the big rigs. Scampering between massive long-haul trucks, I disturbed a slip of a teenage hooker negotiating with a thickset driver. They stared at me balefully but then I heard the hooker mutter, 'Zero!'

'You're shitting me!' growled the driver, pushing her away from him. I dodged sideways, twisting and turning between rigs, then collided with a couple of bearded bums sharing a bottle. One of them grabbed me by the arm and started to shake me excitedly, breathing a pungent mix of malt liquor and halitosis in my face.

'It's you. I knew it was you!' he growled. It was the tramp I had fled earlier. I shoved him in the chest and wrestled free. As he fell back into his companion, I ran. Everywhere I turned there seemed to be more bodies lurking in the dark, more eyes fixing on my flight, more shouts of recognition, shapes looming out of the shadows like zombies in a cheap horror flick. I stumbled, hit the tarmac, and instinctively rolled between the wheels of a rig, lying flat beneath its undercarriage. Feet pounded past.

'Did you see him?' a voice yelled.

'Who?'

'Zero! Zero's here.'

'Fuck off.' A burst of laughter. 'You're crunked and seeing ghosts.'

I lay there catching my breath. It looked like I had reached the end of the road, about to be hauled in by a mob of bounty-hunting hobos. Then I noticed something directly ahead, a small box glinting in a pool of orange lamp light. I crawled forward. It was a battered Marlboro cigarette packet, the lid torn open. Inside, there was a single cigarette.

Maybe there was a God.

Clutching the packet, I crawled beneath the rigs, staying low and out of sight until I reached the ramp. The motorhome park lay directly across the way. I waited till a car crawled past, then launched out and scampered across the road. A cry went up. I kept running. The bulky vehicles all looked the same in the gloom. Where the fuck was the Reverend's? Then I spotted the words 'Sinners Welcome'. That was me. I edged over, pulled the door open and stepped inside.

Marilyn looked up weakly. I pulled the single cigarette from the packet and held it triumphantly. But the expression in her eyes was forlorn. 'I'll take that,' said the Reverend, lumbering from the back of the RV.

'I'm sorry,' I muttered lamely. I wanted to fall snivelling to my knees, reach out for a big bear hug of forgiveness. Where was the love of Christ when you needed it? Suffer little children and all that. But he looked away, too quickly. And that's when I knew the game was up.

'I think we better hit the road,' he said.

'Where are we going?' I asked.

'Out of here,' he said, glancing out front where hookers and hobos were skulking between motorhomes, peering in windows, criss-crossing the road, shouting at one another. Drivers were emerging from the diner and heading for their rigs. Lights were going on in neighbouring RVs. And then he turned back and finally held my gaze. 'You haven't been entirely straight with us, have you, son?'

'No,' I muttered, gripped by an intense feeling of shame.

'The Lord preserveth the simple. I was brought low, and he helped me. Psalms: 116, 6. Well, I am going to get you out of here.'

'Thank you, Reverend,' I gushed.

'You're going to have to lay low. The way they're carrying on out there, I wouldn't be surprised if they start setting up roadblocks. So sit in the can, pull the door shut and I will let you know when it's safe to come out.'

I was genuinely moved by his Christian charity. 'About the cigarette, Reverend, I want to explain—'

'It's all right, son,' he said, waving me towards the tiny toilet cubicle. 'I know Ma put you up to it.'

Marilyn scowled at me furiously.

The Rev opened the cubicle door and, with a firm shove in the back, propelled me inside. It was a tight, airless space, with no windows, and the strong smell of disinfectant overlaying other people's shit. I sat on the small toilet seat as the Reverend closed the door, muttering some kind of benediction beneath his breath. There was a click that took a moment to penetrate. I looked at the lock. The key had been turned from the outside.

'Hey, Reverend . . .' I called.

A rumble told me the RV was starting up.

I tried the door handle. It didn't give. 'Reverend . . . what's going on?' I called. I felt the vehicle lurch into motion. I banged the door. 'Reverend?' I banged it again. 'REVEREND!'

The fucker had locked me in.

16

I spent a long night in a toilet less than a metre square. It smelled bad when I got in and worse after I had taken a dump. Periodically I kicked the door but I couldn't get enough purchase to do damage and there was no response even when I accused my kidnappers of being in league with Satan. So I sat with the toilet seat down and my head leaning uncomfortably on the tiny sink, staring at Formica walls till my eyes lost focus. Night voices chattered in my head, pointing out my flaws as if I wasn't already aware of them, thank you very much. As an escapologist, I was an abject failure. Had there ever been a flight to freedom that involved so little actual freedom? I had swapped one cage for another, each less gilded than the last. Gild was good. Gild meant five-star service, coffee and croissants, a comfortable bed with clean linen. A hot shower.

My eyes snapped open to an ominous stillness. I was kneeling on the floor, body contorted over the toilet seat, head throbbing, every muscle aching. The vehicle had come to a halt. Silence swelled till my ears were tingling. Then there was a sudden burst of voices. The lock clicked. The door swung open. The Reverend stood in the half-light, all six foot six of him. Behind him stood another man, almost as tall but softer, face round behind a primped moustache, midriff bulging against the fabric of a short-sleeved shirt. 'Jesus, Pa, I thought you was shitting me,' he gasped.

'Don't take the Lord's name in vain,' said the Rev.

I propelled myself forward and tried to wriggle past my captor but the Rev clamped those big hands around me, gripping my skinny shoulders like a vice. 'Don't let him go, Pa,' yelled his son, swiping my legs from behind.

The Reverend held me down, praying with the fervour of an exorcist combating the devil himself: 'The message of the cross is foolishness to those who are perishing, but to us who are being saved it is the power of God.'

I spat at my assailants but only succeeded in getting my chin wet. 'You're supposed to be a man of God, you fucking hypocrite,' I whined. 'What does it say in the Bible about kidnapping? Judas!'

'I'm sorry,' he said, face taut with shame. 'There's a reward. I've got to think about Ma. Her medication . . .'

'A million fucking dollars,' said Rev Junior, regarding me with belligerent amazement. 'Jesus fucking Christ, Pa! You can buy a lot of fucking medication with a million dollars.'

'Don't test me, John!' growled the Reverend.

'You watch your tongue in front of Pa, Johnny,' croaked Marilyn, straining to observe the action from her sick bed.

'He never watched it in front of me, Ma,' muttered John, glancing warily at his father as if ready to dodge a blow.

The Reverend snorted loudly, which was enough to make John retreat, sitting on Marilyn's bed to let her stroke his thinning hair. This was evidently the estranged son, the Texan sheriff. Despite a beige and black uniform covered in stars and epaulettes, John had little of his father's imposing gravity. Everything about him was somehow toned down by fat. 'Jesus, Ma, have you pissed yourself?' he suddenly exclaimed, jumping back to his feet.

'Pa said I shouldn't use the little girl's room cause You Know Who was locked up in there,' Marilyn bleated.

'For God's sake, Pa, you ain't never gonna change,' John sniped. 'Here, let me take care of that.'

While the Reverend kept me pinned down, Sheriff John pulled my arms behind me and clamped cold metal around my wrists. It took me a moment to realise I was being handcuffed.

'Do you think those are necessary?' asked the Reverend.

'Best not take chances, Pa,' said Sheriff John, sticking a black patent leather shoe under my shoulder and flipping me over with all the dignity of a newly landed fish flopping on the bottom of a boat. 'I suggest you let me handle this. I am a sworn officer of the law, in case you forgot.'

'I haven't forgotten, John,' said the Reverend. 'I'm proud of you.'

'Yeah, well, fuck you. I didn't do it to make you proud,' muttered John. 'I did it so I could arrest you if you ever raised your hands against Ma again.'

'That's enough, Johnny!' wailed Marilyn.

'A million fucking dollars!' whistled Johnny, prodding me incredulously with his nightstick. 'How you wanna do this? Fifty–fifty?'

'We're gonna share with the whole family,' said the Reverend.

'It's my jail cell, my bust,' complained the sheriff.

'Well, we found him,' wheezed Marilyn.

'Do I get any say in this?' I demanded. Well, it's probably fairer to say I snivelled. I just wanted to remind them who this was really about.

'Shut the fuck up,' snapped the sheriff, which settled that.

'Your sister deserves her share and she's gonna get it,' said the Reverend. 'And so is the Church.'

'Fuck the Church,' muttered his son, then dodged back from the Reverend's raised arm with the lightning instincts of someone who has spent a lifetime anticipating violence.

The Reverend wagged his finger with a sad air of impotence. 'That is enough blasphemy. You can say what you want about me, son, but I will always love you, and so will the Lord Jesus Christ.'

'Fuck's sake, you lot should be on *Jerry Springer*,' I muttered from the floor.

'Another fucking word out of you and you're gonna be picking your teeth outta the end of my stick,' snapped the sheriff. 'Excuse me, Ma. But this little shit has been wasting police time and that's something we take seriously round here. Every law enforcement officer in the country looking for him and he's riding round in your fucking motorhome. I can't hardly believe it.'

'The Lord moves in mysterious ways,' intoned the Reverend.

'He sure as shit does,' said his son.

'That's enough, John!' growled the Rev.

'I'll tell you what's enough, Pa! Fifty-fifty's enough. Now that's fair, that's reasonable. You get your share and you can give whatever you want to Paula and she can just fucking drink herself to death even quicker and leave those poor kids without a mother. You can give it all to the fucking Church, for all I care. But I got plans of my own. I ain't wasting my time waiting for the end of the world. With half a million, I can run for mayor, and that'd just be the start. How d'you like to see a Salt in the State senate? Now you owe me, and maybe this is the Lord's way for you to make reparation, call it what you want. Fifty–fifty, right down the middle. I got people to take care of on my end, so what's it gonna be?'

The Reverend looked at Marilyn for support, which was not forthcoming. 'Whatever you say, son,' he sighed.

'Well, all right,' said the sheriff.

The two men regarded one another thoughtfully, then the Reverend opened his arms and enveloped his son in an awkward hug.

'We love you, Johnny,' sniffled Marilyn.

'You wanna help me get the prisoner inside?' requested the sheriff, wiping what looked suspiciously like a tear from his eye.

Early morning sunlight hit me in the face as I was frog-marched across a wide street towards a block of squat, low-lying redbrick and concrete buildings. I glanced up the road, which ran in a straight, flat line to a distant horizon, but the sheriff grabbed hold of the back of my neck and forced my head down. I was bundled through doors into an open-plan office that reeked of utilitarian tedium, dust and neglect. The only two occupants stood as we entered.

'Oh my,' gasped a flat-faced woman in a floral dress and a tower of hair. 'It's true.'

'Need some assistance there, boss?' asked a lanky young uniform with narrow eyes and pimply face.

'Open up the cell door for me, will you, Seymour?' grunted the sheriff.

'Old Freeman Tally is sleeping it off down there,' said the young deputy.

'How many times I gotta tell you, Seymour, this is not a fucking motel,' snapped the sheriff.

'He's less trouble in than out,' sniffed Seymour.

The woman stepped forward and curtsied. 'Welcome to our station, Zero,' she said, proffering what appeared to be a flyer with my picture and information about the reward. 'Can I get your autograph?'

'My hands are cuffed,' I said.

'Oh, well, maybe later,' she trilled, brightly.

'That's enough of that, Rita,' said the sheriff. 'We're gonna treat him like any other prisoner. Everyone is equal in the eye of the law. And I want this kept quiet till I decide exactly how to handle it, so don't be calling your sisters.'

'She already called them,' said Deputy Seymour, winking at his co-worker.

'Jesus fucking Christ!' snarled the sheriff.

'That's enough of that, John,' growled the Reverend.

'Sorry, Pa,' said the sheriff. 'You just call them back now, Rita, and say it was a case of mistaken identity.'

'If Rita's sisters are on the case, the whole town has probably heard by now,' sniggered Seymour, unlocking an imposing door.

'I hope you enjoy your stay,' called Rita, as the sheriff propelled me down into a gloomy basement.

There were three barred cells, one of which was occupied by the prostrate figure of a wiry, grey-bearded black man, sleeping noisily atop a wall-fixed bed. He appeared to be wearing nothing but dirty underpants and bright red moon-boots with no laces. Seymour unlocked an adjoining cell, while the sheriff removed my handcuffs and shoved me inside. 'Get his personal effects, Seymour,' he ordered.

The deputy unclasped my watch and inspected it with awe. 'How much a thing like this cost?' he asked.

'More'n you earn in a year, I'll bet,' said the sheriff. 'Take his belt, in case he tries to self-harm.'

He tugged my leather belt out and my jeans slid down my hips. 'Empty your pockets,' ordered Seymour.

'They're empty,' I said. But he pulled them inside out anyway. Marilyn's four dollars in small change fell out.

'I thought you was supposed to be rich,' said Seymour.

'Rich folks don't carry money,' said the sheriff. 'They got other people to carry it for them. Better get his shoelaces.'

Seymour bent down and fiddled with my laces, until my sneakers were left flopping from my feet. When he was done, he stepped back from the cold, bare cell and the metal bars clanged shut. 'He don't look much like he looks on TV, does he?' said Seymour.

'Come on, now, Seymour,' retorted the sheriff. 'They have all kind of special effects to make people look good on the box. Everybody knows that. It's just an illusion.' And with that my gaolers left.

I sat on the edge of the thin, hard bed and stared at graffiti-covered walls. There was a dirty sink and a toilet with no seat wafting the smell of sewage up my nostrils. I started to cry and didn't even bother holding back. I was as alone as I was ever going to be, so I let the snivelling turn to sobbing until convulsions of despair sent me sliding to the concrete floor. I didn't know where all these tears were coming from – I just wanted my mummy to wrap me up and hold me, I wanted to smell the warmth of her neck and not the shit from the bottom of the toilet, not the antiseptic of hospital bleach in that room where she lay cold and still and God evaporated before my child eyes, sucked away in a howl so blistering and bereft even the memory of it made me recoil.

I never really thought about my daddy in pain. He was such a fucking rock, so hard and unyielding you could have scaled him with pitons, hooks and ropes. But I heard him cry, just that once, and I never wanted to hear that sound again. So what was this sound I was making now?

'It's all in your mind,' a deep, scratchy voice sounded, resonating in the concrete box. For a moment I wasn't sure if someone was really speaking or I was listening to a half-remembered sound bite in my own head. 'No use bawling, boy. Dry your tears, wipe your fears, don't wanna give folks the idea you never been in jail before,' the disembodied voice continued.

'I never have been in jail before,' I said.

'A virgin, hey?' said the voice. And there was a cackling laugh that I didn't like at all.

'I wouldn't say that,' I retorted, clambering quickly to my feet, alert to danger.

'All the world's a jail, and all the men and women really prisoners. That is the word of the Bard, William Shakespeare, he shakes his spear, he knows no fear, and that right there is the goddamn truth!' said the voice.

'All the world's a stage,' I corrected him.

'Damn right, boy. Now you're getting it. A stage on the way to fruition, evolution, revolution, the chrysalis and the butterfly, which are you? You gots to choose. There are many stages but most never make it out of the cocoon. Too many people afraid of change when they should be afraid of staying the same. Fear is the key: it can lock you up, it can set you free. Fear traps us in the prison of the mind. Jail is the only reality. Don't matter if you're in or out, either way you're in, see?'

'Well, I'm pretty sure we're in,' I said. I figured I was talking to my neighbour in the adjoining cell.

'The sleeper awakes!' declared Freeman, excitedly. 'See, that's why I like it in. At least you know where you are. It's a start. What they get you for?'

That was a good question. Had I broken any laws? I wasn't even sure if I had actually been arrested. 'I don't know,' I admitted. 'I didn't do anything.'

'An innocent man, hey?' sighed Freeman.

'I guess.'

'Wake up, fool!' he yelled in disgust. 'There is no such thing as an innocent man. Haven't you been listening to a single word I said? It is all in your mind! Be the victor not the victim. Everything is a projection of consciousness. Understand that and you will set yourself free. All confused people can desert planet evil. The whole world is a mirror to your mind. Consciousness is the ground of being. Consciousness is the only reality. You made this prison. You are here for a reason. You just got to figure it out.'

Freeman almost made sense. 'So what have they got you in here for?' I asked.

'Vagrancy and drunkenness,' said Freeman. 'It don't matter. I can get out any time I like.'

'How do you do that?' I said. 'Just concentrate and make the walls disappear?'

'Don't be foolish, boy. I call my lawyer.'

'Well, call him for me, will you, Freeman,' I said. 'I could use a good lawyer.'

'How d'you know my name?' snarled Freeman.

'I just overheard—' I tried to explain.

'Are you a spy?' he demanded. 'You working for Sheriff Thugman and President Mugman? Trying to get me to tell you my secrets? I will not wear the Devil's suit, I will not drink the Devil's soup, neither do I wear the Devil's boots, I will have nothing to do with the Devil youth. Damn you to the seven pits of hell, I send you to the Phantom Zone for seven years of seven evils, seven times seven is seventy-seven, you shall shake in an earthquake like you never shake before. You are just a figment of my imagination. Fuck you. Fuck you.' He was shrieking now, rattling something against the bars of his cage. I shrank back to the rear wall. 'I'm on to you, Sheriff Thugman!' screamed Freeman. 'Get your stooge monkey boy out of here. I know you're watching. You got cameras in the ceiling. You can't fool the all-seeing eye . . .'

It appeared he was right about the cameras, because Seymour came running down the stairs. 'Calm down now, Freeman, step back from the bars,' the pimply deputy ordered, while Freeman wailed and clattered. 'You go acting all crazy, the sheriff's gonna stop letting me bring you in here. You get sectioned, you'll go back to the county home. You don't want that, do you? Just back off, now, sit back down on the bed, that's right . . .'

'I am not talking to you,' said Freeman, albeit in a much calmer voice.

'Well, why not?' asked Seymour. Stupid question. I could have told him the answer to that.

'Because you don't exist,' said Freeman.

Rita had followed Seymour down to the basement. She hovered shyly in front of my cell, a mobile phone in one hand. 'Can I take your picture, Zero?' she asked. 'Do you mind? I am such a fan.'

'I don't think that's a good idea, Rita,' said Seymour.

'I ain't interested in what you think, Seymour,' said Rita.

'You don't exist,' Freeman reminded him.

'Sure,' I said, peeling away from the wall. 'Take my picture. Do you want to be in it with me?'

'That would be real nice,' blushed Rita. 'I can't open the cell though.'

'Just lean up against the bars,' I suggested.

'I do not think that this is a good idea,' repeated Seymour, firmly.

'Don't be silly, Seymour,' sniffed Rita, handing him the phone. 'Here, take our picture.'

'The sheriff might . . .' Seymour half protested.

Rita leaned against the bars on her side, and I leaned against them on mine, and our faces almost came together. 'What the sheriff don't know ain't gonna hurt him,' said Rita. 'All he's interested in is the reward. You think he's gonna share that with us?' Seymour pressed the button. A flash went off.

'No pictures!' yelled Freeman.

'Oh, I wasn't ready, Seymour!' complained Rita. 'Take another one.'

I put a hand through the bars, and wrapped it around Rita's large waist.

'Say cheese,' said Seymour. The flash went off again.

'No pictures!' yelled Freeman.

'Do you want to get a picture, Seymour?' I asked.

'Ah, I better not,' he answered, reluctantly. 'It's upsetting the other prisoner.'

'C'mon, Freeman won't mind one more. It's all an illusion anyway,' I insisted. So Seymour posed at the bars and Rita took a photo. Then we got one of all three of us, with Seymour holding the cameraphone at arm's length. Freeman called, 'No pictures!' every time the flash went off but with decreasing conviction. 'Can I see them?' I requested, when the photo session concluded. Rita handed me the mobile, and I turned it over in my palm. 'Nice phone,' I observed. 'And you get a signal down here?'

'I get a signal anywhere with that phone. Right in the middle of the desert sometimes. Up a mountain, even.'

'Do you mind if I make a call?' I asked as sweetly as I could.

Seymour protested half-heartedly but Rita said it couldn't do any harm, the sheriff had already been in touch with my manager. Beasley was on his way from New York with the reward and the media had been alerted and would be swooping in from Dallas and Austin and all points of the compass at any time. It was only fair to let me call my lawyer.

Except, as I sat down on the bed in the cell, I realised I didn't have a lawyer to call. I didn't know anybody's number. I always had other people to do my calling for me. I racked my brain but all I could shake loose were the digits of two phone numbers. One was our old home phone from Kilrock but my brother Paddy lived in his hotel now and I'd bought my old man a new house I'd never even set foot in. The other number locked in my head was even less use. It was also from Kilrock, in the days before everything turned to gold and shit. Almost robotically, I stabbed it out, punching in the Irish code.

'Is that an international call?' fluttered Rita, sounding mildly alarmed.

'I'll pay you back,' I said.

'He's only got four dollars,' sniggered Seymour.

I could hear tones ringing far across the Atlantic. Ringing and ringing, back into my past.

'Hello?' said a voice I recognised straight away.

'Mrs Haley,' I said.

'Who's that?'

'Pedro.'

'Oh my word,' said Eileen's mother. 'Pedro! Where are you, child? Are you back? Everyone has been so worried about you. Your poor father . . .'

'Have you seen him, Mrs Haley?'

'Well, we don't . . . we're not really . . . we don't exactly frequent the same establishments,' she said. What she meant was that she went to church and he went to the pub. 'But I saw him on the *Late Late Show*, and he was telling yer man how worried he was about you. He looked very upset.'

I found it hard to imagine my father worrying about me. I was used to upsetting him, for sure, usually resulting in strings of invective and a clip round the ear. But he never seemed to worry about me when I was there, so why should he care if I went missing? 'Listen, Mrs Haley, I'm sorry for calling you. It was the only number I could remember. Look, could you find my father, and tell him I'm all right, and I'll be in touch soon. Could you do that for me?'

'Of course I can, child,' said Mrs Haley.

'Tell him I want to see him. Tell him . . . tell him . . .' But I couldn't tell him I loved him. Those were words never spoken between us.

'Are you all right, Pedro?'

'I've been better,' I said, tears welling. 'How's Eileen?'

'Well, I can't . . . you know, she doesn't live with us any more. She moved . . . to Dublin.'

'I think about her a lot. I'd like to see her sometime.'

'I'm not sure that would be a good idea, Pedro,' she sounded sympathetic but defensive. Who could blame her? I had broken her daughter's heart. 'Things are different now. Her life has changed, she has other . . . I just don't think it would be a good idea.'

She has other what, I wondered, with a stab of jealousy. Other people in her life? Another man? She could be married, for all I knew, fat and happy with the children she had always wanted. Maybe she was a nun, having renounced men altogether. I preferred that idea. 'I just want to tell her—'

'What in damnation is going on here?' yelled the sheriff.

'What was that, Pedro? I didn't catch that. It's not a very good reception. Where are you calling from?'

'Jail,' I said.

'Oh my word,' said Mrs Haley.

The cell door banged noisily open.

'I wanted to tell her . . .'

The sheriff snatched the phone from my hand.

'. . . I'm sorry,' I said.

'Hello?' I heard Mrs Haley call out. Then the sheriff cut the call off.

'Jesus Christ Almighty!' bellowed the sheriff. 'I leave you alone with the prisoner for ten minutes and he's making fucking phone calls from his cell!' Flustered and angry, he demanded to know who I had called. Only when he was satisfied that the mysterious Mrs Haley was not a member of the legal profession did he settle down. 'Listen, kid, you'll be out of here this afternoon,' he said. 'Your manager is on his way. He was very relieved to hear from me, I can tell you, very appreciative. He's been worried about you. I mean, Jesus, you've had the whole country on a fucking wild goose chase. What were you thinking? You can't just go running off like that!'

'Why not?' I said.

He didn't answer, just backed out, locking the cell door.

'Am I under arrest?' I asked.

'Let's just say your legal status is unresolved pending investigation by my department.'

'Bullshit!' growled Freeman.

'That's enough outta you, Tally!' snapped the sheriff. 'Any more backchat and I'm gonna call a doctor in here and get you hospitalised.'

'Tell it to my lawyer,' growled Freeman.

'I don't see no lawyer here,' retorted the sheriff. 'Where is he, Freeman?'

'You gonna deny me my civil rights, Sheriff Salt?' demanded Freeman.

'How can I deny you something that don't exist?' teased the sheriff. 'It's all in the mind, Freeman, ain't that what you tell everyone? All in the mind.'

'Well, I want to call a lawyer,' I blurted out.

'You had your call, kid,' smirked the sheriff. 'I'm sure your girlfriend's ma will get back to you when she's taken her bar exams.' And with that, we were left alone in our cells again.

'So, is that fucker your illusion, or mine?' I mused aloud.

'We co-create reality, good and bad, black and white, yin and yang,' said Freeman, apparently judging my question worthy of serious consideration. 'Opposites co-create each other. Who is Superman without Lex Luthor? See? It is – good and evil turned around, each one is part of the other – that is creation. Where there is no opposing energy there can be no creation. Your enemy is your ally. It's the mystery of karma.'

Beasley was on his way and I didn't have the strength or patience to follow Freeman's mystic convolutions. Life was complicated enough without tying it up in karmic knots. I mean, if there was one thing that sounded worse than dying permanently, it was surely coming back to repeat the same mistakes. 'Whatever you say, Freeman,' I sighed. 'Either way, he's a fucking Nazi prick.'

'You can see!' Freeman laughed. 'Good brain, perfect brain to make perfect rain, perfect lightning and perfect thunder, perfect hailstone, perfect bloodstone and perfect fire and perfect prayer. To be sane is to be insane.'

'Jesus, Freeman, you are doing my head in.'

'I apologise. Do you wish for me to contact my lawyer?'

'How are you gonna do that, Freeman?' I asked.

'There is always a way. I've been here before.'

I wasn't sure what kind of lawyer would have this lunatic for a client but I didn't exactly have too many other options. 'Sure, Freeman, I'd appreciate it. Tell him you've got a guy called Zero in the cell next to you. He'll probably think you're crazy.'

'Oh, he thinks I'm crazy anyway,' said Freeman.

I laid back on the rancid bunk and studied the graffiti. Blow jobs were promised, or threatened. Jesus loved me so much it hurt, apparently. Some jailhouse philosopher proposed that death was not the end, to which a later inhabitant of the cell had appended the thought that it was just the beginning of something worse. And there was a phone number, underneath which was scrawled *Homer Pax could spring Judas from hell.* Which was an impressive endorsement, only slightly undermined by the amendment *yeah but he told Jesus to plea bargain and see where that got him.* Still, some last vestige of preposterous hope fluttered when I heard a muffled conversation from the cell next door: 'Homer? You hearing me? It's Freeman, damn right. They got me locked up again. . . I been here all night, goddammit, but, you know, it's somewhere to sleep and they gimme breakfast. . . I'm talking to you now, ain't I? Sheriff Salt refused me my civil rights, point blank, said they was a figment of my imagination . . . I have my ways and means, you know . . . You hear of a dude called Nothing?'

'Zero!' I shouted.

'Zero, sorry, Zero the hero, the man without fear-o, Zero, Nothing, Naught . . .'

'Just tell him Zero is in the cell next door and he needs a lawyer!' I yelled.

'They dragged this dude Zero in here, got locked up against his will, and he's in bad need of yo' help!' said Freeman. 'I'm figuring I could use a little bit of assistance at this point myself. What d'you say, Homer?'

A long period of silence followed, broken only by occasional grunts from my jail mate.

'So what's he say?' I pleaded with a needy desperation that surprised me.

'He's on his way,' announced Freeman.

'You serious?'

'I am always serious!' said Freeman.

'You're a fucking godsend, Freeman,' I gushed. If the lawyer could get here before Beasley, maybe there was hope, just a glimmer of a chance that I could keep on running. That's all I wanted. The chance to run.

'There is no God,' Freeman berated me. 'How many times I gotta repeat myself? Jehovah, Allah, Muhammad, Buddha, The Prophet, Tarzan, Superman, Spiderman, whatever you wanna call him, they's all just manifestations of the consciousness. Ain't you been paying attention?'

'I'm sorry,' I said, still excited. 'How the fuck did you get hold of your lawyer? Have you got a mobile stashed in there?'

'Don't be a fool,' said Freeman. 'You are better than that.'

'Then how?'

'Telepathy,' said Freeman. 'Consciousness connects everyone. You gotta learn to ride the interstellar radio . . .'

My mind tuned out somewhere around there. They were coming for me now. Beasley would be on a private plane, thinking private thoughts, looking down on terra firma like lord of all he surveyed, flexing and unflexing his fingers, considering his moves. Flavia Sharpe would be there with her minions, sipping an in-flight drink, tapping on her phone, spinning angles in her mind. Helicopters would be racing ahead from Dallas and Austin, packed with camera crews and news reporters, dashing to be first to the scene. How close were they now? Local stringers would be in cars on the highway, pedal to the metal, punching in satnav coordinates for a small town in Texas. The knot was tightening. The word was on the wire, flashing at warp speed down cables buried beneath the Atlantic and Pacific, bouncing off satellites, instantly relaying my exact coordinates to anyone on the planet with access to a television, radio, phone or computer. I was probably the only interested party who couldn't tell you exactly where the fuck I was, and that was fine by me. I did not want any of it any more. I just wanted to be left alone. I wanted to be forgotten. I wanted to be un-famous.

Voices echoed through the basement, sounding like a party of people descending to the cells. Freeman yelled, 'I do not cast pearls before swine because swine do not know what pearls are!' This was it, I thought. Showtime. But still I couldn't stir.

'Release my clients immediately or I am gonna bury your sorry ass under so many lawsuits you're gonna be running your campaign for re-election from the bankruptcy courts,' a voice rang out.

'Homer!' yelled Freeman. 'I knew you wouldn't let us down!'

17

Things turned around so fast, I thought they were going to present me with the keys to the jailhouse and lock up Sheriff Salt instead. Homer Pax was a lumpy, shapeless man in a cream suit, hands fluttering theatrically as he verbally bombarded the cowering sheriff in a high, camp voice, accusing him of state-sponsored kidnapping, police brutality and all manner of corruption, mismanagement and dereliction of duty for personal gain, citing chapter and verse of legal precedent in a bamboozling monologue, while Freeman banged the bars and howled with delight.

Still the sheriff clung forlornly to the keys. 'Don't you think we should await the arrival of the boy's manager? We can all sit down together in my office and sort this out in a civilised fashion, Homer, what do you say? This young man's disappearance has been a cause of great concern to many people—'

'People don't disappear,' countered Homer. 'Clearly my client is not invisible.'

'He went missing!'

'He may have been missed, Sheriff, but as long as he knew

where he was, then he was not missing. A consenting adult going for a walk without telling anyone where he's going does not, as yet, constitute an offence in any state in this free country . . .'

Salt sulked in his office while Freeman Tally and I signed for our belongings. Shoelaces, a belt, a watch and four dollars were all I had in the world but Freeman was another matter. Standing six foot four in red moonboots, grey beard separating into wiry horns, he solemnly dressed himself in the regalia of a thrift-store witch doctor, his tattered coat held together with so many safety pins, badges, CDs and old coins, he looked like an advertising hoarding for the madhouse. In a final flourish, he placed a pair of novelty store X-ray glasses on the bridge of his nose with the exultation: 'Now I can see! What once was inside is now out. Freeman is a free man! Tally ho!'

It was all too much for Reverend Salt. 'You gonna let a pansy lawyer and this mad old coot walk our meal ticket right out of here, boy?' he snapped.

'I would strongly suggest you refrain from casting aspersions against my clients,' murmured Homer.

'There's a million-dollar reward!' yelled the Reverend.

'Shut up, Pa,' snarled the sheriff.

We staged an exit, with Freeman dispatched in full psycho regalia to greet reporters from the local newspaper while Homer led me out back. Rita and Seymour waved from the door.

'How did you know I was in that jailhouse?' I asked as we drove off in a scarlet Honda 4x4. 'Did Freeman really get in touch with you?'

Homer let out a peal of delighted laughter. 'Did he tell you he can contact me telepathically? I always hear when dear old Freeman has been arrested. He's my favourite client, albeit my least lucrative. One of Rita's lovely sisters called to report his incarceration and happened to mention your name. There are no secrets in a small town, believe me. I've been stuck here for so long, tormenting Sheriff Salt is practically my only entertainment.'

The town quickly gave way to desert plains. Homer flicked on the stereo and an exquisite melody filled the car. 'Leonard Bernstein,' I said, automatically. '*West Side Story*.' It's like a nervous tic, identifying music.

'You're a fan?' asked Homer.

'Who isn't?' I grunted.

'Most young people your age don't even know who Bernstein was,' he said, in a tone that implied this was an outrageous indictment of the education system. 'Their idea of Broadway is the cast of *Glee* singing excerpts from *Mamma Mia*.'

'My mother. . .' I started trying to explain. But what had my mother to do with *West Side Story*? My mind flooded with an image of a woman in a red dress, spinning around our kitchen, singing, 'I want to be in A-mer-ee-ka! Everything's free in A-mer-ee-ka!' And there was laughter. And it must have been me who was laughing. I was spinning with her, giddy with pleasure.

'Do you need a tissue?' asked Homer, cautiously.

Those fucking tears. I poured it all out in a torrent: my flight from New York, misadventures with gangstas, bluesmen, witches and priests.

'So let me see if I've got this absolutely straight,' Homer summarised, as we turned into an imposing gateway, leading to a large ranch house. 'You have abandoned a lucrative tour, on which many people depended upon you, and for which hundreds of thousands of fans purchased tickets, in order to hitchhike solo across the continent all the way to darkest Brazil to prove your devotion to your fiancée, who, according to unreliable reports from scurrilous sections of the media, may have had her affections swayed by the attentions of another?'

'I have to do this,' I said, with a conviction the source of which I barely comprehended myself.

'That is so romantic,' sighed Homer.

At Homer's insistence, I took a hot shower while he made some calls. Wiping the bathroom mirror, I regarded my tired face, blurry through streaks of condensation. I didn't look much like a poster boy now, if I ever had, but I shaved and scrubbed up as best I could. Afterwards, I sat in his study, draped in an oversized bathrobe, stuffing my face with a sandwich. 'It's my private sanctum,' declared Homer, with bashful pride. 'I don't bring clients here, certainly not the rabble of cowboy wife-beaters and Sunday-school embezzlers you get around these parts. But I thought . . . *you* might appreciate it.'

'It's very nice,' I offered lamely, idly stroking a tatty, theatrical feline head mounted on a wall stand, as if Homer had returned from a hunting expedition having bagged the cowardly lion from the *Wizard of Oz*. Walls loomed purple and puce, twisted glass cabinets displayed odd collections of kitschy tourist trinkets and sleek modern sculptures, while Homer perched on the edge of a desk apparently fashioned from the hide of a bull and still bearing pointed white horns at one end. I had shot videos on sets less bizarre than this. 'Did you decorate it yourself?'

'I come here to ponder and listen to music,' said Homer. The bluster from the sheriff's office was gone now. There was such softness and mischief in his round face and dark, sunken eyes that he looked like a friendly troll in his secret lair. Pride of place went to an old stereo beneath a wall of carved oriental wooden shelves crammed with a library of old vinyl. I skimmed through: *Silk Stockings*, *Hellzapoppin'*, *Carousel*, *South Pacific*, *Finian's Rainbow*, *The King and I*, *Guys and Dolls*, *Man of La Mancha*, *Cabaret*, *Jesus Christ Superstar*. They were all original cast productions of theatrical musicals.

'Do you have a personal favourite?' asked Homer.

'Not really,' I said, but even as the words came out of my mouth it felt like a lie. And there was the woman in the red dress again, shimmering through a memory haze, singing giddy lines about going anywhere I asked, just as long as I loved her. And I was singing with her, singing male lead, and I knew every word, to her delight and mine. And could that really be my daddy's gravelly voice, croaking along in the background? My old man never sang, not unless he was crocked, and then it was usually rebel songs or U2's 'Sunday Bloody Sunday' with added profanity. I could see the cover of a CD with a man in a white mask, occupying pride of place in the small rack in the living room, back when there was still music in our house, back before it all fell silent. I wonder what happened to that CD? I suddenly felt like I could sing every song on it. '*The Phantom Of The Opera*,' I said.

'Oh, I would never have taken you for a Lloyd Webber fan,' said Homer, with a hint of reproach. 'Ah well, you're still young.'

He picked up a pen shaped like the Statue of Liberty and tapped a pad of Little Orphan Annie paper, an unlikely signal that it was time to get down to business. Declaring he would be remiss not to advise me to end my escapade, recognising my responsibilities to various entertainment outlets and media partners, many of whom might be inclined to sue for lost revenues, he came to rest on a theatrical, tantalising 'however'.

I wasn't ready to give up yet. And neither was Homer, who was forthright about his own interests. He declared himself the best lawyer in the county, his legal skills being the only reason his presence in this backwater was even tolerated. He had operated a successful practice in Atlanta for many years but returned to the family home after his father suffered a stroke and his mother was diagnosed with a long and debilitating illness. They both passed away, last year, within a week of each other. And now, well, he felt stuck. He was keen to return to a big city practice but had his heart set on New York and I was exactly the kind of client who could turn him into a major player overnight. He was made for entertainment law, in his humble opinion, but there wasn't a lot of call for it in cattle country. He was sure Beasley had my management contracts well sewn up but the way he had been able to remotely cancel my credit card suggested close examination of my income flow might yield interesting results. Did I actually own a house? Apart from the one my dad lived in, I didn't think so. Did I know my own bank balance, or indeed have access to my own accounts? But I had never needed to, I had a limitless credit card, and Beasley made funds available as required. Beasley took care of everything. He thought the artist shouldn't have to worry about mundane matters and that suited me fine. 'I don't suppose you carry your own passport?' enquired Homer. 'No, silly question.'

Homer wanted me to sign a power of attorney, so that he could represent me in a breach of trust action against Beasley. He firmly believed there wasn't a contract written that he couldn't wriggle out of. In return, he had another client, who owed him favours, and who could probably be prevailed upon to get me out of the country and all the way to my lady love in Brazil, no questions asked. And so I signed the dotted line, just the way I had signed all my paperwork with Beasley, without reading the small print.

We took off in the Honda from the back of his house, driving cross-country. Just in time too, because as we reached the brow of a hill, I turned back to see a small fleet of TV broadcast vans, festooned in aerials and satellite dishes, throwing up a cloud of dust as they swarmed up Homer's drive. His housekeeper had been left with instructions on how to deal with a media invasion. Deny everything. 'That's the same advice my PR always gives me,' I pointed out.

We drove for half an hour, staying off road most of the time, until we came down a long dirt track to an imposing barrier of trees and iron fencing that completely cut off the view. A dark, pretty, oval-faced woman opened the gates, holding tight to an ugly black dog that bared its teeth like it was looking forward to its next meal, which might be us. She nodded to Homer and looked me over coolly, without smiling. I felt like I recognised her but I wasn't sure from where.

We drove on to a tall, battered old barn overlooking a long stretch of bare dirt. The Texas sun was high and hot but we ducked into the airless gloom of an office. Behind a heavy old desktop computer, making no move to get up and greet us, sat a wiry, weather-beaten man with careful eyes. A long white scar sliced through his leather skin from a corner of his mouth all the way to his left ear, even trailing a path through a pencil moustache perched on his top lip. An unlit cigarette poked at an angle below, as if to complete a vanity of raffishness. Homer introduced him as Grover Van Horne.

'I'm Zero,' I said, extending a hand, which Grover made no move to shake.

'I know who you are, boy. You're trouble, and right now I'm supposed to be staying out of trouble, according to my goddamn lawyer.' He looked pointedly at Homer.

'Now, Grover, do try and remember your manners,' said Homer. 'Imagine you're in court, that ought to help. How's business?'

'You know what people been saying since the trial,' grumbled Grover. 'I can't even get a bit of honest crop dusting. They take me for a damn smuggler.' Homer raised a sceptical eyebrow, which inspired Grover to thump the table in protest. 'I just move cargo about, I don't ask what's in it. Didn't you prove that in a court of law, dammit!' His unlit cigarette fell out of his mouth while he was shouting but he just picked it up and stuck it back in.

'Well, maybe we can help there,' said Homer. 'As discussed on the phone, I would like you to put your services at the disposal of this young man, take him wherever he needs to go, don't ask too many questions and you will be properly remunerated down the line, when the dust has settled.'

'It's five hundred a day for me and the Baron, twice that if we're crossing borders, plus fuel costs, and gas ain't cheap anywhere these days. You good for that?'

'Who's the Baron?' I asked.

Grover laughed. 'You wanna meet the Baron? Follow me, boy.'

He led us through a side door, into the barn. There, looming out of the shadows, was a red twin-propeller aeroplane, barely bigger than Homer's car but in considerably worse condition, with metal patches on the fuselage, rust on the wing tip and a thick black polythene sheet over what should have been a passenger window. 'Beechcraft Baron, best damn light twin ever built,' declared Grover, proudly. 'Been flying this baby since eighty-eight, and the Baron's never let me down.'

'Are those bullet holes in the tail?' I asked incredulously.

'We been through a couple of scrapes, the Baron and I,' drawled Grover. 'Don't worry about that, it's an aerodynamic thing. So why don't we talk real business, Homer? If your client can put some money up front, we can load the Baron up with gas and I'll take him all the way to Disneyland, if that's where he wants to go, put him right down on Mickey Mouse's front lawn.'

'Brasília,' I said.

'Brasília, as in Brazil?' said Grover, doubtfully. I nodded. Homer had looked it up on the Internet. This was the inland city where the film production office was based, the last point of real civilisation before the Amazon, where Penelope appeared to be holed up in some kind of resort clinic. With her fucking co-star.

'As I already explained, Grover, my client is not in a position to pay your fees upfront,' said Homer. 'I can offer you my personal assurances, however.'

'Yeah, you know how many times I've heard that? No offence, Homer, God knows I owe you a debt of gratitude for keeping my ass out of the slammer, but aircraft don't run on personal assurances.'

I suddenly thought of something. 'I've got a watch!' I shouted out, excitedly.

'Well, bully for you, boy,' drawled Grover. 'Great for telling the time but it don't get the Baron airborne.'

'It's an expensive watch,' I said, taking it off and shoving it at him.

'Do you see pawnbroker's balls hanging over the door?' snarled Grover.

'Gentlemen, please,' protested Homer.

'This watch is probably worth more than that heap-of-shit crate,' I said.

'You watch how you talk about the Baron,' said Grover. 'He's sensitive.' But he took the watch and studied it curiously. We returned to the office, while he checked out the Patek Philippe Rose Gold Nautilus on the Internet. 'Jesus, what kind of idiot spends forty-five thousand on a watch,' he grudgingly grumbled.

'Not me,' I said. 'It was a gift.'

'It don't tell the time no better than my Seiko,' he muttered but I could detect a covetous look as he tried it on for size. 'And the Baron would set you back a hundred grand even in present condition. Damn thing's a million dollars off the factory floor. How's a man supposed to pay for something like that without dealing in a little contraband now and again, eh?' I wasn't quite sure who he was talking to now, himself most likely. 'Anyway, I can't make it to central Brazil in one trip,' he sniffed. 'With all my modifications, I can get a couple of thousand miles out of the Baron but Brasília's gotta be nearly twice that. And there's flight plans to consider, notifications, paperwork . . .'

Homer winked at me. 'Come now, Grover, as your lawyer,

we both know how many times I've got you off the hook for incorrectly filed flight plans.'

'I could maybe do a little business down south. We can refuel in Colombia, it's just a hop from there.'

I felt a lurch in my heart.

'Isn't that a bit dangerous right now?' fretted Homer.

'Colombia's always been dangerous. You think a little natural disaster makes a difference to Colombians? You've met my wife, Homer. Actually it could make things easier. With all this humanitarian aid, flights are going in and out and no one's worrying too much about paperwork. We could make ourselves useful, take in some water, I hear they need drinking water and there's plenty out here on the field. And Consuela's been collecting blankets and medical supplies, she's had a big charity drive going on at church. She's been fretting about it ever since the first quake, bugging me to get the Baron down there. Hey, darling!' We glanced around to see the dark woman at the door, dog still tight on the leash, the pair of them glowering in at us. 'Guess where we're going, darling,' announced Grover, brightly. 'We're going home! Colombia, babe!'

Her dark face was suddenly transformed by a dazzling smile. Now I knew who she reminded me of. My mother.

18

It was noisy in the Baron. And fucking cold. By 6,000 feet, I had lost all feeling inside my trainers. I had flown in private planes many times before but usually in the kind of gold-plated luxury where, if you complain about a slight chill, the stewardess will pour you a hot toddy and sit on your lap. I was wearing one of Grover's leather flying jackets. He had insisted he wasn't taking me to meet the most beautiful woman God ever made (to which his wife snorted, and Homer diplomatically murmured, 'present company excepted, of course') dressed like a goddamn pansy ('No offence, Homer,' he quickly added, and Consuela smirked). But I was starting to shake and it wasn't just the vibration of the plane, which felt like we were skimming the clouds on the back of a lawnmower with loose screws. 'Get the kid a blanket, Consuela,' yelled Grover, his voice a metallic hiss in my headphones. 'I don't want to have to explain to Penelope Nazareth how we had to amputate her fiancé's dick cause he got frostbite over Mexico.'

Consuela, travelling silently in back, pulled a blanket from behind her, and wrapped it carefully around my shoulders.

There wasn't much room for manoeuvre in the Baron. My seat up front with Grover seemed to have been constructed across a wing strut and I had to slouch for a clear view through the cockpit glass. We were squeezed tight in front of a dashboard of baffling dials and a china figurine of the Virgin Mary, eyes closed, hands pressed together in prayer. I suspected that was Consuela's touch. It was a six-seater but Grover had long since removed three seats to make more room for cargo, whatever that might be. I got the impression Homer had kept him out of jail on a narco bust. Shit, there was every chance I'd snorted bucketloads of the stuff he brought into the country. Homer, in any case, had remained behind, to manage the media bloodbath. The little plane was stuffed with crates of bottled water, piles of blankets and boxes crammed with medicines which Consuela had been stockpiling. From the footage I'd seen on TV, what the Colombians really needed were bulldozers to knock down ruins and rifles to shoot the looters but I understood the impulse. She wanted to go home.

Grover explained that ordinarily he wouldn't risk putting down in Olaya Herrera, Medellín's domestic airport. José María Córdova International was out of the question: too many soldiers, too much paperwork. He knew some little strips in the mountains above the *comunas*, but he wouldn't get a refuel without an exchange with local gangsters, and crazy as he might be, he didn't see the point in flying coca to Copacabana Beach and back. So we'd take our chances with the aid crews, let Consuela do her bit for international relations, while he went into Medellín and rustled up business for the return leg.

'Are they still doing that kind of business in Medellín?' I said. 'I thought they were in the middle of a national emergency.'

'Kid, the day the coke stops coming out of Colombia, then you'll find out what a national emergency is,' Grover chuckled. 'The whole damn US of A will go into withdrawal. There'll be crack riots on the lawns of the White House. Prohibition, that's what this great country was built on. And they dare to call me a damn smuggler? I'm a national hero is what I am, a proud servant of the American Dream. They should give me a goddamn medal, what do you say, Consuela?'

'*Chinga a tu madre*,' came a disembodied voice in the head-phones. I knew what that meant. *Fuck your mother.*

Grover laughed some more. 'Consuela don't approve of the drug trade, do you, darlin'?' I caught the drift of her reply. Something about *vampiros*, blood and Colombian babies.

Grover still had an unlit cigarette poking from his lips. 'Are you ever going to smoke that thing?' I asked.

'I don't smoke no more,' he retorted. 'Filthy habit. Gave up under the influence of a good woman.'

'So why have you always got one stuck in your mouth?'

'In case of emergencies,' he winked. 'You want one?'

'It's never been my vice.'

'Clean-living boy, huh? Consuela would approve.'

'I wouldn't say that, exactly,' I muttered. 'So what's Consuela got against . . . you know?'

'Ah, You Know. I ain't heard that one before. YeYo, I believe the kids call it these days. The White Lady, the Snow Queen. Consuela lost two young brothers to the coke wars that drove her whole country *loco* for a while back there. Baby assassins, younger than you. They used to say a kid from the *comunas* was an old man at twelve, cause he's got so little life left ahead of him. In the bad old good old days, you could get shot in the head for singing "My Way" out of tune in a karaoke bar. Seen that one myself and goddamnit if the motherfucker didn't deserve it. But mostly it was drug deals, and most of the killing was done by *bambinos*. Yeah, everybody scrapping tooth and nail for the right to supply Devil's Dandruff to stars of stage and screen. But you wouldn't know nothing about that, now, would you, boy? Clean-living young pop star, like you.'

'So if it's so fucking bad, why do you do this?' I asked.

'Oh, I'm just the ferryman, crossing a river of death,' sang Grover, who seemed to be enjoying himself. He had visibly unwound almost as soon as the wheels had lifted off the strip. 'We don't sully our nostrils, do we, Consuela, my love? Don't get high on your own supply, first rule of business. Wasn't always that way, freely admit it, though not in any court of law, but I'm a reformed man since I met my lady love here. You don't mind if I tell the kid how fate brought us together, do you, sweetpea?'

Taking silence as consent, Grover began to tell me about the bad old good old days, when coke barons were more powerful than the government, drug-smuggling was the only local industry that mattered, and Medellín was renowned as the most dangerous hell hole on Planet Earth, world capital of kidnappings and homicide, practically the private fiefdom of the late Pablo Escobar.

'*Espero que arde en el infierno,*' came the voice from the back.

'Indeed, sweetness, I am sure he is rotting in hell,' agreed Grover. 'If he hasn't taken over the place by now.'

'Doesn't she speak English?' I asked.

'Oh, she speaks the lingo pretty good, when she has to,' said Grover. 'Consuela chooses to converse only in her native tongue, as is her patriotic right. And why not? It's a beautiful tongue. You know what the great Colombian poet, Fernando Vallejo, said about his beloved country? *Para los ladrones no hay mejor reino en el mundo y no hay otro mundo más allá de éste.* "For thieves, there's no better kingdom in the world, and there's no other world beyond this one."'

Consuela's family were from the impoverished lowlands, a village down south in the Amazon basin, but, like so many before, they moved to the city for the chance of a better life, which would be funny if it wasn't so sad, in Grover's opinion, leaving the most fertile region on the planet to earn less than minimum wage halfway up a mountain in the Capital City of Death. But everybody's got a right to sanitation and television, don't they? Plus there was a civil war and all kinds of revolutionaries and bandits to contend with, so life wasn't exactly a bowl of bananas down there in the jungle.

Medellín was a thriving, colonial city, with palaces, treelined streets and modern tower blocks. But these weren't the kind of places peasants from the lowlands were welcome. So they went higher up the mountains that towered over everything, and made their own homes out of whatever materials they could lay their hands on, which was always plenty in this kingdom of thieves. So Medellín became a city within a city, encircled by barrio after barrio of hovels, piled one on top of the other, brick, concrete, breezeblock, cardboard, tin, polythene and people, more and more people, pouring in from all over the country, playing their music too loud, cooking their stinky meals, shitting and pissing where there was no running water, drinking *aguardiente* and *tinto*, hundreds of thousands, maybe a million (who was counting?) hungry peasants trying to turn a buck, honestly if the city would let them, dishonestly if that was what it took, cause this was the kingdom of thieves after all, and there was no dishonour in taking what you could get from those who probably stole it in the first place. Still a third-world city's not a city without its own shanty town, where life is hard but fair, the people poor but happy, and maybe it would have stayed that way, and Consuela and Grover would have gone through their lives blissfully unaware of one another's existences, had not the good citizens of North America discovered disco music went better with coke, and proceeded to snort the soul out of Colombia, sucking it up both nostrils with a force that shook the Andes worse than the hurricanes that rampaged across the peaks. And Consuela's little peasant family, *padre* and *madre* and beautiful *hija* and two angelic little *hijos*, found themselves resident in Comuna 13, the worst of the worst, the black heart of a narco empire.

'Her brothers were probably a couple of little psychos,' said Grover. 'I don't know, I never met them. Maybe they would have wound up whacking out monkeys and parrots down in the jungle. But they grew up in a barrio where the kids had more words for murder than eskimos have for snow, so they played with machetes and knives and killed their friends for fun, they killed over girls and insults and bravado, but mostly they'd kill who the grown-ups paid them to, buzzing about on mopeds, playing *policias* and narcos with real guns and bullets.'

'They were not bad boys,' said Consuela, in English, by which I understood she was addressing me.

There was nothing special about her brothers' story, according to Grover. Baby brother got sent to hit some local badass and wound up getting dropped himself – came up riding pillion on big brother's moped, pulled out his pistol and got popped in the back of the head by some kid standing guard on the corner. He was nine years old. There were over five hundred murders in Medellín that month, which was no more or less than usual. The cops had given up investigating, ambulances had given up collecting bodies, corpses were given a number and tossed in mass graves, which is where Consuela's little brother was probably rotting now, just another sad stat in the murder capital of the world. Only Consuela didn't see it that way. She wanted revenge, which many Colombians consider more than just a right, it's practically a sacred duty. But she wasn't interested in her brother's killer, who was only ten years old himself. She armed herself with a carving knife stolen from one of the rich homes she cleaned, and went after her brother's boss, a local hoodlum and minor lieutenant in the Medellín Cartel who went by the name of Cesar. And who, as it happened, was also Grover's contact for a little business in Comuna 13.

'Of course, I didn't know any of this,' continued Grover. 'I'd only met Cesar half an hour before, and we were hunkered down in a back room bar, sizing each other up over a couple of *cervezas*, when I saw some mad bitch with a kitchen knife making her way to our table. So, being a younger man yet to learn the virtues of thinking first and acting second, I jumped up to stop her. She gave me this for my troubles.'

Grover ran a finger along the scar that split his face. I glanced back at Consuela. She stared me down with unapologetic defiance.

'So what happened?' I demanded.

'Cesar's gang disarmed her and dragged her out into the yard. She was screaming her head off, and there were chickens, I'll never forget that, lots of damn chickens squawking, and what with blood all over the place, my blood, it looked like some kind of voodoo sacrifice. I asked if they were going to kill her but Cesar said it would be a waste of a fine piece of ass, they'd gang bang her, and then kill her. Cesar invited me to go first, which was only polite after what she'd done to me, and what I'd done for him.'

'What did you do?' I wasn't sure if I wanted to hear the answer.

'Oh, I wasn't in the mood for love,' said Grover. 'I asked them to give her to me. I told them I was going to get the ultimate revenge, I was going to make her marry me, that way she'd suffer her whole life and not just a few hours. Ain't that right, darling? What could the guy do? He didn't like it, but I saved his life, so he gave Consuela to the gringo. And we lived happily ever after. Romantic, huh?'

'Jesus Christ,' I said, trying to take it all in. 'I thought my family was fucked up.'

'Yeah, everybody does,' said Grover. 'You want some coffee? Hey, Consuela, what kind of hostess are you? You got the thermos back there?'

I drank hot black liquid with shaking hands, trying not to spill any on the control panel. Down below, a narrow strip of land cut through the vast blue sea, Panama maybe. Geography wasn't my strong suit. 'I thought you said there were two brothers?' I asked, pondering Grover's tale.

Neither of them answered me. Grover was staring intently at his instrument dials. I looked back but Consuela was hanging her head, her face obscured by black hair. 'So,' I nudged. 'What happened to Consuela's other brother?'

'Cesar had him killed as revenge,' said Grover. I could hear another noise faintly coming over the headphones. It sounded a lot like weeping.

'Don't they say the violence is over now?' I said, desperate to change the subject. 'That's what the news reports have been saying, "just when Colombia was becoming a tourist destination again, it gets hit by the forces of nature", all that crap.'

'Oh yeah, it's a whole new country,' said Grover. '*El presidente* cleaned it right up. Plan Colombia, fighting fire with even heavier fire – it takes a death squad to stop a death squad and if you violate some human rights, well, nothing comes for free, everybody knows that. The cartels have gone, or at least they've gone underground. The civil war's pretty much over, cause they've bribed the factions to join the government, so now everybody's got their nose in the trough, and the only things worth fighting over are kickbacks. They've been laying down roads in the *comunas*, and if they have to bulldoze a few neighbourhoods to do that, it's all in the name of peace and progress. They've been doing a great job of papering over the cracks. Before the quake opened them all up, anyway.'

I'd picked up something along these lines, probably sitting up at four in the morning watching CNN with my eyes pinned open by Colombian powder, while they showed disaster footage with my song as the soundtrack and Beasley rattling on about how we could never afford a video as spectacular as that, and the pair of us laughing like the whole thing was being staged for our benefit. With five hundred miles of tremors across the Andes, the Colombian government had its hands full coping with relief efforts, and had been accused of ignoring the poorest barrios. Medellín was the worst hit, with skyscrapers down and problems with the water supply. When a catastrophic mudslide buried some squatter camps there had been rioting and looting, with packs of near feral kids running wild. Scenes of the army shooting live ammunition at children rocked the world, there were rumours of vigilante groups treating the kids like rabid dogs, which is how come the whole Orphans of Medellín thing kicked off, just at the time my single was on the way to number one. I felt sick to think we'd actually had strategy meetings about that. Consuela tapped me on the shoulder and pointed at a brown and green landmass, rising from the blue ocean. 'Colombia,' she said. 'Home.'

I laid my head against the vibrating glass, and gazed at the spectacle of fields, scrub and forest speeding beneath us, the soil and rock from which my mother sprang spread out beneath my fingers like a papier-mâché model. It didn't seem real, more like a child's amusement, like the Nativity they used to put up in Kilrock town hall at Christmas and you'd walk around the glass case, eyes wide, pointing to tiny painted figures, calling out, 'Look, Mama, sheep, cows, look, Mama, look, there's a whole family in the house, waving at us . . .'

And she looks. And she puts her soft hands on your shoulders. And you breathe in the smell of her, the most beautiful smell you've ever known, the only smell you've ever known, the warm clean smell of soap, the acrid hint of cleaning fluids, the rose petal perfume she dabs around her neck, the lemon smell of black hair that brushes against your cheek. She's there with you, and you don't even have to turn to see her. She's always there.

'*Santísima Virgen María, Madre de Dios, nos guíe y nos proteja . . .*'

I don't know how I fell asleep in that rattling crate but I woke with a start. A stream of Spanish prayers were steadily murmuring in my ear, mingling with the noise of the Baron, sporadically interrupted by a 'Shut up, dammit, I'm trying to think!' from Grover. We were descending through a mountain pass, a looming presence of rock falling behind and below, while the panorama of a metropolis opened in front. It was obvious something was wrong, that is, way more wrong than it should have been. There were pillars of smoke rising in the sky, towering black fingers billowing up from a desolation of rubble and wreckage. 'They've been hit by another aftershock,' yelled Grover. 'The control tower's down. Runway looks bad.'

The ground was rising fast to meet us, buckled and riven by savage cracks, the broken shells of other aircraft, fires burning, a building of glass and steel leaning at an improbable angle. Something with a force you couldn't even begin to imagine had ripped right through the airport. And I was suddenly aware of speed, the rush of engine noise and blood and prayers in my ears, the wind battering our flimsy shell of a toy plane. Shouldn't we be slamming on the brakes about now? Or better yet, rising, rising above the distant mountains, rising above the clouds, turning back from this wasteland that had been trying to drag me to my doom, blocking our ears to the siren song, battling free of the magnetic field that had wrapped its coils around my heart and sucked me in from ten thousand miles away. 'You can't land here,' I shouted.

'I can't NOT land here,' Grover retorted. 'The Baron's bone dry, it's a miracle I even got us this far.'

'Dios te salve, Maria, llena eres de gracia . . .'

'But you *can't* land here!' I screamed. 'We'll never make it. You're gonna kill us!'

'Don't worry, kid, I could put this baby down on the side of a cliff,' snorted Grover, grimly.

The broken ground rushed up. I think I started to scream. And my world collapsed to a pinpoint of fear, a black hole at the wrong end of a telescope, and I could see my father in there, and I could see my brother, and I could see Beasley, and Penelope, and Eileen, and fucking Kilo and The Terranauts, but I couldn't see my mother – where was my mother when I really needed her? She was nowhere, the place where we all go, the endless nothing, the big fat zero. And her soft bosom was just bare bone. And her smiling face a grinning skull. And she had left me. She left me. She abandoned me. And now she was taking me back.

'Mama!' I screamed.

We bounced off the ground. The world was shaking. We tipped and spun. We bounced again. And there was dust billowing, brakes were screeching, propellers were beating, and beating, and beating slower, and slower. And we were coasting to a stop.

'What'd I tell you, kid?' said Grover. But he didn't look triumphant. He looked as pale as a ghost, like he couldn't quite believe that he was still alive.

'Santa María, Madre de Dios, ruega por nosotros pecadores,' sighed Consuela.

If the Virgin Mary was listening to her prayers, she didn't show it. She had tilted forward and was smiling beatifically at the floor.

'I think I'll have that cigarette now,' said Grover, then realised it was no longer in his mouth. He started to grope around at his feet. I looked out through the tiny aircraft window, through the dust and the chaos. I had arrived where I didn't even know I wanted to go.

I was home.

I was in the land of my mother.

19

Grover told me to remain out of sight while he organised refuelling and Consuela located an aid worker to deal with their humanitarian offerings. 'They're going to need a little more than blankets and band aids,' I said, gazing at the dust clouds rising over what was left of the city.

'Just wait in the plane,' snapped Grover. 'Anyone approaches, act dumb. That should come natural. Get in back, keep your head down, and don't answer to nobody but me.'

It was probably good advice. It was possibly even well intentioned. But I was sitting jammed against the blankets, thinking about what lay outside, the country that gave me my brown skin, the secret nation of my genes, and it was groaning in pain, it was howling with sirens and grief, and I had to get out and see for myself. Even the fact that Grover, the paranoid bastard, had locked the rear and pilot doors couldn't stop me. I used an emergency axe to hack the thick black polythene with which he had fashioned a temporary rear window, squeezed through and dropped to the ground. There were people nearby but none of them even looked my way, or if they did, they didn't register anything unusual in the sight of a red-headed pop star climbing through an aircraft window. There was just too much to behold, more than the brain could comprehend, an enormous, mind-stunning vista of collapse and destruction everywhere the eye could see.

Let's start at the beginning. The closest point of devastation, the only thing I could focus on for now. Grover had taxied over to a hangar, or what had been a hangar, but was now broken-down walls and a ceiling only suspended from the ground by the planes crushed beneath it.

It would have been the most enormous piece of wreckage I had ever seen. It should have been enough to take the breath away on its own. But next to it, pitched forward at an angle, listed a huge square building of concrete and glass, which must have housed the control tower, its big radar dish still spinning uselessly on top. Furniture had tipped through broken windows, so that office desks, chairs, sofas and filing cabinets littered the ground, glittering in a blanket of shattered glass. There were bodies under desks and spreadeagled across upturned tables, twitching and groaning, and others moving among them, helping them to their feet, shifting them out of the danger zone, in case the building regained its downward momentum.

And beyond the airfield lay the city, spread out in a tangle of broken pieces, like a badly arranged jigsaw of smashed concrete, twisted lamp posts and structures split apart, honeycombs of houses with innards exposed. Every now and then the eye would alight for relief on a building standing tall and proud, as if in defiance of the worst that nature could do. And over all of this hung the blackness of a smoke cloud, spreading across my vision as if the sky was closing in, fed by raging infernos below.

I crossed a highway, buckled and cracked, jammed with cars going nowhere, some still on their wheels, some on their roofs, some perched vertically on crumpled fenders, as if arranged by a mad sculptor. People stood around, gesturing uselessly, weeping or shouting or staring in bewilderment. There was dust in the air, dust everywhere, a thick cloud of concrete dust that had been shaken up by the earth's hammer blow and was slowly, slowly settling down, coating everything and everyone.

I clambered across rubble, fresh rubble, with bits of toilets and baths and TV sets and fridges poking out, and people squatted in it, sifting rubble in bare hands. I came down the other side, and walked along a narrow street where all the houses on one side had collapsed, one into the other, like a row of dominoes, but all the houses on the other side stood pristine and untouched, windows unbroken, even a little angel on a water fountain still pissing into his pond, as if mocking the misfortune of his neighbours.

And that's where I saw my first corpse, a man of indeterminate age lying on the sidewalk, skin as waxy as a frozen supermarket chicken, so obviously not there any more, so obviously dead, though there was no indication of what felled him. Perhaps it had just been his moment, and he'd gone down as the quake struck, clutching his heart and cursing his bad diet, and missed the whole thing. A pack of children circled around him, and, yes, pack is the only way to describe them, ragged and barefoot and feral, sniffing the air and licking their lips – they prodded at the body then darted in, emptied its pockets, and took off down the street, one of them holding a wallet aloft and howling victoriously.

And people picked among the ruins of their homes, retrieving whatever was still intact, piling belongings on the sidewalk, creating outdoor replicas of their living quarters, before collapsing in saved armchairs or rescued beds to stare up at the sky and shake their heads in numbed silence. Some gathered in groups to help others in need, tending to the hurt and wounded, yelling at each other in agitation, as if energy and activity might keep the worst at bay and put off the moment when they had to take stock of their own losses.

And at the top of a hill stood a little church, with its steeple sheared off and driven point first into the ground. A plaster cast Christ had crashed down to earth and lay in the church-yard, still nailed to his crucifix but broken in two, deaf to the prayers of His people, as he'd always been deaf to mine. There were Christs everywhere in this ruined city, peeking out through broken windows, hanging from doors where there was no building left standing, posing on podiums in gardens filled with debris and baring sacred hearts in cracked murals on collapsed walls. Most of all, Christ was to be found dangling on rosaries around the necks of people who still muttered prayers while fingering their magic beads, despite the evidence all around that the bastard Christ and his savage old Father and that sneaky prick the Holy Spirit had not just forsaken the citizens of Medellín, they'd actually visited the wrath of the gods upon them, with not one, not two, but three earthquakes in a row, and a mudslide to boot. Still they prayed, thanking the good Lord for delivering them, like a man in a head-on collision that has smashed his legs and torn his right arm from its socket, crawling from the wreckage to thank the drunk driver who hit him for leaving him with at least one functioning limb.

The pack of children ran past me again, swarming across the cracked pavement and descending like a ravenous horde on the smashed-open front of a neighbourhood supermarket, whooping and laughing as they caroused through the aisles and clambered across tipped-up shelves, filling their hands with whatever they could snatch, and then charging, yelling, back out on to the street, where a befuddled grey-haired man in pyjamas stood shaking his fist in a gesture more of impotence than anger. A cop on a motorcycle started up, as if to give chase, but then stopped, climbed off, went into the store and helped himself to a pack of cigarettes.

And that's when I saw my second corpse, and my third, and maybe my fourth and fifth, it was hard to tell among the tangle of limbs in a car flattened beneath a telephone pole brought down by the collapse of an apartment awning, although the rest of the building remained more or less intact. I was already losing count by the time I came face to face with a woman sitting in a comfortable armchair, bolt upright, dead eyes open and staring, as if she couldn't believe what she was seeing. There was a mangy, brown dog at her feet, tail twitching, and at first I thought it was sleeping in the sun, blissfully ignoring the chaos, but then I realised it too was dead, and the hairs of its tail were blowing in the breeze. I swear when I looked up there were vultures circling high overhead, waiting for their moment to pick the bones of the city clean.

And I passed another car, front flattened beneath slabs of concrete but its boot sprung open and full of fruit, where an old crone in a shawl of red and gold was calling out prices like a hawker at a market. I wanted to stop and buy one of her mangoes, so bright and juicy and delicious, but all I had was four dollars in my jeans, and they had been laundered by Homer and the money came out in a soggy ball, so now I didn't even have a cent to my name. I tried on my famous smile but the old lady looked right through me. Nobody could see me now. I had been rendered invisible by the sheer incomprehensibility of disaster, by the blindness of shock and grief, as if a veil had been dropped over all of Medellín, and nobody could see anything but their own pitiful horror.

And wasn't this what I wanted, after all? To be anonymous again?

Suddenly the noise started to break through and I could hear helicopters overhead, and fire trucks hosing down a blazing petrol station, and ambulances fighting their way through streets littered with immobilised vehicles, and crews of rescue workers digging in the detritus of collapsed apartment blocks. Outside a ruined cinema advertising a Disney double bill a crowd pressed against safety barriers, straining for a view into the crumbling building, and the sound they made was the most horrible sound of all, an orchestra of weeping and wailing, a wall of tears. I kept moving, I kept moving, I had to keep moving, I didn't want their tears to set off my own, cause if I started crying now, I feared I'd never be able to stop.

I had walked such a long way, the streets were narrower and steeper and the houses, those still standing, smaller and closer together. I was in one of Consuela's *comunas*, one of the most dangerous places on earth, according to Grover, but I felt completely safe, protected by the collective pain of a whole city. At last I came to a halt before the ruin of a house that looked like it had never been much of a house in the first place, a hopeful construction of adobe, concrete and corrugated iron that had come down in one bump, while its two-storey neighbours remained standing.

There was a woman sitting in front of this wreckage, covered in dust and dirt, face smeared with blood, one arm hanging uselessly by her side, slack mouth emitting a keening wail. I reached out to touch her and dragging some words from my past, from a time my memory could no longer access, I said, '*¿Que pasa, madre? ¿Te puedo ayudar?*' What's up, mother? Can I help?

'*A mi hija,*' she gasped, suddenly sharp-eyed and hopeful. '*En la casa! A mi hija! Mi niña!*'

Her daughter was still in the house, if you could call this pile of disarranged building materials a house. There were steps leading to a blue door but the whole front wall had collapsed backwards as the house fell in on itself. I wrenched the door open but it was just rubble beyond, with no way in at all. So I scrambled on to the roof. There was a man already there, a short, fat man, digging frantically with bare hands, body damp with sweat, blood under his nails, gasping for breath. I fell in beside him, tossing bricks down the side of the building. He held my eyes for barely a second but what passed between us was the kind of communion that occurs when musicians strike the same chord, a unity and sense of purpose that nothing is needed to be said. '*Estamos próximos, mi niño,*' he cried out. '*Estamos próximos.*' We're coming, my child, we're near!

And so we worked together on that roof under the sun, taking it apart broken brick by broken brick, digging our way down into the building beneath. I don't know how much time passed, and we didn't seem to be getting anywhere, but we kept at it, we kept digging, and soon there was another person on the roof with us, an old man, his moustache coated in dust, taking stones from us and tossing them down. For a moment I had the mad idea that we were going to dismantle this house brick by brick and reconstruct it in the street. But then a kind of narrow tunnel opened up and sunlight glinted through the wreckage into what might be a room below. I thought maybe I could get in there, if I crawled on my belly. The old man was saying no, it was too dangerous, keep digging, the rescue crews will arrive. But the girl's father was nodding, eagerly. You can do it! Can you hear her? She's crying? Can you hear? I couldn't hear anything but I got down, wriggled through, and crawled into the darkness.

Sometimes I act like I've never been afraid of anything but the truth is I've always been afraid of everything. I am filled with fear, it is the oxygen I breathe, it is the blood that pumps through my veins.

I am afraid of the dark.

I am afraid of the spotlight.

I am afraid of being alone.

I am afraid of being in a crowd.

I am afraid of being ignored.

I am afraid of being discovered.

I am afraid of being loved.

I am afraid of being unlovable.

I am afraid of dying.

I am afraid to live.

For fuck's sake, what is wrong with me? Fear fills me with self-loathing, self-loathing fills me with anger, anger fills me with adrenalin, adrenalin makes my heart beat faster, my heart floods my body with blood, fear is in my blood, it courses through my veins making me dizzy and crazy and tipping me over the edge and that is what it is like every time I go on stage, like a high diver springing off the board in the middle of the night, not sure whether anyone has thought to fill the pool below. Because most of all I am afraid of being found out. And so I pitched into the hole.

Did I mention that I was afraid of the dark? Things were poking me in the ribs, brushing against my face, sharp things, hard things, rough things, and I was staring hard into the darkness, seeing nothing, but crawling towards it anyway. The house was groaning, I could feel it moving, and what if there was another tremor? What if God, the almighty bastard, hadn't finished with Medellín yet? What if He was just waiting for me to crawl into this hole to bring the whole thing down? What if this was where it ends, where it was always going to end, under a ton of concrete, buried alive in the home of the mother I abandoned? But that wasn't right: she abandoned me! Just like she abandoned everything and everyone who ever mattered to her. She left her home in Colombia. She left her mother and father and sisters and brothers and cousins and all the kin I had never even met, if she even had any. And then she left her husband and her sons. She left me. See, you can't blame me for running. It's in my genes.

I started to mutter a prayer beneath my breath, the first time a prayer had crossed my lips since childhood, since before the great reckoning with God the cruel Father, God the useless Son and God the Holy fucking Ghost. I wasn't going to pray to that Trinity, no matter how bad things got, but I couldn't see the harm in appealing for the protection of the Blessed Virgin Mary, Mother of Christ, who never asked to be dragged into this holy mess in the first place. Just an innocent virgin child, knocked up by the Angel Gabriel in the only recorded instance of divine artificial insemination. I wonder if he used a syringe? Did he blow heavenly sperm through his angelic trumpet? The gospels are vague on this and many other interesting points. Mary, Mary, not a bit contrary, who suffered her whole life for the privilege of watching her only begotten son die, slowly and painfully on a cross that was probably hammered together by her husband, whispering in Jesus's ear, 'You never were a son of mine, ya bastard. Let your own father help you now.' Though the gospels are discreet on that too. Now there's a tale worth telling. Someone ought to write a musical about that. Or had they done so already? And in the darkness, I heard myself singing, 'Jesus Christ, Superstar! Walks like a woman and he wears a bra!'

And my mother slapped me across the face. What did she do that for? It's just a song they sing in the schoolyard. It doesn't mean anything, Ma!

And I can hear her and Daddy going at it in the next room, voices rising and falling in waves of accusation and counter-accusation, pleading and supplication. I know they are arguing about me. I'm responsible for this; I'm sure of it. So I crawl to the central heating vent that circulates air around our building, I open it up and listen. I can hear every conversation in the flat, and some from flats on the same floor and flats below, as the vents weave their tangled way through the whole apartment block, issuing forth a soft rumble of TV sets and radios and disembodied voices. Through it all, with the super-fine focus of a child who lives by his ears, I hone in on the only conversation I want to hear, echoing down metal pipes, my ma and da in what they foolishly imagine to be the privacy of their bedroom.

'If my mama could hear the filth that comes out of her grandson's mouth, she would die of a heart attack on the spot, *el Señor cuidarla y protegerla*.'

'They don't even know their grandmother, and she doesn't know them.'

'And whose fault is that?'

'Come on, Maria, it's a kid's song, for fuck's sake! He doesn't even know what it means. He's six years old.'

'It's not the song, Patrick, it's everything: this country, it rains all the time, the sun never shines, I'm cold in my bones. I want to go home. I want sunshine. I want my mother.'

'You think they'd be better off growing up in the fucking jungle, picking coca leaves for a few pesos so some fucking rich kids in Manhattan can snort their brains out?'

'I didn't grow up in the jungle, Patrick. What would you know about that? You've never been there.'

'And I'm never gonna go there. And neither are the boys. I've heard enough of your stories to know what it was fucking like and it wasn't fucking paradise. So if you want to fuck off back to Colombia, then you fuck off, but the boys are not going anywhere, they'll be staying right here with me. For fuck's sake, Maria! We came here to make a life!'

'You call this living?'

I stopped in the hole. I was stuck. I couldn't go ahead and I couldn't go back. I could feel something pressing down, pushing the air out of my lungs like the voices from the past were pushing my thoughts out of my head. I needed to focus, I needed to breathe, I needed to find the child, and I needed her to be alive, cause I couldn't go through all of this and pull out a corpse, and take up a limp brown doll to her father, and hear him wail, like my father had wailed, that awful crying that filled the hospital corridor, that terrible sound of hopeless, helpless abandonment. And those wild eyes, locking on to mine. 'You did this! You did this! This is all your fault!'

'Hail Mary, full of grace, the Lord is with thee, blessed art thou amongst women and blessed is the fruit of thy womb,' I was muttering, the words tumbling out from the recesses of my mind. And like an echo down the years, I could hear my mother muttering the same prayer, kneeling before the little blue and white porcelain statue of Mary which presided over a recessed corner of her bedroom, bedecked with flowers and beads and candles, wrapped in twinkling fairy lights, a magical shrine that always drew me to it, though I wasn't allowed to touch because this little statuette was her most precious object, the only thing she had brought with her all the way from the distant home she used to tell me about, where the sun always shone, and everyone was protected by the grace of the Blessed Virgin. '*Dios te salve, Maria. Llena eres de gracia: El Señor es contigo. Bendita tú eres entre todas las mujeres. Y bendito es el fruto de tu vientre. . .*'

And with those words still whispering in my ear, the bricks beneath me gave way, and I pitched down into the darkness, landing with a thump while debris rained on my head. I lay there for a while, because it was all I could do, eyes adjusting to the gloom. Light was breaking in from the hole above me, and I could see a pathway back to the blue and the face of the anxious *padre*. His mouth was moving but I couldn't hear him above the blood thundering in my ears, all I could hear was my mother still praying for my protection: '*Santa María,*

Madre de Dios, ruega por nosotros pecadores, ahora y en la hora de nuestra muerte.'

I was in some kind of a room, the ceiling sagging about three feet off the ground, but still holding, propped up by mercifully solid pieces of furniture. And slowly I realised the voice I could hear wasn't my mother's at all. There really was another voice, reciting Ave Maria in a terrified whisper. I felt a surge of mad hope. 'Where are you?' I called. The praying stopped. I thought for a moment. '*¿Donde estas?*' I asked again.

'*Aquí,*' came a pitiful little voice. Here.

I could have wept with joy and relief. I probably did, but it was so hard to tell what was going on in that black hole, I couldn't be sure if the wetness on my face was blood, sweat or tears, or all three. I crept towards the voice, talking all the time, offering whatever phrases of reassurance I could conjure from my forgotten childhood Spanish, phrases I must have heard my mother say: it's OK, little one, I'm here, there, there, don't cry, everything's all right now, where does it hurt? Mama's going to kiss it better. I crept under an upturned arm-chair, around an upturned cabinet and felt my way towards a solid wooden bed that was proudly holding up the ceiling. Reaching underneath, I touched the outstretched fingers of a tiny hand.

'*¿Papa?*' said the child.

'It's OK,' I said. '*Tengo ahora.*' I've got you now.

So we crawled out, the little girl and I, back up through the passage I had made. Sometimes I pulled her and sometimes I pushed her ahead, and being smaller, and more limber, she began to scamper as we got close to the light, and I could see her daddy reach down and she was scooped up into the blue, her little legs disappearing from view, and I could hear such a cry of anguished joy, of such terrified relief, it was like bells ringing.

There were no cheering crowds. The old man with the dusty moustache helped pull me out of the hole, patted my back and smiled, and that was about it. I clambered gingerly down from the roof, slowly becoming aware of my body, as if I was returning to myself, only to discover I had been done over in my absence, covered with cuts and bruises. I stood on the pavement swaying, aching, dizzy with dehydration. The *madre* with her broken arm and *padre* with torn fingernails expressed eternal and undying gratitude, and called upon the Virgin and the saints to bless and honour me forever and ever, amen, but they had to get to the hospital, if it was still standing.

All over the city such reunions were taking place, I supposed, some families being brought back together with ecstatic gratitude at their survival, some with sorrow and outrage at their losses. This little family were among the lucky ones, if you can call anything about having your house fall on your head good luck. And so, after hugs and blessings, they set off, the little girl looking at me shyly but clinging tightly to her father, and he to her, like they were never going to let each other go. She was such a small, brown-skinned thing, caked in dirt, hair matted with plaster, bright eyes shining, brimming over with love and fear. I could see her looking back at me as they set off down the hill. 'What's your name?' I called after her. '¿*Como te llamas*?'

'Maria!' she called back.

'That's my mother's name!' I shouted but she was already too far away to hear.

The old man brought me a glass of thick fruit juice from somewhere. Perhaps he was one of the lucky neighbours whose houses were still standing. I sat there, as the afternoon grew cooler, drinking the pungent, delicious liquid, wondering if this was the purpose of my whole journey, to come to this place, at this moment, to save this life? Would little Maria have died in there, buried under a fallen ceiling, if I hadn't run out of an awards ceremony in New York a week or more ago? But I don't believe in fate. Not fate, not God, not anything or anyone. Although, on consideration, I might be prepared to make an exception for the Virgin Mary.

At last, I peeled myself up and began to walk, so tired and hungry and beaten down I had to keep moving or I would have just passed out and slept where I lay. Still no one said anything to me, no one pointed me out as I passed. Frantic activity went on all around, oblivious to the glorious power of my celebrity, turning a blind eye to a face that launched a thousand magazine covers. Medellín was tending its gaping wounds and I was a ghost, walking through a life that could have been my own if my mother had never left Colombia behind, for reasons I had never been able to understand, to raise two children in dreary, rainy Ireland with my old man, a bitter old Paddy who could probably organise a piss-up in a brewery but wasn't much good for anything else. No earthquakes in Ireland though. No hurricanes, no mud slides, no baby assassins. At least, not round our way. We did have a dead dog once.

I found myself walking alongside a main road where traffic was starting to move again as abandoned wrecks were cleared. I had no idea where I was going, I was just shuffling in the same direction as other waifs and strays. Then a truck pulled up alongside and I thought, this is it, I've been recognised, which was kind of a relief, because I was too exhausted to run any more. The driver jerked his thumb, indicating I should get in back. I looked up to see that it was a cattle truck crammed with people, all as battered and shattered as me. Hands caked in dust reached down and I took my place among my fellow victims. Gazing down, I saw myself white and grey and brown with the detritus of the building I had crawled through. And I started to laugh. A man patted me on the knee, saying, 'Esta bien, nino. Lo peor ya pasó.' I grinned at him stupidly, and felt my face and hair. No wonder no one had recognised me. I was plastered from head to toe. I really did look like a ghost.

The truck drove on towards the outskirts of the city, and pulled into what appeared to be some kind of refugee camp, bustling with soldiers and aid workers, a mass of tents spreading out up the twilight mountainside as far as the eye could see. We disembarked and were herded towards a vast, open-fronted marquee, where we queued to be doled out rations, shuffling wordlessly along, defeated by the day and lost in our own private thoughts. A smiling but weary young woman in a sleeveless UNHCR jacket filled a plastic bowl for me with a slop of some kind of beans. '*Por favor, mantenga en movimiento,*' she said kindly, her stilted accent suggesting she was no more local than I. A fresh-faced man about my own age handed me a hunk of bread and a small bottle of water. I stared at the familiar label. It looked like one of Consuela's bottles. 'Do you need to see a doctor?' asked the woman. '*¿Un médico?*' But I shook my head, no, and hurried off to consume my precious meal. I don't know what it was but I didn't really care. It was food, and that was good enough.

Night was falling fast, a galaxy of twinkling lights appearing on the dark mountainside. I watched with childish rapture, transfixed by the power of electricity, as if the switching on of street lights was the most entertaining thing in the world. There were people all around, taking up whatever space they could find, and a boy squeezed in and hunkered down next to me, hungrily devouring his own meal. He looked about seven years old but with the self-possession of a streetwise hoodlum. 'What are those lights?' I said to him. He regarded me curiously. Remembering where I was, I translated, '*¿Que son esas, uh, uh, luces?*'

'You fucking stupid, *hombre*? Is *comunas*, everybody knows the *comunas,*' he retorted, shaking his head as if it was just his luck to be stuck next to an imbecile.

'You speak good English,' I complimented him.

'You speak very bad Spanish,' he replied. 'Over there is El Popular, over there La Salle, and this one, La Franca, I think.'

'It looks pretty from here,' I said.

'Is very pretty, *señor*. Most pretty place on earth.'

'Where do you live?' I asked.

'Is gone,' he shrugged. 'I live here.'

'Where's your *madre y padre*?'

'Gone.' His bottom lip started to jut out and tremble. Suddenly he didn't look so tough.

'Family? You got family here? Brothers, sisters?'

'Gone,' he repeated. Tears welled in his eyes.

'Who's looking after you?' I asked, thinking please don't start crying now – if you start, I'll start, and then who knows where it will stop? The whole mountainside will be bawling for its losses.

'I don't need no one look after me,' he snapped defiantly. 'I look after me, OK? Who look after you, stupid gringo? You look like you in trouble more than me.'

'What about aunts or uncles? There must be somebody,' I insisted. I didn't want to have to take responsibility for this kid just cause he sat down next to me.

'*Mi abuela*, what do you say? My mother's mother.'

'That's good,' I sighed with relief. 'Where is your grandmother?'

'Too far,' he shook his head sadly.

'Where?'

But I knew the answer before it even came out of his mouth. The fucking Virgin wasn't going to let me off the hook that easy.

'La Esperanza,' he said. My mother's home town.

'What's your name?' I asked.

'Jesus,' he said. Hey, Zeus!

It figured. 'I've got a brother with the same name as you.'

He shrugged. 'Is common.'

'Not where I'm from, it's not. Come with me, Jesus.'

'Where we go?'

'I need to clean up,' I said. 'Where are the showers? There must be somewhere I can wash?'

'I show you,' said Jesus. 'But try any funny business, I cut you *pipi* off.' And he pulled a blade out from his shorts and flashed it at me, baring his teeth.

I queued for my turn in the communal showers. The water was cold but it was good to feel the layers of dust and grime coming off. My body was livid with bruises, blood swirling in the drain from open cuts on my hands and chest and legs. My T-shirt was little more than a filthy rag but I squeezed back in to dirty jeans and Grover's torn and frayed leather jacket. Jesus had been looking at me slyly ever since I emerged from the shower, a little smile on his face. 'What is it?' I asked.

'I know who you are,' he said, grinning. Then he took hold of my hand.

As we made our way through the camp, a ripple of recognition started to spread, more and more kids gathered around, running to follow, jostling for position close to me. I felt like the Pied Piper. A child came up, solemnly holding a battered acoustic guitar, and shoved it in my hands. '*Cantar para nosotros, Zero,*' she said, and the call was taken up by other children, *cantar para nosotros, cantar para nosotros,* sing for us, sing for us. So I put the strap over my shoulders, tuned it as best I could, and started to play 'Never Young'. And as I sang the kids joined in, a whole choir of orphans, as if it was their song all along:

> *We were never young,*
> *We were born into a world*
> *You had already destroyed,*
> *Life has just begun,*
> *It's the beginning of the end*
> *For all the girls and boys.*

More and more people gathered around, drawn into the noise and spectacle, jostling to see if it was really true, was the *loco* gringo pop star Zero really here in the camp? Some big lights came on, lighting up me and my makeshift choir. A camera crew pushed through, shoving unceremoniously to the front. When the song ended, there was a huge cheer. Hands grabbed at me from all sides, while Jesus clung tightly to my waist. A woman pushed a microphone in my face and I looked straight into a lens. 'Zero,' she said. 'People have been searching for you all over the United States of America. What are you doing here?'

'I'm singing for the children,' I said. Another cheer went up.

'But how did you get here?' she persisted.

'Colombia drew me to her.'

The jostling was getting dangerous now. There were too many people pushing in, too much excitement. The guitar got snatched out of my hands and was fought over by a crowd of older children, till the neck splintered and the whole guitar came apart. I hoisted Jesus onto my shoulders. 'I'm sorry, I have to go,' I said to the reporter.

'Where are you going?' she pressed. 'Come on, talk to me, Zero, tell me what your plans are?'

By her accent, she was a US Latino, probably working for one of the American networks, too dark and pretty for front-line news, out here gathering human interest stories while the big hitters were down in Medellín digging in the rubble. Well, she had lucked out, and she knew it. 'What's your name?' I asked.

'Gabriela da Silva, FNY News.'

'Do you have a car here, Gabriela? Some kind of transport? Get me to Herrera airport and I'll give you an exclusive interview, all right?'

As we bumped down the road in the TV crew's jeep, Gabriela peppered me with questions, which I answered as straightforwardly as I could. No, I didn't know why I ran away, I just had to get some space. No, I hadn't gone mad, at least, I didn't think so. I wasn't depressed, I wasn't suicidal, and actually, now that I thought about it, I felt pretty good, better than I had in years. Maybe I was just confused for a while. Yes, I wanted to see Penelope, and I'd get there in the end, even if I had to walk the whole way. No, it wasn't all a gimmick to sell more tracks, I wish I was that smart. Yes, I was sorry for my fans who had bought tickets for my concerts but that's showbusiness and this is life, and sometimes you have to put life first. Yes, I was shocked by the devastation I had witnessed in this beautiful country – other people's troubles have a way of putting your own in perspective. No, I wasn't ready to go back and face the music. Anyway I've always got the music with me.

'Have you learned anything on your journey?' asked Gabriela, the human interest newshound, batting her lashes. She was very pretty. If I had met her two weeks ago, I'd have had her knickers around her ankles by now.

'Yeah,' I said, after some thought. 'You can't run away from yourself.'

I signalled to the cameraman that the interview was over. 'You know what the real story is here, Gabriela?' I said, pointing out to the city. 'The incredible heroism of these people faced with unimaginable catastrophe.'

'Don't kid yourself, Zero,' she said. 'People get tired of disasters, unless it happens to someone they know. We'll see what they lead with on the bulletins tonight.'

'It's a sick world,' I said.

'Thank God,' said Gabriela.

She really was a girl after my own heart. 'You're wasted down here, Gabriela. You should be doing *Breakfast With Gordy*.'

'Who knows,' smiled Gabriela. 'After this interview, I might be.'

I asked if the crew had a map of Colombia and folded it out on the back seat, my index finger trailing through the southern region while Jesus clambered over my shoulder to get a look. We drove into the airport, weaving around an obstacle course of tipped-up planes and fallen-down buildings. My heart gave a leap when I saw the sleek red form of the Baron, still parked in front of the collapsed hangar. We pulled up and there, sitting on a fold-up chair, sipping from a metal flask and puffing on a cigarette, was Grover. 'I thought I told you to wait in the damn plane,' he drawled, as I jumped out of the jeep. I noticed his jacket and hair was full of dust, like he'd been doing some digging of his own.

'Where's Consuela?' I asked.

'She's with her people,' he said. 'Where she needs to be.'

'Is she coming back?'

'You never know with women, now, do you?'

'That why you've taken up smoking again?'

'It seemed like the right time. Who's the kid, kid?'

Jesus was holding tightly on to my hand. 'He's our new passenger,' I said. 'You fuelled up, Captain?'

Grover laughed, wearily. 'Yeah, I'm ready to get the hell out of here, whenever you are.'

'Well, there's been a change of plan,' I said, pulling out the map and running my finger down to an insignificant dot, its name printed in letters so tiny they were almost illegible. La Esperanza.

'I want to go there.'

20

We slept in the Baron and took off at dawn. Grover had effected what repairs he could but the polythene flapped noisily and Jesus looked panic-stricken as we got airborne. It didn't take him long to adjust to his new circumstances, however. At first he sat on my lap in the back, silent and wide-eyed, gazing in wonder at the mountains below. Soon he was clambering all over the aircraft, peering out each window in turn, before claiming the seat next to the pilot as his own. Grinning at Grover, he took hold of the co-pilot's control column, studying the dials so intently you could have sworn he was flying the Baron. Grover found him a frayed old cap, which Jesus wore with pride, pushing it back every time it fell over his eyes. The Virgin had been straightened up to resume her observational role on the dash. There was a slight chip on the end of her nose but otherwise she looked as serene as ever.

The landscape below was magnificently inhospitable, alternating between vast grey rock as jagged and alien as the mountains of the moon, white wastelands of snow-covered peaks and slopes of dense vegetation in bands of lustrous green. Was this really my country? I felt like a visitor from another planet.

We had been in the air an hour or more, Grover poring over flight map and compass, when he started to circle around a patch of sloping jungle. 'This godforsaken *pueblo* of yours oughta be here somewhere, kid. If it still exists.'

'Of course it exists,' I shouted over the noise of the engine. 'It's on the map.'

'Things change in Colombia, kid. They've had fifty years of civil war. That's a lot of displaced people. Who do you think lives in the *comunas*?'

Then Jesus let up a shout, pointing excitedly, and we banked around and buzzed low over rooftops and yards. There wasn't a road that I could see, just a dirt drag dotted with what looked like goats and pigs scattering from the roar of the Baron.

Grover assured me there would be a strip where we could put down. 'Trust me, kid. This is *coca* country.' Eagle-eyed, on our third circle, he picked out a short, thin clearing in thick foliage high above the village, and swooped in, speeding low over treetops. The landing didn't look possible. We were coming down fast towards a narrow, bumpy dirt track, pitched at close to sixty degrees up the mountainside, with thick foliage pressing on all sides. But Grover grinned all the way, barely jarring the Baron as he touched down, braked and came to a heavy halt in front of a wall of trees. 'That's what they pay the big bucks for,' he drawled, proudly.

We clambered down to the improvised runway. There was no one around. No sound but the shrill chatter of birds and other creatures stirring among the trees. According to Grover, we were about 3,000 feet up on the west side of the southern Andes, in one of the poorest and most neglected regions of Colombia, still prone to sporadic fighting between government troops, guerrillas and narco gangs. 'I hope you know what you're doing here, kid,' he said, lighting a cigarette and pulling in a big lungful of smoke.

'Hey, Grover, cigarette for me?' Jesus piped up hopefully.

'Filthy habit,' said Grover, shaking his head. He coughed hard a couple of times, to emphasise his point.

'Where to?' I asked.

'Let's see now, does this fancy timepiece of yours have a compass?' Grover studied the Patek Philippe on his wrist. 'I'd say thataway,' he pointed.

'No, no, this way, stupid gringo,' shouted Jesus, taking off in the opposite direction.

'Have you been here before?' asked Grover.

'With *mi madre*,' shouted Jesus. 'By bus. It take many days. Not like beautiful aeroplane!' He spread his arms wide and buzzed ahead of us, as if he was flying home.

There were no signs of life as we tramped down the dirt track but we could hear animals fleeing our heavy footsteps, the shriek and click of birds and insects. The sun was high, the sky was blue, it was a beautiful day. We hiked a couple of miles down the mountainside, Jesus never tiring, until the red dirt trail opened up wide enough to be a road, and we three travellers walked into the village of La Esperanza.

A guidebook would be unlikely to describe La Esperanza as 'traditional' or 'picturesque'. It was more functional and haphazard. There were forty or more dwellings spreading in all directions off the main dirt road, some solid adobe bungalows but most just shacks built from rough wood planks and corrugated metal, everything slightly warped and twisted, gaudy colours fading in the sun. Chickens scratched in the dirt, dogs lazed in the shade, pigs snuffled in straw-laden pens. A skinny cow regarded us coolly, then went back to masticating. There were mules tethered to rusting cars only fit for scrap. Laundry hung from lines spread hither and thither, colours faded with wear and washing. Women looked on uneasily, frozen in the middle of domestic tasks, some weaving and sewing, some scrubbing, some tending animals. Small children, displaying none of their mothers' reserve, came scampering out to race around us. A group of elderly men sat smoking in the shade beneath a large open structure of wooden poles suspending a corrugated roof, and they too watched silently, making no move towards us. Dominating the village was a small, gracefully constructed white church with a thick thatched roof and freshly whitewashed adobe walls. In its shade stood a solid, oblong building with a smart, civic air and rows of wide-open windows, at which could be seen the eager faces of children, peering at us, pointing and chattering. A hand-painted sign over wide red doors declared it ESCUELA DE SAN PATRICIO. What the fuck was Ireland's patron saint doing up here in the Andes? Incongruously, flying above the civic building, alongside the Colombian flag of yellow, blue and red, was what looked distinctly like an Irish tri-colour: green, white and orange. Parked next to this building was a white minibus which, apart from a little mud spatter around the wheels, and a hand-painted La Esperanza, looked as if it might have just been delivered fresh from the factory floor. The seats were still covered in plastic shrink-wrap.

'I smell coke money,' muttered Grover, warily.

The doors of the school crashed open and forty or more children exploded out, dashing to surround us. There were kids aged from four or five to maybe eleven or twelve, boys and girls, colourfully dressed in T-shirts and shorts. Their boldness seemed to release the adults, who moved to join the gathering. I looked into their beautiful faces, the dark eye-brows, wide cheekbones, high-bridged noses, aquiline jaws. This was the blend of native Indian and European locals called *mestizo*, the same features I saw in the mirror every day.

No one was calling my name or humming my tunes, yet they seemed agitated by my presence all the same. A girl grabbed at my hair and shouted *El Rojo*, The Red. It spread like a whisper from one to the other, *El Rojo, El Rojo, El Rojo*. Jesus was hopping up and down, I couldn't tell whether from nervousness or excitement. I scooped him up in my arms and held him aloft. *'¿Alguien conoce a este niño?'* I asked loudly. Does anyone know this child?

'Jesus!' shrieked a plump old woman, stepping up to take him from me with strong arms and a smile of toothless joy.

'Abuelita!' gushed Jesus, hugging her tight.

'Goddamn, I love a family reunion,' drawled Grover.

A path was cleared through the crowd so that another old woman could be escorted to the front, children hanging on to her wiry arms. She was small and leathery, grey flecking her long black hair, but she had been a beauty once, and there was a hint of vanity in her print dress and bead necklace. She was clearly of high standing in this village, one of the elderly men pushing children away so she could reach me unmolested. She studied me intently. '*Sabía que vendrías un día,*' she said.

I knew you would come one day.

She took me by the hand and led me towards a pink adobe cottage. It was a simple little house yet conspicuously the nicest in the village, with its own low wall around a carefully cultivated garden. There was a mural, primitively yet boldly painted by the front door, showing the Virgin Mary in blue and white holding a naked baby with a full head of flaming red hair. He was the first ginger Jesus I had ever seen. El Rojo.

The cool, shady interior was simply but warmly furnished, with woven rugs and blankets artfully arranged into a kaleidoscope of colour and pattern. She led me on, into another, smaller room. Candles burned beneath a statuette of the ubiquitous Virgin, blue and white and beatific. Behind the statuette, the wall was covered in photographs, carefully assembled to make the shape of a cross. I stepped closer to examine the pictures in the dim, flickering light. It was hard to breathe. I knew most of these photos. I had seen them before, a long time ago. There were photographs of birthdays and holidays and Christmas meals and play dates and new school uniforms and silly faces and kisses and hugs. And, in all of the pictures, there were members of a family, smiling happily. A father. A brother. A mother.

The old woman reached out and touched a picture of a brown-faced, blue-eyed, red-headed boy, uncomfortable but proud in a shirt, tie and green Kilrock Junior uniform, on his first day at school. 'Pedro,' she said. And turned to smile at me.

'Grandma?' I replied, trembling.

I don't know how long I stood in that room, looking at the pictures while my grandmother ran her fingers through my hair. I don't think I had seen a single one of those photographs in over a decade. The family albums never came out after my mother died. Her face had slowly faded from my memory, her brown eyes had been erased, her wide mouth rubbed out, the freckles across her broad nose had vanished one by one. Her lustrous black hair had lingered longest but it too had disappeared in time, until all that was left was an empty red dress, and then nothing.

I delicately unpinned one of the pictures from the wall and stared at my mother's gorgeous face, caught in an unguarded moment, hair blowing so that a strand trailed across her mouth, laughing unselfconsciously, so young, so free, so happy, so alive. In the background, I recognised the streets of New York. I wondered when my mother had been there, and who had taken that picture, from before I was even born.

My grandmother stroked my neck. '*Ah, Maria,*' she said. '*Mi Maria. Te pareces a ella.*'

You look just like her.

I had to get some air. Outside, a big wooden table was being assembled under the old men's awning, and it looked like a feast was being prepared. Women were bringing dishes from their houses – there was already bread and meats and tomatoes and potatoes and pomegranates and mangoes. Bowls of thick bean stew started to arrive. Grover was tucking in, knocking back cups of clear liquid with the old guys, a roving eye taking in the unselfconscious beauty of the younger women. 'All right, kid?' he asked, as I slumped down next to him. Children kept coming up and touching my hair, smiling and saying El Rojo.

'I don't know,' I admitted. 'I don't know anything any more.'

'Yeah, this country will drive you *loco*, every time. Come drink some of this fine *aguardiente* with me and my *amigos*. They got the good stuff up here in the mountains. Make you see straight again. Or double. I can't remember which is better.' He waved an arm, and one of the old men filled my cup. I took a slug and felt a burn hit the back of my throat and explode in my chest. It was like sour vodka. I put it down. I needed to keep a hold on things.

'There's a joke they tell in Colombia,' said Grover. 'When God made the world, He gave Colombia two oceans, the Pacific and the Caribbean, three mountain ranges, the bluest sky, the greenest emeralds and oil and gold and the greatest abundance of wildlife, forests and rivers anywhere on the planet. So the Archangel, who's doling it all out, he says, wait a minute, *Señor*, are you sure you wanna give all these fabulous riches to one country? Isn't that a little unfair to the rest of the world? And God thinks about it, and He says, "You're right! But wait till you see the people I'm gonna put there!"'

Grover let out what sounded like a low, bitter chuckle.

'I don't get it,' I admitted.

He looked offended. 'The people, kid. The Colombian people. The laziest, most violent, mistrustful, thieving sons of bitches ever to put down in paradise.'

'The people seem pretty fine to me,' I said.

'Yeah, beautiful people, every goddamn one of them. They give the world ninety per cent of its cocaine, and for that, the world is truly thankful. And if, along the way, they have broken all records for the murder and kidnapping of their fellow citizens; fought civil wars for so long that nobody can remember who's fighting who or for what; killed, enslaved and displaced millions of poor peasants . . . well, why dwell on the negative? *Salud.*' He knocked back another cup.

'You married a Colombian,' I reminded him.

'Only after she tried to kill me,' he pointed out. '*Salud!*'

'How much of this firewater have you drunk, Grover?'

'It don't take much these days, kid,' he admitted sadly. 'Ain't touched a drop in fifteen years.'

'Jesus Christ, man, pull yourself together,' I said. 'Consuela leaves you alone for one night and you're drinking and smoking like a trooper.'

'Well, I don't know if she's coming back,' he confessed, sadly. 'Never could figure out if that woman ever really wanted to be with me, or was just paying a debt. We should've had kids but . . . well . . .' He lost himself briefly in some private torment, a grimace flickering over his face. 'Will you be my kid, kid?'

'I'm sure she loves you, Grover.'

'Oh yeah? What makes you such an expert on love? All those dumb pop songs? How about Penelope Nazareth? Tell me about the great movie star. Does she love you? Damn, kid, I used to moon over her back in the day. What do you think she sees in a skinny runt like you?'

'I don't know,' I admitted.

'She's been through a few like you in her time, the old girl, ain't she? No offence, kid. Wasn't she married to Johnny Pitt or Brad Depp? Or was that a movie?'

'It was a movie,' I said. But there had been a few like me in my time, as Beasley was wont to point out.

'Damn, kid, you and me we should just settle down here in the mountains, pick a couple of beautiful peasant girls, just a couple each, and live like kings.'

'Where are all the men?' I asked.

'Working,' he said. 'An honest day's toil for a dishonest day's pay. There are coca plants to be cultivated. And there's probably some little *bossas* hidden around here somewhere, where they cook up the base, then wait for a guy like me to take it north, where some little jerk with a pass grade in high school chemistry will turn it into white gold.'

'*Coca!*' agreed one of the old men enthusiastically, bashing his mug off Grover's.

'This doesn't look like some hardcore drug operation to me,' I said, sceptically.

'Listen, kid, no offence meant. Coca's been growing in these hills since before man even arrived. It's just a leaf. Grows wild around here. Coffee too. They probably grow a little plantain, cassava, sugar cane – everything we are eating here they grow themselves. Resourceful little bastards. But the only thing anyone wants to take off their hands is coca. And they don't want to pay too much for it, neither, and if they can get it for nothing they will. So the guerrillas come in for their cut, and the cops come in for their cut, and the local government comes in for its cut, and every now and then the military fly over and spray the mountain with pesticide cause el presidente has to be able to lock arms with his *compadre* in the White House and tell the world they're doing all they can to fight the War on Drugs, even though everybody knows they are lying through their coke-stained teeth. We lost that war before time began, cause it's a war against humanity itself. It's like telling your cock not to get hard at the sight of a beautiful woman. We were born to get high, dammit. From the first time some damn caveman stumbled on a bush of fermented berries we've been getting out of our skulls every damn chance we get. Life is hard. How you supposed to make it to the end of the day without a little drink?'

'I thought you did fifteen years, Grover,' I said, trying to calm him down. Our hosts were starting to look alarmed.

'For the love of a good woman,' he said, slugging back another cup. 'You know what joke God really played on this country? It wasn't the people. Nothing wrong with these beautiful people. Best damn people on earth! He gave them the

sun, and He gave them the sea, and He gave them the mountains. And then, to even things out a little bit, he gave them
the coca leaf. Yeah. That put the cat among the pigeons. And
through all of the corruption and stupidity and robbery and
murder that drives this multi-billion-dollar business, a guy up
here in the mountains could work with his bare hands all
month to cultivate enough coca to earn his family . . . what?
Fifty dollars? How much cocaine would that buy at one of
your Hollywood parties, kid? Less than a gram, I bet.'

'I wouldn't know,' I said.

'Clean-living kid, huh?'

'I'm a pop star, Grover. I don't pay for my drugs.'

He laughed. 'I like you, kid.'

An old man with a thick, proud moustache patted Grover
on the shoulders and nodded sympathetically. I don't know
how much he had understood of Grover's rant, if anything,
but he seemed to be mulling it over. '*Siempre duro*,' he said,
'*Siempre duro*.' Things are always hard. I had heard the expression somewhere before. But the way he spoke the words, it
was not a cause for complaint, just a fact of life.

Grover rattled his empty mug but a tall, straight-backed
woman stepped forward and took away the bottle. 'I think your
friend has had enough,' she said, in careful, precise English.

'I'll tell you when I've had enough, dammit,' said Grover,
but when he looked into her proud, calm face, he mumbled
an apology and tucked sloppily into the food instead.

'What your friend says is true,' the woman said. 'Life has
always been hard in La Esperanza but there is no shame in

that. Life is hard everywhere. Many young people leave, cause they think there will be an easier life in the city. It does not always work out that way.'

Her name was Doña Cecilia Augusta and she was one of two teachers who ran the Escuela de San Patricio. She herself had left La Esperanza as a girl but she had returned, bringing some tattered dreams and educational skills to the village. 'I will never leave again,' she says. 'I have seen too many terrible things down there. Up here in the mountains, the soldiers come, the soldiers go, but we are always here, like the trees and the birds. Where else is there to be?'

'And my mother?' I said.

Doña Cecilia smiled. 'I knew your mother,' she said. 'She was a little older than me but she was a beautiful girl, brave and kind and resourceful. She left a long time ago, after her father died. Maria was an only child, there was no bread-winner in the family and she didn't want to work in the fields, nor did she want to marry, so she chose to leave the mountain and earn money and send it back to her mother. You did not know this?'

'I don't know anything about my mother,' I said.

Doña Cecilia said something to my grandmother, who hadn't let me out of her sight the whole time. The old woman nodded, got up, and walked back to her house.

'How did my grandfather die?' I asked.

'Everybody dies,' said Doña Cecilia. 'It is not important how.' But she spoke to the old men in Spanish, and the *hombre* with the thick moustache went into an animated monologue that seemed to go on for quite a while, and involved guitar playing and shooting. 'He was killed by some soldiers,' announced Doña Cecilia at the end. 'I don't know which ones, they are always changing.'

My grandmother returned, tenderly clutching a bundle of envelopes tied up with a red ribbon. She placed the bundle gravely before me, like a sacred offering.

My hands trembled as I tugged out the first envelope, examining an address scrawled in childish yet painfully neat handwriting. There was a faded yellow-and-blue stamp, and a florid postmark on which I could just make out the last part of the date, 1989. I gently extracted a single sheet of paper from inside the envelope. It was ringed in pink, with floral margins. A girl's paper.

'*Estimado Madre*' I read. '*Le escribo para hacerle saber que estoy a salvo y bien.*'

'What does it say?' I asked. My eyes were so full of tears the words were swimming on the page. And anyway, although I could understand most of what I heard around me, I had never learned to read Spanish.

Doña Cecilia took the letter from me, and read out: 'Dear Mother, I write to let you know I am safe and well.'

Doña Cecilia explained that there was a postal delivery to La Esperanza on a truck, once a month, or at least most months, and there was usually a letter, sometimes containing some dollars, whatever she could afford, sometimes containing a money order that could be cashed whenever one of the men visited the nearest town, a treacherous drive down the

341

mountain. And there were pictures of her life and stories of her adventures in America and then in Ireland. All of the village was proud of Maria, and what she had made of her life. The letters came every month for thirteen years. And then they stopped.

'Would you like me to read to you?' asked Doña Cecilia.

I nodded numbly. I couldn't speak.

'We will sit in your grandmother's house. It is the nicest house in the village,' she said.

We sat there all afternoon, the schoolteacher and I, while she read to me in her perfectly enunciated English, and my grandmother sat with us, nodding and smiling, as if she could understand every word.

And so, after more than a decade of silence, I heard my mother speak again.

21

Dear Mother, I write to let you know I am safe and well.

*The journey was long, so long, and tiring, so tiring, but
wonderful too, driving across this beautiful country of ours,
skies so wide, mountains so blue, just to be a dot in the
landscape makes me feel tiny and enormous, like I am a
part of something bigger than myself. My bones are still
rattling from Emilio's bus. I spent three days shaking up and
down, shaking up and down, even shaking in my sleep, and
shaking awake. Emilio says he is the greatest and safest
driver in the world but I think he is just the shakiest. But he
is a kind man, and he looked out for me all during the trip,
just as you asked him. All the people on the bus were kind.
We shared food, and told each other about our lives. Some
gave me addresses in Medellín, to help me look for work.
When soldiers got on to check our papers, one old fellow
told them I was his granddaughter and they should treat me
with respect. They were just joking with me and even shared
some chocolate. I don't think they were very much older*

*than me. Boys with guns. That's our country, Mother, it's
scary sometimes. I miss Father.*

*What can I say about Medellín? It is beneath a range of
mountains but nothing like the mountains of home. They
are grey instead of blue, dark and brooding, standing guard
over the city. But the city is climbing up the side of the
mountains, the city gets everywhere. It's a jungle made of
brick and glass and concrete and steel. The monkeys and
birds flit about, hanging from the wires, perching on the
windowsills, chattering loudly to be heard above the noise of
the traffic. There are buildings taller than the trees in our
forest, where you could fit everyone in Esperanza on just
one floor and still have room left over. I know it sounds
frightening but I am not frightened. Some people say you
can get lost in the city but I have this feeling, a special
feeling, that I am going to be found.*

*Well, I found a room anyway, which is a beginning. It is
in a place called El Popular, which, as you can imagine, is
very popular. The room is small but it has everything I
need, a basin to wash, a bed to sleep, and the Virgin to keep
me company. I say my prayers every night, Mother, and I
pray for you and all our family and all my friends. I have a
window that looks out on Medellín, and I am still amazed
about how it fills up my eyes. At night the whole city lights
up, it is like nothing I have ever imagined. It spreads out in
every direction you look, houses and people and streets and
roads and people and people and more people. I've heard
the old men speak about it so many times, I've read about it*

in books, and still it is hard to believe there could be so many people crowded into one place, racing about like ants when you poke a nest with a stick. Everyone is busy, busy, busy all the time, with somewhere to go and something to do. There is plenty of work, at least, which is good, because tomorrow I will find a job. Say a prayer for me, Mother, I am nervous but excited about my future. I will send money as soon as I have some. I love you, always and forever. Maria.

It was strange to hear my mother's voice bubbling through those letters, young and excited and nervous, always emphasising the positive. Details were sometimes a bit sketchy, with strange gaps in the information she offered, and I got the feeling she was trying to spare her mother the worst. It turned out it was not so easy to find decent work but she was getting by, doing cleaning jobs, and you could tell she was dazzled by the city, the way she reported little things that struck her, like the constant traffic, the handsome soldiers, the hustle of markets, the smell of perfumes and hand creams and luxuries she had never known before. But something must have happened because she wrote that she had decided to continue her travels, saying that Medellín could be a rough city, and the boys did not always behave like gentlemen.

'What age was my mother then?' I asked.

Doña Cecilia consulted my grandmother. 'Seventeen,' she informed me.

I had never imagined my mother at seventeen. Younger even than I was when I left home to tour with The Zero Sums.

And I thought I was such a bold adventurer, on the road at nineteen, even though there was always a hotel, always my band around to share highs and lows, always someone looking after me. What must it have been like for my mother, poor, barely educated and alone, travelling through unknown territory with just the hope of a better life waiting somewhere?

Letters came from Panama and Costa Rica, telling of journeys in buses and trains and on the backs of trucks, sometimes travelling with livestock. In Panama, she saw the sea for the first time, and spent most of a letter trying to describe it to her landlocked mother: something so big it stretches beyond what the eye or the mind could comprehend, big enough to lose mountains in, and always moving, always shifting in your vision. She loved the sea but she was afraid of it too, because she had never learned to swim. She was finding jobs in bars and tourist hotels. The pay wasn't good, and she was sorry she couldn't send more money, but the things tourists left behind when they checked out, why, a girl practically didn't have to buy anything for herself. They must be very rich in the United States, where most of the tourists came from. The letters were full of gossip about that vast nation to the north, where everyone lived in a big house with hot and cold running water all the time. Or so it seemed on television, the wonder of wonders, which showed stories all day long of beautiful ladies and handsome men who never went anywhere without music, all kinds of music, like she had never heard before. Papa would have loved the television, she was sure. One day, she hoped, they would have television in La Esperanza, then her mother could see for herself.

Mexico City overwhelmed her: the skyscrapers, the lights, more people than you could even imagine were in the world. She felt like she was living in the future. She got a job on a production line making plastic dolls that cried and wet themselves. They were sent north to the USA, where she thought they must really love children to want toys like these. And she was working in a nightclub as well, where there was wonderful music, all kinds of music – mariachi, jazz, swing and pop – and oh, how she loved music, but how she missed her *padre*. She did not like the way Mexican men treated their women and she did not plan to stay there long. She was saving up, she had heard of people who would take you across the border for a thousand dollars, and then, anything was possible. But how long would it take her to earn $1000? She might be stuck in Mexico for years, with the promised land almost within touching distance, so close she could feel it. There was a song girls sang in the club, from an old musical, and she liked to join in the chorus, about living in America, where everything is free. One day, *Madre,* one day.

For a while, the letters from Mexico fell into a pattern, talking about musicians in the club and friends she was making. It seemed she might be settling into her life, living in an apartment with two other girls, earning honest wages. Even the Mexican boys weren't so bad when you got to know them. Then she met a man who said he could get her a ticket to New York. To fly, in an aeroplane! All she had to do was carry some things for his friends. Her mother was not to be worried, it was strictly business, but she wanted her to know that, whatever happened, she really, really loved her.

Oh no, I thought, my mama was a drug mule.

She made it to New York. She kept the statue of the Virgin with her all the time, to guide and protect her. The man did not pay what he had promised but at least she was in the city of her dreams, which was everything she had imagined and more. There were underground trains and yellow taxis and music coming from cars and shops and apartments. And the food, Mama, the food! Garbage cans were overflowing and there were rats the size of dogs picking off the leftovers. Nobody could ever starve in America.

She got a job working as a cleaner in a hotel where there were lots of Latino people, which is what Colombians and Costa Ricans and Mexicans were all called in New York, and they stuck together. When she was tired, when things weren't going so well, she thought of something the old men in the village always used to say, *siempre duro*, life is always hard. It was so true, even in America, but she knew this was only the beginning. There was a song they sang in New York: if you can make it here, you can make it anywhere. She believed it. It was like a prayer for the future. She had started singing at nights in a Colombian restaurant, with some Colombian musicians, singing the old songs that filled her with longing for home. People seemed to like it. They told her she was very pretty, and she had a nice voice, and if she stuck at it she could go far.

'She was a singer?' I asked in amazement.

'All of your family are musicians,' said Doña Cecilia. 'Your grandfather, may he rest in peace, was a wonderful musician and his father before him. Music runs in the family. Are you a musician too?'

I nodded dumbly.

'Your grandmother has many instruments here, you must play us a song later,' said Doña Cecilia.

My mother's confidence, her language and handwriting improved, letter by letter. All that reading she used to do as a child in school was paying off, she boasted. She was learning to speak American in night classes, and was getting so good at it the manager moved her to reception. No more cleaning, now she had a smart uniform and talked to the guests and they talked to her. Some were famous stars. You were never supposed to admit you recognised them but she did anyway. She knew them all from television, which she watched religiously during her spare time, trying to catch up on everything she had missed growing up in the mountains. There was such a lot to learn, like what to wear, and what to drive, what to eat, what perfume went best with what lipstick and what detergent to wash your clothes with. The advertisements were the best for that but she also liked MTV, a channel that just played music the whole time. Any hour of the day and night, there would be someone dancing and singing, and they always had fabulous clothes and beautiful hair. She loved pop music, especially Michael Jackson, who was a white man who was really black, or a black man who had turned white. Anything could happen in showbusiness and it didn't matter, people loved you if you could sing. Papa would have been a pop star in New York, she thought. They played music in the hotel all the time, softly through speakers in the background, very strange music that didn't really have a beat at all. It was a very strange hotel, really. It was dark all the time, they kept the lights very low, and she worried that might be because it wasn't very clean, and she had to talk to the Latino girls very strictly, to keep them on their toes. Even the porters wore suits and looked very elegant, maybe because none of them were really porters. They were actors and musicians and writers and painters, super talented guys who did their real work on nights off. This was the amazing thing about New York: everybody was really somebody else, just like her. And it was there, in her hotel, she met a handsome Irish boy named Patrick Noone.

A boy!

It wasn't so hard to picture my mother as young because I barely had a sense of her at all, but it was impossible to conceive that my father might have once been young too. He worked as a porter in the hotel, apparently, and he was full of fun and always joking and teasing her, but in such a nice way that she knew he liked her. I wondered if this could really be the same sour Paddy Noone who had raised me, who was about as much fun as a death at a birthday party. She said he loved music too, which was news to me. His favourite was an Irish band called U2, who had a singer named Bono, like a ticket, who dressed like the devil and always wore dark glasses, even at night. That's how you knew he was a star. But it wasn't really her kind of music, too fierce and scary. She liked songs she could sing while she worked. Patrick took her to see *The Phantom Of The Opera* in the Broadway theatre on their first date, and you could tell my mother was very taken with this, cause she spent several pages relating the plot in great detail. The songs were so romantic they made her cry but she couldn't stop listening to them, because Patrick had bought her the CD.

Letter after letter was filled with my father, and to believe my mother he was the most dashing and romantic suitor who ever made suit. And the thing she liked most about him, weirdly, was that he was the only person she knew who didn't want to be anyone else. He liked being himself, working in a hotel, living in New York and being with her. Mother, she announced solemnly in a particularly florid missive from 1992, I think I am in love.

Her letters were growing giddy. She had joined up with one of the Colombian musicians from her old restaurant gig, only he had moved on and wanted to form a duo playing electro-Latino hip-hop music, which was too complicated to describe in a letter, but he had big ideas about the future and thought she could be a star. Imagine! Her voice would be on the radio, her face would be on MTV. She would be rich and famous and build a palace for her mother, and install television in every room.

Then disaster struck. Mother, I have some news, began the letter. She had a show playing a warehouse party in the Bronx, which was a very cool part of New York, and they were being well paid. Only it turned out to be an illegal party, filled with Latino immigrants, and it was raided by police and everyone was arrested. And she didn't have a Green Card so she was being held in an immigration centre. She lost her job in the hotel. She wasn't even allowed back to her apartment to get her things. They told her she would be deported. Oh, Mama, she would never see Patrick again. But she told her mother not to worry, not to shed a tear, she was safe, she was being looked after, and at least she would soon be back in Colombia and they would be reunited. She might even be home before this letter.

'So did she come home?' I said.

'No, she never came home,' said Doña Cecilia. And she showed me the next letter, with a stamp from Ireland.

It was the longest letter yet and full of news. Patrick turned up at the centre, even though it meant he would be deported too, because he did not have a Green Card either. But he brought a priest and an immigration lawyer and it was hard for her to tell her mother this, she felt deeply ashamed, but she was pregnant and Patrick was the father. They were married in the immigration compound and afterwards they danced to a song on the CD player, 'All I Ask Of You', from *The Phantom Of The Opera*. It would be her and Patrick's song from now on. Then they were put on a flight for Dublin in Ireland, which would be her new home. And the letter was signed *Señora Maria Noone*.

And so the newlyweds arrived in Ireland with nothing to live on but love. They travelled out west to stay with Patrick's folks but that arrangement didn't last long, because, as I knew from my father's dark mutterings, my Irish kin were not enthusiastic about welcoming a South American peasant into the family. Oh I knew all about that, all right. The Irish took a perverse pride in calling themselves the blacks of Europe but they were as white as the potatoes they stuffed in their stupid faces and every minority needs another minority to persecute. I thought of my brown-skinned mother arriving in small town Kilrock and wanted to weep for her hopeful innocence.

They got jobs in a hotel, Patrick as a porter and a cleaning job for her. It was a step down from reception but she was sure everything would work out in the end, when people got to know her. Ireland was very green, as green as the forests that covered the mountains back home. And if the sky was almost always grey, well, at least her husband's eyes were blue, and she could lose herself in them. And if it rained all night and day, well, there was sunshine in his smile to warm her heart. And if their apartment was cramped and cold, all the more reason to take refuge in bed. And what could it possibly matter if people were sometimes unkind, and looked at her like she was a freak, or looked right through her and didn't see her at all? All she needed was Patrick, and all he needed was her.

And then there were three. My brother came along, and they named him Patrick Jnr, after his father, and Jesus, after our Lord and Saviour, and he was a fat white baby, who looked so like his daddy it was strange to think she had carried him inside her brown belly. There were letters full of nappies and first steps and first words but it wasn't hard to detect darkness looming beneath her repeated declarations of the joys of motherhood, as if she was trying to convince herself as much as her mother. She often dreamed of home, and home was always La Esperanza, and when it rained in the mountains it was a relief, not the constant drizzle that enveloped Kilrock like a cloud that would never move on. Life was hard and money was scarce and *siempre duro*. Oh, and by the way, she thought she might be pregnant again.

And so it came to pass that a child was born, and the child was me. I listened with amazement as she described my arrival as if it were an epic religious battle. I was taking so long a doctor wanted to cut me out, but she refused, and Patrick stayed and held her hand while she pushed and pushed and prayed to the Virgin Mary, who had never let her down so far, and all of a sudden there I was, skinny and brown with a great shock of red hair on my head, black eyes popping in amazement, like a little alien who had just landed on Planet Earth. I was such a scrawny little thing, so small and vulnerable, her heart went out to me, and she knew she would have to love and protect me forever. She was afraid I was never going to catch a breath, she wondered if my lungs would even have the power to take in air, but the cry that I let out, oh, *Madre*! Such a noise! And she smiled a secret smile, because she knew that I was from her side of the family. But

Patrick said the red hair proved I was from his side. What a strange creature I was, their own *mestizo* baby. And she named me Pedro after her dear father, and Patrick chose the name Ulysses after a big book he carried with him all the way to New York and back, because in Ireland they said it was the best book ever written, but he never got past the first few pages, and now, if he had his own little Ulysses, he could put it away and not think about it again.

And so the letters went on, and they became a litany of happiness, without quarrel or complaint, except about the weather, which she never got used to. There were no fights reported, no glowering arguments between husband and wife about where they should raise their children, no twinges of doubt that she had married a man content to work as a porter and never try to better himself. Instead they were filled with the everyday joys of family life, underpinned by her slow but rewarding integration into Kilrock's community, especially through voluntary work at St Patrick's Church with a kind young priest, Father Martin, who practically made it his mission to help people see past her skin colour and into her pure heart. The Irish weren't so bad when you got to know them, which was a good thing, because there were three Irishmen she loved more than anything in the world: her handsome, noble husband and two healthy, happy boys. Especially Pedro, her secret favourite.

And here, at last, was something I never imagined I would hear in my life, my mother's words describing her love for me.

Little Pedro, Madre, he is such a scamp, he drives his father crazy. He won't do a thing that Patrick tells him, till I think his daddy's head is going to pop in frustration. But all I have to do is smile and speak to him softly, and Pedro does whatever he is told. Patrick says he is a mother's boy and it's just lucky he has such a wonderful mother.

He lives in his own imagination. He doesn't need friends to play with, he can occupy himself for hours and hours, playing games in his own head. In Pedro's eyes, our little apartment is a palace, and Kilrock is the greatest kingdom on earth, and those funny little Irish hills are towering mountains he has to conquer. This morning, he was dashing around, mumbling and shouting and singing to himself, as usual, and Patrick says, 'What planet is that boy on?' and Pedro stopped, blinked, and said, 'Earth, silly Dad!' I love that little boy's mind. I tell him I want to know everything that is going on in there, so he draws me fantastic pictures of dinosaurs and spaceships and alien creatures and says, 'There, Mama, that's what I saw today.'

Pedro is very clever, the cleverest in his class for reading and writing, all his teachers say so. He takes after me, Madre! He writes poems for me, and they are so lovely and funny. Here is one he gave me today:

> *Every boy has got a mother*
> *But I've got a mother like no other*
> *Her hair is black, her skin is brown*
> *The prettiest mama in our ugly old town*

Mama and me, brown as can be
Swinging like monkeys in the funky tree
Oh how happy we're going to be
My brown mama and her brown baby.

He makes up little melodies and sings them to me. He loves to come and hear me sing with the church choir, and always joins in, and asks Father Martin when he can sing in church. I think he will be a musician, like his grandfather. Patrick says not to encourage him. He said we only hear about rich musicians but most are poorer than us, like the bands who come and play in the hotel and are always trying to get free beer. He says Pedro is too much of a dreamer already and life is hard enough even without dreams. But I am not listening to him. I have been teaching Pedro to play guitar, and we play and we sing and we laugh, how we laugh, Madre.

I could see the guitar now, in the bedroom, next to the Virgin. A little Spanish guitar that my mother bought in the charity shop. It only has five strings, one of the plastic machine heads is broken and it never stays in tune but that doesn't matter to us. I can feel my mother's arms around me, holding me from behind, hair falling on my face, hands holding my hands, helping my fingers find the chord shapes. 'One day I know he will make me very proud,' she wrote to her mother.

And I heard a voice whispering in the lengthening shadows. 'Make me proud.' I looked up at Doña Cecilia through tears.

Oh, the tears, Mother, no wonder there were so many tears, I'd been holding them back for years and years and years. Now I couldn't stop them coming.

Doña Cecilia had the next letter in her hands. And with shock, I realised it was the last unopened letter. I didn't know if I wanted her to read it, because after this, my mother would fall silent again. I was filled with fear about what that letter might contain, what terrible events were about to bring her story to an end. I realised I didn't even want to know the answer to that mystery, because there was a part of me that had never truly believed she was dead at all. All the time, all these years, I kept a precious little nugget of hope buried so deep inside I didn't even know it was there myself. And it was that little nugget that brought me here, guided me across continents, all the way to the village of my mother's birth. And the hope, so bitter, so absurd, was that I would find her up here in the mountains, waiting for me, knowing one day I would come. Because she had never really left me. She had left Ireland, because that country had been so cruel to her, and she had left my father, because he was just a brooding, angry, small-minded hotel porter who wouldn't let her take her children to her village in the sun, and she had left my brother, because he was my father's son. But she had never left me, not me, not her beloved Pedro, because she knew in her secret heart that our bond was so strong I would find my way back to her one day, I would find my way home.

And here I was. And all that was left of that hope was the letter in Doña Cecilia's hands, the paper sheet she was carefully unfolding, gently smoothing out with the palm of her hand. And clearing her throat. And taking a sip of water. And I wanted to tell her to stop. I wanted to beg her not to read it. But though I opened my mouth, no words came out.

'*Estimado Madre,*' she began. I closed my eyes, waiting for the blow to fall.

But the story had no ending, it was just another letter, full of mundane domestic detail. Patrick was healthy and well, and Patrick Jnr had started secondary school and looked so handsome and grown-up in his new uniform. *And Pedro wants a bicycle* wrote my mother from beyond the grave.

He goes on and on about it. Patrick tells him he can share Patrick Jnr's bike, which, of course, is too big and Patrick Jnr will never let him ride it. But what Pedro doesn't know is that Patrick has built him a bicycle from scrap. He is so good with his hands. It is a lovely thing to see him take old rusted parts people toss away and weld and hammer and bolt them into the most beautiful machine I have ever seen. I love to watch him work with such concentration and joy. Patrick can mend anything and people bring him broken things all the time. Father Martin lets him use the garage behind the church. He says Patrick should set up a business and stop letting everyone exploit him but Patrick says it is just a hobby. But what a wonderful hobby. I can't wait to see Pedro's little face light up when we show his new bicycle to him.

Which was strange, because I couldn't picture my old man ever picking up a tool. Shelves could buckle and bend and they'd stay that way forever, you just had to learn how to balance things on them so they wouldn't fall off. The sofa in our apartment was propped up with bricks on one side. The hot tap stopped working in the kitchen sink and never got replaced, we just used the cold tap instead. You had to take the lid off the toilet cistern to flush it. The picture of domestic bliss that my mother's letters described was a fairytale to me. All I could remember was an empty flat with three angry people rattling around, shouting at one another. And I didn't remember any bicycle. I used to walk everywhere.

Yet something was tugging at me, spinning like spokes in my mind.

And suddenly I could see myself freewheeling down an Irish road on a summer's day, wind in my hair, filled with the thrill of speed. And it was, indeed, a beautiful thing, a bright red frame with gleaming chrome handlebars.

I was coming down a hill like a speed demon, like a rocket man, like a bat out of hell, standing high in the pedals, roaring with pleasure. And there was someone on the bicycle behind me, sitting astride the saddle, arms wrapped tight around my body. And she was screaming too. Screaming with exhilaration. Screaming with fearful excitement. Screaming for me to stop.

Oh, Mama.

And the wheels were spinning upside down on the road, spinning like they were never going to stop. And I could hear my father's voice, echoing down the hospital corridor.

'You did this.'

There was nothing more in the letter. Just '*Afectuosamente, Maria*'.

'There were no letters for a long time,' said Doña Cecilia. 'Months went by. And then this arrived.'

My grandmother had produced a final envelope, which she sombrely handed to Doña Cecilia. I recognised the handwriting. I had seen that spidery, uneven scrawl so many times before. It was a letter from my father.

It did not contain much detail. It was written in quite poor Spanish, Doña Cecilia explained, but she would translate as best she could.

It was dated November 2004.

Dear Mother,

I am so sorry to have to tell you that our beloved Maria has passed away. There was a terrible accident from which she never recovered. I know she loved you very much and her thoughts were with you always. We will miss her.
Your son
Patrick.

'And that's it?' I cried, angrily. 'That's all he had to say? You never heard from him again?'

'No,' said Doña Cecilia. 'No more letters. But every month since then, money arrives. Sometimes it has been twenty dollars, sometimes a hundred dollars or more. And then, two years ago, more and more started arriving, as much as $1000 a month. One envelope contained a money order for $10,000, so much money your grandmother did not know what to do with it. There were many meetings among the village elders and it was decided we must honour your mother's memory. So we have fixed up this beautiful house for your grandmother and we have built the school in honour of San Patricio, the patron saint of Ireland. There are two teachers now, not just me, and we have a roof and walls and books, and all the children of Esperanza are getting a good education. The older children go to school in San Bernadino in the valley and we bought a bus to take them there. Some have even started university in the city. This money has changed our lives forever. Your father must be a very rich man. You know nothing about this?'

I shook my head in disbelief. I had never stopped to wonder what my old man might be doing with the money I told Beasley to send him, just to keep him off my back. I assumed he was drinking it.

'Of course, we fixed up the church,' continued Doña Cecilia. 'It is dedicated to the memory of your mother. Would you like to see it?'

Doña Cecilia led me out into the darkening evening and walked me across the village, with my grandmother beside me, holding my arm. The sun was setting, and there wasn't much natural light inside the church, yet a sacred stillness infused its thick white walls with a sense of space and peace.

I approached the altar in a trance. There, standing in an arched alcove was a statue of the Virgin Mary, in blue and white and gold, hands clasped in prayer. I knew that statue very well. A small replica stood on a cabinet in my parents' bedroom in Kilrock. 'This is Maria, Blessed Virgin of Esperanza,' said Doña Cecilia. 'She watches over us and protects us.'

A sound broke through the silence, gradually filling every corner of the church, reverberating in the evening air, a thunderous noise descending on the village. I turned and ran outside.

The trees were bending, leaves blowing across the red dirt, animals scattering, children pointing up to the sky. A bright white light beamed down from above, picking out my upturned face.

Grover lurched over to my side. 'Looks like someone found you, kid,' he said.

A large black helicopter slowly descended towards the village.

22

The chopper touched down on a patch of dirt beyond the church, blades spinning dangerously close to little dwellings, the wind knocking over crates and chairs set up for the fiesta. It was a military transport helicopter with an all-too-familiar logo on the side, a Z set in the centre of a zero. The men of La Esperanza had returned wearily from their labours and formed a spontaneous barrier in front of the women, although excited children were harder to rein in. Big doors flew open.

First on the ground was Tiny Tony Mahoney, scanning for danger. The little fucker was actually carrying a gun, which set a ripple of nervousness through the villagers. '*Está bien*,' I called out, stepping to the front, holding up my arms in what I hoped was a gesture of authority. Tiny Tony waved the pistol towards me, scowling. 'Put the gun away, Tony,' I shouted above the cooling engines. 'You're scaring the children.'

Next down was Beasley, big, bald and sweaty in his inappropriate suit. He nodded to Tony, who tucked his pistol in an underarm holster. He still knew who gave the orders. Beasley never travels alone and sure enough down came his assistant

Eugenie, unusually crumpled and flustered, and my PR Flavia Sharpe, dressed as if for a power lunch rather than a trip to the jungle. They were joined by a nervous, bespectacled man I didn't recognise. All fell in behind Beasley as he strode purposefully towards me. I couldn't tell whether he wanted to kiss me or kill me. 'You can run,' Beasley roared, 'but you can't run fast enough or far enough to get away from me!'

I briefly wondered how had he found me here? But the answer was right behind him, clambering gingerly down from the helicopter, the very last man I'd ever expected to find on a mountain in Colombia. A scrawny, ragged, flush-faced figure with flecks of grey in thinning ginger hair came stumbling towards me, like he was still trying to find his feet after a week at sea.

'Hello, son,' he said, carefully.

'Hello, Da,' I said.

'I was worried about you,' said my father.

'I'm sorry, Da,' I said.

We were saved from further awkward intimacy by the descent of another figure from the helicopter, the most beautiful woman on Planet Earth, cinematic goddess, sex queen, love of my life, my fiancée and (according to various sources) adulterous slut, Penelope Nazareth.

It was like my whole life flashing before me. 'Who else have you got in there?' I said to Beasley. 'The Zero Sums?'

Penelope's approach had all the poise of a predatory feline on a catwalk. Here was a woman who knew how to dress for every occasion: patent leather jungle boots, slinky designer combat pants, clingy vest showing off her wasp waist and gravity-defying cleavage, artfully cropped and curved calfskin jacket, wide-brimmed hat and pert Polaroid sunglasses. Well, the sunglasses weren't strictly necessary at dusk but you would expect nothing less from a Hollywood legend.

'We need to talk,' insisted Beasley. But for once he was out of his league.

'Baby,' she gasped, brushing my manager aside and pulling me into her embrace. 'I've been beside myself.' Then sotto voce in my ear: 'Boy, do you know how to stir up publicity, my little savage.'

There was something different about her but I couldn't put my finger on it, I was too distracted by the cameraman capturing our touching reunion for posterity. I hadn't seen him before. Did he work for Beasley or Penelope? Either way, he didn't work for me. 'Get that fucking thing out of my face,' I growled.

He ignored me and kept shooting. Looked like nobody was taking orders from me any more. At least Grover knew whose side he was on. 'You heard the kid, put away the camera or I'll shove it so far up your ass you'll be filming what you had for breakfast.'

The cameraman glanced uncertainly at Penelope but drew a blank. Grover winked at him and he sighed and let the camera drop. Good choice, I thought. There was something about Grover you did not want to mess with sober, let alone half-cocked. I wondered if I could put him up against Tiny Tony.

'Gonna introduce me, kid?' said Grover.

'Uh, Penelope, this is Grover, my pilot,' I said. 'Well, not my pilot, exactly, he's his own pilot, you know . . . it's a long story.'

'I bet,' drawled Penelope, arching a single, sexy eyebrow. I was beginning to remember why I fell so hard for her.

'I've seen all your films, Ms Nazareth. Or may I call you Penelope?' said Grover, gripping her fingers with a dandyish touch. 'You are, without doubt, the most beautiful woman I have ever laid eyes on, not to mention the finest screen actress of our times and I'll fight anyone who says otherwise. It's an honour to meet you.'

'Thank you, Mr Grover, the pleasure's all mine,' purred Penelope. 'Do you think you could help with my bags? They're in the helicopter.'

'It would be an honour, Penelope.' This was a side of Grover I hadn't seen before, the slimy toad.

'What a delightful man,' said Penelope, as Grover lurched drunkenly towards the chopper. 'Although I couldn't help but notice he appears to be wearing the watch I gave you as an engagement gift, *mon cher*.'

'It's another long story,' I said.

'What isn't?' drawled Penelope. She didn't seem particularly interested in hearing it. 'Where are we staying?'

'Are these people your friends, Pedro?' asked Doña Cecilia, stepping forward. Seeing as no violence had broken out, the villagers were quickly adjusting to the new visitors. 'We can put the lady in your grandmother's house, if you wish.'

'The lady!' Penelope whispered to me under her breath without breaking her smile. 'Doesn't she know who I am?'

Beasley was growing impatient. 'Excuse me, Penelope,' he said, breaking in. 'But we have a lot to talk about, Zero.'

I shrugged. 'Now might not be the best time.'

'Now is the only time,' snapped Beasley.

Suddenly, there was an almighty BANG! followed by an explosion of coloured light over our heads. Birds shot up from the trees. Tiny Tony whipped his pistol out, while the kids applauded enthusiastically. 'Relax, Tony, it's a firework,' I sighed. I guess the fiesta had officially begun.

'What's going on?' piped up an LA blonde I recognised as one of Penelope's assistants. 'Is there a hotel?'

'Jesus Christ, how many of you are there?' I snapped.

'It's a party of ten, not counting the pilots,' declared a sing-song voice.

'Kilo, for fuck's sake, what are you doing here?' I gasped at the appearance of my personal bag man.

'Don't ask me! We've been chasing you across half of America,' he pouted. 'You should be in Seattle tonight, playing to twelve thousand screaming fans, and believe me, I'd rather be there. I have friends in Seattle.'

'Sorry,' I shrugged, duly chastened.

'There is a *fiesta* in Pedro's honour,' explained Doña Cecilia. 'As you are his friends, of course you are all invited.'

'Who is this *lady*?' sniffed Penelope. 'Is she your new assistant?'

'This is Doña Cecilia,' I explained. 'She's the local school-teacher.'

Penelope peered at her through her sunglasses. It was getting dark quickly, and I didn't imagine she could see much. 'You can take your sunglasses off now, Penelope,' I said. 'Nobody here knows who you are anyway.'

'I know who you are!' shouted Jesus, hopping up and down at my feet.

'What an adorable child,' said Penelope, smugly.

'You got a cigarette, Señora Penelope?' asked Jesus, winking saucily.

Grover pitched up hauling two stuffed Louis Vuitton cases. Penelope had never been known to travel light. 'I need to freshen up,' I heard her say as Doña Cecilia escorted her to my grandmother's house. 'Is there a shower?'

Someone had started a generator and twinkling coloured lights came on over the dining structure. More food was being spread out on the table and two men began playing fast, rousing tunes on acoustic guitars, with lots of short sung verses and lusty cries of 'Oh!' while another accompanied them on pan pipes. More fireworks exploded in the sky. People started to gravitate towards the food, including members of Beasley's party. I don't think I had ever seen my manager look so uncomfortable, struggling to exert control in a situation where everyone was ignoring him. 'I must admit I'm surprised to find you in such good shape,' he said, throwing a big arm around me and locking me tight. 'Nevertheless, I want you to check into a clinic. The good Dr Gillette here has agreed to certify you mentally incompetent.'

The weasely stranger in glasses stepped forward on cue to shake my hand. 'It's a thrill to meet you in person,' said the doctor. 'My daughter is a big fan.'

'Doesn't he have to examine me before he can declare me incompetent?' I asked Beasley.

'Well, technically—' started the doctor.

'You don't seem to understand the gravity of the situation, Zero,' boomed Beasley. 'We are being sued by every venue in the US and unless we can persuade tour insurance to kick in for medical reasons, they're going to bankrupt us, number one album or not.'

'I am perfectly competent, Beasley,' I said. 'I may be saner right now than I've ever been.'

'Look, there's no shame in a nervous breakdown,' insisted Beasley. 'Some of the greatest stars of all time have had them. Look at Britney Spears. It did wonders for her career, completely repositioned her in the marketplace. Tell him, Flavia.'

My PR stepped in. 'According to market research, this whole flight from fame stunt has polled incredibly well not just with teenagers and young twenties, who one might expect to go for the rebel star bit, but with older music consumers too, the forty-to-sixty age group, who are suddenly looking at you as a potentially more serious artist.' Flavia didn't look me in the eye once during that whole exchange. I hoped she was as ashamed of herself as she should be.

'I'm perfectly sane,' I insisted.

'I was afraid you might think that,' said Beasley. 'Unfortunately, your actions suggest otherwise. As your manager and your friend, I am concerned you might be a danger to yourself, which is why I have reached out to your family, and asked your next of kin to take the required legal steps to have you hospitalised for your own safety.'

My dad smiled apologetically. 'I was worried about you, son.'

'Now would those be the laws of the USA, Ireland or Colombia?' I asked Beasley. Cause I'm not sure your doctor's got any jurisdiction here.'

'Actually my practice is in Brazil,' said Dr Gillette.

'Which is just a short hop across the border by helicopter,' said Beasley, in his lowest, most lethal tone. 'And since nobody knows you're here, then nobody can say for sure where we found you.'

'Nobody knows I'm here?' I exploded. 'This whole fucking village knows I'm here. And you know what? They think I'm baby fucking Jesus. You try taking me out of here in your chopper and see what happens. I'm not the only one who can disappear up in the mountains, fat man.'

'You fucking ungrateful little shit,' snarled Beasley and something flashed beneath his skin, red and dangerous. For a second I thought he might launch himself at me in a murderous fury but he just as quickly regained composure. Maybe it had just been a reflection from the fireworks but I stepped back all the same, out of the reach of his thick fingers.

'Look, Beasley, I don't know what you're up to but you can speak to my lawyer.'

'I want to talk to you about that. Who is this Homer Pax?' said Beasley. 'He's making a bloody nuisance of himself.'

'Well, you better get used to it, cause he represents me from now on. Enjoy the party. I want to talk to my da.'

'Wait!' demanded Beasley as I turned my back on him. 'We can work something out. We just need a story we can agree on, and all stick to it!'

'Will you ever tell him to fuck off, Da?' I suggested.

'Fuck off, Mr Beasley,' said my father.

'Hey, Da,' I said, taking him by the arm. 'There's someone I want you to meet.' And I led him to where my grandmother was standing with Doña Cecilia, watching the festivities unfold. '*Abuelita*,' I said, feeling the language on my tongue. '*Quiero que conozcas a mi padre, Patrick.*'

A tremble ran through my grandmother and she reached out, as if in shock, and pulled my father to her before he had time to resist. '*Mi hijo*,' she gasped. My son. And my father let her hold him, standing under the stars, his body shaking in her wiry arms.

It was around then the feast really got going. I think Grover might have been responsible, grabbing hold of the roundest, fleshiest woman and whipping her off in a dancing whirl. Kids raced to join them, the musicians kicked it up a gear, and I learned something about Colombian peasants that they don't tell you in the guidebooks: they know how to party hard. The *aguardiente*, home-brewed *cerveza* and bootleg chicha was flowing, a fire crackled and roared, the smells of roasting meat filled the air, insects buzzed around lamps hanging beneath the eaves, everything swaying to the whirl of bodies as the music grew louder, wilder, more supple and sensuous.

'The musicians are your cousins,' said Doña Cecilia.

'I have cousins?' I asked, surprised and delighted.

'Everyone here is related,' laughed Doña Cecilia. 'I am probably your cousin!'

'In that case,' I said, 'Will you do me the honour, cousin?' And we took a spin around the dance floor, which was not a floor at all but a bit of open dirtland.

'The lady is very, very beautiful,' said Doña Cecilia, as we danced. 'Is she your lady?'

'I guess so,' I admitted.

'But you are so young to be with a lady like her,' said Doña Cecilia. 'She is old enough to be your mother, no?'

'Don't let her hear you say that,' I warned.

Penelope emerged from my grandmother's house, looking extraordinarily gorgeous in an outfit that might have been designed for just this occasion, an elegant mix of Hollywood gypsy and million-dollar mountain queen in loose, flowing fabrics. Children surged around her, touching her glittering dress, and she glided through them, gauze and chiffon billowing, skimming fingers and heads as if bestowing blessings. I couldn't help but notice her assistant stayed close, discreetly spraying Penelope's hands with germ-resistant sanitiser. 'Oh, these children are impossibly cute, poor things,' cooed Penelope as she billowed into my presence. 'It's so wonderful to see them smiling after all they've been through. Perhaps we should adopt one or two?'

'The orphans are in Medellín,' I pointed out. 'These kids live here, with their families.'

'Oh well,' she shrugged. 'I'd make a lousy mother anyway. Who does a girl have to fuck to get a drink around here?'

I thought it might be a good idea to stay sober but when Grover waltzed past dancing with a goat, I sensed resistance was futile. A swarthy *hombre* with a handlebar moustache poured us tumblers of clear liquid. *'Para esposas y amantes, que nunca se encuentren!'* he roared, clinking our glasses.

'What did he say?' asked Penelope.

'Something about "wives and lovers, may they never meet",' I translated.

Penelope knocked hers back in one. That woman could drink, as I had witnessed many times before. In fact, she could drink, snort, pop pills, shoot up and still look like a cheerleader on a health kick in the morning. 'Do keep up,' she insisted, so I tipped my glass back and felt the liquid explode in my chest.

Our glasses were immediately refilled. It was going to be one of those nights. We toasted health and we toasted love and we toasted friendship and drinking and getting to heaven half an hour before the devil found out we were dead. Every man in the village wanted to drink a toast to *la bella dama* and El Rojo and I feared we were going to have to get through them one at a time until (asking me to translate) Penelope raised her glass to 'all the men, women, children, goats, mules and chickens of beautiful La Esperanza' and dragged me out to dance.

Acoustic guitar licks fired rhythmic triggers in my brain as she obliterated everything in my field of vision, all of my senses filling up with her. There really was something different about her, something I couldn't put my finger on. I let myself be sucked into the centre of those enormous dark eyes, long lashes beating like the translucent wings of black butterflies, luscious red lips like pillows you could rest your weary soul on, the warmth of her breath, the rising and falling of her breasts. As we spun giddily around, her silken black hair flew free, brushing against my skin, just like my mother's hair . . .

I broke away, shocked at the image. But she reached gracefully out, lightly touched the tip of my fingers, and smoothly drew me back into her orbit. I was her dancing satellite. She was the Earth, and I was the Moon. So what was that great white orb in the sky that made me want to howl with hurt and loss and outrage at the tricks life plays? How could she do that to me? How could she leave me when I needed her most?

I broke away again. Penelope regarded me quizzically while I grabbed a guitar from one of my brethren musicians and attacked it with rhythmic fury, strumming like I could capture the night in my fingers, making chord shapes that conjured up the stars, and my cousins played along, laughing, trying to keep up with my shifts and changes, and the people stamped and clapped. I jumped up on to a table, melodies and harmonies flying like sparks from my fingertips. And I opened my mouth and I wailed. I sang without words because there were no words for the things I was feeling. I sang for my poor lost mother, and I sang for her poor lost son, and I sang for all the poor lost orphans in the world. When I was done, a cheer went up, 'El Rojo!', and I raised my guitar above my head, like I was bidding farewell to Madison Square Gardens. Thank you and goodnight!

I looked out into the faces of the people, my real people, and I was filled with love, a feeling so benign and enriching I wondered if it would ever be possible to capture it in music? Perhaps fearing I might be tempted to play an encore, one of my cousins gently removed the instrument from my grip. I lurched off, found a dark corner behind an adobe wall, got down on my hands and knees and threw up.

'You made me look bad in New York,' said a voice. I looked up to see Tiny Tony, glowering quietly in the shadows.

'You can't blame me for that, Tony,' I said, wiping my mouth. 'You should have a word with your parents.'

'You little gobshite,' snarled Tony, knuckles clenched. He looked like he was going to hit me, like he had been storing up a blow since I ran out on him.

'Hold on,' I gasped, and puked up another gut full of alcohol. It seemed to put him off his stride because he turned in disgust and walked away.

'You know what, Tony?' I called after him. 'You're fired!'

'I don't work for you,' he spat back. 'I work for Beasley.'

'Well, that's great then,' I said. ''cause he's fired too.' But I said it quietly, in case he changed his mind and came back and hit me.

I sat for a while, sweating alcohol. Then Kilo appeared, squatting next to me, unfolding a travel case vanity mirror and tipping out white powder. 'This'll get you back on your feet,' he whispered.

'Fuck off, no,' I protested feebly. 'I can't touch that.'

'Suit yourself,' said Kilo. And he whipped out a rolled-up note and proceeded to hoover up half the stash. 'I'll say one thing about this ridiculous country, you haven't tasted cocaine till you've tasted one hundred per cent pure Colombian!' He shivered with satisfaction. 'It's like champagne to your fingertips.'

I looked at the remaining line of white crystals. I thought about all the misery they caused, the wars, the murders, the madness. I thought of how the poor farmers on this mountainside had been trapped by the world's voracious appetite for their coca leaf, labouring for a pittance to feed their families so the decadent children of the West could get high. I thought of my mother, forced to leave her home, risking life and liberty to fly into New York as a drug mule. It was bad, bad stuff. And then I thought what the fuck, grabbed the straw and inhaled.

And with a sprinkling of fairy dust from Kilo's magic wand, I was back to my best, or worst, Zero the Hero, El Rojo, knocking back shots and dancing an Irish jig for the kids. I seemed to have lost my leather jacket somewhere and I was naked from the waist up, but never mind, either the night was warm or I was on fire. I lurched and fell at Flavia's feet. 'Are you enjoying yourself, Flavia?' I enquired politely, as she helped me up.

'I never mix pleasure with business,' she responded coolly.

'That's what I always liked about you, Flavia,' I said, grinning stupidly at her.

'You're behaving like a selfish prick,' she said. 'You should talk to Beasley. You've achieved things in a few short years that most musicians never manage in a lifetime. It's a mistake to break up a winning team.'

'I don't know if I want to win any more,' I mumbled, shuffling guiltily. 'I don't even know if I want to play the game.'

'Oh what rot!' Flavia tutted. 'You've always been a player. The first time we met, I could tell right away you were ready to do whatever it took. You and Beasley were made for each other.' And with that, she walked off.

'I'm nothing like Beasley,' I protested. But nobody was listening to me, which I was going to have to get used to. 'I'm nothing like Beasley,' I told Jesus, who was hanging around, puffing on a big cigar. 'Where the fuck did you get that?' I said, taking it from his mouth.

'The fat man,' Jesus protested, coughing up smoke.

Beasley was slumped at a table with the old men, slugging back their bootleg brew. It appeared to be some kind of drinking game, which he was losing badly. All his pumped-up energy had dissipated. He was like a deflating Michelin man, you could almost hear the air hissing as his rubbery frame shrank. His assistant, Eugenie, looked utterly miserable, sitting bolt upright next to him while a hairy old coca farmer patted her thigh proprietorially. She cast me a silent appeal for help. Had I ever fucked her? I couldn't remember. I was pretty sure neither of us had seen Beasley this drunk before. I suppose she was afraid to leave him in this state, either out of loyalty or fear of being fired. '*Deja a la chica,* uh, *muy solo, por favor,*' I said to Eugenie's amorous old suitor. Leave the pretty girl alone, please. He shrugged apologetically and removed his hand.

Beasley tipped his bald head towards me, eyeballs rolling, sweat bristling on his scalp. 'How long did it take us to build this?' he slurred. 'And you're going to throw it away, over what? To live on a mountainside like a peasant? It's a waste of God-given talent.'

'And here's me always thinking you worshipped the devil,' I said.

'You can't have one without the other,' said Beasley.

'You want me to hit him, Mr Beasley?' offered Tiny Tony. But Beasley waved him away.

'What is his fucking problem?' I asked.

'You hurt his feelings,' explained Beasley, sadly. 'Mine too.'

Oh, what the fuck was going on? I wasn't used to feeling sorry for Beasley. It must have been a hallucinogenic property of the drink. I could feel the poison bubbling in my bloodstream, warping and distorting reality. Two insects buzzed around a hurricane lamp, engaged in a weird ritual dance. I climbed up on a table, to get a better look, sticking my face into the light. Their colours shone bright and hard, like polished gems of cobalt and emerald. Wings beat frantically, feelers and antennae wrapped around each other, and they were secreting some kind of goo. I couldn't tell if they were fighting or fucking.

I tried to remember why I was here. In the distance, I watched Grover dancing with Penelope, putting on the moves like a gigolo at Studio 54. 'Go home to your wife, Grover!' I shouted. He turned and waved. Penelope danced towards me and the whole party seemed to be dancing with her, like they were her chorus line, dragged wherever she went. I knew all about that magnetic pull. It looked like some badly choreographed horror video, with Penelope in the role of Amazon Queen and all the village men as her zombie love slaves. I blinked and she was Circe, and they were her animal lovers. I blinked again, and she was a Hollywood goddess and they were her entourage from hell. But where was her leading man? Surely not Grover, stroking his pencil moustache?

Suddenly, there was Penelope, right beneath me, cooing seductively, 'Save me from this rogue, darling.'

'Why don't you get Troy fucking Anthony to save you?' I hissed.

Her eyes flashed. 'Get down off that table and behave like a man for once.'

'Don't you fucking talk to me like that,' I shouted back. 'You're not my mother!'

She looked shocked. Heads were turning to see what the fuss was about. I jumped down and howled into her face, 'You are not my mother!'

'I have never pretended to be,' she said, before sweeping regally away.

I looked up to see my old man watching with reproachful eyes from the other side of the dancers. Jesus Christ, he could still make me feel like a guilty schoolboy from a hundred yards. 'I'm sorry,' I called out.

Grover was waltzing with the goat again. 'Gonna have to do better than that, kid,' he drawled. 'Unless you wanna start double-dating with a couple of barnyard animals?'

I caught up with Penelope near the entrance to the church. 'I'm sorry. For everything,' I said.

Her face was tight with fury. 'For goodness' sake, what kind of woman do you think I am?' she said. She glanced around, attempting to hold a smile on her face, for the sake of her audience, only to find nobody was even looking our way. Grover and his goat had their attention now. She pushed open the church door, and we stepped inside, where we could be alone. Candles were burning, filling the small chapel with a yellow glow, casting flickering shadows on the thick white walls. The noise of the party seemed a world away from this sacred space.

'You, of all people, should know better than to believe what you read in the gutter press,' said Penelope, huffily. 'Troy is a wonderful, handsome man, a fine actor, and he has been a great friend to me while you were off gallivanting around the world, but he is not now and never has been my lover!'

'I'm sorry,' I repeated.

'He's far too old for me,' she said, pouting.

'He's the same age as you,' I pointed out.

'That's below the belt,' she said coldly. 'And as for all this mother-figure business, well! I can't think of anything more insulting.'

'My mother was a very beautiful woman,' I said.

'I am sure she was but—'

'This is her church, you know. The village dedicated it to her.'

'That's very . . . sweet. I'm sure she was a very special person.'

'She was a saint,' I said.

'Well, that settles it,' said Penelope. 'I am definitely not your mother.'

'I think we've got that established,' I agreed.

'You make me feel like a cradle-snatcher,' she complained. 'Why are you looking at me like that?'

I started laughing. I couldn't help myself. I had suddenly figured out what was different about her. The wrinkles around her eyes had disappeared. And come to think of it, I didn't remember her lips being quite that full. 'Have you had surgery?' I asked, reaching out to touch her cheek.

Penelope recoiled angrily. 'You're insufferable.' But there was a sudden vulnerability about her. 'I've had a little work done, yes. Does it show?'

'You look gorgeous, as always,' I reassured her.

'I could have done without this hullabaloo. I plan a quiet retreat to a clinic in Brazil at the end of shooting, only to find the press camped on my doorstep, demanding quotes.'

'I'm sorry,' I repeated, lamely.

'If it hadn't been for Troy, I don't know how I would have coped. He's been a rock.'

'What was he doing there?' I asked. 'Getting a chin reduction?'

'That's enough,' she said.

'I'm sorry,' I repeated. I'd been saying sorry a lot tonight. I had a feeling I was going to be saying it a lot more in the near future, to a lot of people.

'I'm glad you're OK,' she said, softening.

'I'm not sure I am,' I admitted.

'Well, maybe I can do something about that,' she said, pulling me towards her.

'Not in church,' I protested, as she kissed me. 'My mother might be watching.'

Penelope led me by the hand to my grandmother's little *casa* which, judging by the clothes draped over every surface and magazines and scripts piled up on the table, Penelope had colonised, leaving Granny to bed down with relatives, of which, fortunately, La Esperanza was full.

She dragged me into the bedroom, casting off garments like a burlesque angel, silk and chiffon slipping and sliding across her perfect skin. God, she was fucking gorgeous. Invisible fingers unbuttoned my jeans and slid them to the floor. Then she was standing before me, magnificently naked. She was heavenly warrior and sacrificial virgin, brazen harlot and vulnerable ingénue, she was everything a man could ever desire. She was mother, and I was her child, and I knelt down to suck the manna from her breasts. 'Oh, I do like a hard young body,' she growled, greedily pulling me into her. Then softly, sadly, whispering in my ear, 'But everybody gets old.'

'Everybody except you,' I lied.

*

In the morning, I sat awake as the first rays of cold sunlight streamed through the open window. My mouth was raspy and dry, my head throbbing like an outboard motor, puttering along a dirty river, but the full hangover hadn't set in yet. Maybe I was still drunk. I wondered if Kilo was around, and whether he had anything to alleviate the impending pain. But whatever was coming, I knew I deserved it.

Penelope lay naked beside me, hair cascading across the pillow. Her mouth was open and she was snoring lightly, a little spittle of drool at the edge of her lips. But she looked beautiful. I touched her face, running my fingers over the smooth skin where crow's feet had been erased. She stirred slightly but didn't wake. I got up, still wobbly on my feet, but with a feeling I had to act now or I was going to be stuck here forever, trapped in an endlessly repeating loop. I rooted among Penelope's clothes for something I could wear, settling on some sheer black matador pants with silver brocade and a scarlet zip-up hoodie decorated with tiny silver skulls. Women get all the best clothes.

At the doorway, I turned to look back at her long, curving body, so utterly perfect and sexy. And I knew it was the last time I would see her naked. Well, outside of a cinema anyway.

I walked out into the new day. Chickens picked about among the detritus of the night before, dogs snuffled leftover food. A few bodies lay where they had fallen, sleeping it off in the dirt and straw. A group of bleary-eyed drinkers still sat around the big table, seeing in the dawn in a ragged blur of toasts. They raised their glasses to me, 'El Rojo!' I was not altogether surprised to see Grover among them, sitting with his new companion, the goat, which he had wrapped in a poncho and appeared to be hand-feeding. Tiny Tony lay unconscious at their feet.

'What happened to him?' I asked.

'He opened his damn mouth one too many times,' said Grover.

I laughed. 'Do you want a job running my security detail?'

'I'm a pilot, goddamnit,' growled Grover.

'Sho am I,' slurred another man, raising a befuddled head from where he had been resting it on the table. I guess nobody would be flying anywhere for a while.

'Where is everybody?' I asked.

Grover waved his hand, vaguely. 'Around,' he drawled. 'Have a drink with us, kid.'

'Go home to your wife, Grover,' I suggested.

'Why would I? I got everything I need right here,' he retorted. 'Good liquor, good company and the love of a good lady.' I assumed he meant the goat.

I needed water. One of the locals showed me how to work the pump, and I splashed my face and filled a mug and drank as much of that mountain liquid as I could. The door of an adjacent shack opened and Eugenie appeared at it, blinking in the light. She had lost the frazzled edges of the night, looking strangely radiant in a T-shirt and panties. The drinkers applauded appreciatively, and she blushed and retreated inside. As the door swung shut, I got a glimpse of a handsome, muscular village boy behind her.

'Ain't love grand,' drawled Grover, nuzzling his goat.

I wanted to visit the church. I wanted to feel the presence of my mother again and it seemed the most likely place to find her. I needed to do some thinking. And maybe ask for forgiveness. As I passed a pig-sty of rough boards and corrugated metal, I thought I saw the shape of Beasley inside, fleshy, naked and snoring in the straw. I hoped the pigs were safe.

As the church door creaked shut behind me, I realised I was not alone. My old man was already there, sitting on a bench before the Virgin. I sat beside him. He turned to me, his face tight, eyes watery. He looked like he might have been crying.

We sat in silence. But it was a good silence, not the kind of glowering, unspoken pain that had driven me out of our house. But I had to ask. I had to ask the question that had been scratching at a cellar door, deep in the subterranean bowels of my mind. Scratching, scratching, scratching, demanding to be let in. I didn't even want to know the answer. But I had to ask. 'What happened, Da?' I said. And I could hear the tremble in my voice. 'Did I kill Ma?'

My father turned, as if really noticing me for the first time. 'Don't be stupid, son,' he said, with what sounded like genuine surprise. 'She was a grown woman. You were just a small child. If there was anyone to blame for what happened, it was herself. Stupid. It was all so stupid.'

'So what happened?' I asked.

And he told me.

He had been making a bicycle for me in Father Martin's shed. The plan was to give it to me on my ninth birthday. But somehow I found the cursed thing, snooping about the churchyard probably, trying to figure out the big secret. Father Martin was always forgetting to lock that shed. And there was the bike, and I must have guessed it was mine, so where was the harm in taking it for a spin? Only my father hadn't quite finished with it. You always put the brakes on last, you see? It's just the way it is. The very last thing.

And the memory came surging back, battering down the cellar door and steaming like a freight train through my mind. My father's lips were moving but I couldn't hear him speak. I was riding that bicycle home to show my ma. I was so excited and proud. I'd learned to ride on my brother's bike but I'd never had one of my own. Such a beautiful machine, red and silver, the kind of bicycle a boy dreams about. And so what if there were no brakes? If I needed to stop, I could just put my feet down.

Then the door slammed shut again. I sat there, shaken to my core. My father was still talking, saying he could only imagine my mother had been carried away with my delight. She should have known better than to go riding around on a bicycle with no brakes. She should have had me off that bike in a second flat and tanned my backside for taking it without asking. But her judgement was always suspect where I was concerned. So instead she sat behind me on the bicycle seat, while I pedalled her around, showing off my skills. We must have been a sight on that little bike. Some of the neighbours saw us and said we looked like we were practising for a circus act, wheeling around the estate, laughing.

'She had a great laugh, your mother,' he said. 'I loved to hear her laugh. But nobody could make her laugh like you.'

And then we cycled out onto the road and took off down Kilrock Hill. It was a steep hill that, quite deceptive, the way it started at a gentle incline but then really took a dip.

And there we were, wheeling down that hill, picking up speed the whole way. I could almost feel the wind in my face. I could almost feel my mother's hands round my waist.

We could have ridden right into town down that hill and eventually it would have levelled out, and we'd have gently coasted to a stop at the Town Hall. And on another day, that's what might have happened. And if he'd have got home from work and found out what we'd been up to, he'd have given us both a piece of his mind for being so reckless.

But not that day. There was a lorry coming up the hill and a car going down, and there wasn't room for both to pass. The drivers got out and were arguing with each other about who should back up. And they both saw us coming.

'Stop,' I said to my father. I didn't want to hear any more.

'You couldn't stop,' he said. 'There was no brakes, you see? There was no fucking brakes.'

So I rode into the back of the car, screaming.

'I got called to the hospital,' said my da. 'The hotel manager drove me. The guy was a pompous prick. Your ma never liked him. But he drove me to the hospital, fair play to him, talking to me the whole time, telling me it was going to be all right.'

And my father shuddered, like something was breaking out of him. 'I thought I was going to lose you both,' he cried. And I could see those wheels spinning, spinning, spinning on that upturned bike. My mother lying in the road, head twisted, nose broken, blood in the road, blood in my eyes.

'I'm sorry, Da,' I said. It was all that I could say. It just wasn't enough.

He wiped his eyes. 'Let's go for a walk,' he said. 'Churches give me the fucking creeps.'

Out in the morning light, he looked me up and down sceptically. 'What the fuck are you wearing?' he said, as he tapped out a cigarette.

'Don't start, Da,' I warned him. The hangover was kicking in now. It was going to get rough.

We took an orange dirt path that led out of the village. As the sun rose over the mountains, the colours of the thick vegetation were coming to life, a thousand subtle shades of green and red among the flaming trees and wild flowers, birds flitting like phantoms through the branches. We watched vultures wheeling overhead, black silhouettes dipping and rising in the endless blue, seeking out the dead.

I seemed to remember the inside of an ambulance. I could conjure up an image of a hospital ceiling, people looking down at me, lights, voices. But there was nothing else there. Just a fading, bleached-out dream.

'Your ma was in a coma for ten days,' said my father, picking up the thread, although it was taking a real effort for him to talk about things he'd left untouched for so many years. 'She fractured her skull, there was haemorrhaging – it was bad, very, very bad. I never left the hospital. They said I should go home and get some sleep but I was afraid she wouldn't be there when I got back. We prayed, you know, by the bedside. Father Martin was there with us, saying the rosary over and over, telling me not to give up hope, Jesus Christ was looking after her, she'd come back to us. I think he was half in love with her himself, you know. I think he might have lost his faith in that hospital. All those prayers. But she never woke up.'

'I can't really remember anything about it,' I said.

'You were banged up pretty bad yourself,' said my father. 'In and out of consciousness, but, you know . . . kids are resilient. You were with her at the end. She'd have appreciated that.'

'I always felt like you blamed me,' I told him.

My father sighed, a long, bitter sigh. 'I blamed everybody for a very long time,' he said. 'I blamed God, Father Martin, the hospital, the driver who was too fucking stubborn to move his car and . . . yeah, I suppose I blamed you, for a while, anyway, even though I knew you were just a child. It wasn't your fault. Most of all, I blamed myself. For bringing her to Ireland, for not fixing the brakes, for just not being there. I was supposed to protect her. I promised to take care of her. I promised.'

This was about as much as I could ever remember him saying in one go, at least while sober. We walked a little further, and left the dirt path, following a trail through thick vegetation. An escarpment fell off to one side, and we paused to take in a breathtaking view of the mountainside falling away, deep into a verdant valley. My father nodded approvingly. 'It's a beautiful country, so it is. Your ma always said that about it, and now I can see what she meant.'

'How come you never came here?' I asked.

'Ach, we were always broke, what with mouths to feed, and sending money to your grandma,' said my father, dismissively. But he seemed to realise this wasn't a good enough answer. 'I suppose I was afraid of the place. It was the murder capital of the world, your own grandfather was killed by soldiers. I was afraid if we came out here, even for a visit, your mother wouldn't want to come back, and I wouldn't want to stay.'

'I can remember you arguing about it,' I said.

'Can you now? I can't remember that myself.' We walked on. 'I mean, married life, everybody argues from time to time, it's no big deal.'

'It seemed like a big deal to me,' I said.

'Your mother had a temper on her,' he said. 'It wasn't all sweetness and light, I suppose. She'd get depressed about the weather. And the way people talked down to her. Her job prospects. You know, silly things. Every time we'd have a big disagreement, she'd threaten to leave and bring you boys back to her own mother. But it was just words people say when they're upset. She never meant it. Well, she never left anyway. She loved me and I loved her, and that's the way it was.'

'And then she died, and left us all,' I said. I didn't mean it to come out so angry. But there it was. She left me, and I didn't know if I could ever forgive her.

My father looked at me thoughtfully. 'It was an accident, son. Accidents happen.'

'*Siempre duro*,' I said, bitterly. 'Things are always hard.'

'Your mother used to say that,' said Da. '*Siempre* fucking *duro* indeed.'

We were walking among rows of plants that were obviously being cultivated by the village farmers.

'What's this they're growing here?' said my father, pulling the branch of a tall, thick shrub to examine the bright red berries and smooth, oval leaves.

'Coca,' I said.

'What, like you make Coca-Cola from?'

l laughed, which surprised me. I didn't think I had a laugh left in me. 'Something like that,' I said.

He looked at me slyly. 'I'm not that stupid. I was young once too, you know.' And he winked.

'I don't want to think about that, Da,' I protested.

'Did I ever tell you how your mother got to New York?'

'You never told me anything,' I said. 'But, you know, I figured it out.'

He turned to look me in the eyes and almost started to speak, then he looked at his feet, then he looked up at the sky, then he tutted as if annoyed with himself. 'I'm sorry I haven't been a better father,' he said at last. He exhaled hard. He seemed relieved to have got that out of the way. 'The thing about parenthood is . . .' But he didn't seem to be able to think what the thing was.

'The thing about parenthood . . .' I prodded.

'Ach, the thing is, we're all just making it up as we go along.'

'Like life,' I suggested.

'Yeah,' he said. 'Exactly like that.'

We walked back to the village in silence. I wondered if that was it, we'd had our conversation now, and we'd just go back to tip-toeing around each other. But as La Esperanza hove into view, he suddenly piped up again. 'So, what about this Penelope Nazareth, then? Are you really gonna marry her?'

'I don't think so, Da,' I admitted.

'Good,' he said. 'cause she stayed in the hotel where your ma and me worked in New York, you know. And to tell the truth, she was kind of a bitch.'

23

Anyway, I went back to Ireland. I flew home to the Emerald Isle, my real home, far from the towers of New York or the mountains of Colombia. I agreed to be admitted to a discreet rehab and recovery clinic in Roscommon. I was privately assured that it was really like an exclusive spa hotel, only with no minibar in your room.

I had my own therapist assigned to me, Dr Paige Underwood, and she diagnosed me as having suffered a nervous breakdown due to acute stress, exacerbated by alcohol and substance abuse, with underlying family and relationship issues. I don't know. Maybe I did have a nervous breakdown. It sounded good on the insurance paperwork anyway, so Beasley was happy.

What bothered me were the issues. Everybody's got fucking issues these days. If you don't like what you see in the mirror and try to do something about it by working out or dieting, you've got body dysmorphia issues. If you just don't give a shit, eat too much crap and put on weight, you've got low self-esteem issues. What if you just like junk food? Then you've got junk food issues. If you don't want to sit still and listen to someone waffling on about fucking issues, well, you've got concentration issues. Or avoidance issues. Or commitment issues. If you dare to question how a woman you've only just met is supposed to know you better than you know yourself, you've got female authority issues. And if you get angry about being incarcerated in an institution and having to listen to all this shit about issues, well, you've obviously got hostility issues. I hate fucking issues. But, of course, that only means I have issues.

But the doctor and me, we could never quite agree on what the issues were. Dr Underwood proposed we start with well-documented substance abuse issues and sexual addiction issues. But I'm a fucking pop star – those aren't issues, those are part of the job description.

And I insisted there was no way I was doing group therapy and talking about my issues among complete strangers who might secretly tape them and sell them to the press. So she added trust issues to the list. I said now you're talking, Doc, I have a hard time trusting anyone after my own personal webmaster, Spooks McGrath, turned out to have been keeping records of every private conversation for two years and was currently having his salacious memoir, *I Was Zero's Doppelganger*, serialised in the *Daily Telegraph*. So she had to concede I had a point.

So Dr Underwood came up with a novel approach to group therapy, which involved an actual group. My old band The Zero Sums were rounded up and brought in and they were supposed to tell me how they felt about my dumping them, and I was supposed to say sorry and we were all supposed to hug and make up. Dr Underwood stressed that this was a safe environment where we could all speak the truth, and for a while I sat there and took it like a man while they told me what a selfish, egotistic, pompous prat I had been to work with. Only I had a few home truths of my own to impart, like the fact that I didn't see the point of being in a band where I could play all their instruments better than they could, the drummer couldn't keep time, the guitarist was off his tits on ketamine, the keyboard player had personal hygiene problems and the bassist was a moron who was only tolerated because he had a hot, slutty girlfriend and we all used to hump her behind his back.

'Is that true?' the poor fucker shouted, and his bandmates had to sheepishly admit it was.

'How is Sally these days?' I asked. And then, sensing I might have really put my foot in it, I added, 'She's not still your girlfriend is she?'

'No,' he said, ashen-faced. 'We got married.'

Anyway, that didn't go so well.

As for dealing with substance abuse issues, the whole clinic was awash with class As. There were parties going on in the patients' rooms every night. Well, what do you expect? The place was full of drug addicts, for fuck's sake.

The sex addiction therapy was going quite well, all things considered, until I made a pass at the doctor. I thought she was kind of hot, in her tailored business suits and black-framed glasses and pinned-up hair. 'I'm much too old for you,' she gasped, when I tried to kiss her in the middle of a session.

'You know I have a thing for older women, Doctor,' I said. 'It's my Oedipal issues.'

'Complex,' she corrected me.

'Yes,' I agreed, slipping my arm around her waist. 'I am.'

Who knew they teach self-defence in medical school? She kneed me in the groin with such clinical efficiency, I didn't think I'd be able to walk for a week, then calmly continued the session while I rolled about dry-retching on the floor. She said it was further proof of my sex addiction and, if I preferred, she could refer me to a male analyst for further treatment. I said all it proved was that I was a horny young buck going stir crazy and did I really need some psychiatrist explaining that my extreme reaction to Penelope Nazareth's imaginary adultery was a manifestation of the grief I felt over abandonment by my mother? I didn't want to analyse it; I wanted to write songs about it. Which I took as proof that I was getting better, so I checked myself out and went and stayed in my brother's hotel.

That was an improvement. That was a proper talking cure. I hadn't spoken to Paddy much in the years since leaving home, and maybe not even in the years at home, either. There was so much silence in the flat where we grew up, two lost boys depending for survival on a man who was even more lost than us, raging at the empty space the only woman in our lives had left behind, unable to even comfort one another.

But finally there we were, Paddy and me, sitting up in my suite every night after he'd finished his work, sharing a bottle of wine and talking about our mother and father and our upbringings and jealousies and insecurities, getting it all off our chests. There was so much to catch up on. A whole lifetime. It was a revelation for both of us. I had felt so alone in the world, I felt like an orphan, and now I had found my brother, who had been there all along. We were so different but we were also the same, the same eyes, the same gestures, the same history. We even invited my old man around sometimes and all managed to sit together and share a bottle of wine and not get into a single fight. Mind you, on those occasions, we mostly sat and watched football matches on the television and shouted at the screen as a substitute for shouting at each other. But sometimes, if we were lucky, Da would loosen up and tell us a story from his life with our mother, and manage to get through it without wincing, or crying, or even swearing. Then, one day, he came around with some shoe boxes full of old photos, and we all pored over them together. And there was some crying done that day. But I finally felt like I was getting back my memories of my mother, however vague and impressionistic. Little triggers would almost conjure her up and I could think about her without being filled with anger or grief or anxiety. Well, some of the time.

So why did I still feel so empty? Like there was a hole inside that could never be filled? Maybe I needed it just to function, a greedy vortex sucking in the world then spewing it out as musical anti-matter, my own supermassive black hole. Was I secretly afraid that without the pain I really would be nothing, no one, Zero? The Shitty Committee may have been struck from the register of my subconscious and for their dumbness I was truly grateful, but sometimes the silence itself became oppressive, like a pillow suffocating me in my sleep, and I would wake gasping for air, filled with a strange conviction that I had lost something really important, and if I just lay there, lay very, very still, I would remember what it was.

But I knew what it was. Surely deep down I knew?

Paddy had a girlfriend, Fiona, who worked for him in the hotel. She was smart and friendly, even if she had terrible taste in music. She only listened to jazz and didn't know any of my songs. They were sort of engaged but in no hurry to tie the knot. 'Do you not want kids?' I asked.

'After the mess our old man made of us,' said Paddy, 'I haven't exactly been in a rush to repeat his mistakes. How about you?'

'I still feel like a kid myself,' I admitted.

Anyway, I had all the kids in La Esperanza to take care of. I had instructed Homer to set up a fund to formalise my support of the school and look after all their education and medical needs. We were also in talks about building an orphanage in Medellín. I often thought about little Jesus, and little Maria, and wondered what their lives would be like if I hadn't stumbled into them? I actually felt some responsibility towards their futures, and that was the most grown-up I had ever felt about anything. 'I'll tell you one thing,' I said, with sudden determination, 'If I do ever have a kid, I'm never going to let them out of my sight. Never! I don't want them to feel abandoned, the way I've felt all my life.'

'You know, Pedro, our mother didn't abandon us,' Paddy reminded me, as people had to keep reminding me. 'And neither did Da. He did his best, even if it wasn't up to very much. Anyway, it's not like you've got such a great record of sticking by people.'

I knew that was true. There was a constant thorn in my conscience, memories that haunted me like a terrible refrain, a sad song you have to keep playing, even though it's making you miserable. One night I told Paddy there was only one person from my past that I really wanted to see just to apologise for everything I had done, and that was Eileen.

'I don't think that's such a good idea,' he said, which surprised me.

'She's been on my mind a lot,' I told him.

'Well what about what's on her mind? You really hurt her. I think you should leave her alone. You're just going to open up old wounds.'

'I knew you always fancied her,' I said, sulkily.

'Half the boys in town fancied her,' he retorted. 'You didn't know a good thing when you had it. You fucked up there, Pedro. But it's all in the past now. And some things are better left that way.'

But I couldn't leave it alone and brought it up again over dinner with Paddy and Fiona the next night. I said I wanted a female opinion. 'Paddy's right,' said Fiona. 'You just can't go waltzing back into an ex-girlfriend's life. You don't know what she's got going on, you might upset a delicate balance.'

'I might not,' I said. 'D'you ever think she might actually be happy to see me? She was the love of my life.'

'Oh, for fuck's sake, you were just kids,' grumbled Paddy. 'What did you know about love? Or life?'

'And anyway,' said Fiona, 'hasn't she got a family of her own now?'

'You didn't tell me that,' I griped to Paddy.

'Did you think she was going to sit around and wait for you to come to your senses?' sighed Paddy. 'You blew it. Just move on and leave her be.'

'So who's the lucky fella, then?' I grumbled, feeling a pang of jealousy I had no right to. 'Anyone I know?'

'You're such a chauvinist,' said Fiona. 'The first thing you want to know is what man's having his wicked way with your ex. Why would you assume it has to be a fella? We've got all kinds of couples in Ireland now. We're very progressive.'

'Are you saying Eileen's a lesbian now?' I said, not quite following.

'Fucking hell, boy, we're not saying anything of the sort!' exploded Paddy. 'If Eileen wanted anything to do with you, I'm sure she'd have been in touch by now. The whole world doesn't revolve around your fucking ego, you know. People move on.'

'I just said I'd like to see her,' I wheedled.

'For what?' said Paddy, witheringly. 'So you can fuck her about again?'

I changed tack. 'My therapist said I have to make reparations to the people I've done wrong. I want to say sorry, that's all. I feel like I've been saying sorry for the past two months to everyone I've ever offended, and that is a big long list, but Eileen should be top of the list. She's the only one I really, really want to say sorry to.'

'You haven't said sorry to me,' said Paddy, huffily.

'What have I got to be sorry about? I bought you a fucking hotel, didn't I?'

He shrugged. 'Fair enough.'

If I couldn't see Eileen, at least I wanted to see my mother's grave. The problem was I had effectively become a prisoner in the hotel. I wasn't sure which was worse, the paparazzi hiding in the bushes or the fans holding vigil by the gate. Journalists kept checking in under false pretences, and it got so I couldn't even use the bar or the restaurant. Paddy was delighted, of course. Business was booming, and he didn't react well to my suggestion that we kick everybody out and I take over the whole place. 'You know the thing about a silent partner,' he said. 'They're supposed to keep silent!' So instead, I occupied the top floor. But I was in danger of turning into Elvis up there, with blacked-out windows, not knowing whether it was day or night, writing songs and living on room service.

I instructed Homer to buy me a house but he didn't appear to be making much progress. Which wasn't actually his fault. The usual procedure in house-buying, he pointed out, was to first decide where you wanted to live. And I hadn't made my mind up about that. Or anything else. It was as if I had fallen into the doldrums, caught between the twin ports of Prevarication and Procrastination with no wind in my sails. What was I going to do next? Where was I going to go? Who was I going to be? I needed something to happen, a freak wave to come crashing across my bows and get me moving.

Not that anything had really stopped. The album just kept selling, I couldn't have slowed it down if I wanted to. It was turning into an old-fashioned blockbuster. Every time it started to flag, something else would boost it. They cut a video for my single 'Life On Earth' using footage shot by news crews in Medellín and it was huge just about everywhere on the planet. Then our film came out, *#1 With A Bullet*, and was a smash hit, despite getting panned by critics. The title track lived up to its billing, giving me my third number one of the year. I didn't need to do any promo because I was never out of the news. The Perry women from Siren Creek all appeared on Oprah dishing the dirt on my week as their lover, then did a family spread for *Playboy* magazine, and my record sales jumped on both occasions. Devlin signed that deal she had always dreamed of, and had a minor hit with 'Not For Sale', with some critics hailing her as an authentically primitive new voice of Americana. Aunt Velma got an exhibition in a gallery in New York and sold her painting of me for nearly quarter of a million dollars. Last I heard, she's going to have an exhibition in Paris. And I believe even Marcy has a new career as the star of a hardcore porn pastiche entitled *#1 With A Dildo*.

The rap crew from Philadelphia, Master Beatz and Roc Bottom, had a hit with a novelty record, 'Pimpin' Zero', using an uncleared sample from 'Never Young'. Beasley wanted to sue them but fuck it, it's just music, and I was glad it was being put to good use. Maybe they could use some of their royalties to pay SinnerMan's bail. Even old Clarence Urreal 'Honeyboy' Burnside got signed to Fat Possum records. Billed as the last authentic living bluesman, he became the oldest person ever to win a Grammy. He actually thanked me in his speech.

And while we're catching up with old friends, Grover eventually made it home in one piece, after Doña Cecilia cut off his supply of hooch and practically booted him off the mountain. According to Homer, he cut a lonely figure out there at the airfield for a while, forswearing alcohol and nicotine and all worldly vices, until Consuela called from Medellín and told him he could come and get her if he still wanted her, but she wouldn't be alone. They flew in four orphans. Homer had his work cut out fixing it with immigration. But I'm sure Grover has it in him to make a good father. Well, put it this way, he couldn't do a worse job than my own.

I don't know what became of Reverend Salt and I really don't care. He's probably holed up somewhere, praying for the end of the world, while Marilyn's sneaking cigarettes and wondering why it's taking so long. Anyway, I don't want him taking any credit for my conversion. Not that I'm saying I believe in God, you understand, but after everything I've been through I'm just not so sure what forces are at work in this world, whether they come from within or without, and does it really make any difference? Anyway, there was something Doc Underwood asked me that made a lot of sense. 'Why are you so angry with God if you don't even believe in Him?' I'm evoking the Hamlet defence: 'There are more things in Heaven and Earth, Horatio, than are dreamt of in your philosophy.' See, Ms Pruitt? I was paying attention. I'd like to talk it over with Freeman Tally someday. I'm heartened to hear from Homer that he is still at liberty, sowing discord and conspiracy theories.

As for Beasley, well, he wanted me to record some of my new songs, put out a special extended version of the album, then reschedule the tour. And I'm warming to the idea, if we can somehow tie it in with my new charitable initiative, the Motherless Child Foundation.

Yeah, Beasley is still in the picture. He and Homer are inching towards an arrangement where Homer protects my interests and Beasley continues to guide the musical opera-tion. I think they'll work something out, especially since I hear Beasley introduced Homer to Andrew Lloyd Webber and they've started discussions about whether they can turn my odyssey into a Broadway musical. Anyway, if I'm going to stay in this business, better to have the devil working for me than against me.

And what else am I going to do? Music is the only thing I know. But I want to do it properly, I want to do it for the right reasons, and I want to do some good. I want to make my mother proud.

There was a lot to think about, but a besieged hotel in Kilrock probably wasn't the place to do it. Bono had offered to lend me his house in the South of France to continue recuperating and I was ready to take him up on it. But first I wanted to say goodbye to my ma.

So one evening, under cover of darkness, Paddy smuggled me out in a catering van and we drove up to Kilrock cemetery. The gates were locked but we bunked over the wall, and made our way to the graveside with a bunch of roses and a guitar. Paddy led the way, his torch beam flashing over broken gravestones, plastic flowers and overgrown plots, till he stopped and said, 'Here we are.'

It wasn't much to look at, a square white marble stone that was starting to look a bit weathered. There was an engraving of the Virgin Mary in one corner, eyes closed in beatific repose. And a simple inscription: *In loving memory of Maria Beatriz Noone, Taken from us before her time. 12.11.2004, aged 32. Watch over us from heaven. Love never dies.*

I sighed. I didn't remember burying her. It was strange to think that whatever was left of her was somewhere beneath my feet, fading into the Irish soil, thousands of miles from her Colombian mountains. And there she would lie forevermore, with a view of an old Irish church, and the wet hills of Kilrock.

It was a clear, cloudless night. There was a full moon overhead and a sprinkling of stars. We stood there in the dark, coats zipped up against the cold. 'The grave's been kept nice,' I said, for want of something to say.

'I come here when I can, you know, buy a few flowers and that,' said Paddy.

'I don't even remember being here before,' I said.

'Yeah, well, Da didn't like to come up here. I don't think he liked to remember. He took down all the pictures, he acted like she'd never been there at all. Everybody's got their own way of dealing with things and that was his. But I liked to think about her, so I used to come here on my own.'

'You're lucky,' I said. 'You remember her.'

'Yeah,' he said. 'She was lovely. She was a lovely ma.'

And we both stood and contemplated the stone. 'Do you want to be alone?' asked Paddy.

'Yeah, just give me ten minutes,' I said.

He headed back to the van. When he was out of sight, I considered my options. I decided I was done with beating my breast and wrenching my hair and stamping the earth and howling at the moon. So I said, 'I've written a song for you, Ma,' and sat down on the grass, and picked it out on acoustic guitar.

> *On the darkest day*
> *Curtainfall*
> *At the end of the play*
> *Heads laid on the block*
> *The ticking of the clocks*
> *Keys turn in the lock*
> *The flashing of a blade*
> *Don't be afraid*

In the midnight hour
Waves crash
Neath your ivory tower
A ship is on the rocks
Your captain's in the docks
His last card's been played
His last prayer's been prayed
Don't be afraid

Cause where we go, we all go together
It's a river that runs on forever
And never has strayed
Don't be afraid

And everybody feels
Everybody's pain
And everything that's been
Will be and be again
We've got stardust in our veins
It shines to light our way
To where all things are made
Don't be afraid

Cause where we go, we all go together
It's a river that runs on forever
And never has strayed
Don't be afraid

I waited for some sign that she had heard me but there was nothing but the wind rustling in the trees. 'Ah well,' I said, 'it's just a work in progress.' I lay down on the grass and stuck my fingers into the earth. If I could have, I would have shed a tear for all the days we never had together, and never would have. But I was all cried out. So I told her I was sorry for ever thinking she had abandoned me and that I knew she'd never leave me again.

The wind whistled emptily through the trees. A dark cloud passed across the night sky, blotting out stars and almost extinguishing the light of the moon, till all I could see was a silver shadow up above, and then nothing, as the night plunged into pitch black. I heard an owl hoot its hollow call but the sound was suddenly distant and muffled, as if I had been cut off from the world. Then the cloud shifted, and the moonlight fell upon me, and that's when I saw her.

As I lay on my back, she rose up over me, like a giant getting slowly to her feet, until she was towering overhead. And her body was in the trees, and her face was the moon, and her hair reached out its tendrils to the stars. And she was all around me in the night and the wind and the rustling leaves. 'Make me proud,' she whispered.

Then she was gone.

When I got back to the car, my brother was on his phone. I had the urge to tell him what I had seen, or felt, but I knew how it would sound, and I didn't want to go back to the clinic. Anyway, I felt good, light-headed, almost . . . happy. So

I carefully placed my guitar on the back seat and slid in next to him. 'Where to now?' I asked.

'There's one more stop we've got to make,' he said.

As we drove away, I glanced back. I thought I saw the black shape of an owl rise above the trees. But it was dark and I couldn't be sure.

I was lost in my own thoughts as we drove through Kilrock, through streets unchanged since my childhood, turned into a lane and pulled up outside a house I knew almost as well as my own.

'The Haleys?' I said.

'Eileen's come up from Dublin,' said Paddy. 'She's agreed to see you.'

'Fuck.' I was suddenly afraid to get out. 'Are you going to come in?'

'No, you're all right, I think I'll sit this one out,' said Paddy.

'Are her ma and da gonna be there? Mr Haley always looked like he wanted to cut my dirty fingers off for touching his daughter. I may never get out alive.'

'You've got to face the music sometime,' said Paddy, unhelpfully.

He told me to call later when I needed to be picked up. He'd go and have a quiet pint in the local. And left me standing at the gate, wondering what I was letting myself in for. I was so nervous, I had to just stand there shaking for a few minutes, building my confidence. I thought I saw a curtain twitch, and the idea that it might be Eileen in there, looking out, wondering what was keeping me after all these years, finally stirred me. I walked up and knocked on the door.

The light went on in the porch. Mrs Haley answered, thank God. She was a big woman with a broad, serious face I remembered so very well. 'Pedro, it's nice to see you.'

'It's nice to see you too, Mrs Haley,' I said, and it was true. I remembered the warmth with which that woman always treated me, the stray orphan her daughter brought home, because if Eileen had seen something worthwhile in me, that was good enough for her.

'Give me a hug, boy,' she said, wrapping her big arms around me and pulling me into her house. 'Jaysus, you gave me a fright calling from prison that night. We were all so worried about you. They said prayers in the church, did you hear about that? I don't suppose so. I'm sure they were praying for you all over the world. Well, Eileen's waiting for you in the living room. Would you like a nice cup of tea? I'd offer you something stronger now that you're all grown up, but I read in the paper that you're an addict, is that right? You're in Alcoholics Anonymous, is it?'

'A cup of tea would be lovely, Mrs Haley,' I said.

'Well, go on then,' she said. 'You know the way.'

'Is Mr Haley in?' I said, warily.

'He's upstairs with his grandson,' she said, and winked. 'Don't worry, he's got his hands full! The lad's a little rascal. It's time you went and said hello.' I was starting to think this had maybe been a bad idea. She left me standing at the threshold, outside the door of the living room, where Eileen and I had sat so many times, necking in the dark after everybody had gone to bed. I slowly opened the door.

She was sitting alone on the sofa. She looked just the same, only better.

'Eileen,' I said, weakly.

'Pedro,' she said.

And she stood, and we moved together, awkwardly at first, not knowing what the form was for such a reunion, but we hugged and it was good to feel her in my arms, just like I remembered her, just the right size and shape – we knew just how to hold each other because we had done it so many times before. But then the moment passed, and we broke away and sat opposite each other. I looked at her dark eyes, her pale, oval face, the small nose with the sprinkle of freckles, and I tried to take in what had changed about her. But, of course, everything had changed. She'd had her heart cruelly broken by her childhood sweetheart, she had left home, she had lived and loved and had a child of her own to take care of. She wasn't a girl any more. She was a woman, and the sea blue of her eyes was as calm as it was deep.

I don't know how long I sat there staring into those eyes, so familiar yet so unexpected, while she smiled at me the way you might smile patiently at a slow child. It may have only been a minute but time had become elastic, it was being stretched so far that night I half expected it to snap and send us plummeting back into the past, back to the days before I had fucked everything up. But then Mrs Haley brought the tea in on a tray, and apologised for her living room being a bit of a mess but there had been kids running rampage all day, it's not often she even sees Eileen up in Kilrock any more, cause she was living in Dublin now and she had got a good job and—

'Ma!' said Eileen.

'Sorry, sweet,' said her mother. 'But it's so nice to see you two together—'

'Ma!'

'Oh yes, well, sorry, I'll go and check on the baby,' she said. Eileen rolled her eyes as her mother left.

'So you've a kid now?' I said.

'Yes,' she said, warily.

'How old is it?' I said, then felt like an idiot. 'I don't mean "it", like that, I mean, babies, you know . . .' I was like a tongue-tied fourteen-year-old, trying to make small talk.

'Paddy says you've got something you need to say to me,' said Eileen.

'Sorry,' I said.

'Is that it?' she laughed. She actually laughed, and my heart leaped. 'Christ, Pedro, you can do better than that.'

'No, I meant sorry for asking about the kid,' I tried to explain. 'I mean, it's great that you have a kid, you always wanted one, I know, and . . .' I stopped and took a deep breath. And I saw our teenage years together ripple before me, all those years of near unspoken communion, when we were just in it for each other, joined at hip and heart, and at the very same time I saw her crying outside a clinic in London, and crying in my bedroom when I turned her out, and looking back at me from the street below with such a look of sad reproach, and I thought how strange it was for me to have gone halfway across the world and to have ended up back here, and I thought, you can't run away from yourself. You really can't. And that's what I tried to tell her, nearly five years too late.

'Eileen, I want to say sorry because I hurt you, and I hurt myself at the same time, and I didn't even know it. You are the most important girl in the world to me. You gave me the confidence to be who I am, and you are the person I have loved most in the whole world, only I didn't know it until recently, and I'm really sorry for treating you like shit. I'm sorry for breaking your heart, I'm sorry for dumping you as soon as things started to happen for me, I'm sorry for making you have an abortion in London, when I know you didn't want to, and for being selfish, and thoughtless, and for never getting in touch again, and . . . I'm just . . .' I tried to find the exact right word to convey the abject and sincere depth of my contrition but nothing was forthcoming.

'Sorry?' she suggested.

'Yeah, I'm about as sorry as a boy can be,' I admitted.

'Ah well, we were young,' she said.

Is that it? I thought. Was I forgiven, just like that? And I felt a little upset at the same time. An apology like that deserved more than just a shrugged dismissal. I think I would have felt better if she had screamed and wept and called me an ungrateful, immature shit and got her dad downstairs to kick me out the house. But that obviously wasn't going to happen.

She was just looking at me, with a kind of sad curiosity. 'Was it everything you dreamed it was going to be, Pedro?' she asked.

'You mean, after I left you?' I asked.

'Yes,' she said. 'Did you get everything you wanted?'

'Yes, I suppose so,' I said.

'I'm glad,' she said, and sounded sincere.

'Only it wasn't what I wanted,' I added quickly.

'I'm sorry,' she said.

'For what? You've got nothing to be sorry for.'

It was that innocuous remark that finally seemed to draw her out. 'How would you know?' she said, with just a bit of an edge, a shadow of meaning I couldn't quite place.

'You're right,' I agreed. 'How would I know anything about you? No one will tell me a thing. I don't know if you're married, I don't know what you do for a living, I don't know how many kids you've got. You probably know everything about me now, and I don't know a thing about you, and I think about you a lot—'

'I'm sorry for not staying in touch,' she said.

'Oh. Right. Well. You're forgiven then,' I said.

She laughed. A lovely chime of delight, I knew that laugh so well. There was something about this situation I wasn't reading right. 'It's nice to see you, Pedro,' she said. 'Really. Of course, we see you on the TV all the time.'

'We?' I ventured carefully. 'Is that your husband? Or your boyfriend? Or your girlfriend, or whatever?'

She laughed again. 'Do you want to meet him?'

'Your boyfriend? Not really, to be honest.'

'No, silly,' she laughed. 'My son.'

'Is he not sleeping?' I said, not sure where this was going.

'I wish. He refuses to go to sleep until he meets you. He's always singing your songs. I couldn't get away from you even if I wanted to.'

I snatched at that one like a lifeline. 'Does that mean you don't want to?'

'It just means he likes your music,' she said, firmly.

'What age is he?' I asked.

'Four,' she said. 'Ma!' she called up the stairs. 'Can you bring Peter down now to say hello?'

'Four?' I repeated, doing the math.

'There's something I need to tell you, Pedro,' she said, seriously.

I looked at her curiously. Eileen. My Eileen. She was trembling.

The door opened, and a little boy appeared.

And I knew him.

'I never did go . . .' she was saying, '. . . in London . . . the clinic. I mean, I went in, but I couldn't go through with it.'

I knew the moment I laid eyes on him. It wasn't just the red hair and the dark skin. It was the way he moved, it was his whole being. We fixed eyes on each other, and it was a lightning bolt across the room.

And he ran straight to me, and jumped into my arms.

And I knew him.

My son.

I sank back into the chair, and held his little body in my arms. I could feel the bones in his back, the softness of his skin, the fragility of his existence. And I looked into his eyes, and felt I was staring into the onrushing headlights of the future. I started to panic. What did I know about parenthood? An abandoned son with an abandoned son of his own? What was I supposed to do now? How could I run away from this? Where was the door? But I felt Eileen's hand on my shoulder and started to calm down. Whatever happened next, I was going to do the right thing. I was going to make my mother proud. Maybe my father too.

I remembered what my old man said about parenthood, and it suddenly sounded more like wisdom than an excuse. We're all just making it up as we go along.

'Zero,' said my little boy, putting his tiny hands on my face as if to make sure I was real.

I laughed. 'Zero plus one,' I said.

Unbound is the world's first crowdfunding publisher, established in 2011.

We believe that wonderful things can happen when you clear a path for people who share a passion. That's why we've built a platform that brings together readers and authors to crowdfund books they believe in – and give fresh ideas that don't fit the traditional mould the chance they deserve.

This book is in your hands because readers made it possible. Everyone who pledged their support is listed below. Join them by visiting unbound.com and supporting a book today.

Keith Adsley

Percy Aggett

Claire Alderson

Sarah Alexander

Rosa Alvarez

Roger Ames

Finn Arnesen

Louise Aubrie

Tracy Balsamo

Ian Barker

Peter Bartrop

Mike Bawden

Joe Baxter

Tom Baxter

Emily Beck

Chris Boehning

Dimitrios Bogiatzoules

Wendy Boland

Dita Bouviar

Wendy Broadhurst

Scott Calhoun

Anto Casey

Gennaro Castaldo

Stephen Catanzarite

Chalk Press
Tom Chaplin
Jurga Cipaite
Mary Cipriani
David Cleland
Gina Cloe
Paul Cocks
David Comay
Paula Cook
Andy Cowan
John Crawford
John Crone
Mark Crossley
Ted Cummings
Tim Cunningham
Angelo D'Arezzo
Linda Dahl
Nick Davey
Richard Dawes
Mike Day
Turner Deckert
Dianne Delahunty
Noel Delahunty
Talie-Orfée Després
Alison DeWolfe
Naomi Dinnen
Bernard Doherty
Kacey Donston

Peter Dowd
Ruth Drake
Graham Dumble
Sandra Dunnington
Liz Eades
Gloria Else
Claudia Espinosa & Brian
    Aby
Gary Farrow
Robin Elin Fennell
Gary Finch
Abbey Fisher
Maria Flynn
Richard Ford
Maddy Fry
Vicky Fullick
Nick Gatfield
Mark Gourley
Aaron Govern
Mareike Graepel
Fernanda Araujo Guedes
Pereira
Ian Hall
Sarah Hall
Courtney Hamilton
Rieko Hara
Helen Harbison
Sue Harris

Ian Hartley

Imogen Heap

Anthony Heath

Jennifer Herl

Tom Hickox

Sonia Hines

Mary Hogan

Gavin Hogg

Rob Holden

Pete Holidai

John Holland

Sarah Holmes

Brad Hood

Claire Horton

Tom Hostler

Liam Hudson

Stacey Jaros

Anne Jenkins

Cameron Jenkins

Jason Jestice

Eugene Jordan

Jrodconcerts

Rick Jude

Andres Kabel

Seth Kalichman

Alicia Kamenick

Michelle Kaminski

Harry Kantas

Hannah Keeney

Christine Kelly

Dean Paul Kelly

Gary Kemp

Dan Kieran

Tassoula Kokkoris

Paul Kramer

Rupert Lang

Jill LaPoint

Michael Lasley

Sherry Lawrence

Bob Lawrie

Frazer Lawton

Mike LeZoo

Alon Loewy

Luke Lowings

Dermot Lucking

Fabiano Mad

Vidhya Magendran

Landy Manderson

Greg Mason

Andrew Massey

MBC PR

Conor McAteer

Chris McCormick

Ivan McCormick

Jim McCormick

Juliet Blue Bennett

McCormick

Louise McCormick

Stella McCormick

Susan McIntyre

Tom McRae

Euan McRorie

Daniel Menahem

Allison Menjivar

Kas Mercer

James Middleton-Burn

James Minshull

John Mitchinson

Ed Montano

Trevor Montgomery

Pete Morgan

Tom E Morrison

Donald Moxham

Beth Nabi

Carlo Navato

Tim Neufeld

Linda O'Brien

Andrew O'Hagan

Fintan O'Neill

Emily, Jon and Axl Owen

Scott Pack

Hanna Pallua

Kathy Papasotiriou

Joanne Louise Parker

Scott Pattison

Margit Paul

Alan Perks

Christian Petersen

Adrian Phelan

Melissa Pierick

Christopher Pleydell

Justin Pollard

Málcolm Porter

Petra Posa

Marco Prehn

Andy Prevezer

Janie Price

Rose Ramos

David Ramsay

Leo Regan

Alan Riegler

Erik Rosema

Jil Runkel

Alberto Russo

Tal Sagorsky

Aaron Sams

Sabine Schieweck

Sonja Schiftar

Paul Schofield

Wesley Schultz

Alan Searl

Jasmine Sharp

Tom Sheppard

Sara Silver

Eileen Smee

Jennie Smith

Joyce Smith

Donna Springer

Fergus Stankard

Nick Stewart

Niall Stokes

Susannah Stubbs

Evey Sully

Adam Sutcliffe

Beth Talisman

Rob Task

David Taylor

Dale Tedder

Alan Teixeira

Mike Scott Thomson

Annette Trento

Siobhan Tucker

Colin Tunnah

Alexander Turner

Olaf Tyaransen

Tony Vanderheyden

Philippa Varcoe

Wim Verburg

Tim Vernon

Lori Vinton

Angela Vredenburg

Steven Walker

Dave Waltman

Michelle Watson

Selina Webb

Florence Welch

Rob Wheeler

Dylan White

Margo Wickens

David Williams

Steve Winter

Andy Wright

Martin Wroe

Lisa Zagami

Oliver Zimmer

Joni Zurawinski